The Empty Dark

Pat Arneson

The author wishes to thank:

Mike Arneson, my partner in everything.

Greg Kersten—President, OK Corral Series, Founder of Equine Assisted Psychotherapy (EAP), Equine Services, Inc., EAGALA;

Guy Kaufman—Founder, Executive Director Changing Gaits;

Kelsey Miner—Beta reader, visionary; Sean Miner—Author, journalist, editor; Katie Zezulka—Research Support;

Joey Zezulka—Mechanic, endless source of useful information; Cathy Cleary, MD;

Karen Phillips—PhillipsCovers.com, cover artist.

Additional thanks to those too numerous to mention,
who provided ideas, technical information and instruction,
and encouragement.

Chapter One

The sirens grew louder. More joined in, overlapping. I turned in that direction and lowered my weapon.

"Focus." Max was unyielding.

"They're getting closer," I said.

"You gotta focus. What are you going for—torso or head?" Max waited a beat. "Focus, Maguire. Center mass or head?"

I replaced my hearing protection, exhaled, and aimed for the chest. Focus. I steadied myself, put my finger on the trigger, squeezed. Five shots, center mass—or so I hoped. I glanced at Max.

"I think you got him, Maguire." Vig pumped an arm in the air. "Yeah! One down!"

"Don't encourage her to be bloodthirsty." Max shielded his eyes with a hand and peered at the wooden backstop where my target was fixed with duct tape. "We're going for defensive skills."

"Oh, I know." Vig raised his hands in a gesture of innocence. "I'm all about defense." He turned one hand into a mock pistol and fired it over his head as he walked away. "Proactively."

When Vig got halfway to the house, I leaned in to speak quietly. "Ok, seriously. What is Vig's full name?"

Max focused on his own target. "Viglione."

I waited for more, but apparently it wasn't coming. "The man has to have a first name."

Max adjusted his headset to cover both ears as he aimed his weapon. He blew out a long, slow breath, squeezed the trigger, and squinted at the backstop. He turned to me and uncovered one ear. "He doesn't like his first name. I wouldn't bring it up."

I scampered after Max as he walked toward the target. I didn't want to raise my voice. "What does his wife call him?"

"Vig—unless she's super pissed at him. Then it's Viglione." Max laughed. "I usually run like hell."

The screen door slammed. Vig's wife appeared with a thermos and a couple of mugs.

"Jules!" Max called out. "You're saving my life!" He winked at me, knowing I'd overthink the whole thing. He used her first name, but not because she was female—I was Maguire to all of them. Maybe they just couldn't both be Vig. Maybe if anyone called her Mrs. Vig, she'd take them out.

Jules waved the mugs at Max. "I got you, Turner. Get it while it's hot!" We moved to the circle of wooden benches, and Vig appeared with two more mugs.

I blew over the surface of my steaming, black coffee, tucked a strand of my rusty mop behind a freckled ear, and studied our hosts. We were all about the same age—40ish, give or take. With glossy black hair and a rich bronze complexion, Jules had an attitude of assurance that made flannel and lug boots look sexy.

Jules and Vig were both as solid as the chunk of a tree trunk Vig pulled over for a footstool. They worked their own land. Jules was an expert shot, easily as adept at the range they had built as either

Vig or Max, both former Marines who tended to suck in air and back up several steps when Jules got angry.

Jules looked down their long, gravel driveway toward the main road as a squad car and an ambulance passed quietly. She propped her feet up on a log. "Whatever it is, it's not an emergency anymore."

Another squad car pulled into the driveway, abruptly cutting off our conversation. A sheriff's deputy climbed out, stopped a respectful distance away, and eyeballed the array of weapons laid out on the tailgates of two pickups.

Vig stood slowly, keeping his hands visible. "Hello," he called out. "How you doin' today?"

Jules and Max didn't stand, but moved their coffee mugs farther out from their bodies—resting on their knees, leaving their hands clearly visible as well. I imitated them.

The deputy scanned the property—the range, the surrounding area, us. His eyes lingered on Vig's face, probably due to the black eye. The cast Vig had when I met him—a boxer's fracture—was gone, but he had a heck of a shiner. The deputy nodded at Vig. "Nice looking range you got there. Doing a little shooting?"

"That's right." Vig lifted his mug. "Taking a little break. Get you a cup of coffee?"

"Maybe next time, thanks. Wondering if you noticed anything unusual the past few days? Unusual traffic, machinery?"

Vig thought for a moment. "I can't say I have." He gestured toward us with his mug. "My friends here are just visiting today, they live down by Jack Pine. My wife was out of town the last few days. I've been in and out, but I can't say—oh, scrap guy came out with a truck."

"Scrap guy?"

"Yeah, that's not unusual, though. There's old metal in some of the fields—abandoned farm equipment, junker cars and trucks in some of the groves and shelterbelts. People know where they are. People beyond the property owners, I mean. There's a Chevy guy, knows where there's an old Impala and a Bel Air, like that. Swore me to secrecy."

"You got a name for the guy you know was out here?"

"He gave me a card once," Vig said. "Explained why he was prowling around out there. In the kitchen, I'll grab it."

The deputy nodded. "Anything you got on the Chevy guy, too, if you don't mind. Anyone you know comes out here."

Vig went to the house, and emerged a few minutes later with a sheet of paper. He handed it to the deputy, who thanked him and looked around the property again. His gaze paused on the equipment shed.

"Alright, you think of anything, please give us a call. You all have a good day now." He gave a quick nod and turned back to his squad car.

We watched as he backed out to the main road and turned onto the hardtop. Vig and Jules shrugged and exchanged glances. Max looked thoughtfully down the road.

I'd had enough practice. My primary experience with weapons was a cap gun, and even that was limited. More often than not, my friends and I had unrolled the thin, red strips of paper and smashed the little dots with a hammer. The smell of gunpowder made us feel daring and bold, and Papa—the uncle who raised me—never yelled about the black marks on the sidewalk. I smiled, thinking about it. The others went through a few more magazines before packing everything away.

Max and I left after another round of caffeine—Max driving and brooding while I drank the coffee Jules poured into a travel cup for me. "Something's off with Vig," Max finally said. "I want to make an excuse to go back tomorrow, see if it still hits me that way."

I didn't know Vig well enough to speak to that. "What seemed off?"

Max frowned. "Nothing obvious. Just—" he paused at a stop sign, waited for a truck to pass, then turned onto another back road. "Like an underlying tension. Like he's trying to hide it."

"Well, I'm a handy excuse if they don't mind us using the range again." I shoved my coffee into the cup holder. "Not like you're lying if you say I need practice, having shot exactly twice in my life. And basically sucking at it."

Max nodded slowly.

"You could've argued a little bit," I said. Max didn't answer. I thought about imitating his standard "Maguire, you want to get out of your head and talk to me?" But he was worried. I didn't have the heart to poke at him.

We reached the ranch and I climbed down from his truck. "Let me know about tomorrow," I said. Max nodded vaguely, and I headed up to my apartment.

I've had a lot of temp gigs as a clinical therapist—it's what I do. This one seemed frankly ridiculous, in a "this is what it's come to" kind of way. A horse ranch, out in the woods and fields of central Minnesota, for three months. An experiment. An outrageous thing to do, really—I knew as much about horses as, say, wildebeests. It would be good for me, I'd thought. A step back from decades of work with trauma and violence. A steep learning curve would be a different kind of challenge. I'd bring down the continuous, toxic flow of adrenaline and the stress hormone cortisol. So, I got certified in equine assisted therapy (a whole new concept in itself) and applied for the job. A reset, I thought. A nice break.

A reset it had certainly been. I needed a whole new skill set, felt completely incompetent, and found a person dead in the tack room. By the end of the summer, I was enmeshed in a double murder investigation. Nearly got killed myself. Nothing restful about it. Nothing.

I loved my little apartment over the barn, though. One of the best perks of the job. As ranch manager, Max lived in the fifties-era house across the gravel parking lot, just steps away if I needed anything. Max and I quickly became close living on-site. We led therapy sessions together, and talked through dark nights of mutual insomnia. Processed our own trauma. Bickered, laughed.

The staff had been a family when I came—Walt Bravo, my boss, was the founder and director. Thoughtful mentor, endless source of wisdom. Plus, I'd seen him pick a man up and hurl him out of the barn. Ida Gill— a rebellious, mouthy mother hen—was staunch, smart, observant. And Max. They all did client sessions, but needed my license and clinical expertise, just for a few months, until they hired someone more permanent. And then they took me in.

I came very close to walking away from that initial three month gig—something I never previously considered, with any job. But when it all shook out, when they asked me to stay for a full year, I said yes.

I reached for a framed photo of Papa, took it down from the shelf, and blew off the daily layer of dust. "Kind of an interesting morning," I told him. "Wonder if we'll find out what was going on with the cops?" Papa smiled, because that was the picture I chose. I put it back, picked up a more serious one, scooched my butt up on the counter, and studied his face. "I did a little better today. I'm getting the hang of the whole recoil thing." I wiped the frame with the hem of my shirt. Papa took me in when I was four years old, when my mother died and my father vanished. Papa didn't just raise me—he was my family, my home. My world, until he died just over a year ago. Living alone, I could talk to him all I wanted.

My photographs of Papa shared space with a new picture—a framed, awkward selfie Max took of the four of us laughing, Walt and Ida shaking their heads about technology these days. Papa would have loved it. I grabbed a cold drink and headed back out. Halfway down the steps, I noticed an extra truck in the parking lot. Ben Murphy, private eye.

Ben and Max leaned on the fence, chatted, scratched a couple of horses who inserted themselves into the conversation. Both men were lean and solid—Ben a little taller, a little heavier built. His dark hair was short—his style, backwoods federal agent. Ben was always clean-shaven, with a fair complexion that burned easily.

Max had olive undertones to his skin—an asset for someone who lived mostly outdoors. His dirty blond hair curled a little over the collar of his flannel. His neatly trimmed beard almost covered scarring on his face and neck. A military tattoo peeked out one rolled-up sleeve. They both wore boots, but Ben's were cleaner.

Max politely gave no indication he thought Ben was an idiot. He was good at that. The men smiled when they saw me. Max gave a nod, pushed off the fence and headed for the barn.

I still suspected Ben might be an ex-fed, but he wasn't talking. He had lived in Max's basement for a while, undercover, pretending to be a ranch hand. Eavesdropped, tossed hay bales, romanced me. When his case was resolved, I found out he'd bugged my apartment. And—this is on me, a hundred percent—I let him talk his way out of it. You ignore red flags, you find yourself out in a hurricane. And here I was, smiling at him.

Ben gave me an appreciative once-over, a quick kiss on the lips. "I'm glad I caught you, I might not be around much for a while. Just caught a new case this morning, high pressure."

"Why high pressure? What's up?"

Ben leaned back against his truck, arms folded casually over his chest. "Body turned up. Way out on the outskirts—I'd have thought it was county, but the case bounced back to Tom."

Huh. That explained the cops by Vig's, and the lack of sirens driving away. Tom Harmon, Ben's childhood friend and current housemate, was the smug, snide, overbearing detective for the police station in Deergrass. The closest little town to us, Jack Pine, wasn't big enough to have cops, and Deergrass didn't have that many.

"Local citizen, anyway," Ben went on. "Fine, upstanding member of society—hence the pressure. Might be the quickest I've ever been hired." He grinned. "Tom wasn't happy about that. Not much of a compliment, a knee jerk reaction to immediately bring in a PI."

And Ben came here. Maybe the deputy who'd checked out Vig's place ran the plates of all the vehicles, and owed Ben a favor since high school. "You didn't hear it from me" kind of thing. Ben saw Max's name and came snooping. Or maybe I was being unfair. I eyed Ben suspiciously—then realized he'd kept talking. Worse, he was waiting for a response.

I paused to see if he would elaborate so I wouldn't have to confess, but he looked amused. I sighed. "I'm sorry, I missed the last thing you said."

Ben grinned. "My fragile male ego is wilting. I asked how your day's been so far."

"Not bad. Max and I were visiting friends of his. Amazing coffee—they order it from Black Rifle. Phenomenal coffee. Bigger areas, you can get it in stores, but—hey!" I had an epiphany. "I could order Black Rifle myself now! I'll have the same address for a year."

As excited as I was about the coffee, I was being deliberately obstructive. Perhaps prematurely—if Ben had started a sparring match, I'd missed his opening move. I was determined not to tell him we'd been so close to all those sirens. "What do you know so far?" I asked.

"Very early on," he said. "Local businessman, pretty clear homicide. Shallow grave. That's about it. How was your visit? Other than the coffee."

"We were target shooting. It was only my second time using the range, so I'm understandably bad at it. Kind of a whole-brain activity, though. Visual coordination. It's good for me to do things that get me out of my head."

Ben waited for a moment, then smiled when I didn't go on. An enjoying-the-game smile. He pushed off from his truck and turned to leave. "I'll be in touch when I can. Hopefully we can grab dinner, maybe a quick ride on the trails." He raised my chin with a finger, focused his laughing Irish eyes on my face, and kissed me. With that, he swung into the cab and drove away.

Chapter Two

The oversized chairs and sofa in Vig's living room were sturdy and comfortable—generously padded, framed in solid oak. Bold, colorful art brightened the walls—native themes, wildlife, forests. Strong and welcoming, their home reflected them.

Jules put her feet on the wooden coffee table, which she'd probably carved herself. From a tree she took down. She turned to Max purposefully, every part of her radiating an agenda. Vig looked annoyed, but outvoted.

"Turner," Jules said, "You've never talked much about being a counselor. Obviously, it's good for you. You're so much easier in your own skin. Especially the last few months, honestly—something changed."

Max stretched—relaxed, casual. "Maguire, I told Vig a little about how you helped me get my head straight. Explained to me what's actually going on in a person's brain with flashbacks, nightmares, all that. Thoughts that pop into your head. Over-reacting to stupid things, then feeling like an ass about it."

Vig set his coffee cup down and stood. "Jules, we got any chips left? Pretzels?"

“No.” Jules smiled slightly. “Please go on, Turner. I want to hear this.” Vig wandered to the kitchen and started opening cupboards.

“How, if that stuff comes up,” Max projected his voice across the house, “It’s your brain trying to file it right.” He smiled at me expectantly.

“Yes,” I said, not sure if I should talk loudly. I tend to get loud when I’m passionate. I could just start ranting. “Neuroscience. PTSD is actually a disorder of basic memory function. I wish more people knew that.” I set my coffee down so I could wave my hands. “We could really do away with the judgments—the idea that strength, courage, intelligence have anything to do with it.”

Vig leaned against the doorway. “Turner, you know I’m not talking about you—not in any way. Just seems like people use all that PTSD, trauma stuff as an excuse. I never made an excuse in my life.”

I couldn’t let that go unchallenged. “In my experience, the vast majority of people with PTSD pretend they don’t have it. They’ll stand on ‘I’m fine’ to the death—sometimes literally. People who make excuses will blame trauma as often as anything else, but that’s a whole different matter, Vig.”

He nodded, conceding the point.

“So, anyway.” Max met my eyes—get ready, I’m tossing the ball to you. “It’s like parking. At the airport.” He nodded at me.

Parking? I blinked. We looked at each other for a couple of beats.

“You got short-term parking, and long-term,” he said. “And your brain’s moving stuff around.”

“Oh,” I said. “Okay. Memories are stored in certain parts of your brain. Airport parking works, I guess. It isn’t a perfect metaphor—with your brain, everything starts in short-term parking. All the brain's information intake starts there. Some of it gets moved to long-term, that's the filing Max is talking about."

Vig found a bag of cookies and opened them with a loud rustle. "Sorry!" He stuck his hand in, made more noise. "Sorry, sorry." He looked around with an apologetic shrug, and held out the bag. "Anyone?" Jules shot him a look. He stopped.

I struggled against being distracted. "The short-term parking in your brain—the intake—is also the emotion center. So that makes sense, because emotions flare up and fade away. Temporary. Short-term." I nodded, satisfied. "Long-term parking doubles as the rational thinking center. Which also tracks—thoughts can be held for years. Long-term." I checked the room. Max did a little rolling motion with one finger.

I went on. "If something is too powerfully emotional, your brain can't move it to long-term parking—rational thought storage, where memories are supposed to go. Sticks it back in the short-term lot with the emotions."

Jules leaned forward, her dark eyes intently focused. "But short-term parking, by definition, is time-limited."

"Yes!" I focused on Jules. "So, that overwhelmingly emotional experience? Your brain keeps bringing it up, bringing it up, trying to get it filed as a rational thought. Tow that car to long-term parking! Intact memories can't stay here! Move 'em out, move 'em out! Can't get it in, it keeps trying. Flashback. Nightmare. Intrusive thought. Your brain, trying to refile."

Max nodded. "So, you wanna detach some of that emotion from the memory. One way, take what feels like a flashbang and somehow form it into words. Makes it easier for the brain to refile. I fought back real hard on that one, but it sure as hell worked for me. Hated every minute of it, but it really made a difference. I guess some people write it out. I'm more of a talker."

I wasn't sure where Max intended to go with this. Vig was annoyed by the infomercial. Jules ignored Vig. Max plowed on. "But you gotta have some kinda feeling of being in control. You decide how deep, how fast or slow, for how long. I mean, we try to guide people, but there's a tricky line there. Too overwhelming, it's counterproductive."

"I want to hear about all of this, Turner." Jules threw an even glance at Vig. "But first, tell me how you got so...almost serene. Something changed. My grandma would have said you walk in this world differently." Jules reached out a foot and kicked Vig's leg, startling him.

Max started to grin, but looked away. "For a long time, I turned off my emotions in general. Kept it all on lock-down until it blew, then shut it off again. Felt like an ass, embarrassed, every time. You probably saw that, I never really hid anything from you, of all people. Then I found out I didn't have to keep doing that my whole life."

"That's a big deal, Max," I said. "People shut down, think they don't have emotions. It's a very effective survival skill—until it's not. Never take off the Kevlar, tell yourself it's part of you now. Pretend it's not getting in your way. But it will—survival techniques do that. They do."

I sighed, without meaning to. I suddenly felt the weight of twenty years of clients, pressing on me. Had my own intrusive thoughts.

Saw their faces. Shook it off. "Developing ways to survive is brilliant. Realizing you don't need them anymore, and now they're getting in your way, that's also brilliant."

"That's the damn truth," Jules said. She walked to the kitchen, brought back the coffee pot, and refilled our cups. "That all makes sense. What do the horses do?"

"Thank you." I took a sip, blew across the surface of my coffee, and watched the ripples. "Horses are prey animals, hardwired to sense emotion, intention. They even feel what's going on below conscious awareness. So we watch."

I glanced at Vig. His face was expressionless. "We can point things out," I said, "teach the person to watch the horse with us. 'See what that horse did there? That was a response—what were you thinking about, when the horse moved like that?' Start to reconnect that person with their own feelings, so they won't be all locked up, all shut down. So all that bottled up stuff won't come erupting out anymore."

Max rolled his shoulders, leaned back, studied the ceiling. I took another sip of coffee to keep from smiling. Max let the room fill with silence, let the weight of that stillness do the work. Sometimes we had spontaneous competitions and tried to break each other, just for fun. See who would squirm or talk under that pressure. Walt never admitted to joining us, but Walt could outwait a mountain, and convincingly pretend he'd been lost in thought. Ida refused to play. "Lord, help," and she'd go sweep stable mats.

Vig shifted in his chair. "Every veteran in the world doesn't have PTSD."

"Nope." Max acknowledged that with a tip of his cup. "True enough."

Jules sat quietly, her eyes shifting between Max and Vig.

Max pointed his mug at Vig. "How's that eye feeling? Looks like the color's fading a little."

Jules's mouth twitched.

Vig scowled. "A little scuffle at closing time is nothing, Turner. Shit, I was drinking and brawling when I was sixteen years old. I drink less now than I ever have, in deference to my wife." He nodded in her direction.

"As well you should. She's a hell of a good woman." Max and Jules smiled at each other. Max turned back to Vig. "How you sleeping at night?"

I felt Vig's reaction across the room. The atmosphere changed suddenly. Vig's face hardened. His body tensed. His eyes burned with something potentially volatile. My own adrenaline kicked up. Decades of dangerous settings kicked in. I noticed Vig's shallow breathing, coiled energy ready to spring. Max's feet now flat on the floor, weight forward in his chair. Jules alert to both of them, but gazing at Vig with sadness. Vig shot a look at Jules—what have you said? She gave her head a tiny shake, almost imperceptible, but he saw it, accepted it. Whatever it was, she hadn't betrayed him.

The moment passed. No one spoke. Finally Max let his weight shift back onto the chair. "What the hell was that?"

Vig stared into the air, pain and humiliation in his eyes.

"You know what, I can step out of the room," I said. "You need to talk about something without extra people here, I am absolutely fine with that. Seriously. No offense whatsoever."

"No," Vig said firmly. He blew out a loud breath. "Turner never did anything without purpose, all the years I've known him. Ever. Good or bad, everything's on purpose." He sat quietly for a moment. "He brings something up in front of you, he meant to. I'm fine, Turner."

Max raised both eyebrows at Vig, as though he had done something particularly stupid. When Vig refused to comment further, Max set his cup on the side table—another beautifully carved chunk of wood. Shiny, not scuffed from feet like the coffee table. "Yeah, I gotta call bullshit on that one."

Vig snorted. "How you gonna call bullshit?" His voice grew louder, but his weight was settled back. "I'm extremely happily married. Steady job, couple hobbies. How you gonna call bullshit on whether I'm fine or not? What the hell do you know, I'm not fine?"

Max spread his hands in the air. "I know the room just about exploded when I asked how you sleep at night. Geez."

Vig sat forward, rested his head in his hands. "I—dammit." He looked at Jules and sighed heavily. "I'm sorry. I just—you probably saw the blankets. I been sleeping on the couch." Vig's eyes misted up. He blinked hard, angry about the tears. "I...don't always know what I'm doing at night." His voice grew quiet. "I'd die before I'd hurt Jules. You know that."

Max's eyes widened. He sat up straight. "What happened?"

Vig seemed unable to speak. Jules leaned in. "He has dreams. It's hard to wake him. And he didn't hurt me." She looked pointedly at Vig. "He didn't. I just had to yell for a long time to wake him up. Both of us, dead sleep. He flipped me over on my stomach, knees on my back, pulling my arms behind me, I'm shouting at him." Jules shook her head. "I wasn't hurt. Vig's just worried about what could happen next time."

Vig was so tense, he was vibrating. Max got up and sat on the coffee table in front of him. Vig turned his head, but Max leaned, stayed in Vig's field of vision. Vig gave up pretty quickly and met Max's eyes. "Turner, what do you want, man? I'm tired."

"Let us help you," Max said. "Let somebody. You want, I'll go with you to the VA. Wherever. Come out to the ranch. We can do a thing with the horses." Max turned to me. "Vig loves horses." He turned back to Vig. "There's ways that horses can help, that other people can't do for you. Just give it a shot. Give it a few months—it's not working, at least you tried." He poked Vig in the chest. "See, I know I got you, because there's nothing you won't do for Jules."

Vig shrugged and looked relieved. "Yeah, you're right about that. If it's for Jules, ok. Alright. Let's set it up."

"Tonight," Max said. "There's no sessions at all this evening. We'll pull in a couple horses, set up in the outdoor arena. We gotta grab this while it's hot, Vig. Tonight."

Vig nodded. "Alright, man. I hear you. I'll be there."

Driving back to the ranch, Max wiggled in his seat, one restless hand fidgeting with his seatbelt, the radio, the dash. "Maguire, this is terrifying. You gotta tell me, is this too much? Is this like, beyond our reach? I mean, I know people have nightmares, but God Almighty, Maguire. If he hadn't woke up—it's not like we were cops, just trying to cuff somebody. Combat, they're *always* trying to kill you. He could've—" He shook his head, unable to continue.

"Let him come out tonight," I said. "Let's at least see where we're at. You have to start where people are, and he's willing to do this."

Max nodded, watching the road ahead.

"This isn't a freakish thing," I said. "It happens. A sleep disorder, a PTSD symptom. Okay? It doesn't mean Vig is hopelessly broken. We should keep in mind, though—"

Max glanced at me.

"You decide you're done pretending, you start to actually deal with things you've buried, it can feel worse before it gets better. I warn people, you might get Pissy In the Process—PIP. Tell families, loved ones. This person you care about, who you want to see healed and whole, they might get PIP. Treating injuries can be painful. You just have to be prepared for it, get through it sometimes. Having it feel worse."

"He moves in with me," Max said. "That extra bedroom in the basement. I'm telling him, pack a suitcase. He can live with me as long as it takes. If it gets worse before it gets better, pissy might not cover it."

When we got back to the ranch, Ben was there. Standing between my beautiful red truck and his single cab, long bed, gray one, talking on his phone. He ended his call as I stepped down to the gravel lot. Max gave me a half wave, nodded to Ben, and walked away.

"Hey there," Ben said. "I saw your truck, but the place was deserted. I was just about to take off." He touched my face with the back of his hand and smiled. Charming, give him that. Understanding the mileage he got out of that smile didn't make it less effective.

I pointed my head at my apartment. "Still have time for a break?" Ben followed me up the stairs, and once we got talking, a few minutes became an hour.

In the right mood, Ben was devastatingly funny—without saying a word. A subtle facial expression, the tiniest twitch of his mouth or eyebrow, delivered with perfect timing. My laughter only encouraged him. I tried to make conversation, and he'd throw in the slightest all-body shrug—a glimpse, then gone—or a glance, an ironic, self-deprecating glimmer I nearly missed. He caught me off-guard, and I giggled. Snorted. Ben didn't have to open his mouth to convey intelligence and wit.

I walked him to his truck and let him steal a quick kiss before he opened the door. He paused as Vig drove into the parking lot. Ben scanned the truck, eyed Vig. Noted the license plate. I shook my head. He just can't stop himself.

Vig was tough guy nervous. He noted Ben's scrutiny with a side-eye and drew himself to full height as he stepped onto the gravel. He almost swaggered to the fence for a muscley side-hug with Max, and visually assessed the surroundings—when he identified no threats and turned back to Max, I half expected him to shout, "Clear!"

Max pretended not to notice. "C'mon over to the outdoor arena. I've got a couple horses waiting for us."

Quincy was Max's personal horse. Maverick was Walt's, and the most experienced therapy horse on the ranch. They wore halters but wandered freely in the roped-off arena, a sand-covered circle seventy-five feet in diameter. Maverick lifted his head when Max approached, and watched him for cues. Quincy pretended to ignore us. “Ok,” Max said. “Let’s start with catching a horse.”

Vig noticed the lead rope lying in the sand. He picked it up and the horses came to attention. “Does it matter which one?”

“Nope,” Max said. “Just catch one horse.”

Vig and the horses studied each other. “What’s the brown one’s name?”

“That’s Maverick.”

“Hey, Maverick.” Vig walked over. He got close, but the horse eyeballed Vig and moved away. Vig paused, then approached again. “C’mere, Maverick. Come on over here.” Vig’s voice was friendly, but both horses kept several feet away from him. “What’s the grey one called?”

“Quincy.” Max settled in, leaning on a wooden fence post.

Vig talked quietly, walked slowly, but neither horse allowed him to approach. After several attempts, Vig turned to Max with a palms-up gesture of futility.

“So, Vig,” Max said. “How are you feeling right now?”

He shrugged. “Fine. Trying not to be frustrated, but I’m totally fine.”

“Horse calls bullshit,” I blurted. I didn’t mean to say that out loud. Vig and Max both stared at me. My face burned. I cleared my throat. “Horses can play ‘I Call Bullshit’ better than anyone in the world. They apparently don’t think you’re fine.”

Max grinned, turning back to the arena. “The horse senses your energy, Vig. You act all calm when you’re jacked up inside, the horse doesn't like that discrepancy. Makes you unpredictable. Hell, that's how mountain lions act. Creep up all quiet, and lunge." He climbed through the rope fence. "Let's bring it down a little. Now, I want you to pretend you're in a sniper's nest."

I gaped at Max. He'd lost it. His concern for Vig had pushed him right over the edge.

"No one can see you," he went on. "You're real covered. But you wanna be ready for the target, so you need to breathe yourself into absolute stillness. Give me some sniper breathing."

I opened my mouth to ask him just exactly what kind of therapy he thought that was, but Vig nodded. He focused on the far treeline and breathed—deep, slow, quiet breaths. I watched the tension gradually ease from his shoulders and neck. The horses watched, curious. After a few moments, Quincy walked up and nudged Vig from behind. Vig jumped, then laughed when he saw the horse inches away. He stroked Quincy's neck and gave him a scratch. Quincy nuzzled Vig's shoulder.

"You seriously changed your vibe there, Vig," Max explained. "Now, how do you feel?"

Vig smiled sheepishly. "Relaxed. Way better—but I really did think I was fine, I wasn't just blowing smoke."

"I know you did. That's the whole point. You spend time with these horses, they'll show you tension, anger, just nerves. Any of that, they might move away. So that's your cue that you gotta bring it down. Alright, now we're gonna do something else." He waved a hand broadly at the array of cones, PVC pipe, barrels, lead ropes and stanchions he had assembled along the fenceline. "You can use any of this stuff here. You're gonna make an obstacle that represents settling into civilian life after deployment."

Vig snorted and drew back a few inches. "Shit. How much of a mess you want?"

Max shook his head and climbed back out through the ropes. "It's your mess, man. You decide. Every piece you add, though, I want you to think of something specific that it represents."

He used everything, including the nearby chairs. The horses occasionally wandered through and knocked things over. Quincy picked up a piece in his teeth and tossed it. Vig stopped building to put things back as he'd arranged them. Maverick leaned on a high stack and toppled it. Vig waved his hands in disgust.

Max grinned. "Vig, does this remind you of anything in your life?"

"Yes, dammit!" He didn't elaborate. Max smiled, but didn't push. I knew he'd circle back to it later. Vig finished his obstacle, one of the most complicated, convoluted messes I'd ever seen. Lead ropes were tied between obstacles, a web over a debris pile. Vig turned to Max for direction.

"Ok," Max said. "Now take that rope we didn't use, clip it on either horse, and walk the horse through the obstacle."

Vig stared. "You want me to do what?"

"You heard me." Max leaned on a post. He crossed his legs, one boot in front of the other, and settled in to watch.

Vig had no trouble catching Quincy. He walked up to the obstacle and stood, staring at it. He looked at Max over his shoulder, then turned back to the roped-up pile.

"Kinda overwhelmed, looking at the whole thing," Max murmured. "Watch, though. He won't quit. Twenty bucks says he doesn't ask for help."

Vig held the lead rope with one hand and pushed on a barrel with the other. Several obstacles fell over. He cursed, tried to catch one, knocked another one over. Quincy didn't flinch. Vig tried for several minutes to make a path. Nudged cones, pushed a barrel with one leg while holding a stanchion up with his hip. Set down the rope to use both hands, and Quincy walked away. Vig cursed again, waved his hands in the air, retrieved Quincy, started over. He struggled with it for a good fifteen, twenty minutes.

"What did I ask you to do?" Max called out.

Vig stopped to glare at him. "I'm working on it."

"No, really," Max said. "What are your instructions?"

"Get a horse through the damn mess."

"So, what are the rules?" Max asked.

Vig waved an arm in a broad gesture of frustration and disgust. "You didn't give me any rules."

"What did I tell you, you can't do?"

Vig looked at his mess, looked back at Max. "You didn't."

"Alright, so what's holding you back, here?"

Vig did the arm wave again. He was very expressive. I smothered a smile. Vig picked up a cone and tossed it to the side of the arena, then looked at Max for a reaction. Getting none, he lifted a foot and kicked over one of his own piles, opening a space to make a few steps forward. He waded in, holding the lead rope. Quincy looked skeptical. Vig shoved over a pylon and moved one more step deeper. Quincy planted his hooves. Vig tugged the rope. Quincy snorted.

"Hey, Vig." Max was still relaxed, leaning on the pole.

"What!" Vig shouted.

"What did I say about asking for help?"

Vig didn't answer. He shoved a chair with his foot, and a cone fell off, startling Quincy. Vig stood in the middle of his mess, unable to move forward.

The corners of Max's mouth twitched. "Vig?"

Vig dramatically looked at the sky, threw the rope, waved both arms. "Alright, I can't do it. I can't get out. Is that the point?"

Max stood upright. "No. The point is, you make up your own rules, tell yourself you're failing, but you just made up that whole scenario in your head. How many things did I tell you to do? One. How many things did I say you couldn't do? Zero. How many times did I say you had to do it alone? Zero."

Vig scowled. "Alright, I get it. You never said I couldn't clear a damn path, you just said get through it." He picked up the lead rope again, picked up a cone in the other hand and threw it. He tried to move a chair, then set down the rope to use both hands. He turned and saw the horse leaving, and let out a long string of curses. He saw Max laughing, and cursed again.

"What a dumbass," Max said. "Geez, you're an idiot."

Vig gave him a middle finger. "How the hell is that therapeutic?"

"I technically can't be your therapist," Max said. "That's a—what is it—dual relationship. Consider me your leader."

"We're not in the damn Corps now, Turner. I can tell you to kiss my glorious ass."

"Vig—" Max's grin nearly split his face. "How many times did I say you had to do this alone? What do you call a man who identifies resources at his disposal and refuses to use them, preferring to fail? You are literally stuck in your own mess. You literally can't move forward. Maguire and I are right here. So, what the hell?"

Vig blew out air. "Fine. Turner, Maguire, will you please give me a hand with this?"

"Of course." Max started clearing obstacles, while I retrieved Quincy. The two men quickly cleared a broad pathway, and I handed Vig the lead rope. I picked up a short PVC segment that was leaning against a chair and twirled it in my hands while the guys ceremoniously led Quincy back and forth through the aisle, making it a joke. Taking the sting out of it.

Movement in the parking lot caught my eye. Two squad cars and an unmarked car pulled in and came to a stop on the gravel.

Chapter Three

"Max? Max, we've got an issue, here."

A couple of uniforms and Ben's hotshot friend, Detective Tom Harmon, got out and headed toward us.

"MAX!!" I shouted.

Max and Vig looked up as the cops neared the arena. Max tossed the rope over Quincy's back and stepped forward. "What—"

Detective Tom was holding cuffs. "Enzo Viglione, I'm arresting you on suspicion of homicide."

Vig gaped at him, "What?" He and Max both froze in stunned shock. Vig was clearly bewildered as he was cuffed. He shook his head to clear it. "What?"

Max watched, mouth open, as Vig was led to a squad car. He followed at a distance. "What the hell? What?"

My stomach clenched with rage. Hardly breathing, I stormed up to the detective. "Are you out of your mind? This is completely unacceptable! We are in the middle of a therapy session! There is no excuse for this! Absolutely none!" I stabbed my finger in the air, inches from his face. "What if he was in surgery? Would you barge into the operating room and command the doctor to down scalpels? Would you? I hope this happens to you! I hope you're in an exam room with a gloved finger right up your butt when the goon squad breaks the door in!"

Harmon glanced at me. "You're overreacting."

My face flared hot. Knowing it was turning bright red just intensified my anger. I shook the piece of PVC at him. "You're as ignorant as you are condescending and dismissive! Do you have any idea the damage you are causing? Set aside that this is private property! Set aside that sessions are legally confidential! It matters if you compound trauma! There is no reason you could not have waited an hour for this ridiculous charade! Do you have any idea how hard it is for people to come in here at all? Do you?"

Detective Harmon walked away. I followed him. "Now my client will at least subconsciously associate therapy with getting cuffed and shoved in a squad car! Completely blindsided by some promotion-seeking jackass with a badge! We might as well close the doors and not have clients at all! At least people wouldn't be damaged here!"

Max exchanged hard looks with one of the uniformed cops, but stood, unmoving. "Vig, don't worry, we got you. We'll figure this out."

Vig was calm—or, more likely, shut down tight. "Call Jules."

"I will," Max said. "I'll call her, I'll get you a lawyer. I got you."

"You could have damn well waited." I raised my voice, punctuated my words by stabbing the PVC in Harmon's direction. "He is hardly a fugitive. You know where he lives, where he works. He didn't even know you wanted him! You could've asked him to come in! You could pick him up anywhere without violating a confidential session! There is absolutely no excuse! This is medical treatment! You are trespassing! And you are completely out of line!"

"I'm going to need your notes and files on Mr. Viglione," Detective Harmon said.

"Like hell! Medical notes are protected by law. You can get a court order, or you can take a flying—"

"Maguire." Max interrupted. "Let's take a step back now. We need to focus on helping Vig."

I blew out air, crossed my arms over my chest, glowered. "Get a court order. Or get—" I quivered with the effort of stopping my mouth.

Harmon narrowed his eyes at me. "I can do that. It's going to take time away from actively solving a homicide. I would think a therapist would care about a person losing their life."

"I would think a sworn police officer would care about the law."

He nodded curtly. "Alright. I'll be back."

I glared at the back of his car until it left the property. Max pulled out his cellphone, paused. "He's blowing smoke about getting a warrant. He's gonna be pissed, though, if he does, and finds out we have zero paperwork on Vig."

"I'll make up a blank file for him," I said. "With a big note that says, 'If the detective wasn't such an incomprehensible idiot, we might have had time to write something down here.'"

Max called Jules. I walked away, looked at Vig's truck in the parking lot. Max could drive Vig's truck to his house—Vig had set his keys and phone aside before we started. I'd follow in my own truck and bring Max home. My adrenaline was starting to level off, fury settling into a cold anger. My gaze took in the row of three trucks—Max's and mine dusty from gravel roads, Vig's with off-road mud—and a thought occurred. My stomach tightened again, with returning rage. I pulled out my cellphone and dialed Ben.

"Abby! You done for the night? I was just going to run out for a pizza, you want to join me? I can swing by."

His chipper voice made me angrier. "You!" I took a deep breath, blew out through my nose. I could feel Ben silently recalculating. "You told Tom to come here for Vig. I saw you scoping him out, eying up his vehicle. How dare you? How could you do that? How could you? You knew he was a person of interest, didn't you? Nobody else knew, including Vig! None of us had any idea! You drove away and sent the dogs in—to a therapy session, Ben! Do you have that little respect for what I do? Do you think it doesn't matter? How dare you!"

There was a long silence. I looked at the screen to see if I had lost the connection.

"Abby—"

I hung up, turned off the ringer and stuck my phone in my pocket.

Jules was furious, as loud as Max was calm. Max had a switch that flipped in times of crisis, from emotionally engaged to detached efficiency. He walked Jules through finding a veterans' legal aid program, and stood with her while she called and left a message. He assured her that he would stop at nothing to help sort things out. Told her to call, day or night, even to rant. "You can scream and swear at me at two in the morning," he said. "We're gonna get through this. We'll figure it out, Jules. Don't for one minute think you and Vig are alone."

The drive home was quiet, both of us lost in thought. I turned into the gravel driveway, and stopped. Ben's truck was in the lot. He saw me, got out, and leaned against his tailgate. My heartrate kicked up. I heard, rather than felt, my breathing change.

Max looked from Ben, to me, to Ben again. "Yeah, I'm out. Come on over when you're done." He got out and walked to his house.

I sat for a moment, then drove in and parked next to Max's truck. I took a deep breath and pondered whether there was anything to be gained by using careful, measured words. I walked over and stood a few feet from Ben, arms crossed so he wouldn't see me shaking with anger, and glared at him. Waited for him to speak.

"Abby, can we just talk about this?"

"Go ahead, Ben. Explain why you sent your roommate with an armed escort to disrupt a therapy session, completely disregarding my client's wellbeing."

He straightened and faced me. He took on an open stance with hands raised, palms out in a gesture of nonaggression, goodwill. To make me relax and trust him, I assumed. He'd paid attention in "conflict de-escalation for feds" class. Good for him.

"I didn't tell him to interrupt a session," Ben said. "I didn't tell him not to wait, and grab Viglione when he left the property. I don't tell him how to apprehend anyone, Abby. But can you just look at this from another perspective?"

I willed myself to shift into therapy mode. It had served me well for decades of listening attentively to delusional or psychotic rambling. It would work for Ben. Turn off my emotions. Maybe provoke his emotions—this wasn't therapy, after all—and get him to tell me something he probably wasn't even supposed to know. I exhaled slowly. "When you pretend to visit me, to pump me for information and use me to justify being somewhere, don't kiss me. That's disgusting."

He used his reasonable tone. "This is a homicide investigation. I know your profession is important to you, I know you're passionate about it. But a person was murdered, Abby. That's very serious also. It has to be."

My right eyelid started twitching. "Important to me? To me. This is not about me needing you to validate my career." I watched a dust devil blow in from the dirt road, carried on a gust of wind. I wiggled my toes inside my boots, to ground myself, calm. "Mental health is a branch of medicine, Ben. The arena is an exam room, a treatment area. Safe, confidential therapy is important whether it's my profession or not."

"I'm not contesting that." Ben moved his hands wider, looked patient. "I'm not saying they should have interrupted your session, okay? But you're lucky you didn't get arrested yourself, waving a stick in a cop's face, screaming. You can't do that, Abby. And from another perspective, yes, Viglione is a person of interest. A viable one. More than enough to warrant taking a squad and some uniforms to detain him."

"If you think he's that dangerous, why drive away, Ben? Leave me here out in the middle of the woods with someone you think is homicidal? Thanks a lot for that."

Ben huffed out a breath through his nose, ran a hand through his hair. "Please. As if anyone's going to lay a finger on you with Max around."

I gaped at him. "You drove away, leaving me with someone you thought was a killer, and told the cops to barge in, disrupting therapy, because you're jealous of Max?!"

His eyes bulged. "Jealous? Are you nuts?" Gone the calming posture—Ben waved his arms in the air. "Listen, whatever the warrant was based on, I've seen the guy. Lives a mile from the body dump site. That's right next door! Can't verify his whereabouts. Ex-Marine with extensive combat experience. Vast array of personal firearms. Gets into public fistfights when he's drinking—currently has a black eye given to him by the homicide victim the day before, witnessed by a bar full of people! They're not going to roll up and arrest him at his own wooded property, with his whole arsenal at hand! You got a problem with that, maybe you should check your own save-the-bottom-feeders bias!"

I couldn't breathe. That last comment punched the air out of me. Ben's face immediately changed from irritation to regret. I didn't want to hear his backpedaling. I pointed a finger in his face. "He was alone for the weekend because his wife was out of town. He's a decorated American veteran who served several tours of combat defending thankless, presumptuous people like you. He and his wife built a recreational shooting range on their property and use their registered firearms there, along with other law-abiding, licensed gun owners—like you, Mr. Civilian Detective."

I raised my voice. "If he does have anger issues—which I certainly wouldn't talk to you about, with privacy of health information laws—he's not likely to resolve them any time soon. You've seen to that. Well done," I shouted, stabbing a finger at his chest. "And you're only calling my clients bottom-feeders as a psychological deflection! You can't handle knowing you're worse!" I stormed away, to stop myself. I didn't want to say anything that would actually hit the mark and hurt him. I'm terrible at arguments. I rant, but I never want to draw blood.

"Abby, I'm sorry," he called to my back. "I didn't mean to say that."

I opened Max's door without knocking, locked it behind me, and leaned against it. I heard Ben drive away. Max stood in his kitchen, grim but curious. I had never barged into his house before. "Did you know Vig got that black eye from the murder victim?" I asked.

Max closed his eyes. "Shit." He took a few breaths. "I called Walt."

"What did he say?"

"He was very quiet." Max paused. "He tends to get real quiet when he's angry." He pulled out a chair and sat heavily. "He did say if they come back with a warrant, he will personally interact with them. Hands off for us. Probably just as well."

Ben apologetically, humbly asked me to just disagree with him, and move on. There was precedent for this. We still disagreed about the bugs he planted in my purse and apartment when we met last summer. Ben argued that he had been on a murder case. We hadn't been dating when he placed them. Everyone came up for my coffee klatches, found their way up my stairs. Everyone—including the killer, he never failed to remind me. It was an effective way of doing business. Promoting justice, no less.

Which all sounded great, if you set aside that it was illegal for a reason. He romanced me while listening to and recording private moments—deep, personal conversations he had no right to hear. When his case was resolved and he came by to remove his equipment, he expected me to be irritated—we would argue and move on. He was perplexed when I felt betrayed, humiliated. When shock gave way to fury.

Ben stayed the course. He calmly, patiently insisted that he hadn't merely been using me. I gradually allowed him back into my life, but it cast shadows, and lingered like an aftertaste. He was an expert at the long game, Ben. Knew how to wait until the angry flames became embers, how to turn the fact of his waiting to his advantage. Look dedicated, committed. Make me forget he started the fire in the first place.

Ben smiled warmly and slid sideways through my door, with a bag of groceries in each arm. He was a talented chef, and demonstrated love with food. "I had to buy the bread," he said. "I just ran out of time. It's from the bakery, though, fresh today."

His eyes had dark circles underneath, and lacked their usual twinkle. He set the bags on the counter, pulled me in, and rested his face on my head. His breath ruffled my hair. We stood like that for a long moment.

I wrapped my arms around his waist. Ben always immersed himself in a case. I certainly couldn't fault him on dedication. I wondered what he was doing that left him so exhausted, but there was no point asking. I let him stand and breathe, feeling the warmth of my body.

"Ravioli," he finally said, pulling slightly back. "I actually did a lot of the prep work in the middle of the night. We've got beef and butternut squash for fillings."

"That sounds wonderful," I told him. "Let me help you this time, instead of sitting on the counter watching you cook."

"Not a chance." He turned and unloaded his bags, making a row of jars on the counter.

"I know cooking is something you do for me, Ben. But you're completely drained." I scootched my butt up on the far end and leaned against the fridge, swinging my feet. "I wish I knew what to say that would be encouraging. Or that you'd let me listen."

He pulled out my cutting board and his own rolling pin. "As much as I'd love to, my profession doesn't lend itself to talk therapy." He floured the board and pulled out a ball of dough. "I will say, it's so tiring, having to connive and coax to get real information out of people. It would be so nice to meet one person who was honest. Straightforward."

I bit my lip, squinting with the effort of keeping my mouth shut. I wanted to be supportive. Did he hear himself? Darn those dishonest people he was conniving. As if they were obligated to satisfy his curiosity. Maybe he should get a different job where he didn't intrude into other people's lives, and forget that he doesn't have a right to something just because he wants it. Maybe he'd be happier.

Ben had that tightening around his eyes that meant he was irritated. He rolled the dough flat and thin, didn't look at me. "I hear you thinking, Abby. Mind toning that down a little?" When he did turn to face me, he put on his inscrutable cop face.

I was trying, I really was, but he knew that was an act of war. I countered with a nonreactive therapy face, knowing it would annoy him. He blinked hard and turned back to his dough.

"Let's talk about something other than work," I offered. "Just relax and chat."

He spun the board a quarter-turn, rolled the dough the other direction. Said nothing. His shoulder muscles rippled under his shirt. Finally, he blew out a slow, even breath. He deliberately didn't look at me. "I really don't want to argue, Abby. I apologize for getting snarky, when you held back your opinion."

"You start, Ben. You set the conversation."

He flipped the dough, folded it in quarters, and set it aside. He pulled out another ball of dough. "I don't even feel sorry for this guy that got killed, how about that? It makes everything more difficult. I'll be professional, obviously. I'll do whatever I can to close the case, but I really don't care that the vic's off the planet. Can you know that, and eat my cooking?"

"Of course I can. You're a great cook." I was happy to see the corners of his mouth twitch. "I thought you said businessman earlier, but what, drug dealer? Pimp?"

"Oh, no!" Ben paused the rolling pin, threw up a hand. Ben struggled to talk with his hands full. "There'd be way less pressure if he was an honest bad guy. Pretender bad guys, they're the worst. Real asset to society. Can't find one single person who didn't despise him, but we can't have apparently law-abiding citizens getting bumped off. Don't want to panic the populace. Well, let me tell you, the populace is not panicking. They're all smiling." The rolling pin gained a new energy.

"Okay, you can't say that and leave me hanging. What can you actually tell me?"

Ben paused to wave the other hand. "Well, this much is open knowledge. Doug Larsen. Business owner, life-long resident. On all kinds of boards, commissions. Everyone hated him, everyone kissed up to him."

"What kind of business?"

Ben noted the change in my tone, and shot me a tired grin over his shoulder. He knew he'd hook me with conflicting human emotions and behavior. "Auto parts. Haven't heard that he cheated anyone, but they might not admit it right after he gets knocked off."

I was fascinated. "How are they showing this? The hatred or the kissing up?"

"The hatred, with body language, facial expression, tone of voice. Or just a guarded, satisfied demeanor. A few people had some choice descriptions that would make a trucker blush. Nobody—I mean nobody—has made any pretense of oh, it's sad. Oh, that was a terrible thing. Nobody." Ben paused to spoon dollops of filling onto half of his sheet of dough. He focused on folding the other half over the top, then pressing his finger around each little hill of filling.

"The sucking up," he continued, "people tell on each other for that. Now the guy's dead, it's easy to point fingers at each other. Like a dam bursting, almost." He pulled out a pasta wheel and rolled it over the indentations his fingers had made. "Now you.

Any regrets about changing your temp job routine for a longer stint, to be here for a full year?"

"No," I said, "but ask me in a few months. I'm a little uneasy thinking about twenty degrees below zero, and wind chills." Successfully changing the mood felt like a major win for us. I wasn't sure it should be this much work, but maybe this was just who we were, both of us.

We relaxed through dinner, teased each other affectionately, ate too much. I always ate too much of Ben's cooking. We held it together long enough to do the dishes, blow soap suds at each other, laugh. Tonight we sank into the couch that we often moved to dance in the living room.

And Ben decided to poke me. "We should take a selfie together, so you could have a picture of us up, not just a picture with Max."

I stiffened. "You mean the picture with Ida, Walt and Max? All of my coworkers?"

"You know what I mean."

I slid to the end of the couch. A throw pillow fell down between us. I left it there. "I know you're tired, Ben. Just don't."

"I've been wondering, are we still casually dating?"

I knew what that seemingly innocuous question meant. I'd been clear at the onset of this relationship that I don't include sex as part of every casual date with every guy. "I know you come from a much more loudly expressive family than I do," I said, "but I'd like to get through one date without arguing. Bickering just isn't foreplay for me."

He shrugged. "You go so far, Abby, and that's it. You're like an Oreo cookie. Incredibly sweet, but it's hidden under the hard, crispy part."

"Oh, listen to you!" This was too much. I glared at him. "Are you married?"

"What? No!" He lost his momentum. "Are you?"

"You know I'm not, having already run a check on me."

He missed a beat. "What?"

"I knew it."

He opened his mouth, closed it. His face hardened a little. "What are you on about?"

"Oh, please." I drew my feet up under me and hugged myself with my arms. I didn't care if I looked closed. "Don't try to act like you haven't done background checks on me. I'm sure you know every pertinent fact about me. You investigate everything, you can't stop yourself. It's an obsession. Whereas, I know what you choose to put forward, like your dog's name when you were ten. Half the time I've known you, you pretended to be a ranch hand!"

Ben scowled. "As if you believed that for a minute."

"That's beside the point! You don't reveal yourself, Ben, at least not on purpose. You think you're so inscrutable—you might as well tattoo a badge on your forehead. But you never tell me who you really are."

I had an epiphany, and stopped talking. Ben squinted at me. No matter. I'd just realized I was not without resources, myself. I'd worked with so many people over the years, made so many friends—many of them in various roles in law enforcement or licensure. Why hadn't I thought of this before? I knew at least three of them would do a background check for me on the sly. I smiled.

"What?" Ben made no effort to hide his annoyance.

"I really do appreciate the work you put into these meals, Ben. You do such a good job." Self-satisfaction caused my annoyance to evaporate. I smiled warmly.

Ben scowled, off balance and not liking it. He claimed exhaustion and gathered his things. He did rally for a kiss at the door, but the fun had gone down the drain with the soap suds. I watched him drive away, then opened my laptop and decided who to email.

Ida came in the next afternoon with a cheery hello. She left her boots at the door and padded down the hall. Her salt-and-pepper hair was spiky these days. She pulled it off magnificently, adding a fun touch to her weathered face, her sturdy build. "You're not busy tomorrow night, are you?"

Because it was Ida, I answered before finding out why she was asking. "I'm free. What's up?"

She gave me her encouraging smile. "My girlfriends and I are having dinner—you remember, the Old Bats Club. We'd like you to join us, be an honorary member while you're here. You're a little young, but we're willing to overlook it. What do you say?"

My email notification pinged. I glanced at it, then opened the attachment with delight. "Benson! Huh. I would've guessed Benjamin. There I go, assuming."

"What are you doing?" Ida moved in close.

"Background information on Ben," I explained happily. "He thinks he's the only one with contacts, with his fancy PI skills. He didn't even deny doing a search on me." I read a few choice bits aloud. "We were right," I crowed. "We nailed it, day one. He was a fed! ATF Special Agent. I wonder how I can find out why he left?"

"Hunh." Ida's weighty disapproval didn't dim my enthusiasm, not one bit. She shook her head. "That's a strange way to have a relationship, doing background checks on each other. Lord, help. I never heard of such a thing." That didn't stop her from reading over my shoulder, murmuring at the interesting parts. When we got to the end, she pulled away and pretended she hadn't been glued to the screen. "What do you say? Will you join us?"

"Sure! I love dinner." I smiled at my computer, then at Ida. "If your friends don't mind."

Chapter Four

"No. He's not moving out." Jules stalked across the room. "No, Turner. Before this, I would've gone with it, but now it'll look like I kicked him out. Like I thought he was guilty, like we're having problems. It'll get used against him. He stays here."

Vig sat quietly at the table, as if he were not being discussed.

"I get that." Max was calm, quiet. He had the air of assured authority he sometimes took on. "Look at it this way. This sleep disturbance, it's gonna get worse with stress. Even being released without charges, the stress increased exponentially here. And who's going to know, anyway?"

"The cops will know," Jules said, "And people talk, Turner. You know small towns. Everyone will tell their cousin, their aunt and their grandma. Everyone will know."

"Call it anger management," Max said. "If this ever did lead to charges—which it won't, because there's nothing there—it just makes him look that much better. Yes, he got in a scuffle outside the bar, but he's working on de-escalation tactics. Deflecting provocation. Not getting pulled into conflicts. All that is stuff we really could do."

"And what about his reputation?" Jules said. "People don't forget things, especially gossip that somebody's neighbor's second cousin swore was a fact."

Vig stood, walked over to his wife and reached for both of her hands. "Jules. Listen. I know you got my back. I know you got me. But listen. I don't give a half a damn what people say. The whole point of going to the ranch was, it was for you. To deal with this thing before I ever hurt you. And that's still what it is. That's all I care about. Just you."

They stood in the middle of the kitchen, holding onto each other, for several minutes before morosely joining us at the table.

"How long are we talking about?" Jules asked. "A week or two?"

Max shook his head. "Give us a month, six weeks." He held up a hand, stopping them. "I know. But there's no point playing around. We gotta really do it."

"Six weeks?" Vig was loudly aggrieved. "Turner, I haven't been away from Jules that long ever, without being deployed. Ever."

"It's not like you can't see each other. Every day, if you want. Just sleep at my place, hang out enough to get some sessions in. We can fit a lot of sessions in." Max was quiet, let it settle.

I waited a few minutes while Vig frowned at the table, then turned to him. "You ever get a car stuck in a snowbank?"

Vig pulled slightly back and looked at me like I'd started speaking Swahili. "You do go off on tangents." He eyed me warily, shrugged. "Sure. Buried one practically up to the windshield. Hell of a deal. Had to get a tractor to pull it out."

Max smiled.

"Huh," I said innocently. "You couldn't just hook a tow rope on there and floor it?"

"No, no! Damn, you'd rip the whole bumper off. You might have to get out there with a shovel, clear out a little bit, pull a little more, you got to—" He stopped, scowling at me.

I smiled sweetly. "Ever do a restoration job?" I knew he had a muscle car in the garage. "I've heard it takes time, you want to do it right."

Vig shot me a side-eye. "Screw you, Maguire."

I was delighted. I was accepted, one of them. He hadn't thrown me an F-bomb, but casual rudeness was a step in the right direction.

Ida drove us to a family diner in Deergrass. Two women were already seated at a table in the back of the room. One of them patted the chair next to her. "Abby, you sit right here." She took my handbag and stacked it with the others on a designated purse chair. "I'm Janet Elson. And this is Betsy Clark, and we're still waiting for Fran. She's coming, though. She texted. I have no idea where she is."

Betsy had a neon blue streak in her chin-length grey hair. Ida patted it and sat next to her. "That color looks good. What is that, the royal blue or the vivid blue?" She carefully took it in her fingers, examined it. "It's nice and conditioned, too. Didn't dry out, not at all."

Betsy smiled at me, then turned to Ida. "I'd recommend it for you, but you haven't got enough hair. You can pull off that spiky look, though—I just look ridiculous. How long ago did Fran text? She's not texting while she's driving again, is she?"

Janet peered at her phone. "Just watch me try to do that. Tobias would have my head." She glanced at me. "Tobias is my son. He's a police officer. He sometimes forgets exactly which one of us taught the other to eat with a spoon."

Ida laughed. "Is he still going on about that night at bingo?"

Janet snorted. "He throws it in here and there. Okay, here it is, texted a half hour ago. Just leaving home." She set her phone on the table. "She lives five minutes away, so she'll have a story to tell. We've got some important things to talk about tonight, Abby, that's why we asked for a table away from other people. But we'll wait until Fran gets here. Ida's got something, and then so does Betsy."

I hadn't realized Old Bats Club meetings had agendas, but why not? I knew they went on road trips together. Something about Janet's tone made me suspect they went on missions together as well. Ida was up to something, and she hadn't warned me. Not so much as a hint.

We all chatted until Fran came bustling in, looking harried. "I apologize. I stopped at the store to buy flies—I want to practice my casting over the winter—and the man just would not stop talking." She dumped her coat on the extra chair.

"Probably trying to pick you up," Janet said. "You're the best thing he's seen in the bait section in years."

Fran started digging through her purse. "I might let him. You know how long it's been since I've been picked up? He was a talker, though." She shook her head. "Too much talk, not enough action.

Our generation has to have more in the tank than that, don't you think?"

She pulled things out of her bag and set them in front of her. "Think of the mileage at this table—but there's tread left on the tires. I hope I didn't leave my phone there. And no, I didn't have it out while I was driving, so you can all just stop right there."

She pulled out a package of tissues, a tin of mints, a tiny tape measure. A utility knife. A spork. An oblong, plastic device with a hose tucked inside it—set it right down and kept digging. I blinked. Holy Hannah. Right on the tablecloth.

Janet leaned in. "You need to take charge. Get his mind off his inventory and on to yours."

Betsy chuckled. "Where was this? Just over at Gundersons?"

"Betsy wants to check out his bait," Janet said. "Did you talk about rods?"

Ida picked up the plastic device. "What in the world is this, something to fill your thermos?"

Fran glanced up at me. "Abby, I'm Fran Winters. I didn't say." She moved her billfold and looked under it. "Abby knows what it is." She smiled mischievously.

Betsy and Janet focused on me expectantly. Ida studied the device, turned it over in her hands, pulled the hose through the little hole on one end, finally looked up.

I cleared my throat. "It's a Shewee. Or a Go Girl." They all looked blank, so I tried again. "A Tinkle Belle? A Freshette. Although I haven't seen one quite like that before, with that style hose."

"It's an older model." Fran looked around the table. "Not to put too fine a point on things."

"Let me see that." Betsy reached for it and turned it right-side up. "It's a urinal."

Ida and Janet straightened in their chairs. "Would you look at that," Ida said. "Hand that back over here, Betsy." They passed it around the table, murmuring and tsking.

"I don't know who to grill first." Janet fully extended the hose and pulled it tight against the washer. "What's it doing in Fran's purse, and why does Abby know every version on the market?"

"It's a bit of an equalizer," I explained. "Go like a guy, without undressing."

"Lord, help." Ida leaned forward eagerly. "I never heard of such a thing."

I toasted her with my water glass. "It's a big, wide world out there, Ida. If you want to see it, you have to be able to pee there."

Fran raised her glass to mine. I continued, "I knew a woman in the National Guard who was issued one by the government. It was a lot easier for the guys—they could just pretend they were checking the air pressure in the tires."

They all nodded thoughtfully. I went on, "I once worked with a female deputy who had a hard time finding a place to pee on duty. You can't drop your duty belt anywhere that someone could reach under a partition and grab your weapon. Honestly, if men had to drop trou to pee, these things would be passed out like napkins at McDonald's."

The waitress came for our order, looked at Janet and froze, mouth slightly open.

"Janet, I hope you used soap on that," Fran said. "Put that away."

Janet's eyes widened. She dropped the Freshette on the table. The waitress took two steps back. "I'll just give you a minute." She fled to the kitchen.

Ida and Betsy shook with laughter. Ida wiped tears from her eyes.

"Go ahead and laugh," Janet said. "Tobias will hear about this, you know he will. Every time I move in this town, someone calls him."

"We'll watch for squad cars," Betsy said. "Fran Winters, is that what you were doing in the city park? I thought you were looking for berries in there. I'm telling Tobias that, when he gets here to scold Janet." She picked up her own phone and poked a few buttons. Somewhere in the pile of coats, Janis Joplin started singing.

Fran sighed, stuffed everything back in her purse, and pulled her phone from her coat pocket. "Thank you, Betsy. How long do you suppose it will be before we can eat, now?"

"I think they're coming back to kick Janet out," Ida said. "The rest of us can order then." She wiped her cheeks again, replaced her eyeglasses. "Oh, my."

The woman who came to take our orders, twenty years older than the first, smiled with wry humor. She winked at Janet, although the Freshette had been tucked back into Fran's purse. Janet was the very picture of falsely accused indignation. Fran was delighted. The server would get a good tip.

As soon as the woman walked away, Betsy settled forward on her elbows. "Alright, ladies. Let's get down to business. We have a lot to talk about tonight, too much to cover over dessert. Ida, you have the floor."

Ida quickly became serious. "Well, you all know about Doug Larsen being killed. We need to find out who did it."

I froze with my water glass halfway to my mouth. The others nodded seriously and waited for her to go on.

"Max's best friend is getting blamed," Ida said. "Max is so upset. He's determined to do absolutely anything, won't be able to think about anything else until his friend is cleared. Well, Fran was right, there is a great deal of mileage around this table. We know a lot. There's something we can do, I know there is. Abby's already brought down a killer—"

I gaped at her.

"Well, I did help," Ida said. "We did it together, but we need more resources this time. So. What do you all know about Doug Larsen, that we could start with?"

After a moment, I realized everyone was watching my mouth hang open. "Ida Gill. You lured me here! You crafty old fox!"

"That's fair," Fran said. "You are one. Of course we'll help. Max is like family to you, we all know that. We help family."

"I knew little Dougie his whole life," Janet said. "Abby, you may not know Fran and I were teachers. Career teachers know everyone. It's surprising we don't get bumped off more often, don't you think? We know every family better than they want to admit."

She considered that for a moment, then continued. "Dougie was a red flag from the get-go. He was a mean little boy. I know it's out of fashion to say that, but it's true. 'Doesn't play well with others' was the least of it. Never a sign of remorse, and he really didn't care about consequences, either."

"Same when he was older," Fran said. "Win at all costs. Above other people, thought himself superior. By high school, I think he divided the world into people he thought he could use, and people he disregarded. Which is worse—being used, or being disregarded entirely?"

"I didn't know him," Betsy said. "I was a librarian, Abby. He never set foot in the door, as far as I know."

Fran scowled. "Made a lot of noise about cutting library funding." All of their faces darkened at that. Even Ida looked menacing. I nodded. As soon as I accepted the year-long gig here, Max took me to get a library card. He threw in a highlight tour of all the events and resources they have in addition to books, for free.

"I can tell you that his wife isn't exactly heartbroken." Betsy was interrupted by the server with our food. We all started eating, but when the woman walked away, Betsy continued. "She went right out and bought new clothes. Nice ones, too, and flattering. Turns out she has good taste. I hope she has a good alibi. She took all his clothes out in the middle of the field and made a big bonfire."

"I saw that," Janet said. "You could see the smoke for miles. I drove by just to see what was going on. Of course, there were cops checking it out too, so Tobias came by later to scold me for following fire trucks, which I did not do. Not at all. He was already testy because of my anti-squirrel activity a few days earlier. Anyway, there she stood, feeding jackets and slacks into the flames, piece by piece. Well, she had it under control, so there was nothing to charge her with. More power to her, I say."

"She's got postings on the Buy/Sell bulletin boards at all the gas stations," Betsy said. "Guns and hunting bows."

Ida frowned. "You know, I never heard specifically how he was killed. That would surely help, to know that."

We all thought, but shook our heads. "Well, how are we going to find out?" Janet asked. "Tobias will just get huffy, I can't ask him."

"I'll call my old coworker," Betsy said. "Librarians know everything." Two minutes later, after a matter-of-fact phone call, she announced, "Suffocated. Passed out drunk at the time, wouldn't have been aware at all. Moved out to a field—very shallow grave, just barely covered."

"Well, Betsy! That was very efficient," Ida said. "Didn't she ask why you wanted to know?"

Betsy looked blank. "Why would anyone need a reason to know things? I generally want to know everything. Oh, you'd be surprised what librarians talk about."

No one spoke for a moment.

I steered us back on topic, sharing what Ben told me—he said it was public knowledge. "The field was by Vig's place," I added. "Max's friend. I was there when the cops first found the body. A deputy came and asked if they heard machinery."

"They must have found tracks, like a backhoe," Fran said. "Smaller, maybe—a Bobcat, or a skid loader. Something to lift a body. That would really make it easier, but then why a shallow grave? That means it was shallow on purpose. Make a note of that, everyone."

"I don't understand that," Ida said. "If you want a body to be found, why haul it out to a field and bury it a little, but not really?"

No one had anything to offer. “Okay,” Janet said. “We know what we’re working on. We’ll all see what we can find out. Next topic, Betsy?”

Betsy straightened. “We need to finalize our plans to get tattoos on our bums.”

I dropped my cup.

Chapter Five

Coffee sloshed out, all over the table. Everyone grabbed napkins, scrambled to move dishes. A waitress brought a cloth, wiped the table, and left a pile of paper napkins. "I'm so sorry," I said, when I stopped coughing.

"Not at all," Betsy said. "I caught you unawares."

"Can I just ask—" I paused to choose my words carefully. "Um, how this came about?"

They all exchanged glances across the table. "That's actually a matter of some debate," Fran said. "We can only agree that the origins are unclear. I remember Janet talking about getting a handgun on her bottom, and the words 'hotter than a two-dollar pistol.' It did sound exciting."

"We were meeting," Betsy went on, "like this, except over margaritas. By the end of the evening we decided we'd all get one, together. We just have to firm up the details. Has everyone finalized their choices?"

"I want to know if Abby's in," Janet said. Everyone turned to me expectantly. I was at a loss for words, which has maybe happened twice before, in my entire life.

"Um," I said. "Is it even late enough in the year for Max to cover all the trail rides for a few weeks?"

"I'm sure Walt would step in," Ida said.

"Wait—you're going to tell Max and Walt they need to pick things up, because we got tattoos on our butts?" I couldn't breathe.

"Oh, Abby, you know they both make a living observing tiny changes in stance and behavior. You think they won't notice?"

I pulled back into my seat. I started to curl, as if moving toward a fetal position.

"This isn't quite fair," Betsy said. "Abby hasn't had time to think about it. We know what Janet's getting. Fran, how about you?"

"A motorcycle. I can't ride like I used to, but at least I can sit on one. And you, Betsy?"

"I'm getting a griffin."

Silence. Finally Janet spoke. "A what?"

"A griffin is half lion, half eagle," Betsy explained.

"I think we all know that, Betsy," Fran said. "But why?"

"It's perfect for a librarian. Griffins were guardians of treasure, and in some cultures stood for knowledge and wisdom—but they had claws, and knew how to use them."

"Well, alright then," Ida said. "I look forward to seeing that. Multi-colored, or just the outline?"

"That's an excellent question," Betsy said. "What about you?"

"I just can't decide," Ida said. "Abby, maybe you and I can shop around, find some good ones together."

No one would ever believe this, any of it. Ida would carry on as if I'd already decided, and I'd have a dragon on my butt before I knew what hit me. The entire evening took on a feel of unreality.

"You know, it's just occurred to me," Janet said, "when Tobias lectured me about the squirrels, that would have been the day the body was found. Maybe that's why he was so darn cranky."

"What are you talking about?" Ida wrinkled her brow. "I don't know this story." The others had expressions of hesitant curiosity.

"They just get on my last nerve," Janet said. "Getting in the feeders, scaring the birds away, chewing the openings bigger. I finally just snapped. Grabbed my Red Ryder, went charging out there in my big, old t-shirt and baggy mom shorts." She gestured dramatically, did a quiet imitation of shouting. "Not today, mother—well. Started blasting away at them. They all just scattered. No one got hurt, but try telling Tobias that."

The table was silent as Janet paused for a drink. "I just can't think who ratted me out," she went on. "My neighbor Warren was in the backyard with a friend of his, but Warren's a good egg. It can't have been him."

"I imagine there are plenty of times you never quite know," Ida said.

We had pie and coffee, and paid our bills. There was a squad car in the parking lot—right next to our vehicles. As we stepped out the door, the driver climbed out and leaned against his front bumper, arms folded over his chest. He watched us approach. "I told you so," Janet said.

"Hello, Tobias," Ida called cheerily. "How nice to see you."

"Yes, ma'am," he replied. "Always a treat." Tobias wore three stripes on his uniform, I noted. A sergeant. And fit. Not the exaggerated steroid look, but toned. The short sleeves of his uniform shirt were snug on his biceps. Probably around thirty—ten years younger than me—but oh, my. He smiled at Ida, and a dimple formed. Tobias and Janet waited each other out.

Fran wasn't having it. "What brings you here, Tobias? Passing by, and saw our cars?"

He gave Janet a sideways glance. "Something about a public disturbance? Scaring the waitstaff? Dumping coffee around?"

Janet drew herself to her full height and frowned. "Who really called you?"

Tobias laughed. "Someone off-duty thought I'd get a kick out of my mother playing with a urinary directional device at the dinner table. It's been quiet, so I thought I'd swing by and tease you a little."

I introduced myself. "I actually dropped the coffee."

"No worries." He shook my hand, met my eyes for just a tiny bit longer than expected. Did he? Or was I just delirious after a meal with the Old Bats Club? He definitely sized me up, wondered what I was doing there, wasn't going to ask. His radio crackled. "Gotta go. Have a nice evening, everyone."

Janet sputtered as he drove off. The Bats were huggers, so it took a few minutes to get away. Ida pulled out of the parking lot and glanced at me. "I saw you eyeing him up."

"I'm a trained observer," I said.

"Uh huh." She turned down a side street. "So what did you observe?"

"Well," I said. Not yum. Don't say that. "How much of Janet's complaining about him, his checking up on her, is all a game they play?"

"Ninety-five percent," Ida said. "They both enjoy it, as much as Janet fusses."

Vig was subdued, stepping down from the cab of his pickup. He looked like a Doberman who had been kicked too many times, lost its confident saunter through the junkyard, wanted to go sit behind a wrecked car and let the scrap metal thieves have at it. Max walked up to meet him. "I'm glad you came, man."

I tried to think of something helpful to say. Vig glanced at the barn, distracted by movement. I turned around—Walt strode across the gravel. Built like a brick, Walt was every bit a working boss. His black hair was streaked with silver, cut short, usually under a cowboy hat. His skin had a warm caramel tone, unless he was angry. Walt rarely got angry. When he did, he darkened several shades.

He held out his hand, grasped Vig's hand firmly, and leveled a no-nonsense gaze directly at him. That gaze unnerved many people—Walt, determined and purposeful, was a force. Max became still, watchful. Vig looked wary.

"Mr. Viglione, I'm glad you're here," Walt said.

"Thank you, sir. It's Vig."

Walt released Vig's hand. "Walt Bravo. Please call me Walt. I'm sorry about what happened the last time you were here. I want you to know, I do not support how that was handled, and they did not have permission to be on the property. You are welcome here."

Walt carried such an air of authority, it felt like a benediction. He shifted his weight back on his heels, and with his posture, the atmosphere changed. Vig visibly relaxed. Max beamed happily. For just a breath, troubles fell away.

"I understand I owe you a debt of gratitude," Walt went on. "I wouldn't have Max here, if it wasn't for you. He's invaluable, part of the very heart of this place. Thank you for helping him, bringing him here. Now, Max and Abby likely have plans for this morning, and I haven't talked with them about it, but I'd like to show you something, if you don't mind." Walt turned toward the outdoor arena. "Max, would you mind catching Ollie and bringing him in?"

Max grabbed a halter and rope, disappeared into the trees, and came back with a white horse flecked with grey. It glanced from side to side as it walked. Any of the horses would go anywhere with Max, but this one seemed unsettled. When Max draped the lead rope over Ollie's back, the horse moved to the gate and stuck his head over it. He glanced from Max, to Walt, to the pasture. His intention was clear.

Walt led Ollie to the far side of the arena, and tied the rope to a post. As soon as Walt turned his attention away, the horse tossed his head at an angle, in a way that looked practiced. The rope came untied, and he walked back to the gate. Walt returned him to the post. Ollie waited for Walt to turn his back, then jerked the rope free again, returning to stick his head over the gate. He whinnied. Some other horse whinnied back. Walt walked Ollie back to the post and tied the knot differently, sticking the end of the rope through a loop. Ollie was thwarted. He tossed his head, but couldn't get free.

Walt joined us across the arena. "Now, we're just going to talk here for a bit, and pay no attention to the horse. Just watch him in the peripheral." He talked about the hay stacked in the back of the barn and another shed, and whether it would be enough for winter. Max joined in, commenting on the relative quality of the hay. Vig and I exchanged a glance, shrugged.

Ollie started pacing with his hindquarters, back and forth in his range of motion, glancing occasionally at Walt. He raised a hoof and banged on the post with it, pushed down on the rope fence, stomped the sandy ground. Walt changed his posture and shot him a look, and Ollie stopped—though he did give Walt a side-eye. Walt used his own sharp, black eyes to hold the horse in place for a long moment. Then he walked over, untied the lead rope from the post, and led the horse in a few circles.

"Now, we want to have him do just a little work, so we don't teach him to kick things as a solution to being a little unhappy." Walt broke into a jog, the horse speeding up beside him. They did a few quick laps, then reversed direction for a few more. "Alright now, Max, would you please open the side gate over there, and then the arena gate?"

Max climbed through the ropes of the fence. He trotted over to open the side gate between the corral and the woods. The horse watched with a tension I could feel several feet away. When Max opened the arena gate, Ollie wiggled, glanced at Walt, squirmed.

"Stand." Walt waited until the horse was still, then removed the halter and took a step back. "Alright." The horse trotted through the gate, loped through the next gate, galloped full-out past the woods to a group of grazing horses, and nuzzled a few of them.

"Now, this is something we're working on with Ollie," Walt said, "but I wanted you to see the importance of the herd. Horses are social animals. They're hardwired to be part of a group—that's the context of their existence. And we're the same way. Study after study has shown that people need to belong as well, need to be part of a social context. It's just how we're built."

Vig listened politely, but I could tell he didn't see the point. Honestly, I didn't either.

Walt chuckled to himself. "I saw a horse one time, wanted to get back to its herd so bad. Person holding it wouldn't let go of the rope." The belly of his t-shirt twitched as he laughed quietly. "Ended up dragging the guy—butt tracks all the way across the arena." Walt grinned, shook his head. "Now, when you joined the military, how would you describe the herd you became a part of?"

Vig glanced at Max, but didn't speak.

"Think about how that herd changed," Walt said, "developed over time. The experiences you shared, the trials you endured together. How that impacted your feelings about each other. The group that was formed through it all—think about that group, that herd." He paused for a few moments, to let them process.

"Now," he went on, "consider whether the horse's behavior here reminds you of anything in your own life." Max and Vig had pulled back into themselves, but Vig couldn't mask the pain in his eyes.

"Grief isn't just about someone dying," Walt said. "Grief is about loss. Many kinds of loss. And grief is not willing to be ignored. Takes on a life of its own. Squeezes the life out of some people, but it can be worked out." He paused, visually assessed each of us in turn. "Changing herds is the hardest thing for a horse to go through. It's not an equivalent replacement to just step into. Different personalities, but also orders of dominance that are already established. Often takes some kicking and biting before a new horse has a place. Not the same as its place in the old herd. Bit of a change in identity, and it doesn't come without a struggle."

Walt turned his gaze to Ollie, and seemed to wait for something. We all watched. A horse wandered up to the group—Walt must have seen it lingering on the periphery, eyeing them. Two other horses pinned their ears, lowered their heads, and snapped their teeth at the newcomer. It fled, and they returned to eating grass. Walt nodded. "There's a lack of trust, with a new herd. Trust is built over time. Same with people."

He hooked Ollie's halter on a post and coiled up the rope. "Sometimes you see a person come into therapy with their ears back. Distrustful. Any beginning—new job, school, team. New herd."

Vig was going with it. "Horse loses its herd, can it ever get it back? Like, in the wild?"

Walt nodded seriously. "Herds get separated, there's a reason. Crisis of some kind, like a fire, maybe. Pressure on the herd changes—have to find resources, new way to resolve that pressure. You'll see herds come back together again when it's passed." He glanced from Max's face to Vig's. "One of these massive fires, of course, really significant event, the herd might not be there anymore." No one spoke.

"Young stallions on their own," Walt went on, "Might form their own herd for a time. You may see a stallion try to join a herd, it doesn't work, they go back to the boys' club. Not to stay forever, that's not a life-long herd, but they've got a place of belonging there." Walt nodded, slapped the end of the lead rope gently against his thigh.

Max turned his gaze to the far corral. He looked like he was studying the hay ring. Vig stopped breathing. Walt waited.

"I started doing better when I was back with Vig," Max said. "Not like he held my hand, but at least there was someone I could identify with. Yeah, I get it." He bumped shoulders with Vig. "And you're right about the group. You're there for each other, it gets you through. As much as they irritate the hell out of you sometimes, it hits the fan, they got you."

"But," he went on, "it's also, like, I don't know, it becomes who you are. You identify yourself— literally, the group literally becomes your name, and you're proud of that. Then, what? They're gone. I don't know why I'm not." He looked away, composed himself. "Come back here, I'm not saying people don't care. People don't get it. Isn't their fault. They can't—they fit, and you don't. You're the one that changed. And the people who changed with you, they aren't there."

Vig opened his mouth, closed it again, blinked hard. The quiet stretched out. The birdsong in the woods seemed amplified, the sound of galloping hooves on dry ground, wind in the tree tops. I moved my arms, and the whiffing of my sleeve against my jacket sounded loud.

"I felt so damn guilty," Vig finally said. "Not only did I get to come home, I came home to Jules. Not everyone had that. Luckiest man in the world. And I was desperate to come home to her, I really was. I should've been happier. I thought something must be wrong with me."

"Natural part of dealing with loss," Walt said. "It's real, and it matters. That isn't a fault that's in you somewhere. A person no longer has the group they were so bonded with, yet their old place in the prior group doesn't quite fit like it did. Something they wanted so badly feels different, now. Tremendous amount of grief there, completely apart from anyone dying. It's natural, and it can be worked out. Needs to be worked out, or it's an open wound."

I spoke up. "Vig, that was brilliant." I met his dubious look. "I mean it. Emotions can be such a convoluted mess, sometimes it takes months for people to figure out what they really do feel. You just called it out. Then you nailed the thought process that led you there."

I reached a hand into the air, pretended to grasp something, hold it, look at it. "Pull an actual thought into the open, figure out what its operational role in this battle is—how it's impacting you, what the consequences of that thought holding ground are—you can think about how you want to change it or eliminate it." Vig and Max exchanged a glance. Max's looked suspiciously like "I told you so."

I ignored them, except to raise my chin stubbornly. "Different battlefields call for different weapons and strategies. You learn and adapt. If you don't know how thoughts and emotions work on each other, you learn. Just like the specs of any weapon. Internal battles are just as real, and just as deadly, as external ones." They both looked decidedly noncommittal.

I shook my head, unwilling to yield. "We all know of threats in the physical world that were treated dismissively or minimized, or that came in under the radar, but they caused incredible damage. Same thing happens with internal threats. People can blow it off, say this is all a bunch of hoo-ha, or that even acknowledging the battle means you're weak, but this war takes casualties every single day. I'm never going to stop talking about it. People can be trained and equipped."

For what felt like an hour, no one spoke. Finally, Walt stepped forward. "I want you men to think about this together. Take a little time and talk through this whole concept. You both know exactly what we're talking about. Work it out. The two of you are a real small herd— might want to think about adding to it. Could be other folks around, in a similar situation."

Vig slightly leaned against Max, shoulder to shoulder. They stood together in the sand.

"Now, Max," Walt said, "would you please get Quincy in here?"

Max climbed up on the nearby wooden fence and cupped his hands around his mouth. "Quincy!" he shouted. "Quin-nnnn-ceeee!" Max's grey horse, standing with a group in the sun-shine, raised his head and looked at Max. "Quincy, come here! Come on, buddy!" Quincy regarded Max for a moment, then trotted down the path and in through the open gates. He stood next to Max, with a quizzical look in his eye.

"Why don't you do a few circles with him," Walt suggested.

This should be interesting—Max didn't have Quincy's halter. I'd seen him loosely wrap a lead rope over a horse's neck to guide it somewhere, but Max didn't pick up a rope. He just started walking, looked back at Quincy, gestured with his hand, and Quincy followed. They walked, jogged, zig-zagged a little just to show off. Then Quincy stopped. He gently nosed Max's shoulder, turned, walked a few steps away, and threw Max a questioning glance.

Max gestured with his head, and Quincy trotted out of the corral and back to the pasture. He glanced over his shoulder at Max just once along the way.

Walt turned to Vig. "You'd be hard pressed to find a relationship anywhere with more respect and trust than what we just witnessed. Now, Quincy came in here because he decided to. He worked with Max until he chose to disengage. Where did he go?"

"Back to his herd," Vig said. "Yeah, I see what you're doing. Didn't go isolate, off on his own. He's good there." Vig watched Quincy for a moment. "He came out because Turner asked him to. Did a little work and quit—stopped, I guess. Different than quitting."

Walt leaned back against a pole—relaxed, casual. He nodded, seemingly to himself. "That's how therapy's going to work, too, if it is going to work. Some folks, there's a certain comfort level in knowing that. No one can make them do anything. Just show them respect, try to earn their trust. Lead them as far as they want to follow. No one can truly change another person—Abby's right, it's about training and equipping. There's another thing to just think about. Now, I'll leave you be. Please remember that you're always welcome here."

Walt returned to the office in the barn. The three of us stood and looked at each other. "You know what," I said, "Walt's given you enough for today. I'm also going to tag out, let the two of you work through all that together."

No one protested. Max and Vig walked through the woods and the fields, visited various horses along the way, talked about things I didn't need to hear. They finally ended up at the parking lot. Vig pulled a suitcase out of his truck. He and Max walked toward the house.

I sat out on my step that night, leaned back against the side of the barn, and listened to the dark. I did it in the city, too, but city darkness was harder to find. Rural darkness had different sounds—the rich, full hoot of an owl, sometimes a pair of owls, calling. Thin cries of coyotes, overlapping. A quiet rustle of horses moving through brush. Or just the wind. And different sights, dimly appearing as my eyes adjusted to the night.

I knew an old woman who talked about the dark. A long time ago, now. Her deeply wrinkled, chestnut face reminded me of a shrunken apple head—but not a scary one. She embodied calm. Her bright, sharp eyes saw everything, yet even after a long life on this earth, her basic essence seemed to be kindness.

She said the dark of the world always has something in it. Even deep inside the earth, where there is no light, there are sounds. Empty darkness, she said, can only be found inside a person. Grief, the pain of loss, creates a hole—a hole, she insisted, that could be filled with one of two things. Love—not superficial love, but the deep, abiding kind that covers, heals, binds things together, holds light, restores life. Or fear—the kind that hides itself behind lies, masquerades as other emotions. It's a circular illusion: the fear of what might be lost, if one admits to fear. So, call it anger. Give it that face, that name. Pretend it's a shield. Pretend it's not filling that hole, and spreading outward, deepening the dark.

Walt saw Vig as a man who was grieving. Struggling with loss, telling himself he shouldn't be. The old woman would have seen Walt's brand of wisdom as a form of love, the kind that could take a beating, and hold. Fear and love can't remain together, she told me. The challenge is in calling fear out for the lie that it is, because it will tell you to be afraid of the love. Embrace me instead, fear says, and fills the empty dark.

Chapter Six

Ida kicked gently at my door the next morning. Her hands were both occupied, holding a baking pan—a thin, disposable one—covered in foil. "I need to put something in your refrigerator. I hope you have room." We moved things to clear a shelf. "This is our way in, Abby. I'll be done with my client session in a couple hours."

I searched my memory. Had I forgotten something? "Our way in where?"

Ida beamed. "We're going to visit Doug Larsen's wife. Widow, I suppose, although that generally suggests some degree of feeling bad about it. I'm not sure what to call her."

"I thought you didn't know her!"

"Well, we've never met," she said, "But I made a nice hotdish. That's what you do when someone dies. You bring over a hotdish. She'll take it, watch and see."

I rubbed my forehead. "I hope she didn't keep any of his shotguns."

Ida laughed. "Just follow my lead. If she doesn't go for it, I'll play the eccentric old lady card. You can pretend to be the niece who tries to keep me from wandering off."

I drove. Ida protested—she knew where we were going—but I insisted the niece would not let the dotty aunt drive. "I'll say you talked me into it, convinced me she was an old friend. Besides, I don't have a hatchback anymore. That was always your excuse to drive everywhere. My truck is just as roomy as yours." I put the hotdish on the floor in the back seat.

I didn't need her directions, once we got within a few miles. We followed a pillar of smoke to a tidy bit of acreage just outside Deergrass—the rural address probably led to relaxed burning laws. I drove down a long, gravel driveway. "Should I go up to the house or stop where she is, by the bonfire?"

"Just pull over here." Ida got out and approached the woman, who paused with a pair of heavy, insulated coveralls held halfway to the flames. I followed in Ida's shadow. The woman seemed only mildly curious at our arrival, sizing us up before tossing the coveralls into the fire. She brushed her hands on her pant legs.

"I'm sorry to interrupt you," Ida said. "You look like you're getting a good, satisfying job done."

I gasped, hissed "Ida!" Then I realized that was exactly how the fictional niece would react. I'd pretend I did it on purpose.

The woman laughed. "You're the first honest person who's come up my drive. Want a cup of coffee?"

"We'd love one," Ida said. "And we brought you a hotdish. You probably don't have time to cook, with all the housecleaning you're doing."

We introduced ourselves as we walked to the house. She wiped a hand across her cheek, pushed her hair back from her face. One of her eyeballs had a red spot. Extreme stress can contribute to a subconjunctival hemorrhage. Then I noticed what looked like a rash around her eyes. Huh. I stepped closer, waited for her to look at Ida, then glanced at her face. Not a rash. Pinpoint red spots, in clusters. Petechiae. Tiny, broken blood vessels. My brain immediately spun through reasons for increased pressure in the head. Strong coughing fits? Vomiting? Strangulation?

She seated us at a wood table, stained a rich, warm brown, but nicked and scarred. Phyllis—that was her name, not Doug Larsen's anything—set the hotdish on the stovetop and turned on the oven to preheat. "I haven't eaten yet today, so thanks for this. Every time I open a new closet or drawer, I just want to keep going." She slid out of her jacket, hung it on a doorknob, and pushed up the sleeves of a worn, faded turtleneck.

Ida studied a large box of Carhartts and Realtree camo. "Are you going to sell those?"

"No," Phyllis replied. "That's the flame-retardant box. They'll just muck up my fire, and they're illegal to burn, even outside city limits. I'm trying to think of the best place to donate them, that would've irritated Doug the most." She handed me a cup—part of a cheap department store set. She'd probably smash the lot of it, when she finished with his clothes.

I set it in front of me. "Have many people come up your drive, being less honest than Ida?"

She snorted. "You know it. Everyone wants a scintillating bit of gossip to impress people at the café."

I mentally refocused, then chastised myself for not expecting her to use words like scintillating. Standing in a field, burning her husband's possessions, didn't dictate her vocabulary. It would be interesting to see where Phyllis was in five years. Why not ask? She liked honesty. "Do you have plans for your own life now, Phyllis? Or is that premature?" Normally I'd shift into grief counseling mode—don't make any big decisions or changes in the first year, be patient with yourself. Phyllis had probably waited too long already.

She filled the carafe of her coffee maker, and focused on the water level while she answered. "First, I'm going to clean house, as Ida put it, quite thoroughly. That may take a while. I'm sure I'll keep finding level after level of things to eradicate. After that—" she poured the water in, measured grounds into a filter, started the coffee brewing. "I was one year shy of an undergraduate degree, still young, sweet and impressionable, when we married. I may have to redo a lot of credits, or maybe take a new direction. Lot of work, either way. However—"

She took three small plates from the cupboard. Something caught her eye—she frowned, examined one of them, and must have found a speck. She walked across the faded, chipped linoleum, stepped on the pedal to raise the garbage can lid, and dropped the plate in. She took a new one from the cupboard, studied it, and set the plates on the table with a plastic container of cookies.

"However, after decades of not having access to one cent beyond a housekeeping allowance—because I was so stupid as a youngster and a long chain of events I won't go into—I now have checking, savings, a retirement account, and—when someone other than myself is convicted—substantial life insurance. So, to answer your question, Abby, I'm going to do whatever I bloody well please. Help yourselves to the cookies."

I happily took a chocolate chip. Ida took two ginger snaps. "Phyllis," Ida said, "do you have an idea about who killed Doug?"

"Good luck," Phyllis said. "Far too many possibilities for me to sort through. He slept around for years, picking up drunk women in bars. Getting women in bars drunk, so he could pick them up—it made him feel clever. He'd press the drinks, turn on the charm."

The oven beeped. Phyllis opened it, took an oven mitt from a drawer—heat pouring out the open door—and moved the oven rack. "Doug apparently has illegitimate children all over the county—many born to married women, mind you. Add that to the people who worked with him, hunted with him, served on committees and councils with him, or were ever ahead of him in traffic. Anyone's guess." She shoved the hotdish in the oven and sat.

Phyllis shifted her weight in her chair, crossed her legs, uncrossed them. Slid a finger underneath the turtleneck, pulled it away from her throat. "If it wasn't for the insurance, I'd hope they never figure it out."

She kept her hand up and held the turtleneck away from her throat, but up against her chin. I can't stand full turtlenecks myself. I hoped she'd buy a whole new wardrobe. Being nosy—it's my nature—I watched her in my peripheral vision and waited.

Phyllis shifted, and I surreptitiously eyed her throat. Shadows? I focused, tried not to be obvious. Waited for her to move just right, and she finally did. Not shadows. Ovals, maybe an inch and a half in length. Dark green, yellowing. I struggled to swallow the food in my mouth, and left my cup half full.

We chatted for a polite amount of time, Ida eating two sugar cookies. We wished her well, and left. Ida waited until we were in the truck. "Well, that's a solid maybe in my book," she exclaimed. "Probably! She might have done it, Abby. Are you okay? You suddenly got quiet."

"Did you see her throat?" I asked. "The red spot in her eye, around her eyes?"

"I saw the eye and skin irritation, yes. I thought she was reacting to all that smoke, but just kept at it. And she wasn't comfortable in that turtleneck, I hope she throws that in the fire. Why?"

"Ida, she's been choked. She had bruises on her throat, thumbprints. And that wasn't skin irritation, it was broken blood vessels. She was strangled, Ida."

Ida didn't respond until several mile markers had gone by. "If it weren't for Vig," she finally said, "I wouldn't spend one second trying to find out who killed that man."

"Well, I agree she could have done it. She's smart, has enough motive for ten people. He must have had some kind of hold on her, to keep her in the marriage so long. Him being passed out drunk and a machine being used to move the body, the smallest of women could have done it. But if the cops are that impressed by Vig's circumstantial evidence, and she hasn't been arrested, I bet she has an alibi."

"So maybe she has a lover herself," Ida said. "He knows she's being abused. They can be together, share the insurance money. I hope it wasn't the lover who hurt her. You know some women have multiple abusers at the same time. We'll say it was Doug. She gives herself a solid alibi while the lover knocks him off. You don't think she had a tin of poisoned cookies just handy in her kitchen, in case someone came snooping? She didn't eat any."

"I only ate one," I said. "If you keel over, I'll tell the EMTs what to look for."

"Hunh. They probably came from other people, just like our hotdish. Hopefully no one wanted to poison her," Ida said. "Well, alright. We'll see if Betsy's librarian friends know if Phyllis was having an affair. I wonder if anyone knows why Doug and Phyllis never had children? I didn't want to mention it. Just imagine having two strangers in for coffee and telling them something like that. But how does she know about all those children? Did he tell her? Rub her face in it, say he kept getting other women pregnant, but not her?"

"That's an excellent point," I said. "And that's horrible." I slowed at an intersection, and turned toward the ranch. "I sincerely doubt there were paternity tests done, so if he told her there were children, he was just being vicious. Emotionally and physically. But I also wondered about the information dump—oversharing as deflection, to hide her own guilt? Or just letting go of stifling inhibitions, no longer fearing consequences?"

Ida looked back over her shoulder. "There's still smoke. I hope she's containing that fire. Things can get out of hand in a hurry." She resettled, leaned against her door. "You know, Johnny and I never were able to have children, but he was very kind about it. Well, who knows if it was him, or me. Things were different in those days. If it just never happened, that was that. But Johnny made me feel like I was worth a hundred children to him, and that did help."

I drove quietly for a moment. "I didn't know that, Ida. That must have been hard."

She made a "hmm," acknowledging my words, not wanting to go into it. "If they couldn't have children, and he taunted her about it, I'm surprised she didn't kill him sooner."

"It's going to be hard to keep an open mind, now," I said. "We can't assume that she killed him, or even had a lover do it for her. We have to stay alert."

Max and I fell into a pattern of bickering. He snapped whenever I came near him, and—years of therapy experience flying away like a hat in the wind—I snapped back. We bristled at each other until Max stalked off angrily, leaving me to feel guilty for not disengaging first.

Remorseful, I walked across the gravel parking lot to Max's house. I'd go make peace, while we were both calm. I knocked on the door. Someone who sounded like they had their mouth full yelled to come in.

Vig sat at the table, eating cheap macaroni and cheese—the box was still on the counter—and studying a graphic explanation of how to turn your pants into a flotation device. In case he, I don't know, fell overboard. He looked up when my stomach growled loudly. "More on the stove. Help yourself." He smiled as my face flushed. "Nothing to be embarrassed about, Maguire. We all get hungry."

I gave his leftovers a stir with the spoon leaning against the side of the pan. "I hate to take your lunch. You sure you don't want seconds?"

Vig waved expansively with the survival guide, and shoveled a large forkful of pasta into his mouth. I grabbed the pan and sat down next to him, scooped up an artificially orange pile with the serving spoon, and awkwardly tried to stretch my lips around it. Failing that, I tipped my head up and let food slide off the spoon, into my mouth. Vig stopped chewing and watched me. After a long moment, he swallowed. "What are we now, barbarians?"

I narrowed my eyes at him and lifted the pot to my chin, so I wouldn't spill on my jeans. Vig's grin filled his face, made it to his eyes. "This is nice. A whole side of you I hadn't seen before. Don't look too close at the box, though. Turner said you're kind of a health nut."

I scraped cheese sauce off my face with the spoon and rolled my eyes eloquently.

Vig nodded. "Yeah, exactly. I'm a big fan of fruit and all that—Jules has me eating all kinds of healthy stuff—but I'm not giving up fast food, or mac and cheese. I figure expanding the ceiling doesn't raise the floor."

I paused to process that, then licked the spoon clean before pointing it at him. "I like that, Vig. I didn't know you were a philosopher."

He waggled his eyebrows at me, setting down his survival guide and fork. He rose to his feet and glided to the cupboard in one fluid motion, then dug out a second pan and another box of mac and cheese. I swallowed a mouthful. "I'm sorry, Vig. I thought you were done."

Vig waved dismissively. "No, no, I reserve the right to change my mind on important matters." He put water in the pan. "Like lunch." Vig started the burner, sat, and studied me quietly for a few moments. "Having you here is real good for Turner."

I snorted and set my pan on the table. "That's the last thing he would say."

"Why's that?"

I crossed my arms over my chest, not sure why I felt defensive.

Vig shook his head and slouched in his chair. Slid his butt forward, stretched his back, propped one leg on another chair. "I bet Turner never told you he outranks me."

No, he hadn't. Did it matter? "It's never actually come up."

Vig nodded as if I'd proven his point. "Plus, rank aside, he's the one we followed. Every one of us would've followed him into hell." He tilted his head, smiled wryly. "We did, actually." He paused, seemed to study the crop art rooster on the wall. "Afraid of nothing, but smart. Takes a minute to think about things if he can." He shrugged, stood, went to check on his water. "Sometimes you can't."

I waited, but he didn't elaborate. "Vig, what are we talking about here?"

Back turned to me, he shook his head again. He dumped in the macaroni. It hit the hot water with a whoosh. "Doesn't even get the concept of giving up on someone, leaving them in the shit." He took a clean spoon and stirred. "Turner's not mad at you. He's upset because he figures you and Ida are getting into things. Doesn't want you involved, but he knows you're scary smart, and you might be able to help me." He turned to face me, punctuated his words with the spoon. "Cognitive dissonance."

He sat down, squarely facing me. "He doesn't know whether he wants to recall you or deploy you, and either way he blames himself for something. But maybe that's my question, too. Maybe Turner shouldn't associate with me right now. This whole thing came out of nowhere. I don't want Turner getting pulled into something I don't even know what it is, or where it's coming from. I know he thinks he owes me, but I couldn't repay him in ten lifetimes. He can't owe me."

I studied him. "Vig, if you're talking about leaving, I think it's a little late for that. You and Max were solidly connected in the eyes of that—" I rubbed my temple. Name-calling is not productive. I sighed. "That detective, as soon as that deputy pulled into your drive and saw us there. The day they found the body." I couldn't read the look on his face. "You might as well do what's most likely to help you," I said. "Wasting money on a motel room somewhere won't make any difference."

Vig sagged. His energy slowly dissolved. It took me a minute to process that. "Ok, I get it," I told him. "You want to do something." I twirled my spoon in a circle. A little dab flew off. I set the spoon down. "Listen. No one kills over old car parts, do they?"

"You mean the Chevy guy. Not around here." He gave my raised eyebrows a half smile. "People get killed over five bucks or a loaf of bread, somewhere in the world. Here, people want a certain car because someone in their family had it when they were growing up. Or they think it looks cool, or they want to go fast, want something small and lightweight. No one's going to watch their family starve because another person took the used parts or the scrap metal first."

"Do you know why they arrested you? Was there anything not circumstantial?"

He scratched his ear. "Well, you know I had a run-in with the guy, over at The Nail—that's a dive bar. I walked away, left my ball cap sitting on the table. Forgot about it, really, but it was just a cheap one. Friend of mine has one just like it, so we wrote our names in them with a Sharpie. Joked about it." He blew out a breath, sat back. "Well, hell. The guy grabbed it, apparently, after I left. Tried to save face by stealing my hat, or something. Put it on his head, picked up what was left of my beer and drank it. That's what I heard. So, they found my hat next to his car. Car door hanging open, I guess. Not much I can say about that."

Huh. I spent a moment imagining that. Wondered if, like Ben suggested, there was more he wasn't telling me. "Don't take this as accusatory," I said. "Better to have information, than not. I'm just saying." He scrunched up his face, tried to make it funny. I went on. "Have you ever left the house, sleepwalking?"

He lost all humor. "No." He looked glumly at his feet. "Never."

"Okay, tell me about the fight." I picked up my spoon and pointed it at his face. "The black eye. What were you fighting about?"

Vig opened his mouth, closed it again. He checked his pasta, drained the water, silently added the other ingredients. He dumped a steaming pile onto his plate and made a few quick gestures with his pan, as if using it to push my hands away. I pulled back. He scooped the rest into my pan and sat down. He waved his hands in frustration, then finally met my eyes. "I swear to God, Maguire, I never even met the guy. No idea who he was. He's hassling this young woman, she's clearly not interested, he's not listening. Everyone's pretending not to notice. He's putting the moves on her, pressuring her, she turns away. I'm starting to get up, head over there, and he grabs her arm. Starts throwing racial crap at her." He looked away, deliberately turned the anger in his eyes to the far wall, away from my face.

"I can't stand that," he went on. "Native gal. He's calling her Pocahontas, calling her a squaw." Vig let loose a string of profanity. "There's no excuse. Well, Jules is Ojibwe, so it could've been her, just as easy. Except Jules isn't powerless. I just can't stand there and let that happen to someone that can't protect themselves. So I went over there and drew the guy's attention to me, so she could get away. And she did, too. She took off the second she could."

He turned to look at me through the waves of steam rising from our food. "Guy wanted a fight, so we took it outside. I got him to swing first. He escalated it, every step, I made sure of that. Lotta people saw that. And here I am, getting accused of going after him in secret? Like I'd have to wait and sneak up on him, dark of night? The hell is that?"

Chapter Seven

Janet texted in proper sentences, with no shortened words or emojis. That seemed mildly incongruent with her personality, but she was also a retired teacher. She wanted me to come over, pretend I was just stopping by, and meet her neighbor—in a half hour, could I make it? I threw on presentable clothing and headed into town.

I followed Janet into the kitchen. An older middle-aged man sat at her table. Stocky build, a bit rounded at the beltline. He had thinning dark hair, glasses with thick plastic frames, blue Dickies work pants and a button-up shirt. He buttoned his cuffs at the wrist, not rolled or pushed up on his forearms, which gave him more of a formal appearance. He reminded me of Papa's friends who occupied our kitchen and garage throughout my childhood, worked on vehicles, drank strong coffee from a Thermos. Illogically, that made me inclined to like him.

"Abby, this is my neighbor, Warren Koenig. He brought my garbage cans in from the curb for me, so I thought he deserved a little coffee break." Janet shot me a significant look. "Warren, this is Abby Maguire. She's a therapist, works with Ida Gill. You remember Ida. Out at that horse ranch. Now Abby, I was just asking Warren about Doug Larsen. You know the whole town's talking about him. Did you know him, Warren?"

Warren finished chewing, swallowed, and took another rhubarb bar from a Corningware platter. "Of course. I knew him since we were kids, Janet. We've been involved in the same things for decades—hunting, community events, planning committees. Nobody's likely to miss him." He shook his head. "If anyone claims they will, that's who the police should focus on, if you ask me." Warren looked at his bar, but didn't take a bite.

Janet set a napkin in front of him. "Who do you think did it? You knew a lot of the same people. Who do you suspect?"

Warren set his bar on the napkin, but pulled it closer, as if one of us might snatch it. He straightened in his chair. "It's all about mindset, Janet." He glanced at me. "Abby. When you don't see what you're looking for, you need to change your angle, change your scope. This will be about hunting. I mean in general, the mindset of a hunter. People who've hunted their whole lives, if they ever really paid attention and learned how to think like a hunter, they know certain things."

I tried not to look as confused as Janet did. I sat across from Warren. "What do you mean? I'm not a hunter. Help me understand what the mindset is."

He nodded. "They ever figure this out, it's going to be about nature. Just watch. You want to understand human animals, you have to look at the natural world. Tell you what I mean. Take things down to their basic level, it's amazing how much of life is all about camouflage. You know how a cat kicks dirt over its own scat, to bury it? That's to keep it safe from bigger predators."

Warren sat back for a moment, studied us. "Doug was a predator by nature. People had to hide themselves around him, to be safe. Ever heard of a California ground squirrel? This animal will chew up rattlesnake skin, spit it back out, and rub it all over its own fur. So it smells like the very thing that could destroy it. You see? With Doug, you had to not just hide your own crap, excuse my language, but really hide your own scent. Make yourself stink like him so he wouldn't turn on you."

This was interesting in a revolting way, but I wasn't sure it was relevant. That must have showed on my face. Warren's voice turned from lecturing to persuasive. "I never saw one single person act like themselves around Doug. That's camouflage." He stabbed a finger at the table to emphasize his point. "Octopus and lizards, they'll change the color, even the texture of their skin to blend into the background. Other creatures, their behavior will change."

His words grew louder, more energized. "Lizards become more tree-dwelling when ground-dwelling predators are introduced into their habitat. Their standard behavior changes. Or the kangaroo rat, it becomes less nocturnal during a full moon. See, that's a more active kind of camouflage. There are crabs that will stand, holding plants or stones to blend in with the background. You can't see me, I'm a rock."

He waved his arms in the air, swayed back and forth. "Some lizards and bugs act like plants blowing in the wind so they effectively disappear. Or, here's a good one. There's a mimic octopus that makes itself look like an animal that's dangerous, or foul tasting. Whatever the predator really won't care to mess with, it makes itself look like that."

"Warren Koenig! What in the world does this have to do with the price of rice?" Janet frowned at him.

He stopped, deflated a bit. "The point is, people are extremely good at changing their behavior to avoid predators, too." He waved a hand at me. "As a therapist, I'm sure you know that. Look for the camouflage." He picked up his bar, took a bite. Picked up his coffee cup, looked in it, set it down.

Janet got up and refilled his cup. She shot an annoyed look at Warren and put the carafe back on the heat plate of the coffee maker. "But who do you think did it, Warren? Looking at everyone in the county who wanted to avoid being mistreated by Doug isn't helpful at all."

Warren peered at her over his glasses, which had slipped down his nose. "I'd hate for anyone to have a finger pointed at them, Janet. Look to see who gets a parade in their honor in a couple months. Then you'll know folks've figured it out."

Ben and I met for a quick grilled cheese in Deergrass. As bar and grill food went, it wasn't bad. He glossed over the details of how things were going. I understood that—I glossed over the details of doing therapy at the ranch. I talked more broadly about working as part of a team for most sessions, alone for a few. The flexibility and freedom—doing cognitive behavioral therapy in a lean-to, having a teenager open up while scratching a horse. Working on grounding exercises sitting on horseback in the woods, or the pasture. Or on a moving horse, pairing breathing with the horse's steps. I loved it.

Ben never pressed me for details about sessions. He never told war stories, either, which I liked. A lot. Guys who leverage other people's tragedy to make themselves look impressive are a huge turn-off. Give him credit, Ben never noticeably tried to look cool.

But then he got that look in his eye. That sharp look. He dropped his napkin on his empty plate and pushed it away. "You've been spending a lot of time with Ida's friends?"

I blinked, caught off-guard. "Some." I sat back. When had I talked about it? I tried to avoid the matter, so I wouldn't accidentally reference their interest in his case.

"You said something about tattoos." He stretched a little, rolled his shoulders. "What are you going to do about that?"

"I haven't decided." I felt a little off balance.

"You seem defensive," he said. "I'll show you my tattoo—but it might involve revealing something. I know you don't like that."

What just happened? I leaned in. "I'd love to know what your tattoo is, Benson."

Startling him was worth writing off the date. I let it sit. Let him think about it. Watched him put it together—he knew he hadn't told me his full name. His face hardened.

This was stupid. I always tired of the game first. "Ida's right," I said, discouraged now. "Doing background checks on each other really is a bizarre way to have a relationship."

"Doing—" Ben was still. Even his hands didn't move. I'd really thrown him.

"What, did you truly think you were the only one with resources, Ben? Does it upset you that much, to not have the upper hand? Really?"

His face darkened. "So there is a scenario where you look first, before barreling in. I suppose I should be happy about that, the way you cozy up to the prime suspect in a homicide, nose around with the widow. You have—"

He stopped abruptly. He'd told me something. Someone had seen me, seen Ida and me. Was Doug Larsen's widow under surveillance? She must be. Now Ida and I were in a police log somewhere. Well, fine. We got caught being neighborly. Prove otherwise.

Ben studied me. "What?"

I didn't try to hide my exasperation. "You're a civilian now. Why are you privy to police surveillance information? It's not like you're an official consultant. What else does Tom tell you over morning coffee?"

Ben seemed only mildly annoyed by the accusation, so he probably wasn't guilty. Maybe Tom didn't cross that line. Ben probably had informants everywhere.

"This isn't some civil case," he said. "It's a homicide. Knowing people's movements can be very helpful. And don't just assume you know things, alright? Don't just follow assumptions down a wrong trail." He shrugged one shoulder, casual.

I picked up a vibe—something subtle in his manner registered, activated a tripwire somewhere deep in my memory. I stared at him until my brain chased it down: a previous job I had in corrections. Many of the felons who came to sessions had an ulterior motive. No intention of being real. Courteous and respectful to the lady therapist, certain they had me totally snowed. Thought they were slick—but you don't even realize that, ma'am. That's what it was.

"You're being slick!" I blurted.

"What?" He sat back.

"What are you trying to be slick about? I've told you before, you are not slick. And you know what? There's a flip side to thinking you're unspeakably clever. You also think the person you're talking to is stupid!"

His mouth fell open. "What are you talking about?"

I squinted at him. "I see you, Ben. Careful verbals, deliberate nonverbals. I know how interview and interrogation work. But you slipped. I saw something. Don't even think about trying to play me. What are you hiding from me?"

I watched him regroup. "Abby, this was meant to be a lunch date. Not a debriefing, that's not what it is." He shrugged, a whole-body shrug. His hands moved from palms down on the table, to open, shoulder width apart: nothing to see here. "Listen. You need to be careful with Viglione. I don't care if he and Max are combat buddies, that doesn't make him either good or innocent. He's a known associate of some pretty rough people—including one guy with assault on a cop."

A cold residue sat in my stomach. Whatever it was, was gone, but I'd felt it. "We've always understood that we don't share details of our work, Ben. This was different. You're hiding something from me, personally. Specifically from me."

A flicker in his eyes, almost not even there. Gone. "I'm trying to solve this case, Abby. You're right about me being a civilian. Tom doesn't talk to me. Working with the police is a one-way deal for a private investigator, that's a basic ground rule. I give him a tip like any other citizen, he does with it what he wants. If I can help the police, I will, but I'll make damn sure my client knows exactly what I did. They need to know they got results for their money."

His tone was informational. He might have been talking to a group of interns. "I need to have a variety of ways to get information. If you can help me at all, I really hope you will. Can you please just tell me if you had any impressions of Phyllis Larsen? You're very good—don't look at me like that. I'm not flattering you. What did you notice?"

I made him wait. "First tell me why this is so important, it's worth fighting with me continuously. Yes, it's a case. You have a lot of cases."

He struggled with his facial expression—went with reluctantly sincere. "Abby, listen. This is a career-building opportunity. It matters, having a professional reputation. People do talk. Homicide is a big deal, especially—I know, I know. Everyone matters. But professionally, the higher level the victim, the more noise the case produces." He spread his hands again: what can we do? "It's the world we live in. Yes, I came back to a small town, to start over in my old stomping grounds. But I don't intend to stay small professionally. Okay?"

"This, I believe. Thank you." He'd finally been honest. I waved a hand: what can I tell you? "Everyone in the county knows Phyllis is burning or selling everything her husband owned."

He nodded, kept his gaze attentively focused. He knew how to get me. I was a sucker for actually being listened to, the way men listen to each other. As though I had a brain in my head. "She talked like he had something on her," I said grudgingly. "Some unnamed indiscretion of her youth. Controlled every aspect of her life—every penny, every movement, every detail. And now she's free."

He considered that. "And what did you notice, that she didn't tell you?"

I paused, studied him. He wasn't trying to flatter me—another thing he said that was objectively true. I weighed my desire to help Vig, against my hesitance to throw a woman under.

Ben spoke again, softly. "You're sad about something."

I realized he was right, and blinked it away. "Am I talking to you, or indirectly talking to Tom Harmon?"

He put his hand over mine on the tabletop. "I don't tell him everything, Abby. He knows that, but he can't do a damn thing about it. I won't set Tom on her, not to weaponize anything you tell me." He did a little head shrug. "If she's a murderer, I will. I'd have to be sure."

I sighed. "Don't abuse this. She'd been choked. Strangled. May very well have blacked out." I described the subconjunctival hemorrhage, the petechiae around her eyes, the bruising she tried to hide under a shirt. I suddenly thought about Warren. He'd know all about wounded creatures hiding their injuries, pretending not to be vulnerable. To survive. Look for the camouflage, he said. I shook that off, met Ben's eyes, saw anger. Good.

His focus turned inward. Processing, sorting. "Any impression at all, who else might know about the abuse?"

"No. She seemed pretty isolated. She said people keep coming down the drive, supposedly offering support, actually looking for gossip. She said 'scintillating tidbits.'"

I saw him register the vocabulary, make a note of it. Just like I did. "She didn't talk about any real relationships. They didn't have kids. I didn't get any sense she was allowed to have friends."

He nodded again, quiet.

"So, Ben, what can you tell me?" I knew he wouldn't tell me anything. I really only asked to be oppositional.

His eyes refocused. He leaned in, as if that would soften his words. "Abby, there is literally nothing you need to know about any of this. I don't want to see you hurt. This is a very dangerous situation."

"I should go. I hope your week goes better." I picked up my check and headed for the cash register.

"Abby—" Ben followed me, but saved it for the sidewalk, where he took hold of my elbow. "Abby, I'm sorry. Look, I didn't mean to torpedo this whole thing. And I really do appreciate you meeting me halfway."

I snorted. Halfway.

He pretended not to notice. Shrugged, ran a hand through his hair. "Can we do dinner? Not tonight, but maybe tomorrow? Give me another chance at not acting like a caveman. I really don't mean to make you angry all the time."

"I'll have to let you know."

"Look at tomorrow, okay? Shoot me a text." He waved his hands, but in a subdued manner, sadly expressive. I said I would, and watched him walk away.

I pulled out my phone and called Ida. Left a message. "Hey, just letting you know we're probably on a police watch list. Give me a call later." How did it come to this?

I pulled into the driveway and passed Max chopping wood. He had a couple of axes, a couple of hatchets, a pile of logs. Some branches he'd dragged out of the woods. Sounded good to me. I put on scruffy clothes and went to join him. He nodded a greeting and kept working. I started with a hatchet, took off side branches, left the heaviest parts for Max. When I was warmed up, I moved to an axe and started breaking down medium-sized branches. I followed his lead as he carried good firewood to stack in a lean-to by one of the machine sheds. Lesser scraps and brush went into a burn pile.

He planted his axe in a stump. "I'm gonna grab some sodas." He walked to the house and came back with two cans.

I sat on a log and popped open the Diet Coke he handed me. "Ben said that Vig associates with rough people, and one of them assaulted a police officer. What do you think?"

"Oh, bullshit," Max said disgustedly. "That guy is not an associate. We didn't associate with him overseas, we sure as hell don't now. Vig told me he came up to him in a bar. Like, 'Turner, you'll never guess. It's the shit you can't wipe off your shoe, here he is again.'" He took an angry swig of root beer. "Somebody wrote down that he walked up to Vig, now he's tied to the guy? No, Maguire."

"So you don't think he's legitimately connected to someone who could be criminally violent? I just want to be sure, Max. I know you were deployed together, I know that creates a bond—"

"No." Max shook his head impatiently, kicked a loose branch in frustration. "I mean, yes, it does, but it's not just that. First of all, I know Vig. Better than my own family." He squatted, set his can on the ground. Leaned his back against the shed. Took a breath.

"Vig's the reason I came here in the first place. I was in Chicago, he's the one who lived up here. Jules was from here."

Max stood, picked up an armload of wood, dumped it on the pile. Straightened it into a neat row. "I was in bad shape." A long pause. He swallowed, looked away. "One night I..." He threw a hand up, a wide gesture. "Might have been night. Kind of a blur." He moved his shoulders and arms, rearranged himself in discomfort, almost turned his back to me. "Took my Glock out of my mouth and called Vig. He ran out and jumped in his truck, drove almost 500 miles to come get me. Kept talking, said if I tried to hang up, didn't matter if I was on the crapper or what, I stop talking and there's gonna be cops kicking my door in."

Max looked everywhere except at me. "He found me in this nasty little roach nest I was renting, threw me in his truck and brought me home. I was a mess. I stunk. I think Jules burned my clothes. They didn't have room for me, but I stayed there on the couch."

I watched him pick up more firewood. "Did you know Jules before that?"

"No." Max grabbed a bucket and filled it with bits of bark, scraps of kindling. "For a long time, I thought she hated me. She called me a whole lotta things." A rueful half-smile. "Some of them, pretty sure I hadn't heard that since boot camp. I was gonna leave, told Vig I didn't want to wreck his marriage, but he said boot camp was pretty much her love language."

Max shook himself slightly, as if the memories would fall away, drop like cockroaches from his clothing. "Anyway. I got a job as a ranch hand here, for Walt." He paused, jostled the bucket so the kindling would settle. "I don't know why Walt hired me. Seriously." He finally turned in my direction. "Walt got me straightened out. Then he taught me how to do equine therapy myself, gave me a way to walk it down the road. Take it to the next person. I say equine therapy saved my life—you know that means Walt did, but Vig did first. Every person I ever help is down to him." Max held my eyes soberly. "I don't care what it costs, Maguire. I don't care what happens to me. I'm helping Vig."

His gaze was intense, but I met him there. Let him search me for judgement, disapproval, pity, as long as it took to see there was none. Let him find respect and trust—he would never admit how desperately he needed them to still be there. I wrapped him in a hug, stood and breathed the musty air with him. "Okay," I said. "I get it."

We went back to chopping, stacking. Max was quiet, uneasy. The way people are when it costs them to say something, but they do it anyway, and the atmosphere around them changes, and they aren't sure what happens next. He offered up something he saw through a lens of shame, and would take a while to believe it looked different through my eyes. To believe I could see the same story through a different lens. I saw his strength and courage, and in time he'd accept that. I had no hesitation about staying the course with Max. Speaking into that empty darkness, the unknown filled with fear—speaking life into him for as long as it took.

My own fear was a different matter entirely. Call it professional experience or cynicism, but I just can't assume what people say is objectively true. Talk about seeing through different lenses—people distort things all the time, deliberately or not. Vig could skew everything he told us, leave things out. Max would filter everything through a stubborn insistence on Vig's innocence. And how could I judge them? Vig could be guilty, and my biggest concern was for Max.

Chapter Eight

Walt was in his element doing therapy. No matter how the day was going, he came to life in the arena. We brought two horses in for a family session and watched as a woman with four kids climbed out of an SUV. A man drove up behind them in a sports car. He strode into the barn, and walked up to Walt with an outstretched hand.

"Well, we found the place! Sure appreciate you making time for us. Not really sure what we're doing, but my daughter's therapist said we should do a family thing." He looked around. The horses both stood back and watched, with ears straight up and swiveled toward the parking lot. The youngest boy, who looked to be about five, ran in and climbed on the fence. A girl, probably twelve, stood near the SUV with her arms crossed. A set of twin boys around eight years old argued as their mother tried to move everyone into the arena.

It took some time to get going. I finally set them to their first task: "Work together, and use any of the materials in the arena, to build an obstacle representing something your family struggles with. As big or small as you want—something to get around, something to get over, or something to get through."

The father turned to Walt. "What about the horses?"

Walt looked at the horses. They stood near the orange cones, watchful. Swiveling their ears, scoping out the situation. "What are you thinking about the horses?"

"Well, they should be restrained!"

Walt tilted his head toward the row of hooks on the wall. "There are lead ropes hanging there, if you want to take a couple and hook them on the halters."

The man looked from the lead ropes, back to the horses. "Pete! Andy! Go grab a couple of ropes and hook up those horses!"

The twins ran over to the wall, grabbed ropes and started swinging them around, hitting each other. The girl sighed loudly and crossed her arms again.

"Hey! Knock it off!" The father shook his head at Walt. "Boys."

"Oh, for God's sake." The woman walked over and took the ropes away from the boys. "Come here." She approached the horses and tried to open the clip on one rope without dropping the other. The horses walked away. The boys laughed as their mother followed the horses in a circle.

"Let's make our obstacle!" The twins picked up cones and poles. Their father joined them, pulling the girl by the arm. Within minutes, the four of them were bickering. The five-year-old climbed under the fence and ran after a barn cat.

One of the horses stood still for the mother to clip a rope to its halter. She held on to the rope and walked after the second horse. The first horse stopped cold. The woman pulled on the rope, as though she could shift well over a thousand pounds of refusal.

She set down the rope, walked over and took away a pole one of the twins was using to hit his brother. Carrying the pole with her, she picked up the rope from the ground. She held the rope tightly, although the horse hadn't budged.

The second horse backed into the fence. The mother tried to stand in its way, pole swinging awkwardly as she juggled ropes. The horse looked around for an escape route, prancing in place. The din from the obstacle area was growing.

Walt stepped in. "Alright, let's take a time out for a moment." He gestured for the mother to step toward him. She did, and the loose horse ran through the opening that was created. It stopped at the far end of the arena and looked back. Walt went on. "What's going on with the horses right now?"

The family looked at the horses. The horse on the lead rope moved away. The mother tried to pull it back. "They're not co-operating!" shouted one of the twins.

Walt gestured toward the obstacle. Nothing had taken shape. "What's going on with this group of people over here?" There was silence for a beat, as they looked at each other. They all started talking at once, voices overlapping in accusation.

Walt held up a hand for quiet. "What's going on with Mom?"

Everyone turned to look at her. The dad looked surprised, as if he had forgotten she was there. "Lisa, what the hell are you doing?"

She stood with a rope and a pole in one hand, lead rope with horse in the other. "I am doing the best I can! You're the one who wanted the horses tied up! They were fine!"

Walt held up his hand again before the man could respond. "What's going on with the little one?"

The family looked around. Not seeing him, they all started in different directions. "Why the hell weren't you watching him?" the dad shouted. I wasn't sure who he was yelling at.

The mother dropped everything in the sand. "Timmy! Timmy, where are you?"

The little boy climbed back under the fence, holding a kitten. He walked over to Walt, who put a hand on his shoulder.

"Now, if we look at this whole picture," Walt said, "does it remind you of anything in your life as a family?"

They all looked at each other. The mom held the lead rope again. She tried to pick up the other rope and the pole. The horse walked away until the lead rope was stretched tight. The woman turned toward the horse, and hit herself in the head with the pole. No one spoke for several beats.

The dad looked at Walt. "What do you mean?"

"Oh, for God's sake!" The woman glared at her husband, threw everything down and strode out of the barn. We all watched her get in the sports car and drive away.

The rest of the family stared in silence. After a long moment, the dad shouted, "What the hell kind of place is this? I hope you don't think for one minute I'm paying you! A negative review is all you'll get!" He stormed out of the arena, kids trailing behind.

Walt leaned over the rail and watched. The children swarmed around the SUV. The father pointed and shouted.

"Well," Walt said, "I think that went about how it needed to." The horses calmly groomed each other. We put them out and cleaned the arena.

"How do you want to document this?" I asked Walt.

"Descriptively." He smiled. "And then we wait. We may not have heard the last of this."

I heard tires crunching over gravel and looked up. Ben's pickup rolled down the drive. He grinned happily to see me standing by the fence, scratching a horse.

"I was hoping I'd catch you," he said. "Are you free for dinner tonight? I can whip something up, if you don't feel like going out." Another horse came up to the fence to greet him. Lucy, the young, high-energy horse he rode regularly last summer. I tried to ride her once. Well, Walt made me ride her once. I was terrified.

Ben enjoyed Lucy—a highly intelligent animal with a feeling of barely restrained, explosive power. Lucy tested Ben as much as Ben tested Lucy—they both enjoyed it. I'm happy with my Rosie. Also highly intelligent, she has a heck of an attitude. Runs like the wind, but controls herself. Too mature and experienced for shenanigans. A quarter horse, so she also has explosive power when she wants to fly—but even then, she waits for permission. An agreement between the two of us.

"I guess that's a vote of confidence," I said. "Lucy remembers you."

"And still wants to associate with me." He scratched her neck. She leaned in. He scratched a larger area, and they had a moment together in the warm sunshine. Loose hair wafted in the breeze. I couldn't help smiling at the both of them—and taking in all of Ben. Blue jeans and boots. Sexy laugh lines. Shirt sleeves snug on his biceps. A goofy look on his face as he imitated the bliss of the horse.

"You can cook for me." I laughed at his open delight. "You can go easy on the dinner, if you bring dessert."

Ben stepped back, apologized to the horse for stopping without permission, and threw an arm over my shoulders. "On it." He kissed the side of my head, got back in his truck, and stuck his head out the window. "Seven?"

I gave him a thumbs up, and he drove away.

I had time to shower after my last session. I felt amazingly cheerful, two-stepping around the apartment with a towel wrapped around my head. I stopped in front of Papa's picture, touching the top of the frame with one finger. "I am not going to argue with Ben tonight, Papa. Nope, not gonna happen."

By some act of providence, I got clean clothes on and removed the towel from my hair before my date showed up. Batting a thousand so far. I ushered him in and watched him unpack bags while I sat on the counter, swinging my feet.

"I took you at your word," he said. "I hope you're not disappointed. I went for a light meal, quick and easy, and—" He held up a box, beaming proudly.

I jumped down from my perch. "Give me that."

He held it behind his back, but I feinted left, dodged right, and grabbed it. I laughed at him—the fed outsmarted by the therapist. I turned my back, shielded the box with my body, peeked inside, and moaned. A huge chunk of apple crisp, with cinnamon crumbles on top. It was warm. "Grab a couple forks. We're starting right here." I made for the couch and settled in.

Ben fake-scowled, hands on his hips. "Do you have any sense of decorum whatsoever?"

"You go have decorum over there," I said. "I'm eating this with my fingers."

He grabbed forks from the drawer. One clattered across the counter and onto the linoleum. He ignored it, landing on the couch next to me. "Give."

We took turns scooping. I picked the bites with the most crumble topping, and he let me. I wiped apple filling from his cheek. When the box was empty, he gave me a sticky kiss. I settled back against the cushions. "I don't care if we even have dinner now," I confessed.

Ben went to the kitchen and stowed his food in the cupboard and refrigerator. He came back and sat on the couch. "Done. You were right, it was more important to eat that while it was still hot from the oven." I turned sideways and put my feet on his lap. We sat quietly. Ben rested a warm hand on my foot. It was so nice to just relax together. I smiled, and wondered what he was thinking. He started to snore.

Ben was disoriented. He looked blankly around my living room, then noticed the darkness outside. His expression transformed into horror. I couldn't help laughing. "At least you snore quietly." I closed the billing program on my laptop. "It wasn't too distracting."

He joined me at the table. "Abby." He blinked slowly. "I am so, so sorry. Why didn't you wake me?"

"I figured a sugar coma was better than no sleep at all. You're clearly exhausted. What have you been doing, overnight stakeouts?"

"Uh." He rubbed his face, shook his head a little. "There's a lot to run down, when twenty thousand people hated your homicide victim. I spend all my time eliminating probabilities, telling myself it's progress. Only eighteen thousand, five hundred to go."

I set a glass of water in front of him, sat down, and propped my feet on the side of his chair. He took a long drink. "I spend a lot of time," he said, "processing data. Try to focus on footage, get eye fatigue. Listen to garbled conversation, try to make sense of it. Nice to have a fridge and a bathroom handy, but too easy to stay up all night doing it."

I willed myself to keep a neutral expression. Look interested—don't start an argument. Don't ask if it was difficult making out conversations, say, from the device he'd put just a few feet from where he was sitting, right now, drinking my water. Conversations with people seated right where his butt was planted. He sat in the basement of Max's house and eavesdropped as Max told me deep, painful secrets. Had Ben become frustrated, trying to figure out who was up here with me when I talked to Papa?

Breathe. Think about something else. Just breathe. Clearly I still had some healing to do around this subject. I'd have to figure out a way to process it all.

I was thinking loudly again. Ben sat up straight and leveled a steely glare at his water glass. I put my feet on the floor, tried again. "Do you really have a tattoo? I'm surprised it's not on your arm. You have that general military vibe."

"I didn't want obvious, easily recognizable markings, in case I was undercover. I do have one, though." He gave me a half-hearted smile. "Kind of interesting if you get one because you're running around with people twice your age." He noted my grudging nod of agreement, then continued. "You hanging around with Elson's mom—I mean, I know you and Ida really connected. I didn't expect you to get pulled into her social circle. Hanging at Elson's mom's house."

Had I mentioned going to Janet's house? That came from Tom. I would think the Deergrass police would get tired of talking about Janet. Other than shooting a BB gun in her backyard, shouting profanity at woodland creatures, things like that. Why would they care who was at her house?

Ben rolled his head, stretched. "I don't suppose the old ladies have gossiped about anything that could be helpful? Having an ear to the ground sometimes brings the best intel. Any names come up in conversation, could be short-listed to check out?"

"The consensus is someone other than Vig," I told him.

Ben put a hand on my arm. "Look, I'm tired. I don't know if I can say anything you're not going to squint at. I should go. I really am sorry—I've never in my life slept through a date." He paused in the doorway for a tender kiss, a regretful look.

"The apple crisp was amazing," I said, trying to make it better. His smile made it to his eyes. Dessert antics, instead of dinner. We could have fun. Even together.

I loved watching the sun rise as I ran on back country roads. The mornings were getting colder. Max's treadmill was convenient, across the parking lot from my door, but the deep orange glow over the horizon gave me energy. Canada geese honked loudly, starting to join v-formations for their southward migration. Mist rose from ponds that would eventually freeze over. Snow would cover them, cover the roads.

In a storage box somewhere, I had micro-spikes that strapped onto my running shoes, for ice. I'd have to decide how safe I felt on narrow, almost-two-lane country roads carved out by the snow-plow. I shook out my arms, loosened my shoulders, engaged the top half of my body with the rhythm of my legs. My breath formed little clouds in front of me.

In the meantime, there was Ben to think about. Our relationship felt like one of those dances where the partners moved closer together, farther apart, turned their backs, came together again. We both loved dancing. We should have danced last night. We did well together when we danced, instead of trying to talk.

That was a terrible thought. I grappled for a different focus, anything. A pickup drove past, tires loud on the gravel road. The driver moved over, gave me space. Lifted two fingers from the wheel in greeting. I waved a thank you. There was always the butt tattoo—oh, for crying out loud, there had to be something positive to think about.

The investigation, say. I hadn't done research in a long time, but I used to be good at it. Betsy was a librarian. I should pull her in, and find out—I reached a small town, jogged a big circle in the empty parking lot of the bar, and headed back toward the ranch—find out what the local newspapers in the last, say, five years had to say about Larsen. He was a local mover and shaker.

Had he shaken anyone in particular? And did I just decide murder was a more positive thing to think about than my love life and my social life combined? Did that even bear analysis?

Max was in the barn, hanging buckets over railings. "Hold on," I called. "I'll change quick and help you bring them in." I jogged up the stairs for jeans and boots.

The horses spent their nights roaming the woods and pastures. On a busy morning, Max herded them all into the big corral, so the trails would be free. Slow days, he might just bring in what he called the breakfast crew—horses who needed meds or supplemental feed. There was also a lunch crew, and a dinner crew. Max and Walt had recently adapted the list, considering who needed fattening up before winter. I loved helping with horse retrieval—I learned the horses' names and how to tell them apart. Practiced haltering and leading them. Felt triumphantly victorious when I got it right.

"Thanks, Maguire." Max scanned the barn, checking how each horse was tucked into its feed. "I'm going to give them a once-over. When they're done, come on over to the house. I'm making waffles."

"Fabulous," I said. "I'll bring fruit." I looked back at the doorway and watched for a moment as Max approached the first horse to be done eating. He put away its bucket and led it to the other end of the barn. He ran his hands over its flanks, its legs. Picked up its feet and looked at the bottoms of its hooves, a move that still terrified me. He checked for a wide range of things I knew nothing about. Max could do anything with any of the horses. I loved to watch him in action.

I showered off my run, filled a thermos with hot coffee, and collected berries and fruits. Max wouldn't have produce. He made great waffles, grilled a good burger, but that was about it. His repertoire was mostly sandwiches—meat and cheese, peanut butter, jelly on a fancy day. Hands full, I knocked a knee against his screen door and slid in under his arm.

Vig joined us for breakfast, then headed off to work. We all tried for an air of normalcy—Vig was a neat, polite houseguest, but he wanted to go home. I listened as his truck left the parking lot, then turned to Max. "How's he doing? Does he sleep? Has anything happened at night?"

"We sit up talking a lot," Max said. "He really took it seriously, what you said about processing memories, trying to separate off some of the emotional payload. He's really trying." He forked another waffle onto his plate. "It's not ideal, you know? I'm not a clinical therapist, like you. Not always a hundred percent, myself. Sometimes we get each other a little upset, have to go down to the workout room and lift, or hit the treadmill or something. Thing is—" he piled sliced berries on his waffle, drizzled a swirl of syrup over it, added a curlicue in the center. "I'm what we got. Where he's at right now, he can talk to me, so we're doing it. You'll have to see, when we do another session together, how he seems to you."

Max said he'd do the dishes, but I grabbed a dishcloth and started drying. "You're tired, Max. You try to do everything yourself, you'll eventually crash and burn, and we'll be screwed."

He laughed. "At least your motivation is pure."

"You know it. I'm not picking up a horse's hoof, I promise you. I suppose Ida and Walt could move in. They're both fearless. I could be the timid sidekick."

He threw a sideways glance at me, shook his head. Decided not to say it. Just as well—we were having a good morning. My situationally specific, occasional lapses in self-preservation were not a topic for polite conversation. He saw me read his mind, raised one snarky eyebrow, and rinsed the batter bowl.

"What's on the agenda today?" I took the bowl from the rack and wiped it. "Any big projects to tackle, with no sessions until this afternoon?"

"Yeah, cleaning my boots. We'll do yours too." He squeezed out his dishcloth and hung it over the side of the sink. He gestured toward his bedroom with a head jerk. "My kit's in the closet. Leather cleaner, brushes, all that. I'll show you, you ever want to borrow it. You should have your own brush, though, keep the dirt off the stitching. Especially at the bottom. Doesn't matter how expensive boots are, how good the leather is. They all use the same thread to sew them together, and urine is acidic. Even the dirt has traces of urine in it—that'll eat the thread if it sits. Shorten the life of your boots."

I followed him—I'd never been in his bedroom. It was tidy, no-frills. In perfect order. He had a faded, blue bedspread, probably with military corners on the sheets underneath. The walls were bare. I guessed the curtains, blue and white checks almost faded to gray and white, came with the house. The bookshelves looked homemade. I immediately wanted to peruse the titles that filled the shelves, overflowing in neat stacks on top of the bookcase, on the floor, on a wooden chest of drawers.

"It's right up on this shelf, here." Max pointed at a boot box, clearly labeled as leather cleaners. He took it down, then pulled the string to turn off the closet light. The hex nut tied to the bottom of the string swung a little.

I smiled. The house I grew up in had pull-string lights in the closets, the fruit cellar— the whole basement, until Papa and his friends put up some walls, did some rewiring. He did that for me. Considered himself a family man, because of me.

Max's closet shelves also looked handmade. He may not be much of a decorator, but he nailed it on usefulness, functionality. I scanned the shelves. I'm curious. It's just my nature.

My eye was drawn to a small, wooden box—about six inches square, less than two inches deep. The wood was so thin, I thought it was cardboard at first. I picked it up for a closer look—it felt nearly weightless. The tiniest nails held it together. Each surface was intricately carved and textured except for the smooth bottom. I turned it over carefully, found a woman's signature in faded ink: Lou Anna Turner. Next to that was a childish scrawl: Max. I'd never seen anything quite like it. Max turned, saw me holding the box, and froze.

Chapter Nine

I set it down quickly and took a step back. "I'm sorry—I didn't open it. I wasn't trying to snoop, it just caught my eye. Sorry." I babbled, caught off guard by his reaction.

Max reddened. He looked away. "No, it's okay, Maguire. You're good." He picked it up, brushed dust from the sides. "It was my grandma's. And mine, I guess."

I touched his forearm. The hair felt soft over firm skin. "Max, you've never talked about your grandma. Or your family at all. Or anything before the Marines."

He hesitantly met my eyes, shrugged sheepishly. "I guess my family isn't that close. We don't really communicate much."

"Tell me about your grandma."

Max brushed his fingertips over the lid of the box. "She was always—not just there, but so happy to see me. Not like I had a rotten home life, not at all. Just one of a whole bunch of kids. Always had everything I needed, got to be in sports. Nobody treated me bad—sibling stuff, you know? Nothing. Just—"

He ran one index finger along the rough, scored edges. Seemed to refamiliarize himself, as though it had been a long time. "Just, nobody really had time to wonder what I thought about, if that makes sense. Who I really was. Except my grandma. We had the longest conversations about the littlest things. Some ladybug. How come birds' feet don't freeze in the winter. Whatever it occurred to me to think about."

He smiled self-consciously. "I was over there all the time. I wasn't just one of the kids there. I was Max. She, uh—" It suddenly seemed hard for him to talk, as if his throat tightened. He swallowed hard, looked at the faded rug on the scuffed, wooden floor. "She died while I was deployed. Absolutely blindsided me—no idea. Didn't see it coming. She wrote to me all the time, but didn't say she was sick. Didn't want me to worry, I guess. I mean, I never told her the bad stuff either, never would have, so—"

He waved the box gently, shook his head. "I was just so wrecked that I didn't get to say goodbye. Got back, her house was gone, everything was gone. But she put my name on this, so they set it aside for me."

"Max, I am so sorry." I touched his hand that held the box. "This must have been special."

"Our treasures. I suppose it seems silly." He opened it, poked around with a finger, pulled out a green plastic ring. "Got this in a box of Cracker Jack. Some kind of secret agent thing. We'd go to the store, I'd carry her groceries for her, she'd buy me a treat. I loved carrying her groceries, I didn't need a treat. But it was fun, we'd share it. She really liked the peanuts. It made me real happy to give her my peanuts."

He flicked a hand, trying to be dismissive, not pulling it off. "Little kid having something to give his grandma, that she's all excited about. My whole life, I have never been happier about anything, ever. I was an adult before I thought about it long enough to realize it wasn't the peanuts that put that shine in her eyes."

He put the ring back, paused, held the box for me to see inside. Metal bottle caps, from sodas I had forgotten ever existed. A blue jay feather, an acorn. Ticket stubs from a matinee. A couple of baseball cards, and an autographed picture of Max, probably about ten, in a baseball uniform. I thought about little Max, preferring a quiet refuge with one adult who really cared about him, to being part of a loud, boisterous horde doing childhood together. And here he was on the ranch, scheduling people-time into his quiet life.

He pointed to a faded bit of newsprint. "She put this in while I was gone. Some article about me being in the service, all the local kids that enlisted." Max closed the box and set it back on the shelf. He picked up a shoebox, gestured with it. "I was gonna throw these all out, but—" He opened the lid, showed me a careless pile of medals and ribbons, then closed it and shoved it back in the closet. "When I saw that news clipping, I decided to just put them with our box. Like giving them to her. Think about her being proud of me."

Max blinked hard, turned his face away, brushed his cheek with a fingertip. "That's what Vig said. I was just gutted—we had a bad week out there anyway, lost some guys, and then I found out she died. Well, I couldn't sit and cry over my grandma. I actually did, though, just in front of Vig one time, off by ourselves." He swallowed. His voice was husky. "Vig said she was proud of me. Because of how she wrote, sent me socks. She didn't have a lot of money, but she'd send me socks. And a couple times, a box of Cracker Jack."

Max gave up, sat on the edge of the bed, let a few tears run into his beard. "I'm sorry, Maguire. I'm just too tired, that's all. A little touchy. This isn't what we came in here for."

I sat next to him, put an arm around his back. "Thank you for telling me this. And please don't be embarrassed. I still have a little bag of candies from Papa. They're hard as rocks now, but I can't get rid of them. They were in his shirt pocket when I cleaned out his house." Now I waved a hand, failed at nonchalance. "They were always in his shirt pocket. He'd pull one out and pass it to me, like it was our little secret. I was in my thirties, he was still presenting me with a candy, with that same flourish. Like I was five. Like he was giving me the moon."

Max smiled ruefully. "Grandma always had this dish of Tootsie Rolls you could've used as shrapnel. I don't think she knew they were hard. I just acted all happy, and sucked on them for an hour." He leaned his head against mine. After a moment, he stood. "Anyway, I can't let losing her be how I feel, remembering her. She was the best thing in my life for a real long time, so I remember that. And I try to always see kids for who they really are, like to honor her. To be like her." He picked up the leather cleaning box. "Come on, I'll show you how to take care of your boots."

Walt and I had a client in the outdoor arena when the sky went dark. The horse seemed uneasy, which had Walt's attention. I could see him focus, assessing the cause. Then the wind kicked up, carried dust across the corral, bent the trees.

The darkness was sudden. The black sky had a strange, green tinge. “We’d best cut this short,” Walt said. “We’ll credit you this session, don’t worry about not getting your full time in.”

The woman started to answer, but Max came jogging up. “We need to get inside, down the basement. Get the horses out.”

Walt immediately removed the halter from the horse and shooed it out of the arena. Max trotted by, calling the horse to come with him, and opened the gate to the woods. The horse walked out, and Max hurried over to open the next gate, letting all the horses leave the corral.

“Abby, please take Betty here down in Max’s basement, will you?” Walt said. “I’ll just quick get Lego out of the med stall, and I’ll be right in.” He turned and jogged into the barn before I could answer.

“Okay, let’s head in.” I tried to sound confident. We walked to the house with our heads on a swivel, watching Walt and Max. Walt brought Lego out of the barn, took off the halter, and shooed her toward the woods. Lego left at a quick walk, checking behind her a few times, making sure she understood what Walt wanted. She disappeared into the trees as we reached the door.

It felt odd, going into Max’s house without him. I put a smile on my face and led the way to the basement. Betty texted her ride, told them not to come. Told them to get downstairs, themselves. She looked around nervously. “Those two men, they don’t mess around.” She rubbed her hands briskly over her arms, as though she were chilled. “Max says something, Walt doesn’t question, just boom. Almost think they run drills on this kind of thing.”

My phone buzzed. It was Ida, making sure we knew about the storm. "Excuse me," I told Betty. She nodded, while I texted Ida back.

Walt joined us in the storage room, only minutes later. Max had some folding chairs in there. It was also the room with no windows, but we didn't point that out. Wind howled around the house as we settled in. If not for Betty, I'd have my head stuck out the door. I desperately wanted to see what was going on out there, but she had enough anxiety. Walt struck up a jovial conversation, and soon had Betty laughing.

I started to worry about Max. What was he doing? His absence felt prolonged. Was this an emergency, or not? Walt saw me check the stairway repeatedly, and made a little head gesture, obviously meant to reassure.

Torrential rain pounded against the siding. The screen door slammed, and Max came down the steps at a clip. "Whoo, boy!" He shook himself. His clothing was soaked. "I almost made it. Excuse me just a minute, here." He disappeared into another room and closed the door. He came back wearing dry clothes, rubbing his hair with a towel. "Good thing I had a load in the dryer."

"What were you doing out there?" It came out sounding accusatory, scolding. I cleared my throat. "I mean, I was starting to wonder."

Max handed a set of keys to Walt, then handed me the keys to my truck. "Hope you don't mind, Maguire. I ran up and grabbed your keys off your counter, put your truck in the garage with mine. Walt, I put yours in the barn."

I opened my mouth to protest, to accuse him of the same risk-taking he scolded me for—but my words were drowned out by a thunderous pounding. "Listen to that," Max shouted over the noise. The room went dark as we lost power.

"Got to be some golf-ball sized hail there," Walt yelled back, "maybe more. Don't worry, Betty! We've got good insurance. Might just get a new roof and new siding out of this one!"

The pounding grew louder, made conversation impossible. It sounded like baseballs being hurled from the sky. Glass shattered somewhere above us. My eyes adjusted to the dim room—I could see Max and Walt exchange a look. Max had some new windows coming. My irritation about Max taking the time to put my beautiful truck in the garage faded rapidly.

Betty's eyes were huge, but she seemed to be breathing normally. No panic symptoms I could see. Her hands were still, arms loose. She steadily tapped her toes, but it looked like a pretty good coping mechanism. When the hail quieted down, she turned to Max. "Why didn't you put the horses in the barn? Won't they get hurt?"

"We'll go check on them right away," he said, "soon as this passes. Couple funnel clouds touched down, headed this way. Horses could get trapped in the barn, it gets hit by a tornado."

Walt nodded. "They're free to shelter in the trees, or take to the open prairie. Their instincts will guide them to lower spots. Barn's not strong enough to withstand a twister, and things aren't secured inside. Even if the walls or the roof didn't completely collapse on the horse, why, they could get hit by flying debris. Wheelbarrows, feed bins. Lego wasn't sure I knew what I was doing, but she was happy enough to join the herd."

He reached out to Betty and patted her shoulder. "Now, I don't want you to worry. This house is incredibly solid, built in a time when they didn't stint on the concrete. We'll be just fine here."

The wind kicked up again, with a high-pitched keening. Betty grabbed Walt's hand, gripped it tightly. He let her hold it, patted the back of her hand with his free one. She slid her chair closer to his. Something heavy hit the side of the house. I shot a look of alarm at Max, met his eyes just as the howl of a freight train started in, loud, close. Time seemed to stretch out—like it does sometimes, when something happens and you know in your gut that it's bad.

Max's expression was grave. We kept coming back to each other's eyes, held each other's worry. Another loud bang on the side of the house—our eyes flicked in that direction, to Walt and our client, to each other, stopped there. Flicked again toward a resounding crack—likely a tree snapped in half—then back to our silent connection. The screaming wind passed, moved away. No one spoke for a few long moments. Max took out his phone. "Lemme just pull up the radar, here." He stood. "I need to go in a different room. Just hold tight." He walked over to a room with windows. I got up and moved to the doorway.

I was too well-versed in liability risks to leave Walt alone in a basement room with an anxious, clinging female client. You never know how things might get turned around, misconstrued. I stood in the doorway and watched Max, down the hall, holding his phone up to the window, finding bars of coverage. He found a good spot and held it for a few minutes, studying the screen.

I walked back into the room with him, when he returned. "It's moving out," he said. "It's a fast storm. Ten, fifteen minutes, we should be able to head up and see how we fared." Max was antsy now, impatient. He paced the length of the basement, went back to check the radar again, and called the all clear. "I'm heading right out."

Walt stood. "Abby, will you wait with Betty until her ride comes?" We all followed Max up the stairs and out the door. It felt cold, clammy outside, after the front moved through. The air smelled odd. Standing water pooled in the corral and the parking lot. The ground was covered with hailstones—large marbles, golf balls, baseballs. I walked out into the wet grass, over small branches, twigs, sodden leaves. My shoes quickly became soaked. I bent to pick up a few of the largest hailstones, hefted them, one in each hand. Considered my impulse to keep them in the kitchen freezer. I took a selfie at an angle that showed balls of ice covering the ground.

Betty stood by the house and texted her ride. I watched Max and Walt move toward the horses, Max at a run, Walt not far behind. I scanned the house they had disregarded, seemingly without a glance. Someone would have to go up on the roof to check out the shingles, but the siding was clearly annihilated. One of the lean-tos was gone—just gone, but the hay shed was still there. The barn still had four walls and a roof. In the grass next to the driveway, there was a large piece of roof with green shingles—ours were black. I walked back to Betty. "Are you okay?"

"Yeah." She looked around, wide-eyed. "Do you think the horses are okay?" We both turned toward the woods.

"I hope so," I said. "We'll know soon. Max and Walt will find them." I stepped farther from the house, to see around it. Pointed. "There's the tree that broke in half." We both leaned, craned our necks, moved closer. It was the big oak. I frowned. "I really liked that tree." At least it only took out a fence. Max could fix that, but we probably better get to the lumberyard, quick, before there was no wood.

Betty pointed. "There's one thing that slammed into the house, see that garbage can? That coulda come from miles away. I knew somebody had a trampoline in their yard after a storm. They didn't even know anyone with a trampoline." She looked at the side yard. "Never heard of someone finding a roof, though."

We continued our circumference of the house. I stopped. "Found the lean-to." It was picked up and thrown against the house. My phone rang. Ida. I excused myself and stepped away. We were all okay, I assured her. The guys were checking on the horses now.

Ida had lost her chicken coop—the whole thing vanished—but her house was fine. "There were a handful of tornadoes that touched down, I don't imagine you've seen," she said. "We got a few of those long, thin ones skipping around, up and down. Some buildings just demolished, others not even touched. It looked like one went right over the ranch, I had to call and see. I feel just terrible for my poor chickens, but I can't complain, Abby. Not at all. Some people have lost their homes. I'm coming out there, I'll leave right away."

Vig pulled up in the drive, slid out of his truck and trotted over. "What do you need?"

"Is your house okay, Vig? Is Jules okay?"

He nodded briskly. "We got missed." He turned and looked at the lean-to smashed against the shattered siding, the roof in the yard. "Might be a while before we can get adjusters out here. There's houses down."

"Listen, Vig." I showed him the fence with a tree on it. "Can you run and buy some wood to replace this fencing, before the whole county sells out of lumber? We absolutely have to have this main corral functional."

He quickly assessed the damage, mentally calculated, scanned the fenceline he could see. "Okay. If I can't get wood, I'll see about wire and metal posts." He climbed into his truck and drove back toward town.

Betty's ride drove away as Ida pulled in. She looked at the shattered lean-to for a few seconds, the carpet of hailstones, the roof in the grass. Then she snapped into efficiency mode. "We'll get a list of horses from the office to use as a checklist. Make sure we get eyes on every single one, mark any injuries."

"I can do that," I said. "You go help Max and Walt. See if you can find Rosie, Ida. See if Rosie's okay." By the time I emerged with a list on a clipboard, they had started gathering horses in a few undamaged side corrals. Vehicles continued to pull into the drive, volunteers arriving one after another. Within a half hour of the storm passing, we had a dozen unsolicited helpers. They saw the radar, the storm's trajectory, and came. Compared stories, talked over each other, chattered loudly, a frenetic buzz.

Walt gratefully assigned duties: either Max, Ida or Walt would personally examine each horse. Volunteers with halters and ropes found horses in the woods, the pastures. Most of them were still crowded together in lower ground with tree cover. Alert and watchful, they moved along with the horses being led. They followed as a mass, herding themselves toward the barn. An experienced volunteer directed traffic: in smaller, confined spaces, separate these horses. Keep those together.

The least agile volunteer held the clipboard and jotted notes about cuts, limping, apparent tender spots. I saw Rosie and rushed over, ran my hands over her sodden back, watched her walk. She would be looked at much better, I knew, by people far more knowledgeable, but I satisfied my own worries and breathed easier.

With all the horses in, the volunteers surveyed the property. A few stronger people got the chainsaw and moved the tree off the broken fence. Vig brought Jules, their truck filled with lumber, wire and posts. "I figured we better check the whole fenceline," Vig said. "We don't need it all, we can take it back." They swung into action with the fence crew.

A few people drove into town and returned with boxes and bags of food and beverages. They moved into Max's house, cooked on his gas stove, pulled his cooler from the basement and filled it with bags of ice. The refrigerator and freezer stayed closed, to keep them cold longer. Someone drove Walt's pickup out of the barn, which quickly filled with tables and chairs. People worked, rested and ate in turns. I grabbed a hotdog and a Diet Coke.

"They're all okay." Ida appeared at my side. "No serious injuries. Walt's cancelled all riding for a couple weeks, then we'll reassess, make sure we don't put any saddles on bruises. Well, Rebel's in good shape except for a tender spot on one side. Seems to be on the muscle. We'll watch, of course, keep a sharp eye on them all. And I checked Rosie myself, Abby. The girls are just fine."

I threw a grateful arm over her shoulders, even gave her my Diet Coke. She handed it back. "Thank you, but I'm cold and wet. I'll have coffee."

Walt made the rounds repeatedly, thanked everyone, shook hands. The tables and chairs were put away before the last volunteers went home. They left food to last for days, knowing nobody would cook. Max hauled out a ladder and climbed up to look at the roof. Ida stood below and yelled at him. He came down fairly quickly and shook his head at Walt. They walked the grounds, took inventory, spoke kindly to the horses who were unhappy about spending the night in the side corral. Vig and Jules kept at the heavy work until it was too dark to see.

Finally, the power came back on. We all stood together under the yard lights. Numb, silent, we stared at the lean-to that was tossed at the house, the debris from miles away. Walt crossed his arms, clicked his tongue on the roof of his mouth. "Well, we've a great deal to be thankful for. And this is just a hell of a mess."

It rained in the night, but the waves that followed the storm were quieter, easier. I liked the sound of rain on the barn roof. It could be loud—the horses didn't like it—but the steady patter was calming, somehow. It helped me sleep.

When it pounded hard enough to wake me, it didn't startle me awake. Not like a nightmare. Not like a panic attack. Even the wind blowing around the corners, howling up under the eaves, didn't feel like a threat. I thought about sitting in the dark with Papa, on his lap, warm and cozy while it stormed outside. I listened to the rain and smiled.

In the morning, Max took his chainsaw and axe, and set about clearing fallen trees. I drove into Deergrass for supplies, and maybe a quick explore to see who was open, who had damage, who still didn't have power. I scored a parking place at the end of a block and backed in.

A uniformed cop stood on the sidewalk outside the café, facing away, talking on his cell phone. He ended the call and turned—it was Tobias. He graced me with a smile. "Maguire! Elson, we met the other day. How are ya?"

"Delighted to see you." I studied his grinning face. Looked like he was growing a beard. Not bad, but it would hide his dimples. "You on break?"

"Double shifts, all the storm damage, power outages." Elson shrugged dramatically. "Thought I'd stop by my mom's, she'd offer me a home-cooked meal. No luck—she's never home. This spot here's the next best thing."

"Let me buy you lunch," I said. "I've never been here—usually I hit the drive-through at Burgers 'n Bait or Taco Tio. Consider it my version of giving someone home cooking."

"You're on," he said. No social back-and-forth, pretending to refuse. He silently noted my approval, cataloged it. Probably absorbed details all day.

Elson slid into a booth. He seemed unaware of the slight shifting and adjusting of his loaded-down duty belt. It must become second nature. I walked the table a few inches closer to give him space, and leaned back against the padded vinyl. Elson had taken the side with splits in the backrest, off-white cushioning fluffing out in spots. It probably started out white.

The server moseyed over with the comfort of a thirty-year veteran. "Morning, Tobie. Who's your friend?"

"Good morning, Mrs. Thorson. This is Abby Maguire, she's working out at Walt Bravo's place."

She looked me over, nodded. I must have passed muster. "You can call me Hazel, honey. How's Walt doing? Hasn't stopped in for a while."

"He's good. Always too busy, especially now, after the storm. I'll tell him you asked after him."

Hazel nodded again. "You do that. Now, honey, what you want is the burger and fries. Don't know if Tobie told you, we get our beef local and fresh. You look like a 'sub fruit' gal, but the melon's a little green right now. Fries are a better bet. Get you some coffee?"

"Lots of coffee, black. And just a burger today, please."

"Alrighty." She walked away without writing anything down or asking what Tobie wanted. Everything about this was delightful. I studied the surroundings. Elson studied me.

"You in town running errands today?" he asked.

"I need to head over to the farm and fleet, get a list of things for Max. He's cleaning up downed trees today. Plus, I've been advised to get a pair of winter-weight muck boots, a heavier barn coat, and warmer gloves."

"You're going to want all of that," he said. "I was you, I'd get a case lot of hand and foot warmers too, before the hunters buy them all out." He paused, assessing me. "How did you end up running around with my mom and her friends? The youngest one has got to be twenty-five years older than you."

"Ida invited me. She said the Old Bats Club would set aside the problem of my youth and grant me a temporary affiliation."

Elson frowned. "If I called any one of them an old bat, they'd take me out. I tell you what, those gals get together, their sanity level drops proportionately as more of them show up."

I hesitated. "I'm not sure I can disagree with you, based on the evidence I have thus far."

Hazel brought a carafe of coffee, poured us each a cup, and set the carafe on the table. It felt like only moments before she reappeared with our food.

"I met your mom's neighbor the other day," I said. "Seemed like a nice guy."

He grinned. "She's being snoopy. Pumping him for gossip. He's one of the men's group that holds down a table drinking coffee all morning."

I tried to look casual. "I guess he brought her garbage cans up from the curb, so she had him in for a treat."

"Uh huh. I'll bet she did. Well, I do appreciate Mr. Koenig helping her out. It helps me, as much as her." Elson dunked a fry in ketchup and stuck it in his mouth. He nodded while he chewed and swallowed. "I work some long shifts, not always predictable. I try to get over there, all hell breaks loose and I don't make it. It really is nice for me, knowing he's right there. Last week he nailed down a loose board on her porch. She could've tripped on it."

He dipped another fry, held it suspended halfway to his mouth. "I mean, I know she's not that old, she's not infirm, but she doesn't slow down and think. Ever. Just goes full bore. If she had some grand impulse, she'd barrel out the door and whoop! Head over keister." He made a tumbling gesture through the air with the fry, then ate it. "Always been like that—all my life, anyway."

"Do you really call him Mr. Koenig?" That seemed incongruous, but he'd done it with Hazel as well.

Elson smiled and shifted his weight on the bench seat. "Knew him when I was growing up. I can't bring myself to call him anything else."

"He did talk about the guy who was killed." I paused, not wanting to lie to him, not willing to tattle on Janet for her interrogation schemes.

He laughed. "You're trying to be all noncommittal. Don't even try to protect my mom. I know full well what she's up to."

I ate a couple of his fries. "I have no comment on that."

He pushed his plate closer to me. "I'm sure Mr. Koenig did have something to say, and it wouldn't be pretty." Elson wiped a drip of ketchup from his chin. "If anyone had a reason to hate Doug Larsen, Mr. Koenig did. Guy shot his dog."

I missed a couple beats, blinked. "He did what?"

He sat back against the cracked vinyl, shifting sideways when an edge poked his shoulder. He tipped his head up in affirmation. "They used to be part of the same group, went out hunting together. Not that they were buddies or anything, kind of a loosely affiliated group. Larsen said it was an accident—the dog was running through the weeds, retrieving a bird. Said he heard rustling, thought they'd flushed something out. Mr. Koenig was just absolutely devastated. He loved that dog, had it for years. Nice dog."

Elson glanced at a couple of people in the doorway, looked them over for a moment, then returned his attention to me. "Heck, I liked that dog. Mr. Koenig called it murder. Well, I mean, it was a dog. Real nice dog, but still. Reckless discharge of a firearm, firing that low in a group like that." He shrugged one shoulder, made a gesture with his hand: what are you gonna do?

"Warren didn't say anything about that," I said. "Just that Larsen was generally abusive to people. Bullying, intimidation. Did he get charged?"

Elson listened, but eyed the people in the doorway at the same time. "Got his hand slapped. Upshot was, Larsen had to give him a new dog. And he did, a real nice young dog, bred to be a great hunting dog. Mr. Koenig didn't want it. Donated it to some family that had a couple kids learning how to hunt." He shook his head. "That was a helluva thing."

The people he was eyeballing walked out to the parking lot. Elson didn't say anything, but seemed to mentally file something away.

"Huh." I watched as Elson topped off his coffee, then mine. "Warren said whoever killed him should get a parade. He seemed to think it could've been any of a hundred people."

Elson nodded, rubbed a thumb across his two-day stubble. "Or more. That's the problem. Half the county could be a suspect." He stopped himself and gave me a stern look. "Not that I'm discussing this case with you."

I smiled innocently. "Of course not! We're just chatting. Tell me how your day's been."

"Long." He took a bite of his burger, chewed thoughtfully, studied me. The stubble looked good on him. Roughed him up a little, accentuated his cheekbones and his eyes. I fought down an impulse to touch it, and looked away. Stop it. This guy observes everything. Just stop.

Elson gave me a slow smile, then took another bite. I sighed. This was not helping anything. I had to get something useful to report back.

"You grill up a mean burger," Elson said. "I like your version of home cooking. If you were ten years younger, I'd propose to you."

Surprised into laughter, I threw a wadded-up napkin at him. "If you were ten years older, I'd accept."

"People would talk. I'm just a lad." He shook his head solemnly.

I squinted at him. "You've got a little gray in your beard." He didn't.

"Lies." He looked around for Hazel, waved a hand. He looked at my mug. "I need more coffee. You want another carafe?"

"I do. You know, Warren seemed really nice, but he went into this long, involved biology lecture. Does he always do that?"

Hazel paused at our table, hands full of plates. He leaned forward to talk to her, and I picked up a subtle whiff of cologne. Nice that he didn't overdo it. Just enough to make me want to move closer, investigate. My pulse kicked up. A little shiver. I made myself look at the array of high school sports pictures on the wall—decades of them. Hockey. Football. Basketball. Track.

When I turned back, Elson was studying me again. Did he say something, and I missed it? I gave him a friendly smile.

His eyes rested on my face. When he finally spoke, it was only to offer me another fry. I had no idea what was really going on behind that studious gaze. We chatted lightly through another pot of coffee, his radio crackling a few times.

Elson thanked me as I picked up the bill, and whistled as he walked back to his squad car. I imagined him whistling his way through his shifts—not happy, carefree whistling, but more of a declaration into the world. Still here. Undaunted, carrying on. I saw him pick up his mic, say something into the radio, and pull away from the curb.

Chapter Ten

I took Elson's advice and loaded up on hand and toe warmers at the store. The outdoor clothing added up quickly. I was making an investment in this one-year gig—but there were other cold places. I'd think of it as expanding my options.

Unpacking my bags, I heard a knock at the door. It was Walt. I waved him in, and he stood at the entryway, hat in hand. "Say, Abby, you recall that family we worked with a bit ago?"

I smiled. "Vividly."

"Well, the mother scheduled a solo session for this afternoon. I was hoping you could help me out with it."

I was glad to, and showed up early for the session. Our client—her name was Lisa— already sat in the office. She seemed to search for words. "Thank you for seeing me." She looked at each of us in turn. "Especially with how the family session went."

Walt smiled gently. "I'm glad you came back. What are you looking for?"

Lisa paused. "My daughter—" she took a breath. "I need to figure out my part in all this craziness. We act like our daughter's the one with the problem, but that's not entirely honest." Silence. Walt seemed completely relaxed and comfortable, as though he'd be happy to wait for hours. I pulled in some quick, energizing breaths to counteract the contagion of her overwhelming exhaustion. Just being in her presence was draining.

"My daughter opened up," she went on. Her voice was flat, devoid of energy. "Started talking to me after the session. Said she doesn't want to grow up, if that's what being a woman is. You saw how I was that day. How we all were, I know, but how I was. I need to figure this out, give her a better example. Can you help me with that?"

We waited in the outdoor arena while Walt brought in a couple of horses and set them free to wander around us. We watched him set up a very basic obstacle course—all straight lines, no cones to weave around. He dragged over an enormously heavy wooden bridge that I couldn't move, and pulled it to one end of the course.

"Alright, then." Walt brushed his hands on his jeans as he approached us. "I'd like you to grab a lead rope, and choose a horse to work with. Then you're going to lead the horse—" he pointed to the far end, away from the bridge. "Starting there, and when you get to the middle of the bridge, you're going to stop. Keep him standing there for a moment, you decide how long. Then back him off the bridge, and see how far you can move him backwards, through the course."

Lisa looked around uncertainly. I was struck by the difference in her stance and demeanor. With her family—corralling the children, dealing with issues—she'd been authoritative, not stopping to second-guess herself. Even her walk had been confident. She seemed hesitant now, but Walt had chosen horses that both stood still for her.

She hooked the rope to a halter, and easily led the horse through the obstacles. She stopped on the bridge, and looked at Walt. The horse looked at Walt. Walt didn't move. His posture indicated no intention of moving. The horse looked at Lisa. She stood, apparently frozen. We waited.

"Back up," she said quietly. The horse ignored her. She threw another nervous glance at Walt. She tentatively pushed at the horse's chest. "Back," she said to the horse. "Go back." Nothing happened.

They stood on the bridge, immobile. "Back up," she said again, with a slight twitch of the rope. The woman seemed increasingly frustrated, the horse simply bored. Lisa looked at Walt. "I don't know what to do."

Walt moved to stand beside her. "You seem to be struggling with getting him to listen to you, and back off." He looked at the horse, the obstacles.

"I was fine until we got here," she said. "I was doing fine."

Walt nodded. "Until you wanted him to back down," he said. "It appears to me that your level of confidence and authority changed."

Lisa thought about that for a moment, and seemed to sag. She unhooked the rope from the horse's halter and stepped off the bridge. The horse still didn't move.

Walt regarded her seriously. "Does this remind you of anything in your life?"

"Oh, of course it does," she said. "One more way I'm not good enough. One more thing I can't do right. No matter what I do, he's there to tell me how I should have done it." She got a little louder. "One more way I'm lacking, is that what you want to hear?"

She took a deep, slow breath, shakily blew it out. "I'm no longer attractive, I'm no longer desirable, never mind having and raising four children. I don't even know who I am anymore. And you know what I'm afraid of, if we're honest?"

She focused on Walt, who met her eyes silently. She took on a look of desperation. "What if I'm not anyone? What if there's nothing left? Of me." She waved a hand, and the rope slipped away, fell to the ground. Right next to a little pile of manure a horse had dropped while Walt set up the course.

Lisa looked at the rope in the sand, and choked back a sob. One more failure—I could see it in her eyes. What would happen if she allowed herself to know she was angry? She framed this whole thing as needing to fix herself. I thought about horse calls bullshit, but didn't say it out loud.

She leaned over, picked up the rope, and caught some sand in her grasp—and with it a tiny drop of poop. My eyes widened. She didn't even realize she'd done it. She gripped the rope tightly. "Alright, do you want me to try it again? Or do you want me to do something else?"

Warm and sweaty, she was unaware of the bit of manure oozing between her fingers. Lisa turned toward the horse. It didn't move, except to glance at Walt for direction. She made a choked little noise, raised her hands to her face—then jumped, as if she'd been shocked. She gasped, looked at her hand in surprise, then looked around, unsure what to do. Stricken, she wordlessly turned to Walt.

His voice was calm, gentle. "I observe that you picked up that crap without really noticing it, or thinking about it."

She held her hands in front of her face, stared at them, and saw the manure she'd gotten on the rope. "Oh my God." She started to shake, horrified. Walt pulled a clean handkerchief from his pocket, handed it to her, and took the rope from her hand.

"I'm so sorry," she said. "I—I'm so sorry."

Walt chuckled. "Poop isn't that big of a deal around here. Comes with the territory. More important is what you take out of this."

She held his handkerchief between two fingers, not wanting to use it. Walt gestured, smiled, and she started to wipe her hand. Suddenly, the coin dropped. She froze, eyes wide. "This isn't even my crap," she all but shouted. She shook her head in disbelief. Appalled. "It's not even my crap." She looked at the soiled handkerchief. "Oh, for God's sake!" Walt held out a hand, and she gave it to him. "Yes, this reminds me of something in my life," she said angrily. "I get it."

We scheduled more sessions and watched her drive away. Walt smiled, picked up a muck rake, and balanced it in the wheelbarrow. "Just can't make this stuff up."

Ida knocked at the door, then stuck her head in. "Mail call!" I waved her in, and she handed me a small box. "Max asked me to bring it up."

"Yes!" I danced in place. It was from Black Rifle Coffee. I took it to the kitchen and looked for something sharp to open it with.

"Abby, are you busy? I'm heading home, but I want you to come with me. We've got some things to discuss." Ida wore a t-shirt from an Old Bats Club road trip. She made a new one every time the group had an adventure, and gave each member a matching iron-on decal. This one had a photo of the women at a fire hall, posing by a hook and ladder truck, arms wrapped around men who had put on fire hats and removed their shirts. Everyone was laughing. All but Janet looked at the camera—she gazed at her fireman.

Ida saw me staring and grinned. "This was one of my favorite trips. My, that was fun. We'll get you a shirt too, Abby. As soon as you join us for something noteworthy."

"Did you wear that for a session?"

She laughed. "I pulled a jacket over it until the client left."

I forced myself to look away. "Just come in here. I'll make some of this coffee. You will cry, it's so good."

"No, we need good, reliable Wi-Fi. It can be spotty out here. You can show off your coffee in the morning. Come on, get your boots on. I'll drive."

I took my own truck, so Ida wouldn't have to drive me home. I detoured through the Burgers 'n Bait drive-through, and got enough fries for us both. Ida settled in at her kitchen table with coffee and her laptop. I dug in her refrigerator for ketchup.

"Alright, now," Ida said, "we've got some research to do, and we need to get on it. We've got a meeting coming up, and we have to be ready."

I reached for a particularly crispy fry, to stall while I figured out why she needed Wi-Fi. "Do you have a new theory?" I'd told her about visiting Janet, meeting her neighbor, the biology lecture. I hoped Ida would have some insight into the entire situation. She hadn't. I settled into a chair. "You're not doing a web search on natural predators, are you?"

"No, Janet's got Warren right next door, if she wants any further clarification on that whole thing. Abby, we're running out of time. We haven't chosen tattoos!"

I choked on my fry. Ida peered at her computer screen and clicked on things. "Look what I found," she said. "There are whole web sites with tattoo ideas. I'm trying to think what represents me, though. The others didn't have any trouble with that, but I'm just coming up empty." She glanced at me sideways. "Are you alright over there?"

I waved her off while I tried to stop coughing. I pounded a fist on my chest. "You know what you should get? One that says Rebel. It's your horse's name, and it would suit you perfectly."

Ida sat back in astonishment. "Why, Abby! That's such a good idea! I'll search for that. Now, what about you? Then I've got one more thing I want your help with."

"What other thing? I'm happy to assist."

"Don't worry, we'll find you a good one. It will come to us." She frowned at her screen. "Oh, dear. Some terrible things come up for a rebel tattoo."

"Just design your own," I told her. "You can use a nice script for the word, then put a heart or rose or something."

"That's exactly what I'll do. You know, Johnny would've gotten such a bang out of this whole thing. I can just hear him laughing." She chuckled happily, remembering her late husband. "Sometimes it makes things more fun, thinking about it. Now, I don't really know where to start for you. You're smart, you're a fireball. You're just not a butterfly kind of gal—feminine, but not girly, if you know what I mean."

"I'm not getting a fireball on my butt, Ida. And don't think I'm not on to you, just carrying on as though I'd already agreed, thinking your momentum will sweep me along. What's the other thing you want help with?"

She straightened and leaned back in her chair. "There's quite a bit of information online about bum tattoos and toilet seats. I'd really like to mitigate that whole situation. Now, I don't have any experience with these things—that urinal Fran had at the dinner table? I'm going to get one for each of us—the whole Old Bats Club." She acknowledged my grin with a nod. "I need you to help me find them. Searching under purse urinal didn't quite work."

"Try Shewee. One word." I leaned in. "This is actually a great idea."

"Well, here it is. I knew you'd know what to do. And look, they come in a rainbow of colors—except yellow, I guess, which would have been practical. We can get a different color for everyone! Do you think I should include Fran?"

"Yes," I said. "Hers is so old, that model doesn't exist anymore. She might as well join in the fun. And I'd hate to think what might happen if the little washer on the hose got too brittle."

"I'm overnighting them," Ida said. "It will be worth the extra postage. I'm getting you the teal one, Abby, and I'll splurge for the ones with matching carry cases." She continued scrolling and clicking. "Lord, help. Just look at this. You can get a pair of underwear with a fly opening. That would simplify things, but I'm certainly not going to hazard a guess about what size everyone would wear. No, sir. Not touching that one."

Betsy and I met at the library. I found her sitting behind the desk, chatting with the staff as they worked. She waved me over and introduced me to the crew. "Come on back to my office," one woman said. "We'll leave the open computers for patrons."

Her office was a desk and a row of filing cabinets pushed up to one wall of a storage room. She had a computer, a printer, and a landline phone. A chipped mug from a university bookstore held pens and pencils, and doubled as a paperweight for a stack of notepaper. I couldn't stop myself from running my hand admiringly over an old card catalog cabinet. I leaned in and smelled the wood.

"Aha," the woman said. "A childhood spent in libraries, I'll bet." She smiled triumphantly when I agreed. "People look at that piece and assess the antique value, but a true library lover might caress it." She and Betsy nodded to each other, as if sharing a secret understanding.

Betsy plopped herself into the desk chair with comfortable familiarity. "Have you changed the password?" She typed quickly. "You haven't. Good." They bandied search engine terminology back and forth. I surveyed the wall art delineating the office space—framed posters of classic and genre literature, cartoons with nerdy humor.

"Give me a holler if you need anything." The woman retreated.

Betsy slid her chair slightly to the side, so I pulled up another and sat beside her. We both peered at back issues of a local newspaper on the screen. "I'm going to search Doug Larsen," she said. "What do you want for date parameters?"

"Let's start well before he died. I don't think our answer will be in his death coverage. Do we look for a long-term grudge that simmered, or for a more immediate catalyst? We should do both, but where to start?" I drummed my fingers on the desk for a moment. "Let's do the last year."

"Well, alright," Betsy said, when over a hundred results came up. "Let's narrow this down." She clacked on the keys, and we had seventy. She sat back and pondered the screen. "Abby, what would you think about starting here, while I run get us some coffee? We may need to take turns actually scanning, to save our eyes."

"Extra-large, black," I said. "On it." I moved to the padded chair when she vacated it. Doug was certainly a topic of local conversation. I eliminated the more sterile articles pretty quickly. Ben had said from the beginning that Doug was active in civic organizations and served on boards. He also ended up on the sports page, for hunting and fishing conquests. His auto parts company had to close a second location in another town, I noted. It looked like the local economy just couldn't support two stores, but I wrote down the name of the store manager who'd lost a job. I didn't recognize the name, but Betsy might know if he was related to someone even close to being in the frame.

I finished three months and moved aside, letting Betsy take another three while I drank coffee and nibbled smidgens from a piece of coffee cake. I ignored her comment that I might as well just eat it, instead of pretending I wasn't going to. "It tastes better an inch at a time," I told her. "Coming up with anything?"

"Nothing earth-shaking. We'll have to review our notes later, see if anything pops." She kept scanning. I looked around the store room, to give my eyes a break from the screen. I tried to guess what was in various boxes, then got up and did some squats and hamstring stretches.

"Look at this picture," Betsy said. She enlarged it to fill the screen. Doug held a plaque, some contrived-sounding civic award. The people in the foreground wore their best photo-op smiles, but the camera had captured two people on the periphery. A man, taller, tilted his head toward a woman whose face angled up, mouth close to his ear. They were caught in an unguarded moment, expressions of disgust clear on both faces.

Betsy tapped the screen with a fingernail. "He's actually a cousin. On the mother's side—a Swanson, not a Larsen. But related, like it or not. They're both city council reps—she's one of the Koenigs, actually. I wonder if we can leverage Janet's friendship with Warren to find out what was going on here? We haven't even thought about this being a family affair. Extended family, beyond the widow. Do you suppose Warren could be induced to find out what the good councilwoman knows about Swanson's beef with Larsen?"

"What about Phyllis's family?" I asked. "Does she have siblings? Nobody would convict them."

Betsy nodded thoughtfully. "We could be on to something, here." She printed the picture and added it to our stack of notes. She wrote a reminder to look into both families. "We might need to all split up, each of us targeting a prominent local gossip. The danger, of course, is in gathering severely distorted information. We'll have to be very discerning."

We tagged off periodically, and covered the past year. "I have to stop," I finally said. "My eyes are glazed over." Betsy agreed. We gathered our notes, thanked the librarian, and went for tacos.

My hair whipped into my face. I brushed it away, pulled my jacket closed, and hunched against the chill. Dry leaves skittered across the pavement. I'd circled the block twice looking for a parking space, finally ending up down the street. I walked as close to the aging, brick buildings as I could, hugged the edges for shelter, and walked around other huddled people. A gust nearly took the café door from my hand—I barely kept it from slamming against the wall.

The group was gathered around some pushed-together tables. Betsy must have just arrived—she smoothed her wind-blown hair with her fingers.

Fran saw me and reached for her purse. "I found a few tattoos I thought you might like, Abby. I kept a screenshot of them. Hold on, I'll find my phone."

Betsy picked up her phone, called Fran, and Janis Joplin started singing. Fran pulled her phone from an inside pocket of her coat. "Thank you, Betsy." She opened her saved screenshots and handed me her phone. "Here, Abby, take a look at these."

One was a simple sunrise—or sunset, I guess—over waves. "I actually like this one," I said. "But I don't know about it on my butt." I swiped to the next one. "Cheeky?"

Ida laughed. "I like that! You are, Abby!" She laughed harder, took off her glasses, and wiped her eyes. "On your cheek! Oh, please do it! That would be hard not to tell people, though. Maybe you shouldn't—every time you were being cheeky, I'd want to make an announcement."

"A heart with the words Lucky You?" I set down Fran's phone. "I haven't even agreed to do this at all. Not at all."

Betsy pulled some papers from her purse. "Here, I found this online. I printed a copy for each of us." She passed them around.

"Getting Tattooed as a Senior Citizen," Janet read. "Who are you calling old?"

"Well, it's got some good pointers," Betsy explained. "And it starts at age sixty, so we all qualify—except for Abby, of course."

"Exactly," I said. "Except for me."

"Differences in skin elasticity and healing later in life," Ida read. "This really is good information, Betsy. Thank—oh, no! Avoid caffeine for two days ahead of time? And ibuprofen? How am I going to do that?"

"Place your tattoo in an area with sufficient fat!" Janet laughed. "We've got that covered!"

"Speak for yourself." Fran turned hers over. "Thicker lines and less fine detail, for the best healing. Well, I don't suppose my motorcycle really needs elaborate wheel covers."

"Reduce blood flow by raising the area above your heart!" Janet cackled. "You girls go ahead. I'll have Tobias show me how to make a video. I just won't tell him why I want to know."

"I'd like to propose a toast." Betsy raised her drink, and everyone followed suit. "Bottoms up!" Glasses clinked.

"Not to change the subject," I said, glancing out the window. No squad car yet.

"Go ahead, Abby," Betsy said. "Let's move on."

"Betsy and I did some research, and I talked with Vig," I said.

"Excellent," Fran said. "I've been doing a great deal of thinking. Now, Ida, just hear me out—don't get reactive. Is it just possible that Vig was involved?" She held up a hand to stop Ida. "Just for the purpose of discussion. Have we even considered the possibility? We should learn what we can about that bar fight."

"That's exactly what we talked about," I interjected, before Ida could start blustering. I told them about the young woman being harassed, and Vig intervening. There was silence around the table.

Finally, Fran spoke. "Well, you're just making it impossible for us, aren't you?"

"We can't go after him now," Janet said. "If he turns out to be guilty, let's think about who we can frame for it."

"I can think of half a dozen people I'd nominate," Betsy offered.

Ida finally erupted. "He is not guilty! You can see the kind of man he is—exactly the kind of man Max would be friends with. This is a waste of time."

A whistle would've been helpful. A loud one. I held up both hands. "Hold on. Betsy's probably better equipped to talk about our research, then I want to talk about something else."

"Quite right," Betsy said. She efficiently summarized our notes, and passed around the printed picture. They scrutinized it, murmured, exchanged glances. Betsy turned to me. "Abby, you have the floor."

"This isn't as concrete," I said. "More of a philosophical thing, to spur our thinking." They all seemed attentive. "I've been thinking about Warren's idea."

"Oh, Lord, help," Ida complained.

"Just hold on," I told her. "Not the whole wildlife thing—more a rabbit hole I went down after Warren's monologue." I paused. "I haven't actually put this into words before. You might have to bear with me."

"Go ahead, Abby," Fran said. "Just take your time. We really can quiet down and listen, when it matters."

"I was thinking—" I hesitated—"about how frustrating it is to make yourself small, for another person. Diminish yourself. Dumb yourself down. Keep yourself from shining, or even being noticed. Silence your own voice. Oh, I'm not making sense. Just hold on."

No one spoke. I tried to regroup. "Warren was talking about people deliberately fading into the background, trying to avoid attention. Not feeling safe. But people need to be seen. It's a basic part of human nature. Maybe we should think about that—all those conflicting emotions cause so much frustration, anger, resentment. Wanting just basic acknowledgment, but being treated dismissively."

Betsy nodded. "We've all lived as females on this earth for a long time, and now we're old. We certainly understand being treated dismissively, being expected to dim our own lights, to let others shine. Under what circumstances do you suppose it would be a reason for murder?"

"I don't have a hard time imagining that at all," Janet said. "Not at all. There's so much we're expected to just let slide. Someone was continuously told to be nice and not make waves, and finally snapped. If it wasn't so important to help Max's friend..."

"Let's not go there," Fran said. "We really mustn't."

We sat, grim and quiet. "So, you all know what I'm talking about," I finally said. "Perhaps you've noticed it, picked up on it somewhere that never even registered with any of the alpha males involved in this case. They have too much of a shared perspective, might not see the complete picture. Sometimes it takes someone with a different life experience to widen the view."

"To look at things someone else doesn't." Fran nodded thoughtfully. "The root word of ignorant is ignore." She tilted her head, studied me. "I can see why you're a therapist, Abby. That's really very good, and we do need to think about it. Who feels dismissed and angry, but the men solving the case might not even notice them? The killer who just wasn't seen." She took a drink of water, set her glass down carefully, deliberately. "We really mustn't dwell on the entire subject, but just as an observation, we would make excellent killers. Yes, we goof around—largely because we realize what matters, and what never truly did. We're smart, determined, capable of sustained attention—which is more and more uncommon—and completely invisible. Very few people take us seriously at all, even fewer than when we were young women. But we can still think for ourselves, and be flexible."

I glanced around the table. They looked like they were thoughtfully considering the matter. They couldn't be. Could they?

"On that note," Ida said, "being flexible—we do need to think about Abby's question, but I have something for all of you. Because of toilet seats, and open wounds. We want to be ready." She brought a bag from under the table, and presented everyone with their colorful new Shewees.

"Well, this is wonderful!" Fran admired hers. "Thank you for including me, Ida. Just look how technology has changed!"

"I hope Tobias hears about this," Janet crowed. She held it up for anyone in the restaurant who happened to look over. "I almost hope someone overheard Fran. Imagine if he thought we were considering becoming assassins, as well as being able to pee from an upright position."

I could imagine that, actually. I practiced stuffing my Shewee into its case. "Just so you all know, you really might need to try it first in the shower. You have no idea how hard it is to release your bladder, when your brain has been trained since infancy that peeing while standing means an indescribably humiliating event is occurring. Seriously."

"We'll have to find out. You know what we should do?" Betsy smiled as she turned her Shewee around in the light. "I vividly remember how aggrieved I felt in kindergarten, standing in the hall crossing my legs, trying to hold it, while six boys were allowed to crowd into the bathroom. I can still hear the teacher explaining that girls can't stand in a circle around the toilet." I held my breath as the Old Bats eyed each other around the table. "And that was only the beginning," Betsy went on. "Our whole lives, we've stood in long, hot, suffocating lines at public restrooms while men zip in and out..."

"I'm in." Ida stood.

Fran slapped both palms on the table. "Let's do this."

Janet was already halfway across the room. I noticed she'd left her handbag behind. "I'll guard the purses," I offered. This was it. We'd get thrown out. We'd probably make the local newspaper.

Ida grabbed Janet's purse and her own. "Get moving, Abby. This is a moment of solidarity."

"Soli—" I was cut off when Ida pulled me from my seat. Solidarity? "Do not make me a t-shirt, Ida," I said. "I'm not wearing it."

Chapter Eleven

Ben called as I settled down to work at my kitchen table. "Just checking in," he said. "Want to grab a quick lunch one day this week? I was going to suggest the diner in Deergrass, but you're probably tired of that. Maybe the truck stop south of town? No one has better food than a truck stop."

I missed a beat. Of course he knew I was frequenting the diner—Janet was there. Elson was notified about something, every single time. Give her credit, she tolerated this constant scrutiny as graciously as she did anything. It was already making me livid.

"I'll have to check the therapy schedule and get back to you," I said. I'd checked an hour ago, but the urge to push back was overpowering. Ben probably thought it was funny, the old ladies meeting at the diner. Everyone knew a bunch of old men in town met at the café, to gossip over coffee. They'd say to visit, to while away the morning, but they gossiped. This probably wasn't that different. People knowing your business was just part of small town life.

"Abby?" Ben had that tone. He said something, and I missed it.

"I'm sorry, I got distracted. What was that?"

There was a smile in his voice. "Just wondering if anything noteworthy has happened lately. Anything interesting come out of the coffee klatches?"

"Well, let's see." I still felt like being obstructive. "Last time, we talked about gerontological concerns in tattooing, urinary directional devices, and alpha males. Would you like to hear about any of that?"

Silence. "Oh, someone just came in. Better go. Catch you later."

I smiled, put my phone out of reach to help me focus, and booted up my computer.

I sat on the steps outside my door. The side of the barn was still hot from baking in the sun. I leaned against it to watch the sunset. Vibrant pinks and corals melded into rich orange and red. I'd never seen such intensity, before coming here. The last of the fading light sank into the tops of pines and birches. A chill settled in quickly with the dark. I pushed myself up and headed into my apartment. I fumbled with the switch to turn on the lamp, as my phone rang.

I read the screen with delight — Bobby, a coworker and much more, for a regrettably short time. I wondered sometimes if we made the wrong decision, letting each other go.

We were temp workers together. Then gone, in different directions. It became too difficult, unsustainable, but we tried to keep some kind of connection. Bobby eventually got tired of moving and settled down in a mid-size city in North Dakota. He loved it. He had his own space, and let me use his basement for storage when Papa died. I didn't have that much, really, but there were some things I'd kept at home—at Papa's—and a few things of Papa's that I couldn't let go.

We happily chatted for a few minutes. Then his voice became hesitant. "I'm sorry, Ab. I'm putting my house on the market, moving into a condo. I'll have a lot less storage room."

"Of course I understand," I told him. "Don't feel bad at all. I really appreciate the time you gave me." I was in driving distance now, and could haul my things without renting a trailer. "I'll get a couple days off and pop right over."

I cleared it with Walt, and the next morning I threw my duffel bag in the back seat. I love solo road trips, and it was a nice time to take one. The leaves were starting to get some color, reds and oranges rippling in the breeze with yellows and greens. A stand of deep red maples was hit by a gust, and whipped around like flames against the blue sky. The air was cool, the sun deliciously warm. I stopped at rest areas along the way to stretch my legs on walking trails, sometimes through little groves of trees. I dragged my feet through fallen leaves, kicked them in the air, watched them fall again.

I had packed coffee and sandwiches, to avoid fast food. I sang loudly with the radio, until I lost the station. I tried to find another one, but gave up on the fragments of country, talk radio, static. Bugs accumulated on my windshield, almost obstructing my vision. I had to scrub to get them off, when I stopped to fill the gas tank.

I arrived as Bobby got home from work, and proudly showed off my truck—he'd only seen me drive a tired, little hatchback. He was properly appreciative, running his hand over a shiny, crimson quarter panel. "Let's see what she can do," he said.

Bobby and I learned from each other, no egos in the way. One thing Bobby taught me: how to drive fast. I laughed, remembering the fun we used to have. North Dakota has some long, straight roads, he said. Miles long stretches with next to no traffic. He knew some good ones. Of course he did.

Turned out she could do over a hundred. She probably enjoyed it, I happily announced, like Rosie loved to run, to fly. He humored me with an affectionate grin. We took turns, cheering each other on.

Along with long, straight, isolated roads, North Dakota has aerial speed traps—aircraft with radars. You innocently tool along after the fact, three over the speed limit, and a ground cop snags you. They know what you did. We decided we'd pushed our luck long enough. We made it back to his house without incident—hopefully I wouldn't get a ticket in the mail—and Bobby had hamburgers ready for the grill.

"Now, help me understand some things," he finally said, as we finished eating. "First, what is this horse thing? Horses?"

"It's evidence-based, Bobby. Statistically proven, lots of research." I explained the model of therapy, then thoroughly captivated him with stories about learning to ride a horse, put on a saddle, fling manure into a centrally located wheelbarrow. He laughed until he could barely sit up. We moved to the living room to settle on the couch.

"What about you?" I put my feet on his coffee table. "Tell me what you've been up to."

"Not yet," he said. "I have another question. The whole horse thing almost qualifies, but what have you been up to that's outrageous? I do miss that."

"I have no idea what you're talking about."

"You're basically happy—for the most part, it seems. Which means you're not bored. Which means there's something crazy going on."

I hesitated too long. He leaned in, suddenly serious. "Abby, I haven't offended you? I didn't mean to."

"No." I closed my eyes. "You've never said that before."

Bobby put a hand on my knee. "Hey, I didn't mean anything, really. I'm sorry."

"I'm not mad at you. You're right, I haven't told you everything. It doesn't make me happy, though." I liked his hand there. I rested my hand on his. "I'm going to have to think about this, if you think I'm addicted to craziness." People do that. Say they want peace, but adrenaline and stress hormones are familiar. If they start to relax, they do something to jack themselves up again. Comfortable chaos.

Our sodas got warm and flat while I told him about the murders I'd gotten pulled into last summer. He was visibly upset about me getting hurt, but he listened, riveted, while I explained about the latest situation. About Vig. He halfway smiled at the antics of the Old Bats Club, but the laughter had been lost.

"Getting a tattoo on your butt would've probably been enough. Are you going to?"

"I don't know," I said. "I haven't decided."

He took hold of my shoulder with comfortable familiarity, massaged it gently. I leaned in. It felt really good.

"Help me understand why you're doing this," he said. "You've never been that person who has to fix everything for everyone."

Great question. You'd think I would have considered that myself. "For Ida," I finally said. "Max, really. More for him. Last summer, it was mostly for Walt."

"At least that makes sense," Bobby said. "Your career has thoroughly conditioned you to hurl yourself into protecting your friends and coworkers. 'We all go down together' kind of thing." He repositioned me so he could reach my whole back, and dug his thumbs in between my shoulder blades. "Take me through this again. The current one. Walk me through it."

Bobby was, among other things, one of the smartest people I'd ever known. He listened carefully. I knew he was mentally sorting and filing as I went. "Don't forget the effect of people talking," he said. "Fires get lit by people's mouths. Sometimes people talking about an action is what causes the reaction." He stopped rubbing and rested a hand flat against my back, as though he couldn't move and formulate thoughts at the same time. "Okay," he said. "Two things." His hand made a warm spot between my shoulder blades.

"I just want to point this out, Ab. You've done temp jobs for a long time. You go all in, then you leave. Everything starts over. Nothing is permanent." He lifted his hand, leaving a sweaty spot under my thin shirt. He leaned forward to catch my eye. "Just stop and think about what you're doing, going all in. You've walked away after situations nobody would believe. We've done it together."

"We have," I said. "Countless times."

"People have no idea the crazy dangerous things that go on, while they go about their lives. But Abby, you walk in two realities, it skews your perspective. It just does." He sighed, sat for a moment, then started rubbing my back again. "We've had this conversation before. I'm not telling you to get a job knitting doilies somewhere. Can you just consider that you do throw yourself into things, without a thought? Assume you'll walk away in a few months? Rationally, you know consequences can be permanent. Don't give a violent person a reason to come after you. Just think about that." He dug his thumb into a sore spot. "You're solid knots."

"I drove several hours to get here. I got stiff."

"Please." He jabbed harder, making me yelp. "You start using deflection with me, I'll show you the meaning of digging deeper."

"Okay, okay. You said there were two things."

Bobby found another knotted muscle and pressed a knuckle into it. My eyes watered. I clenched my toes, determined not to show weakness, beg for mercy.

"This seems ridiculous to say," he said, "after the conversation we've already had, but what's wrong?"

The knot released. A wave of dopamine flooded my body. I sighed happily. "I'd forgotten I even was tense."

"Exactly my point. You do seem surface-level happy. At a deeper level, something's off. Generally, after insane situations, we wipe our faces, a little dark humor, and move on. Your general approach is to put your head down and ram through things, but I feel something—" He leaned around me again to look at my face. "Hesitant?

Tentative? Almost like you want to be in retreat mode, but haven't given yourself permission. Was it the attack in your home? Having to fight back, hurt someone, instead of using containment skills? What's taken a chunk out of you?"

I didn't answer right away. He didn't push. He set it out there between us. Mine to engage with—or to say something dismissive, leave it. We would be different then. I bit my lip. I didn't want it to stay between us.

"I'm not sure I'm okay," I said, appalled when my voice wavered. I clamped down emotions, made it intellectual—my safe spot. "I guess it's complicated grief, or complex trauma. Both. Losing Papa, it's all mixed up with old, accumulated work trauma that I didn't know was impacting me. I really didn't, Bobby. The new setting hasn't really helped at all." I cleared my throat. "I mean, I'm fine. I am. I do a good job, I'm not falling apart."

"You can still pretend it's not there," Bobby said.

A tiny sideways tilt of my head, not denying something I didn't want to admit. "But sometimes I'm a hot mess. It's hard to fake through it. Triggers blindside me. My anxiety spikes. I feel so stupid—have a whole adrenaline reaction in the middle of something, try to act normal. Some nights I wake up at the peak of a panic attack and can't get my bearings. Maybe I should get a job knitting doilies. Except I can't knit. I suck at crafts. I do, Bobby. I suck."

He almost laughed. More of a loud exhale through his nose. He shook his head.

"Sometimes I wonder if I wasted my life," I confessed. "At the time, it felt so satisfying. Every single day, I made a difference. I liked that. But was there ever a lasting change? Did I spend my life pulling people out of the ocean, just for the waves to wreck the lifeboat? All those years helping drowning people, and now I can't get the water out of my lungs, and I get pulled under at night, in my dreams."

He pulled me into his arms, his voice husky. "Ab, maybe you can't be involved in situations that make it worse. Your brain's screaming at you, slow down, I can't catch up. It keeps getting bombarded. It needs to clear that backlog so you can move forward."

We sat so quietly, I heard the refrigerator hum. Wind kicked up outside. A branch scraped a window. "I really tried to take a step back," I said. "It feels like a vortex. I can't get out."

"Okay." He sighed. "Rationally, you know you're forty years old, it's a bit premature to talk about having wasted your life. Objectively, we know some of the people we worked with had a different trajectory afterwards. It mattered. I'm concerned about the potential for depression, here. We know the traumatized brain develops a negative bias, to survive. Expect the worst, you'll be ready for it. Do you think you're clinically depressed?"

I thought about that. "Not yet," I said.

I felt him nod, his chin moving on the side of my head. "But," he said, "you have that AOP Syndrome that you invented for other people, even though you're the original poster child for it yourself—" he pulled back a little, saw me smile. "Anxious Overachieving Perfectionist that you are, you struggle with not being okay in front of other people. How am I doing?"

"That's all true," I said. I rested there on his shoulder, and listened to him breathe.

The intimacy of our friendship was comforting, restorative, but I slept on his couch. His eyes lingered on mine, just a moment, when he handed me blankets and a pillow. He didn't say it. I took them, wordless. He looked away from whatever he saw in my eyes, but ran a hand through my hair, pulled my head into his shoulder. He kissed the top of my ear and said goodnight. He almost closed his bedroom door, but didn't latch it.

I settled in and stared at that door. I thought about his almost-invitation, not quite a question, not a statement. We wouldn't be together—I wasn't ready to quit my job, move to be with him, fold myself into his choices. Try to erect scaffolding around him and build some kind of life. We both knew that was not coming next.

Yet he didn't close the door. Was he staring at the other side of it? Bobby was sweet, gentle, passionate. We knew each other well. There would be no awkwardness, fumbling, anxious fear of unmet expectations. My fear was—suddenly I knew, and turned my face to the back of the couch. I was afraid it would feel like coming home. It would be an illusion that, fading, might take another piece of me with it. Neither of us wanted to risk losing what we had. Even knowing that, I felt strangely sad, lying in darkness, longing for something that wouldn't fix me anyway.

I drove away after breakfast, when Bobby left for work. We exchanged long hugs and promised to stay in touch, no longer connected by the thread tying me to my possessions. The drive back was quieter—I left the radio off and sat with my thoughts for hours. Fond thoughts of Bobby. Complicated thoughts of Papa, kicked up by moving his things again. Thoughts of people talking, setting fire to situations with their words, causing deadly reactions.

The prairie stretched out around me in every direction. It seemed immeasurably vast. Harvested fields sat empty, waiting for winter. Field corn dried in rows of grays and browns, broken by county highways, lakes, tiny towns. I was tired when I pulled in to the long, gravel driveway. I left everything but my duffel bag, and climbed the stairs to my compact, one-bedroom, temporary apartment over someone else's barn.

Vig fried up a mean breakfast. His repertoire was broader than Max's, expanding to omelets and different versions of fried potatoes. I convinced him to leave the cleanup for us. His work schedule was much less flexible, and he needed to run.

He wasn't aware of getting up in his sleep, he said. Hadn't woken up standing in another room, or anything. But he was aware of having nightmares. "Not sure if that's better, or worse. Maybe I had nightmares all along, just couldn't remember. Maybe it's better, wake up in bed, know what the cold sweat's all about." They both looked at me.

"Could be," I said. "There's a certain logic to that. I know you don't want to hear this, but it really would be a good idea to put the deep dive into past trauma on hold for a while. This whole murder suspect thing would be overwhelming for anyone. Better to work on bringing down the biology—do something to mitigate over-the-top stress. Train your body and brain in different ways of processing it, instead of digging up more right now."

Vig's face became noncommittal. "Yeah, I hear ya. I'll take that under advisement. Better head out."

"He just wants to go home," Max said, as Vig drove away. "Not sure how we're gonna know it's time—maybe when the nightmares let up? I don't know."

Our conversation moved to the practical: I had to empty the bed of my pickup. This is how stagnation sets in, I philosophized, waving my coffee cup expansively. The negative side of ambivalence always wins out, because it's the path of least resistance. Papa's things, I would keep. But some of these boxes were in storage, in one basement or another, for years. I didn't want to part with them, clearly didn't need them in a technical sense. My tonneau cover was not fully waterproof. Waiting for rain to ruin it all before discarding things was cowardly, it just was. It might take some inner examination, but I needed to toughen up. Make some hard choices.

Max blinked at me tiredly through the steam of his own coffee. "I got room in the basement."

"Done." I sat back, smiled, took a long drink.

Max helped me lug boxes down to the utility room. I'd only been in there during the tornado, and hadn't paid attention to the room itself. Usually I walked right past, to use the very efficient gym he made in one of the basement bedrooms. He'd done just as well with his storage area. A wall of sturdy shelves, pallets on the floor. I saw no evidence of water in the basement, but Max was ready. He'd even built a wooden spacer of sorts up one wall, so the tarp-covered door on a pallet wouldn't lean against the concrete where water might seep in. I paused mid-stride, a box balanced on my hip to spare my arms the weight. A door in a tarp? Why? I studied the door for clues, but the cover was neatly secured with bungee cords.

Max tracked my gaze, flushed, looked away. He busied himself consolidating boxes on the shelves. "I wasn't really careful packing stuff in here. There was so much room, I just kind of put things down, didn't worry about it."

I watched him slide boxes over, fitting them together to take up the smallest possible space. What could be embarrassing or private about a door? Now I was even more curious, but his face was red. I never knew with Max where the land mines were buried. "Max, never mind. I don't mean to make you uncomfortable. It's just interesting. You don't have to explain anything to me." I was dying to know.

I put my box on the shelf, turned toward the stairs for another trip, and eyed the door on my way by. Max scowled. The box he moved to a pallet landed too hard, slammed down with a loud bang. Startled, I snapped to high alert.

Max noticed. He was embarrassed. Setting me on edge upset him. His breath got just a bit louder, his movements shorter, tighter with the growing tension in his body—his shoulders, neck, face. His stance changed, weight slightly forward, feet squared off. I automatically scanned the room—marked the exit and our relative positions. My heart beat faster. I couldn't breathe. I fled the basement and leaned on my tailgate in the sun. I had to reel this in. Having a danger response to Max was ridiculous.

He came out and we both jumped when the screen door slammed behind him. Neither of us spoke, but he registered me taking a break from him. Some strong emotion flickered in his eyes, but he shut it down before I could name it. He walked in a wide arc around me and reached in for another box, lifting it over the side of the truck rather than using the open tailgate near me. Seriously? I narrowed my eyes at him. He squinted back.

Fine! I angrily grabbed a heavy case of books I'd been planning to leave for Max. I struggled up the steps and leaned the box against the house as I groped for the door handle. I awkwardly squeezed through the doorway and slid the box against the wall, trying not to drop it. The door slammed behind me. I rested the weight of the box against the railing and took the stairs slowly, one foot and then the other on each step, all the way down.

Max stood at the bottom, arms crossed tightly over his chest. "I would've helped you with that," he snapped. His fists were clenched.

An anxious wave washed over me, pooled in my stomach. "I don't need any help! I'm fine!" It came out louder than I intended. Sharper. Rather than try to fix it, I looked away. I staggered forward a few steps and pressed the box between my chest and the wall, so I could readjust my arms.

He leaned in. "You don't have to yell at me!"

I pulled away and the weight of the box created momentum, pushing me a few involuntary steps backwards. I overcorrected, reeled sideways, caught my foot on the corner of a pallet, pitched forward, dropped the box with an echoing thud, and fell on it. I landed on an elbow, legs bent awkwardly, butt in the air. I tried to right myself, and tipped over sideways. Max stared open-mouthed, arms spread in the universal posture of a person watching a train wreck.

I tasted blood in my mouth from biting my lip when I fell. Tears of frustration welled up in my eyes, but I furiously blinked them back. Max had seen them, dammit. I clambered to my feet and turned my back to him. My hand was scraped and splintered from grazing a pallet on the way down. I shoved the box along the floor with my foot until it reached a pallet with empty space. I was too embarrassed to try lifting the box from the floor. Not in front of Max. I sat on it instead, not looking at him, not looking at his stupid door in a tarp. Not willing to admit how stupid I felt.

"Are you okay?" Max was deflated.

I nodded. I didn't trust my voice. I tried to do stupid calming breathing like I keep telling everyone else in the world to do.

Max stuck his hands in his pockets and studied the floor, like a child caught at something. His shoulders drooped. Silence settled around us like fog. "What are we doing?" he asked quietly.

I didn't answer right away. I let the gloom spread, then finally spoke into it. "Triggering each other."

He didn't respond for a couple beats, then slowly nodded. "I get it." We stayed there, dejected, morose together. I thought about my half-empty truck bed sitting in the sun.

Max turned to the mystery door as if it would tell him what to do. "I just never—" He scuffed his shoe on the concrete floor. "I mean, Walt helped me move in, he was curious too. I was so embarrassed, he just got all reassuring, you know how he does. If he's ever down here, he pretends he doesn't see it."

"Just let it go, Max," I said. "You don't have to talk about it." I tried to look uninterested. Let him have a secret door.

Max shifted his weight from foot to foot. He stuck a fingertip under the top of a box that was folded closed, wiggled it around, frowned uncertainly. He glanced at me sideways. I watched him struggle, but didn't try to help him. I had no idea what would help.

"When I came back—you know, from overseas—I drove past my grandma's house." He tried for nonchalant. Utterly failed. "Drove by a couple times, sat in my truck, tried not to get the cops called on me. Just thinking about her. Then this man walks by with a kid riding a bicycle. They go up the driveway, but the man sees me sitting there. I quick wipe my eyes and start the engine, but the guy comes over before I can drive away. Says hi, am I okay, like that. I'm trying not to sound like I'm unbalanced or anything—still got bandages on my head and neck, pretty sketchy looking. Told the guy I just got back from being deployed. How I didn't get to say goodbye to my grandma, so I just wanted to see her house again."

Max blew out a breath, closed his eyes for a moment. He was humiliated, thinking about it. It started to make sense. I'd noticed something he was embarrassed to own, that reminded him of feeling lost. Vulnerable. Ashamed. "I just wanted to get out of there, but the guy asks if I want to come in. Part of me really did. So I follow him inside. He's got this nice little family. They show me around, they want to hear stories. How I made Hot Wheels tracks down the stairs, the kids liked that. There's still these tiny dents in the sheetrock, where I made a jump and the cars hit the wall. How she let me build models at the kitchen table—they even had her table, I guess it got sold with the house. Little burn marks on it, scuffs and dents. Couple of new ones–they weren't all on me." He smiled at that, as if he couldn't help it. "I got ready to leave, I told them, take good care of this house. It was the happiest place in the world for a long time."

Max became quietly dramatic—waving his hands, using different voices. "So the littlest kid says, 'We didn't paint your door.' The family all gasps. 'Oh my gosh! He's right! The door guy! I can't believe we got to meet the door guy! We've wondered about you so much! We didn't paint it—we just couldn't!' So the first kid takes me by the hand and leads me into the bedroom that was mine when I slept over, they've got three bunks in there. They painted everything—the woodwork, the outside of the closet door, all fresh and bright. But the inside—" He pulled the tarp away, picked up the door, and turned it around to show me the back.

Black horizontal lines up the center of the door were marked with dates, tracking Max as he grew, starting just above my knees. The highest line was around his current height—they must have laughed about that one. Both sides around the growth chart were filled with drawings that grew in sophistication as they moved higher on the door. Something that might've been a dog, I wasn't sure. A little boy and a woman holding hands. A really awkward attempt at a bicycle. A baseball glove. A box of Cracker Jack. Near the top, the solar system—complete with Pluto—and the schematics for a pickup truck.

Max smiled, ran his hand over it. "I haven't looked at this in a long time." He turned away, shook his head. "I saw it then, it was all I could do not to start bawling right there. I'm chewing on my lip, blinking hard, trying to breathe. I'm like, ok, thanks so much, I gotta go. But the dad follows me out and says, 'Listen, take the door. I'll help you take it down, throw it in your truck. We can get a new door.'"

He took a few deep breaths. "So we did. The whole family was beaming, like they were getting something exciting instead of giving away part of their house. I tried to give him money, I could see they didn't have much. I mean, stuff was faded, their clothes were all worn out. They didn't have money for a new door, I knew they'd just do without one. He wouldn't take it. Said it was a mitzvah, in their culture they wanted to do good for people when it mattered. Like a blessing. So I drove away with this door in my truck bed. People kept it in their basements for me, all wrapped up. I never explained it. Even Vig never pushed."

Max squatted, touched the possible dog with his fingertips, and smiled. "Can you imagine just letting a kid draw all over the door in permanent markers? I was real careful, though. I worked real hard on it." He straightened, effortlessly standing from a squat, which I momentarily resented. "I sent them a gift card for the grocery store," he said. "For probably the price of three doors. I always hoped that didn't cancel out their mitzvah. I don't know how all that works."

"Max," I said, "I'm just sorry you feel embarrassed by all this. It's a beautiful door. I love it. I hope it becomes a happy memory again." I had another thought. "Hey! You know what? We should put this up. When you're ready. Uncover it, take it out of hiding. It's a standard size door, right? It could go on your bedroom closet upstairs, become part of your life again. You could open and close it any time you want."

Max didn't look at me, but he smiled. "Yeah." He took my hand, pulled me to my feet, lifted the box onto a pallet. "Let's get the rest of your stuff."

Chapter Twelve

I'd agreed to help Ida with a session in the morning, covering for Max. We grabbed halters and lead ropes, and went out together for the horses.

A very thin, older couple in shapeless, faded clothing arrived on time. Rather than come in, they stood in the gravel by their dented, rusty car and shared a cigarette.

"They do that every week," Ida said. "They say it's the only way they can calm the anxiety before getting themselves to walk in here and work on things."

The clients stubbed out their cigarette and started towards us. They seemed genuinely happy to have me fill in for Max. Rather than appearing more anxious at facing an unexpected therapist, they warmly shook my hand.

Ida used a similar activity to Max's first session with Vig. I was interested to see it play out in another context. The flexibility of this exercise was fascinating—such a great diagnostic, such a mirror to hold up for a client.

Ida let Rebel and Sally Mae roam freely in the arena, and instructed the clients to catch and halter a horse. They both nodded, picked up a halter, and slowly followed the horses around in big circles. Ida leaned over to whisper. "Remember, it's not about the exercise, whether they complete it or not. We're just observing everything."

The couple approached the horses, halters held out, or behind their backs in attempted trickery. They would get close, and the horses moved away again. It was a low-speed chase, but it looked like it could go on all day. I tried to focus on observation. The couple engaged in separate pursuits in the same arena.

The horses stood calmly, moving away when a person with a halter got within arm's reach. "Look for small things," Ida murmured. "Don't wait for the big aha moment."

Each client glanced at Ida from time to time. The man periodically straightened his shoulders, blew out air, furrowed his brow. The woman, after a failed attempt, laughed nervously. She glanced around, to see who was watching. She picked at her drooping sweater, as if removing loose threads or bits of hay. There weren't any. The couple didn't look at each other. Neither of them asked for help. Ida showed no inclination to rescue them.

My own discomfort became a distraction—the longer it continued, the more I wanted to step in, say something, do something. I wiggled my toes inside my boots, willed myself to stay out of it. The exercise went on and on. The pressure became acute. I started counting my breathing, and thought of Max's sniper breathing. Stop it. Focus.

Finally, the man stopped in the center of the arena. "Well, hell." Hands on hips, he stared at Sally Mae. She seemed unaware of him. He turned to watch his wife sidle up to Rebel, step sideways and teeter in the sand.

I barely held myself back from rushing up to grab the woman before she could topple over. At the last second, she put out an arm for balance and righted herself. Her husband shook his head. "Hell with this." He dropped his halter to the ground. "Just hang on here. Hell with this. You hold on." He walked over to the rail and picked up a lead rope.

Rebel watched the man, but let him resolutely walk up and drape the rope over her neck. He held it on both ends, as if he had Rebel captured. "Alright, you come on, now," he called over his shoulder. "Come and halter your horse." His wife walked up and put the halter on Rebel.

"There." The man pulled the lead rope away. "I guess I didn't get mine, but she got hers, so there you go." The woman sighed deeply, patted Rebel's neck, and leveled a gaze of adoration at her husband that rivaled anything Superman ever got from the people of Metropolis.

"Now, I'm noticing something," Ida said. The three of us turned to look at her. "What's going on with Rebel?"

We all looked at Rebel. She moved her mouth, made chewing motions, blew out air. Ida turned to the couple. "Any idea what that means, when a horse does that?"

They shook their heads. "Well, she looks relaxed," the woman said.

"That's right," Ida said. "That's a release. Releasing tension. Relaxing. Why do you suppose she's doing that?"

"Well, I s'pose we finally relaxed," the man said. "We ain't at each other's throats for a change." His wife smiled at him, showing yellowed teeth, with a few missing. He shyly ducked his head, face starting to redden. He stole a quick glance at her, turned a deeper red when he saw her shining eyes. He looked at the ground, cleared his throat. "I guess that horse felt us relaxing a little, between us, for a change. I just figured, hell with this. We gotta do somethin' different, here. Ain't gettin' nowhere."

His wife stepped in and leaned her head on his bony shoulder. He put an arm around her. Sally Mae yawned and started nibbling on Rebel's back. The woman giggled. "We're just having a love fest at the ranch today, ain't we?" She stole another glance at her husband, and I realized they were flirting. Ida beamed.

"Hell, woman," the man said. "Let's go home, shall we?"

His wife reached out to take Ida's hand. "Thank you." She smiled and waggled her fingers at me, wrapped an arm around her husband's waist, and they headed for their car.

Ida watched them drive away. "I'm sorry Max missed that. Those two have been tearing each other's hair out like a couple of feral cats under a full moon, each of them blaming the other. They come every week though, always on time."

"How long have you been working with them, to just stand here and watch it happen today?"

She shook her head. "It's been happening for weeks, bit by bit. They come in, the horses pick up on their anger and move away. They both get mad." She chuckled. "At first the husband accused us of training the horses to move away from him, to make it look like his wife was right and he was wrong. Then they moved away from her too, and she got mad."

"You're joking," I said.

"No, I'm not. He really thought we had some kind of horse conspiracy going on, to side with her. After a while, they figured it out—they were both so full of anger and resentment they were half blind. So they started looking at themselves, instead of pointing fingers at each other." She picked up the halter from the sand, walked up to Sally Mae, and buckled it on.

"I was hoping it would eventually occur to them that they could ask for help, or even advice. It's amazing how long people will stubbornly go on, insist on being self-sufficient, when it obviously isn't working. And we could've gotten some mileage out of the fact that nobody ever said they couldn't work together. Or how his demeanor changed with his focus, and the horse's response changed. Several things we could've worked with, there."

I snapped a lead rope on Sally Mae's halter, and turned to walk her out. "He saw her look vulnerable. His heart toward her must have been softened enough that he couldn't stand there and watch her fall. Ida, I nearly lost my mind waiting for something to happen," I confessed. "If I would've interrupted, said or done anything, they wouldn't have found their solution."

Ida nodded. "Patience. Don't make something happen, let it happen." She attached a lead rope to Rebel's halter. "I hope this is a real turning point, Abby. Life can be hard. I hope they can face it together instead of turning on each other."

I carried that romantic warmth into scheduling a date with Ben, at a neighborhood bar in Deergrass. It wasn't a dive, he told me, but they had no pretensions of grandeur, either. As long as I had clean boots on, I'd be fine.

I spent several hours off-ranch, on my own. It felt like a small vacation. I stopped at the library to pick up an eagerly awaited book I requested on an inter-library loan. I picked up a few books for Janet, delivered them to her door, and came in for coffee and snacks. Plenty of both. When she heard my plan to head for the park, to walk and to read under a tree, she insisted on packing me a lunch.

It was impossible to ever get out of Janet's house in less than two hours, but she was so entertaining, I didn't mind. She told stories from her teaching career—she had some doozies— and she pulled stories out of me that I hadn't thought of in years. Laughing, I finally noticed the time.

"I need to swing by Vig's," I said. "For another book, actually, that Jules is letting me borrow. She's off work and I'm off from the ranch at the same time, so I don't want to miss the opportunity."

"You'd better skedaddle," Janet said. "Don't forget your lunch."

Vig and Jules were both home. I accepted the book with thanks, and turned to leave immediately, to give them time together.

"No, you're fine, Maguire." Vig pulled on a long-sleeve shirt and buttoned the cuffs. "I need to get caught up on some yardwork. Buckthorn takes over, you turn your back too long."

I talked with Jules for another few hours, but she wasn't in the mood for amusing stories. She needed to vent, but didn't want to pile on Vig. We went through cup after cup of coffee. She felt better afterwards. I'd be up all night.

Pressed for time, I skipped the hike. I found a secluded place to park, with nice, soft grass to throw a blanket on, and nice, thick bushes, because I had to pee every twenty minutes. I was slightly buzzing from caffeine, but I set an alarm on my phone and tucked into my book anyway—leaning on a tree, a safe distance from the bushes.

I was well into the plot when I heard footsteps in the grass, pantlegs brushing as someone approached. I closed the book and sat up—it was Ben. He grinned. "Nothing wrong with your early warning system."

I relaxed. "What are you doing here? Nice to see you, I mean."

He sat beside me on the blanket and plucked a leaf from my hair. "I've always liked this park. You see a lot of people just pulled up, sitting in their vehicles with the windows open on a break from work. I think that's the biggest way the space gets used, really. People in the middle of their workday."

"I don't have long," I told him. "I'm meeting someone for dinner."

He grinned. "I hope he knows how lucky he is." He leaned back against the tree, stretched his legs out, kept his shoes off my blanket. I leaned against him. He wrapped an arm around me and pulled me in. We chatted lazily until my alarm went off, a quiet, slow jazz saxophone.

I pulled away, reached for my phone and stopped the music. "Dinnertime," I said. "Meet you there?" He agreed, gave me a quick kiss, and walked back the way he came.

I drove past the tiny parking lot and found a perfect spot down the block, around the corner, right by an alley. Ideal for backing into, when I wanted to leave. I congratulated myself as I swung down from the cab.

Ben already had a table. Facing the door, he saw me and waved. He smiled happily, reaching for my hand as I slid in across from him. "Thank you again, for making time for me tonight."

The menu had something I'd never tried—a hamburger with peanut butter in the middle. Ben laughed at my delight. I turned sideways and surveyed the room. I took in the working-class clientele, the big mounted fish over the cash register, the paper signs thumbtacked to the walls. Meat raffle. Gun bingo.

"Let me know when you're done with your cultural analysis." Ben's leg brushed mine under the table. I relaxed, let the weight of my leg rest against his. It felt nice.

I told him about my drive to North Dakota, how my truck had felt going long-distance. The peace of the open country—endless stretches of prairies and sky. Gold and crimson flames of leaves. How everything I owned was now in one place. I left Bobby and Max out of it, but talked about keeping some of Papa's things. Not wanting to look at them, incapable of parting with them, not sure what I was doing. Ben listened intently, and touched my arm on the table. That felt nice, too. The tenderness in his eyes distracted me, and we sat for a few moments, quiet, thinking separate thoughts.

"Tell me about you," I said. Our burgers came.

"I found myself over by the library the other day," Ben said, as the waiter slid a plate in front of him. "Just following up on something. It didn't amount to much in the end, but I thought it might. I don't get over that way very often, for some reason."

I squirted ketchup onto my plate, and pushed away defensive feelings. Ben was just making conversation. He wasn't trying to maneuver me into talking about the library, because he wouldn't know I'd been there. Would he? Elson was called every time Janet breathed wrong, but Detective Tom Harmon wouldn't have cops reporting about me, would he? Hinky Harmon and Ben had talked about me before, I knew that. I liked to imagine they didn't anymore, but really, the men lived together. They probably talked about everything.

"Abby?"

I looked up from my plate, and set the ketchup down. "Sorry, did you want this?" Ben was definitely scrutinizing me. Was it an ex-fed scrutiny, or a 'man whose dinner partner was lost in her head' kind of thing? I swallowed hard. This is why I don't date.

Ben opened his mouth to say something, but his eyes cut away. I looked to see what had distracted him. A group of people milled around by the bar. For crying out loud, it was like having a burger with Elson. Cops, anyway. Just try to keep their attention.

"Oh, imagine that." I said nonchalantly. "I was just at the library." Ben's focus snapped back to me, sharpened. Well, I had his attention now, didn't I? I squinted at him and waited for him to make a countering move.

He held his burger in both hands and watched me. "I saw the book you had today," he said. "Do you primarily use the library to find escapist reading?"

"I also do research," I said. "It's important to stay on top of things, don't you think?" I dipped a fry in ketchup. "I've rambled on enough. You were going to tell me how you're doing." I settled my weight back in the seat and shoved the fry in my mouth. Watched him hesitate, weigh his options.

"This case is a bear," he said. "I've got feelers out in all directions, multiple ways of pulling in information. Small towns are hard in a way that cities aren't. It helps that I grew up here, but it can still be like running into a wall." He gestured with his burger. "You'd better eat while it's hot. Keep a napkin on your lap, the peanut butter's drippy."

I layered several napkins over my thighs. The filling was runny, but surprisingly good. "I never would have imagined peanut butter with grilled meat," I confessed.

Ben grinned and wiped his face. "Next time, try adding the spicy peppers." He smoothly transitioned to seasonal conversation. Pre-winter yard preparation. Protecting young trees and gardens, or backyard chicken coops. Grouse hunting season. Stages of deer hunting, with different dates for bow hunting and guns. Where to see the best color as the leaves turned, but avoid the sightseeing crowds. The joy of being on a lake on a cool, fall morning.

We lingered over a shared piece of pie, then stepped out into darkness. The earlier sunset seemed abrupt, but I knew in a few months it would be dark by five. Daylight felt precious this time of year. We walked together to the corner, where I gestured with my head. "I'm parked down there."

A group of men stood near my truck, talking loudly. One man sat on the curb, not far from my tailgate. Another leaned against a fence. I paused, irritated by feeling uneasy. Being female in this world is just rife with vulnerability, like it or not.

"Think they've been a bit over-served," Ben said. He took my hand, laced his fingers between mine. "They must have wandered down from somewhere else. They would've been cut off much earlier here. I hope you won't be insulted, Abby—I'm absolutely walking you to your truck. You don't need to be fending off drunks."

"No, I appreciate it. As much as I'd like the world to be different." I squeezed his hand as we crossed the street and headed for my parking place. The men definitely eyed me up as we approached. They also sized up Ben. Most of them moved into the alley, but one particularly inebriated young man gave us a cocky grin.

"He's dropping you off, you can pick me up, baby." He put a hand on my tailgate to steady himself. Ben turned, shot him a hard look, and held it. The man walked backwards and raised both hands, warding Ben off. "Hey, sorry, officer. Didn't mean nothing." He turned to stumble away.

I unlocked my door. "That's a useful skill. I'm glad you retained it. And thank you." I gave him a kiss. He wrapped an arm around my waist, pulled me in for another. He smelled good. He felt good. Ben was amazing at kissing—just the right amount of pressure, not sloppy, not overpowering. Heat grew in the core of my belly. My toes curled.

Ben pressed his forehead to mine for just a moment, then pulled back far enough to meet my eyes. The unspoken question in his gaze was clear. His finger stroked the side of my face, and a tingle spread through me, all the way to my boots.

I opened my mouth, and almost told him to climb in, come with me. Extend the evening, knowing it would go through breakfast. I almost did. Why didn't I? What was this hesitation? I was suddenly embarrassed. Feeling stupid makes me angry. What is wrong with me? What is my problem?

Ben felt the change in mood, and stepped back. "Call me," he said.

I felt even stupider. "Ben—I—" I felt my face dissolve into frustration and regret. I ruin everything. I'm probably incapable of dating.

Ben squeezed my shoulder, stroked my cheek again, gave me an almost imperceptible headshake. "Call me, okay?" He waited on the sidewalk, watched me back into the alley and drive away.

I paused before unlocking my apartment. I sat on the step, leaned back, and listened. It took a minute, but I heard it again—coyotes. One started a long, high howl. Before it faded, more joined in, overlapping in full chorus. It sounded magical, lonely—even though I knew that was city thinking. Ranchers don't romanticize predators. My mind had shifted enough that I hoped they would stay away. I'd been on a horse that profoundly didn't want to walk down a trail and cross the scent path of whatever had been there. Coyote, bear. Probably not a wolf, but what did I know? I sat in the warm night and listened a little longer.

I changed into comfy clothes, made a cup of decaf tea, and focused on a picture of Papa. "What do you think of Ben?" I asked him. I chose a thoughtful picture to talk to, rather than a smiling one. Not that I didn't think he'd smile about Ben. "I just miss having conversations with you," I explained. I blew across the top of my tea, studied him.

"I mostly ask because this would've been a really easy night to bring him home. I mean, we could never go to his place. The sight of his roommate's face would kill the mood like a rat infestation.

But he'd come here, I know he would, and it would probably be really nice."

I honestly could have talked to Papa about the whole thing. When I was old enough, Papa didn't find some woman to come explain to me about sex. He talked with me the same way we talked about everything. Intelligently, respectfully, without a trace of discomfort or shame that might have attached itself to the subject matter.

"You are not a pizza," he said. "Dollar a slice. It's more precious than that—don't just give yourself away. Not everybody who thinks they're entitled is, or ever will be."

I'd been skeptical about ever wanting to do such a thing, but Papa smiled. "Our bodies will tell us we want things. Good things, harmful things. Now, guys—well, a fellow's body will tend to shout pretty loud, telling him what he wants. Might be hard for him to think straight, all that shouting. You just remember, that doesn't make it your issue. Boy or man, he's responsible to manage his own body, no matter what he might tell you. Don't be fooled. Your body is for you."

I'd been thankful for that advice more than once, and Papa was always happy to help me with the differential diagnosis on the matter. "I'm not sure what my problem is," I said. "I just never feel settled on the matter. I could listen to my body shouting, but I'd have to actively stop listening to some other internal voice, that's just kind of muttering something."

And then I knew exactly what Papa would have said. I could almost hear him. "Don't be so quick to think you're the problem, Abby." He told me that more than once. I had no obligation to meet other people's expectations, especially if I had to ignore my own voice to do it. Papa had deep beliefs about listening to ourselves.

Something sparked in my mind, but disappeared when I tried to focus on it. Something about people having a voice—or not having a voice, more to the point. Having their voice drowned out. Maybe turning deaf to it themselves—Papa had been adamant about the troubles arising there.

Not listening to your own self leads to confusion, he'd insisted, and blindness toward something you need to see. Then that inner confusion sets things off-kilter. Makes people angry, deep down. They feel off, but don't know why. Think there's something fundamentally wrong with them. Shame makes people even angrier, and desperate. People will lash out. It will feel like self-defense, and in a way, it is. Shame crushes the life out of people.

I picked up the picture frame, brushed off the barn dust. He would have laughed at how often I dusted his pictures, trying to keep a working man shiny and clean. I smiled at the thought. It was nice to hear his voice, even in memory. "I don't know what it is with Ben," I told him. "Maybe I'm just having trust issues. But there's something here I need to remember, Papa. Something you told me, over and over." I looked at his face, quieted my mind until I could hear him.

Some folks turn to drink, he'd said, to quiet that nagging feeling, that inner discomfort. Might get to where it would cause upheaval to start hearing themselves, start listening. They think they shouldn't make waves. Other people wouldn't like it, might push back. But it's never too late, Abby, for people to realize they matter. Never forget that.

I never had. He was quite a philosopher, Papa. He lived at a deeper level, with his coveralls and lunchbox, his trade school education. And he was always right, in the end. He saw people. Every single time.

You get a feeling in your gut, you listen. He'd picked up the salt shaker and knocked it on the tabletop for emphasis. Something seems off, pay attention. Anyone tells you that's wrong, walk away. You find out later you maybe read a situation wrong, that's fine. Lesson learned. But you never ignore what your inner voice tries to tell you. That can be immediately dangerous, or it can be a slow poison.

Again, I almost saw something—and it was gone. Chasing it wouldn't help. I refocused. Doug Larsen. By all accounts, a bully. Stifled every other voice. Someone was angry, ashamed. Maybe it felt like self-defense.

Chapter Thirteen

Ida phoned in the morning, all keyed up. She and Janet were going down to The Cities—that meant Minneapolis and St. Paul—for expanded shopping opportunities. Ida had a few destinations in mind, and promised lunch at some authentic ethnic restaurant—take my pick. I immediately offered to drive, and collected them both at Ida's.

Janet had an ambitious list. "We might not get all these places," she said. "Traffic is something terrible down there. Takes forever. Stop!"

"What's wrong?" I glanced in the rear view mirror and stepped on the brake. Something shifted in the back of the truck. I did a quick mental inventory. All I had back there was an old milk crate full of jumper cables and bungee cords.

"Pull into the bakery," Janet said. "Can't do a road trip without coffee and donuts. I'm buying."

"I'll go around the block." I took a right turn.

"Stop!" Janet shouted.

I stood on the brakes, looked wildly for pedestrians or stray cats. "What?"

"Oh, I thought there was a parking place. Never mind. There's a motorcycle in it."

"Abby, I thought you and Max emptied your truck bed," Ida said. "Put everything in his basement."

"We did," I said. "It's just a milk crate."

"Huh. Sounded more substantial than that." Ida pointed. "Let's go around this way. We can walk half a block."

I made a quick turn, and something shifted back there again. "Now it's bothering me. I don't remember what's back there." I pulled over and climbed down from the cab. "Just hold on. I can try to get closer to the bakery, I just want to fasten things down back here." I popped open the tailgate, and saw feet—boots, and then pantlegs.

Frustration surged through me. Those drunks around my truck last night! Someone had climbed in to sleep it off. The others probably thought it was funny to close him in. "Hey!" I shouted. "Hey!" I smacked the guy's boot. For crying out loud, what was his blood alcohol level last night, if he was still out?

I hit his foot harder, shifted his leg, angrier by the second. He'd better not have puked in there. "Hey! Get up! Get out of there!"

Ida called back from the cab. "What on earth is going on?"

I walked up to her window, used a normal voice. No point causing a scene. "There were a bunch of drunks last night when Ben and I came out from dinner. One of them crawled into my truck bed! It's a good thing it's not winter! You know how drunk people climb into someone's van and freeze to death. I've gotta get this guy out of here."

Ida and Janet joined me on the berm. I grabbed the guy's leg and yanked on it, whacked him a couple times. "Hey! Wake up!"

Janet rolled back the tonneau cover. "Stop!" she shouted.

I blew out air. Don't take it out on the old lady. "Janet, quit yelling at me to stop," I said. Remarkably calmly, I thought.

"No, stop, Abby!" she yelled.

"What?" I shouted. I held up a hand, took a breath, spoke more quietly. "What?"

Janet pointed. "His head's bloody."

"What?" I peered over the side of the truck. "Oh, hell." She was right. "Well, dammit, they weren't fighting when we got out there. Now my whole truck bed is a bloodborne pathogen exposure incident! Why men persist—" I hit his leg—"in getting into bar fights—" I hit his leg once more, harder. "Wake up!" He didn't move. A knot formed in my stomach.

I climbed up on the tailgate and stepped over his legs. Leaned in and felt for a pulse. He was very cold. His face was ashen. I moved the milk crate, knelt, tried again anyway. I sat back on my heels and thought about CPR for a couple of seconds. I gave his arm a tentative poke. He was in rigor mortis. Hell. He wasn't coming back. "Call the cops," I said.

"Dear God in heaven, that poor soul." Janet paused. "Tobias is going to be pissed."

"Oh, dear Lord." Ida shook her head somberly. "Well, he will be, but there's nothing for it. It's not our fault, what people do when they're drunk. And that's hardly the point now, is it?" She took out her phone.

"I feel sorry for his family," Janet said. "Whether it blindsides them, or they've worried about him for years. Fearing this would happen, and here he is."

The first squad rolled up surprisingly quickly. The cop started toward us, looked us over, paused and pulled out his phone.

Janet tilted her head at him. "You see that? Mark the time. He's calling Tobias."

"I bet he's here in ten minutes," Ida said.

"Five," Janet countered.

They both looked at me. I ignored them, and turned toward the approaching cop.

"Oh, Abby, I'm sorry," Ida said. "We're not making light of the situation, really. This is just terrible, in so many ways."

Four minutes later, Tobias arrived. He was pissed.

I told the responding officers everything I could remember about the drunks. Where I was parked, at what time. I didn't know the street names. You know, beside that bar, you turn left. That alley. No, I didn't see anyone wandering around the ranch last night, or this morning.

Tobias moved Janet to the back of a squad. She insisted on sitting with the door open and her legs out. She squawked about Ida and me not being removed from the action, but Tobias led Ida to a different car—separating us, without announcing he was doing it. His manner was distant, cold, professional. I repeated my whole story for him, defiantly matched his formal tone. He wasn't any angrier than I was.

And then it got worse. Detective Tom Harmon parked behind the squads and headed toward us. An unexplained death—call the detective. The string of obscenities that flew from my mouth was so uncharacteristic, it shocked Elson out of his snit.

"I'm sorry, Maguire," he said. "I'm not trying to make this harder on you. This is just really, seriously bad."

I had no response, so I leveled a glare at him that clearly labeled him an idiot. Which was rude, I know. But really.

Harmon talked with the uniforms, looked in my truck bed, scanned the scene. His gaze moved from Ida, to Janet, to Elson, back to Janet. He walked toward us, without even glancing at me.

"Try not to provoke him," Elson said.

"Sergeant Elson, could I have a word?" They walked away together, and talked in a huddle for several minutes. Finally, Harmon walked back to me. "Run me through this. Explain why I shouldn't arrest you."

I repeated everything. Again. Didn't look at him, trying to shake me. I could see him in my peripheral vision. Don't react. Switch into clinical mode—observe. The full-body, non-verbal attempt to intimidate? Just interesting. The stance, the glare. He can't hit me. All he can do is posture. I liked it better when Ben was doing it to the drunk who wanted to harass me. Don't react. Diagnose him. Shouldn't be hard. Let's start with sociopathology.

"Abby?" Harmon stepped into my personal space. "Abby. Hello?"

"What?" I'd lost track of his question. Of the fact that he was talking. I felt myself tearing up, and looked away. Blinked hard. Damned if I would cry in front of him. I tried to talk, cleared my throat, tried again.

"I don't know what more to tell you. This stupid, stupid man must have been disoriented, alcohol plus a head injury. Climbed into my truck." I angrily met his eyes. "Someone closed him in, though. He didn't do that himself. Some stupid, stupid drunken friend. Probably thought it was funny. Probably recorded a prank video. Probably posted it online."

I could hear Harmon breathing. He studied me. "You seem pretty calm for someone who allegedly didn't know there was a body in their vehicle." I could feel his eyes on me, as he waited for an answer. I couldn't think of a single thing to say, that wouldn't get me arrested.

He squinted. "I'm going to need a better description of these men who were supposedly near your vehicle last night."

I blew out a long, slow breath. "Ask Ben." I focused my gaze on the fire hydrant across the street. "He chased them away with that same scary cop look you're trying on me. He probably photographically remembers all of them. He can probably work with a sketch artist." I crossed my arms, bit my lip. Stopped, when I realized he'd notice me biting my lip.

"So," he said, "Your official statement is that you do not know the deceased. That you have never seen him? Not once, ever. Is that your official statement?"

My face felt hot. Knowing it was turning red infuriated me. "I don't know him. I'm starting to get a better line on you, though. This isn't going to be a single axis thing. I can start with sociopathology, but this is more of a complicated diagnosis than I thought." I narrowed my eyes, studied him. "Do you ever have feelings of paranoia, thoughts that no one in the universe likes you?"

Elson took my arm, led me to a different squad car, and opened the door. "Sit down." He firmly deposited me in the back seat. Harmon's eyes bulged, his face redder than mine. Every single cop turned away.

Harmon went over and talked to Ida for several minutes, then moved on to Janet. I could only hear bits and pieces, until Janet got indignant. "Well, I demand to be fingerprinted! You can just take me to the station right now, Tommy Harmon. And don't think I've forgotten about that incident in the boys' washroom—"

Elson raised his hands, as if he thought he could contain her. "Alright. Let's stay on topic. Come on."

The other cops seemed so disinterested, it had to be an effort. Ida leaned in eagerly. Harmon took a step back and shook his head. "Sergeant Elson, please arrange for this witness to come in to the station and give a full statement."

Sergeant Elson got his mother's legs in, closed the door, and talked to another cop, who got in the squad and drove Janet away. Elson rubbed his temple. He wasn't the only one getting a migraine. I felt worse with every passing second. I got that it was an unexplained death—they just had to officially determine there was no foul play, right? Fine. Of course they had to follow protocol. That didn't necessarily mean anything.

Harmon came back to me. "I'm going to need the keys for your vehicle. We'll have to wait for crime scene from the county to get out here and examine it."

"Crime scene?" I gaped at him.

"I need to know every place you've parked for the past few days. Don't leave anything out—every place you've been. This is incredibly serious, alright? I have to find the actual crime scene." He wrote in his little notebook, eyes ever so slightly hardening a few times. This gave me a perverse sense of satisfaction—he didn't want to send investigators to Janet's house, or to the ranch. He stifled a smile, though, when I mentioned Vig's place.

"Your keys." He held out a hand.

"Wait a minute," I said. "How do you know it's a crime? Did he have ID? Do you know who it is?"

"Do you? You want to amend that statement? Maybe an interview room at the station would improve your memory?" He met my eyes with a challenging stare, inviting me to have a go at him. Daring me. He wanted a fight now.

I suddenly remembered reading something about not making eye contact with an aggressive dog. It took a lot of effort not to tell Harmon about it. I focused on the door frame. "The keys are in the ignition. I wasn't planning on really stopping." He turned and walked away.

The cop returned from taking Janet home. Elson moved Ida and me to that squad. "Okay if you both go to Mrs. Gill's?" he asked, and sent us off. Janet's car was still parked in front of the house.

"Let's go get her now," Ida said. We climbed into her truck and went to collect Janet. Back at Ida's house, we all trooped into the kitchen. Ida started some coffee.

Janet plopped down at the table. "That cop wouldn't tell me when I can be fingerprinted. I couldn't get a thing out of her, Tobias being her commanding officer and all. I was so jealous when you all got printed out at the ranch last summer. I don't imagine you'll have to go in this time."

"We won't," Ida said. She slid a plate of cookies in front of Janet and sat down. "I wonder who else might?"

I had no appetite. "Max helped me unload my truck, but they got his prints last summer, too. My friend will have to go in to a police station in North Dakota and do it, so they can eliminate his prints. He helped me load everything up. How far back do you go?" Just thinking about Bobby getting that call, I couldn't even drink coffee. "When will someone tell me anything?"

Ida tapped her spoon on the table thoughtfully. "And how can we find out? Abby, you should call Ben. Get something out of him." That actually wasn't a bad idea, but I went outside to do it. I called Bobby first.

"Part of a crime scene?" he asked. "How big a part? Anybody who touched your truck bed? What are you into?"

I finally gave in to tears as I tried to explain. Then I realized I was glad I got that out of my system before calling Ben. I filed that thought for another day.

Ben pulled up in less than ten minutes—the benefits of a small town. He sat beside me on the steps and draped an arm over my shoulders. "Are you okay? I mean relatively? I'm just kicking myself. I should have checked the scene better, with all those guys around your truck. I should have walked around it, maybe I would have noticed something. I should have been more alert to the situation."

I pulled back to look at him. "What are they saying? Is it really a crime scene? Who is it? Do you know? Ben—I have to know if he was alive when I was driving home. If he died in my truck while I was sitting in my apartment, obsessing about whether to have sex or not. What a stupid thing to be so distracted by, that someone dies while I'm driving home, just parking, just walking away."

Ben definitely filed that away, the sex part. I saw him mentally stop and make a note of it. "It wasn't just a drunk who climbed in, Abby. The guy's name is Patrick Lutz. Does that mean anything to you?"

I thought. "No. I don't think I've ever heard that name."

He shook his head slightly. "Tom won't appreciate my telling you, but he'll have to get over it. He doesn't need an element of surprise, there's nothing to catch you in. He's just under a lot of pressure—a local businessman killed, and now Lutz, he's the son of another businessman. It's going to be hell. The local power structure will be all over Tom, worried about their families. Wondering if there's a target on their own backs."

The knot in my stomach turned cartwheels. "What are you saying? How do you know he wasn't drunk?"

"He may have been drunk. He didn't die of alcohol poisoning, or choke on his own vomit. He didn't die from being drunk, no one has to wait for the autopsy to know that. The back of his head was bashed in, Abby. You didn't roll him over, you didn't see it."

"How do you know all this?"

He shook his head. "That entire neighborhood watched him being removed from your truck. People are ghouls—stand out in their yards making videos on their phones." Ben studied me, considered whether to go on. "Totally different MO than the first guy, maybe not even related, but someone killed him. They might have just stuck him in your truck because it was handy, right by the alley. Although, why they wouldn't just leave him in the alley, I have no idea. Hey—head between your knees!"

I focused on the concrete between my shoes, a little crack with a tiny weed in it. Don't throw up on Ida's sidewalk. When my head stopped spinning, I sat up. "Who was he? And tell me he was dead when we came out. I don't care if you believe it."

"I really do believe that, and it's counterproductive to think otherwise. Don't torture yourself. I mean it." He lifted my chin to look directly at me, see that I heard him. "You were parked really close to where he worked, at that garage just on the other side of the alley. His father owns the place. At least now there's a connection to look for—auto parts dealer and a repair shop owner's son."

Ben paused, shrugged. "Anyway, a garage has lots of things to hit someone over the head with. Maybe nothing more than an argument. There's a thought—maybe putting the body in your truck was just an attempt to get it moved away from the crime scene, throw confusion on the whole thing." He nodded to himself, liking it. "I should go. Will you be okay?"

I nodded. "Better if you can keep Harmon off me. He's the last thing I need right now."

Ben gave me a half-smile. "You'll have to give a full statement, we both will, but I'll see what I can do. The county's coming in to assist now, anyway. Deergrass has a good department, but the powers that be want more bodies—ah, officers thrown at this thing. Tom wouldn't hate having a county guy deal with you." He closed his eyes, rubbed a temple. Every man I talk to gets a headache. "He'll have you questioned more than once. Just try to do your cold, clinical thing, okay? Go ahead and give them that annoying therapist look, but don't be provoked. Homicide victim in your vehicle, they're gonna try to provoke you."

He drove away. I sat for a moment, thinking of all the ways that people manipulate each other, all the reasons. Then I went inside, to tell them what I'd learned.

Chapter Fourteen

Every time I closed my eyes that night, my own thoughts overwhelmed me. I ended up on the couch with a blanket and a worn, faded paperback. A book I nearly knew by heart. No surprises.

The knock on the door startled me, but in the context of a late night, with my lamp on, knocking meant Max. Must be having a rough night, and need to talk. I picked up my Maglite anyway, before cracking the door open.

Max and Vig both flicked glances at my flashlight, then back to my face. "Your light was on," Max said. "You up for a little company?"

"Yes, please." I opened the door wide and stood back as they filed in and slid off their boots. I gestured toward the couch. Max sat on the far end of the couch, Vig in the chair I'd been going to claim. I sat in the open space between them.

"How many nights you figure you've sat here, listening to me and my tales of woe?" Max leaned back, threw one leg over the coffee table, stretched. "Up all night, make me tea, help me talk, help me get the horses in for breakfast, help me all day, we're both too tired to walk a straight line?"

"I don't keep track," I said. "You know I don't."

"Exactly!" Max and Vig exchanged a triumphant look—a visual fist bump. I started to feel disoriented. Max went on. "I have been shockingly remiss. It's not all about me, Maguire. Those midnight talks never would have started if you hadn't been up having nightmares, but you always make it about everyone else. Never about you."

I glanced at Vig. Back to Max, who nodded. "Vig is here purely for the pleasure of calling bullshit on you," he said. Vig smiled.

I sank into the cushions. "Oh, hell. Don't you think I've been through enough today?"

"Don't you think that's exactly the point?" Max heaved himself up, went to the kitchen and put water on. He dug around for tea bags and mugs, came back and settled in. "Talk to us," he said gently. "Don't let this be one more thing you stuff away. Let us help you put words to it, so your brain can refile things. You deserve to live too, Maguire. Really live."

I picked up the paperback I'd left on the arm of the sofa, moved it to the side table, and thought about how to stall. "I hardly know where to start," I said, largely to myself.

"Just start anywhere. Start talking, and it sorts itself out." Max smiled affectionately, knowing I'd recognize my own words. "You also taught me it can get real ugly when those first emotions get out, but that's okay. It's just all the pressure of keeping them down for so long. Tell you what, you have a horse with colic, you've never been so happy in your life, when they crap all over the barn. Most beautiful mess you ever saw, because they got it out, and they're gonna be alright."

"Man." Vig stared at Max over his stocking feet, propped on the coffee table. "Really, Turner? That's disgusting."

Max raised a middle finger to him, and I laughed. Actually laughed, and then I could talk. It was the perfect atmosphere for me, to safely spill out horror. I left for a day of shopping, but found a murdered human being in my truck.

The words started rolling, and the men didn't flinch. I searched them for signs of potential secondary trauma, saw none, and moved closer to the ugly, heavy things I could never lay on another person. Things from the past, that made the present harder to take. I wasn't graphic or vivid—once you hear horrific things, you can't unhear them.

I only touched on what I saw, heard, experienced—but focused on how I was impacted. I believed they could hear that much, that I wouldn't make their trauma worse by exposing them to mine. It cracked open a door I'd closed.

They were sober, grave when the sun broke over the fields. "Damn," Vig said. "I honestly never thought about civilians dealing with shit like that. I mean, I know cops, but there's probably a lot more. Makes you think."

"You gonna be okay today?" Max searched my face, reached a foot out and rubbed my sock with his. "We're gonna do this some more, but I wanna be sure you're okay to stop here, for the day."

I nodded. "Thank you, both of you. Really. It's going to be a long day now."

"I got the day off," Vig said. "I'll help Turner—we can grab a couple hours sleep between things. Be just like old times, except there's no IEDs out there in the horseshit. You should sleep now, Maguire. Get what you can."

I started them a pot of coffee, and went to bed.

I wrote down my timeline while I could still remember the details, and took it along when Ida drove me to give my statement. Harmon stayed well out of it. Multiple people interviewed me over and over, but they all went with courteous and relentless. They smiled patiently, came from different directions, played dumb, pretended to have misunderstood. Clarified. Asked, and asked again, until I couldn't take it anymore. I'd done all I could. Attitudes, tones, facial expressions washed over me—an odor I could no longer smell, having been immersed in it for too long.

They released my truck, but I felt nervous, driving. Or parking, even in front of Ida's house. I locked the cab and the tailgate. Walked back to make sure it was locked. Went back again, got a rag from under the seat to wipe off black smudges. Fingerprint powder, I assumed. I dabbed at one smudge for a moment, put the rag away, tied back my tonneau cover and drove through the carwash. Three times. Then once more, for good measure. Then one last time. Five should do it.

"Now," Ida said, "Janet asked if we could come over. She's all excited about something, but she wouldn't tell me until we were both there."

Warren stepped down from Janet's porch as we reached her driveway. Another man, younger and slimmer, followed him. They paused on the edge of Janet's yard. "Ida, Abby," Warren said, "I'd like you to meet a friend of mine. Ernie and I worked together for several years. Ernie, Ida here is a good friend of Janet's, and this is Abby. Glad to see you both."

Ernie nodded to Ida, but shook my hand with both of his. "Real glad to meet you, Abby. Much obliged. Really. Thank you, from all of us." He didn't wait for a response, which was good. I didn't have one. I stared at their backs until they disappeared into Warren's garage.

Janet fairly pranced across her linoleum. She closed her door firmly, checked to make sure her windows were closed, and looked suspiciously toward Warren's house.

"What on earth?" Ida looked too, as if the men might have their ears pressed to the door. "What are you up to?"

"Did Ernie and Warren go inside?" Janet, glowing, waved us toward the kitchen chairs and pulled her own chair close to ours. "We're in!"

I glanced at Ida. She looked blank.

"Listen." Janet wiggled with excitement. "Deergrass Days start tomorrow. Parade, food trucks, turtle races for the kids—you know. Fun run in the morning, fireworks at night. All kinds of events."

"I'm all about food trucks," I said. "And I'd love to do the fun run, if registration is still open."

"No idea," Janet said. "But you being a runner is what got us in, Abby." She glanced over her shoulder at the closed door. "You're going to replace Patrick Lutz on the garage's team for the outhouse race! And Ernie will be there too!"

"Ohhh," Ida nodded thoughtfully. "How did you swing that?"

"Wait." I sat back, pushed my chair away. "Are you saying they worked with the guy? And I'm doing what? Are you saying the fun run is called the outhouse race?"

"No, no," Janet said. "The outhouse race is totally separate. There are teams—area businesses, political candidates and their supporters, sometimes a church will have a team. Haven't you ever seen an outhouse race, Abby?"

I rubbed my face and squinted at both of them. Was this a joke? And what would be the point?

"I can see you haven't," Ida said. "The outhouse is on wheels. Someone rides in it, and there's also running involved. Right down Main Street. Is Warren on the team? I can't quite picture that."

"No, he's strictly in an advisory capacity," Janet explained. "They need four people on the team, but no one wants to step up. Some people said they should pull out, but honestly, it's not because anyone liked Patrick. It just made a good excuse to say no. You watch, every one of those men will be there on the sidelines, eating brats and drinking beer." She and Ida shook their heads, as if personally disappointed in the lack of dedication.

"Technically you're a ringer," Janet went on, "but they'll finesse it somehow. No one will question it, under the circumstances. They were going to have to forfeit the registration money, lose the advertising benefit. A lot of community goodwill doing things like this, you know. I told them you're a runner and you'd be glad to support the garage. They were over for coffee, you see, Warren and Ernie—eating me out of house and home, but it was worth it. Just think of the snooping you can do! One of those men knows something, I'm sure of it. You'll have a few hours in an outhouse to figure it out."

"This is wonderful, Janet," Ida said.

I waved my hands in the air. "Stop!" The women both looked startled. "Hours? In an outhouse? Are we not even going to talk about your neighbor and his friend working with the murdered guy? And does nobody think it's a tiny bit inappropriate for me to replace the guy whose body was found in my truck bed?"

"Oh, nobody blames you for that," Ida said. "I think people will admire your spirit of goodwill."

"Absolutely." Janet nodded vigorously. "You could have refused to have anything to do with it, but here you are, supporting a community business that has suffered a blow. Helping them get through it." She pounded a fist on the table emphatically. "Shoring up an important part of the local economy!"

"Oh, good for you, Abby." Ida beamed at me. "Well done!"

"What? I haven't agreed to anything!"

"Don't worry, you'll do fine," Ida said. "You might want to wear older shoes, though. It's not like you'll run any real distance."

"What's going to happen to my shoes? No! I'm not doing any outhouse thing I have to wear old shoes for, replacing a dead guy that was in my truck! No!"

Ida drove us to the downtown staging area the next morning. We walked past a crowd of adults holding kitty litter buckets and five-gallon pails, children reaching in for turtles with numbers painted on their shells. In the center of the crowd, a few men carefully placed a round, metal frame over a spray painted circle on the street. Children reached into the frame and set down their turtles, then stood back. The men lifted the frame, and the turtles wandered in all directions. The first few turtles to waddle over the line were triumphantly raised in the air with shouts of joy.

Beyond this spectacle, there were ring tosses with hula-hoops and painted wooden cutouts of cows. Stick horses—and one unicorn—leaned in a barrel, ready to be raced. Then I saw the outhouses—a parking lot full of them. Some were more like go-karts—wooden boxes with bicycle wheels, in a framework of metal bars. Inside the boxes, toilet seats on plastic buckets. The Porta-Potties and more traditional wooden outhouses sat in frames of two-by-fours nailed together, mounted on wheels. Some had business logos. One sported a giant poop emoji and the words, "Push it!"

Janet came along to introduce me to the team. Ernie and two other men, Roger and Joe, stood by a Porta-Potty with the door removed, the garage's logo painted on the sides. They were all in high spirits, and greeted me enthusiastically. I'd seen Joe before, but took a moment to place him. He'd been in the crowd at the bar, that distracted Ben during our dinner date.

Roger shook my hand. "We're so glad you're here! You and me are gonna be the quick ones. And you'll be riding inside, being the lightest. Ever done this before?"

"I've never even heard of this before," I confessed. "So I'm riding and running? How does that work, exactly?"

"Don't worry," Joe said. "The grand marshal walks all the teams through the course before it starts, all at the same time. Seeing as you're the most agile, you'll be doing the pool."

"I—pool?" I turned to Janet and Ida, but they were gone. I looked around wildly, finally spotting them half a block away, in the corn dog line. "Nobody said anything about a pool. What pool?" I looked down the street. For several blocks, barriers erected along the curbs kept people on the sidewalks. People sat in lawn chairs, stood behind them, sat on the cement. It looked like the whole city had shown up to watch. Possibly the entire county.

Teenage girls, apparently winners of various pageants, set up and monitored the course. Girls wearing crowns and knee-length white dresses set out buckets, guided by older women with measuring sticks. Others used canoe paddles to stir plastic wading pools of brown, murky liquid. What? I glanced down at my faded, worn running shoes. Ida had known something terrible. And where was she? Probably on to the mini donuts by now. She was going to pay for this. She and Janet both.

At the end of the course, younger teenagers in shorts, t-shirts, and tiaras stood by toilet paper rolls on metal stands, attentively listening to an older woman. "They all look very serious," I said. "The girls."

"Oh, ya," Roger said. "Well, they gotta take it serious, for their organizations they're representing. But think about it, they're high schoolers, with the whole world staring at them. Lotta pressure there. Old farts like us, now—"

"Here's the marshal now," Ernie said.

A middle-aged man in faded jeans, a seed company ball cap, and a Deergrass Days t-shirt waved his arms, and the outhouse teams crowded around him. "Alright, then," he shouted. "Now, everyone pay attention. We'll go three at a time." He pointed out three lanes at the sides and center of the street. “Now, this here’s the start. Each team will have three pushers and one rider. Try to keep control. You come out of your lane, that’s a disqualification.”

He walked to a line of thick paint across the road. We all followed in a mass. Farther down the street, each lane had a bucket with a toilet seat secured by several yards of duct tape, and a little pile of brown rubber pieces. I leaned closer. They were...fake poop. They really were. “You’re gonna stop the outhouse here,” the marshal announced. “Now, two people from each team will be tossers. You cannot move on until you get three in, from behind the line here. You step over the line—”

“Disqualification,” the crowd finished with him.

“Don’t you worry about that, Abby.” Ernie patted my shoulder reassuringly. “Joe and me are the tossers.” I nodded.

“Now, as soon as they get three pieces in,” the marshal continued, “the first runner will sprint to the pool, find the corn cob, and deposit it in the next commode.” He pointed at the pools of brown liquid, and another row of duct-taped bucket toilets.

“Hold on,” I said. “Wait.”

“Then, and only then,” the marshal said, “the final runner will sprint with their roll of toilet paper to the stand, remove the existing roll, and replace it with the new one. The paper must drape over the front of the roll. Incorrectly hung paper will result in disqualification.”

“I can do that,” I said. “I’m pretty fast. I should do that one.”

“Nope.” Roger shook his head. “That’s my role. See what I did there?”

I looked at the senior royals, stirring the brown muck with their paddles. My morning coffee rose into my throat. "I—wait. How do I find the corncob?"

"When the new paper is successfully hung," the marshal went on, "the entire team will run back to their outhouse, the rider will enter the unit, and you will push it back to the starting line—again, staying in your lane. May the fastest team win."

The herd meandered toward the parked outhouses. I grabbed Ernie's arm. "Really, though. What exactly—"

Ernie laughed. "Don't worry so much. We won't be in the first group. You can watch how they go."

We were assigned to the third group, and lined up accordingly. I stood by the outhouse and watched. Everyone got stuck at the poop toss—the misshapen rubber projectiles were apparently hard to aim, and bounced unpredictably. Eventually, a chaser darted back and forth, frantically retrieving misses, returning them to the tossers to try again.

When the required three baskets had been made, the next person on each team ran to the pools and—it was all bad. Some knelt on the pavement and swished their arms in the brown muck, feeling for the corn cob. Others leaned their entire torsos in, to broaden their reach. One man jumped into the center and sat, engaging all his limbs in the search, but losing precious seconds climbing out. I bit my lip.

Excitement built to a fevered pitch as the teams completed their tasks, the crowds roaring on both sides. The riders jumped back in, and the outhouses careened madly, barely staying in their lanes as the pushers raced for the finish line. Maybe I could fake a heart attack.

"We're up!" Joe shouted. "Climb in, Abby!"

I jumped in and braced myself on the doorway. The air horn blared, and the outhouse lurched into motion, faster than I expected. I gripped the sides as the men swerved madly in our lane, shouting like commandos, "GO! GO! GO!"

They stopped abruptly at the line. I swung out over the pavement—one foot still lodged against the wall, the other whipping out in a windmill kick that caught Joe square in the back as he rushed forward. I squeaked a desperate apology, awkwardly spun, and landed on the asphalt.

Joe didn't hear me. The men were engrossed in throwing and chasing fake poop. Cries of triumph marked each successful basket. The noise from the sidewalks was dizzying. The crowd screamed, groaned, shouted. Blood rushed to my head. Then it was, "THREE! GO, ABBY! GO! GO!"

I sprinted for the pool and dove in face-first, eyes and mouth clamped tightly shut, and felt the cob under my stomach. I grabbed it, rolled sideways, pulled my feet under me and launched out. The cheers were deafening. I wiped brown water from my face, located the commode and ran. I dropped the cob in as Roger pounded by, toilet paper in hand. My clothes were soaked. Liquid muck ran from my hair, dripped from my arms. I shuddered.

Joe and Ernie grabbed my elbows and pointed me toward the outhouse. "Get in, Abby!" Joe shouted.

My shoes squelched with each step, murky water squirting from my insoles. I climbed in, bracing myself just as Roger thundered back, red-faced and panting, waving the new roll of paper in one swinging hand.

"Hang on!" Ernie yelled. The outhouse jerked and jolted. My wet hands and shoes slid on the plastic. We swerved wildly. The Porta-Potty to our right careened towards us. We nearly collided, but both teams managed a massive push, staying in our lanes. At the finish line I threw myself sideways, and slammed into the wall instead of flying out.

The men erupted into neanderthal roars, chests pushed out, arms in the air. We had won our heat, narrowly beating one team. The third came wheeling in twenty seconds later. Joe slapped my back with a wet splat. "We did it! We did it, Abby!"

They pushed our outhouse to the side, as the other two teams rolled down the street. "We wait here now," Roger panted. He wiped a hand across his brow. "We just watch now, until the semi-finals."

"The what?" I wrapped my arms tightly around me, shivering, dripping. I looked around at the other teams. Wondered about each wet person, and how it had come to this.

"We advanced to the next round," Joe explained happily.

"We do it again?" Little spots danced in my vision. I swallowed hard.

"Not for a while," Roger said. "We can just enjoy the show now, until the first heats are over. This is real good, seeing people excited like this. Something positive. There's been enough trouble."

This was my opening. I couldn't let it go by. I couldn't have bathed in fake toilet water for nothing. "You think there's a killer standing here watching us?" That was a pointless question. With the kinds of therapy jobs I'd had for so long, I knew perfectly well there could be killers around us. Some of them trying to improve their mental health. I asked anyway.

Ernie gave me a side-eye. "They arrested somebody for Larsen."

"Yeah, they let him go, though," Roger said. "I bet they just pulled him in because of that fight over at The Nail."

Joe scoffed. "That wasn't even much of a fight." We all leaned in.

"What, were you there?" Roger asked. "Did you see it?"

Joe nodded, suddenly animated. "Guy stood there and let Larsen get a swing in, then laid him out with one punch. It was beautiful." He demonstrated with a fist. "Pop! On the ground, guy walks away. He left after that, but if he woulda stayed, guy coulda had free beers all night long."

"Do you think that guy killed him?" I asked.

Joe shook his head dismissively. "You don't go kill a guy when you won the fight."

The crowd shouted, and we all turned. An outhouse had swerved out of their lane, colliding with the next Porta-Potty. "That takes them out," Roger said.

Joe went on. "Best thing I ever saw, Larsen getting put down. Bam! One hit."

"I'm sorry I missed that." Roger smiled at the Porta-Potty pile up. "Probably the first time anyone ever stood up to Larsen in his life. Knocked him down more ways than one, huh? Who's King Shit now?" He glanced at me. "Excuse my language."

"So you knew both murder victims," I said. "You think they were connected?"

Ernie turned away, distracted by something across the street. "I'll be right back." He walked over behind the meat market and disappeared into the shadow of the building. He reappeared, talking to someone. I took a step sideways to see better. Ernie pulled a woman into an embrace. Several minutes later, they came up for air. Ernie gestured toward us, probably saying he had to get back. They both turned. My mouth fell open.

Chapter Fifteen

Phyllis Larsen. The first victim's wife. Roger took hold of my arm. "Abby," he said sternly, "now you forget you saw anything there. I mean it. No point starting any trouble."

"They weren't exactly being subtle," I said. "If I saw them, a hundred other people could have, too."

"Everyone's watching the race. I'm serious, Abby. You gotta be careful who you piss off in a small town. You don't know who their cousin is, or who they babysat thirty years ago."

"Roger's right," Joe said. "You just forget that happened."

I blinked. It must be an open secret—the whole lot of them in agreement. Nothing to see here. Move along.

We all turned toward the race. No one looked up when Ernie nonchalantly rejoined us. "You missed a collision, Ern," Roger said. "Now watch and see if they give a do-over to the ones that got crashed into."

They did, which rounded out the teams for the first heat. The crowd settled as the officials organized the second elimination round, but if anything, more people packed the sidelines. We made the first cut and lined up at the start. Roger jogged in place. Ernie posed like a prize fighter. Joe dropped and did five quick push-ups, to the delight of onlookers.

I wedged my still dripping shoes against the sides of the outhouse and gripped the doorway. Cold trails ran between my shoulder blades, dripped from my bra, trickled down the small of my back. The horn sounded, and the crowd erupted.

I hopped out smoothly at the first line and shifted foot to foot, shivering in the breeze. The pools had been stirred again to keep the muck thick in the water, obscuring the corncob. I swallowed hard. For once in your life, just don't think. Don't.

On cue, I sprinted and dove into the pool again, thrashed around a little, and felt the cob under my thigh. I perfected the roll and launch, and fairly flew to the commode. I wiped sludge from my eyes while Roger galloped by. I looked at the crowd and saw Max gaping at me, eyes and mouth perfect circles. Walt stood next to him, laughing uncontrollably. I looked away.

Down the block, another face caught my eye. Phyllis Larsen, keenly focused on me. She couldn't know I'd seen her with Ernie. She probably remembered me showing up with Ida, though, and here I was on Ernie's team. She didn't look happy.

Ernie shouted, "Let's go, Abby!" I turned and ran back to the outhouse. We won the round by seconds, to a deafening roar. I couldn't hear the men's words as they jumped up and down, hugging each other and me.

They pulled the outhouse to the side again. The noise dimmed as the next competitors lined up. "Just one more round now, Abby," Roger said. "There's five winners from this heat, but they go by time to get it down to three. So we have to see if we make it."

I forced a smile, to hide my disloyal thoughts. "Is there a prize for this?"

"A trophy," Roger answered. I could only imagine.

Joe nodded. "You get to display it for a year, until the next race. We already know where we'd put it, right there in the waiting room so all the customers would see it. But high up."

"I guess it would help to have such a positive thing to focus on," I said. "After losing a coworker like that." In the resulting quiet, I heard my shoes squelch with each shift of my weight.

Finally, Roger spoke. "We'd love to have that trophy. And take it away from Swansons, too. Those guys loaded up their team with college football players last year. Shouldn't even brag about that, even if they were technically summer employees."

I was cold, soaked to my underwear, dripping something unmentionable. I didn't feel like playing. "Are you struggling to get the work done after losing Patrick? Suddenly having one less mechanic must be hard for you."

Joe and Roger exchanged a glance. Ernie grabbed the handles of the outhouse and repositioned it slightly. The horn sounded. They all turned to watch the race, their eyes cutting to my face periodically. I'd probably been too direct.

I wiped my forehead with a hand, ineffectively wiped the hand on my wet shorts, and shivered. Roger walked over to a nearby cooler and picked up a flannel shirt he'd tossed there. He draped the shirt over my shoulders. It smelled a little sweaty, but I smiled thanks.

The spectators cramming the sidewalks cheered, clapped, stomped. Most of them would know most of the competitors, probably always had. Years of personal history fed the frenzy, added context to winning and losing. Getting killed, for that matter. Killing. Getting caught, or getting away with it.

Surely most of the people shouting, eating corn dogs and drinking lemonade wanted to know, as they met in the café, the church, the hardware store, that violent criminals around them were taken off the streets. How many of them would close ranks for one of their own?

Roger nudged my shoulder. I blinked. It was quieter again. Roger held out a steaming cup of coffee. I gratefully took it with both hands. Ernie and Joe had wandered away.

"Listen," Roger said. "You're really helping us out here. We might even win, and we woulda had to pull out otherwise. It's just kind of a sensitive subject, you know?"

I nodded, took a sip. It felt warm all the way down, but kicked off a whole-body shiver. "I get that. I'm not trying to be insensitive. I guess it's my nature to wonder about things. I always have."

"Thing is," Roger said, "both those guys that got killed, well, no one wants to feel like a jerk, you know? Don't want to sound glad or anything. Better not to talk about it."

"That's kind of what I gathered," I told him. "But that just makes me more curious, I can't help it. Everyone can't just passively not miss them—someone went to some effort. Do you even have a theory? You must think about it, quietly to yourself. Do you think it was one person? Or maybe the second one was a reaction to the first?"

Roger stuck a hand in his pocket and wiggled some coins around. He watched the officials comparing notes to decide which teams to eliminate. He looked at me sideways.

"I don't think it was something just out of the blue," he said. "Things run deep. It'll turn out to be like one of them sinkholes, that nobody even knew about until the street caves in."

I nodded. "And the same truck that's driven over it every day for the last ten years, suddenly it's too heavy and everything collapses. I see what you're saying." I took a sip of coffee to pace myself, hoping not to seem pushy. "I wonder what the truck was." I looked at Roger. Friendly, conversational. "I wonder what was finally too heavy, this time."

"I wondered that too, actually." He looked around. Joe was passing the mini donuts, headed our way.

"You, you're a counselor," he said. "I'm just a mug that fixes people's vehicles, but you'd be surprised. People don't wanna part with their money, want you to fiddle the insurance, need something repaired but don't trust you with it. Lie about how something happened. We ain't gonna fix it any different, but they got this story makes them seem like less of an idiot. Not like we say anything. Just do the work, let people try to save face."

Roger snorted. "Larsen used to come in, blame the damage on his wife. Everybody knew he just did it driving home from the bar again. We'd just hand him the estimate. Pretty pathetic, some drunk blaming things on his wife. Ernie'd be mad as hell." He hesitated. Opened his mouth, closed it. "I mean—"

"We did it!" Ernie jogged up from the judges' table. "We're still in it!"

Joe stuffed the last bite of something in his mouth as he approached, shaking a fist in the air triumphantly. The men pounded each other's backs, slapping mine with less vigor. Roger glanced at me nervously. I pretended not to notice and pulled his shirt tighter around me.

The crowd had swelled even further, more people arriving for the championship round. They packed in tightly, crammed together, peering over each other's shoulders. I saw previous competitors eating hotdogs, and shook off a wave of jealousy.

Stepping up into the outhouse at the starting line, I felt my adrenaline rise. The electricity in the crowd surged over us. Loud chanting—team names, people's names. I heard "Abby! Abby!" and looked up. The entire Old Bats Club was pressed together, raising drink cups my way. I locked eyes with Ida, looked down at the brown-stained clothing sticking to my body, then back at her with a steely gaze. She grinned with wicked delight.

I turned my focus to the race, the crowd, the starting horn. The outhouse lurched forward, and time became a blur of motion and noise. I sprinted, dove, caught the edge of the pool in my roll-out and partly tipped it, sloshing a viscous wave over myself as I rose. Roger seemed to fly by.

I didn't wait, but ran for the outhouse, hurtled into it, held on wetly, and watched as a brown puddle formed under me. I squatted to lower my center of gravity as we careened toward the finish line.

My feet slid out from under me when we stopped, but my hands held long enough for my butt to hit the outhouse floor instead of the street. It had been close. I wasn't sure, but the officials called in our favor. The men lost any sense of decorum they'd ever had. They'd won the Super Bowl.

Joe pointed at the frame around the outhouse. "Get on up there, Abby! We'd put you on our shoulders, but we'd throw our backs out!"

The frame was rough wood, so my wet shoes wouldn't slip. I clambered up. Ernie, leaner than the others, climbed up beside me. We were surrounded by mechanics who'd begged off, now happy to share the glory. The manager appeared in time to accept the trophy. I searched the crowd, finally located Ida, and gave her a head-jerk. Get over here. Get me out of this.

Give her credit, Ida extracted me as efficiently as she did everything else. We left amid promises of free beer any time, just name it, and headed for her car.

"Well done, Abby," she said. "Well, that was just marvelous. Let's get you over to my house for a good, hot shower. Wait, let me put a towel down."

"Don't think this is over," I said. "Watch your back."

She laughed, and handed me a thermos. "Pour yourself some cocoa. This traffic will take us a few minutes."

The rest of the Old Bats Club arrived in Fran's car. We all filed into the kitchen, but I refused to talk until I showered. I took my time, shampooed my hair three times, lingered under the hot spray. Let them wait. Then I would demand lunch, not having had a single food truck opportunity.

Ida's homemade vegetable soup and cracked wheat bread took the edge off my huffiness. I told them everything. No one had a single smart remark. "Joe was in The Nail when Vig got in a fight with Doug Larsen," I pointed out. "The night Larsen was killed. He was also in the bar where Ben and I had dinner, the night Patrick Lutz ended up in my truck."

"I'll find out more about Joe," Betsy offered. "You should probably move to the background for a while. We don't want anyone to focus on you as a threat."

"I'm a little concerned about the widow giving you the stink-eye, Abby." Fran leaned back in her chair and frowned at me. "Those other men may not intend to tell Ernie you saw his little tryst, but the alcohol will flow freely today, as the trophy relocates. You're a grown woman, I don't need to tell you to be careful. But please, be careful."

Max and Walt couldn't look at me without grinning. I was roped into a ridiculous situation and ran with it—that was all they knew. I certainly wasn't going to enlighten them about the darker side of my association with Ida's friends. I worked with clients, did my documentation, and waited for them to get over it.

Mental stress exhausts me physically, and I felt a growing weariness. Determined to push through it, I went for a sunrise run. Benefits of physical exertion and all that. Sustained effort. You can do this. You'll feel better. Really.

I set off at an easy lope and got into a rhythm, enjoying the peace of the empty road. I covered a couple of miles, gently trotted over a rise, then heard a vehicle behind me. I glanced back at a dusty, old car. I moved to the side of the road, but the vehicle slowed, staying behind me.

A few months earlier, I had been shot at while running—from an old car that stayed behind me. My central nervous system remembered, kicking up the adrenaline without stopping to ask questions first. I stepped off the road, prepared to bolt for the trees.

I looked back, heart pounding—a beater sedan, faded green. The driver, alone in the car, face hidden by the brim of a ball cap, hesitated. Like you do for a deer, not sure if it will leap out in front of you. I waved him past, and waited. He didn't move. Then he slowly rolled by, turned, and met my eyes.

Ernie. He nodded, like a greeting, like this was normal. Just out for a drive, past the ranch, at dawn. After a long stare, he turned to look behind him. I followed his gaze to a long gun in his back window. He met my eyes again, cold, direct. He drove on, turned at the crossroads, and pulled to the shoulder. I couldn't breathe. I forced myself to move, and ran hard. I looked back. His car slowly turned around.

I kept a frantic pace all the way to the ranch, ran up the stairs, and locked the door behind me. Breathing hard, I pulled the little hallway stand in front of the door. I felt embarrassed—what could I do? I had to run away. But sheer panic was humiliating, and I couldn't stop it. I had to shut this down, but my heart was pounding. My legs trembled.

I leaned against the shower tiles. Breathe. Calm the frantic, racing thoughts, slow the adrenaline. Focus. Hot water, cold tile. I dug my fingernails into my scalp to lather my shampoo. Focus. Feel. Switch that brain function.

I tried to recite an Edgar Allen Poe poem we had to learn in school, but couldn't remember. Try history—four score and seven years ago today, our forefathers—what? What did they do?

I grabbed my body wash and a scrubby, and focused on the scratchy feeling all up and down my arms and legs. We, the people of the United States, in order to form a more perfect union, establish justice and something about tranquility something.

No use. I rinsed my hair and thought of an object for every color of the rainbow, twice. Not allowing easy ones, making myself think. Visually searching for them would be far more effective—pair sensory input with information recall—but I was in the shower. I should go buy a purple loofah.

I nailed every verse of Barry Manilow's Copacabana, scrubbing in rhythm, shaking my hips. By the time I listed the diagnostic criteria for major depression, intermittent explosive disorder, and generalized anxiety disorder, I'd done it. Flipped my brain from spiraling emotion, to rational thinking. Reined in the beast. Calmly, I toweled off and considered my next move.

I don't like being in reaction mode. Feeling pushed makes me want to do something dramatic. It's a personality issue, I know. Since I was a kid. I could pretty easily find out where Ernie lives. Take it right back to him. I thought about it while I pulled on jeans and a t-shirt.

A knock on the door. I froze. Another knock. I slipped into the hallway, picked up my Maglite, and pulled the furniture away from the door with a loud, scraping noise. So much for stealth. I hefted my Maglite, holding it ready to swing, cracked the door, and peeked out.

Ida's eyes cut from the flashlight, to my face, to the obviously displaced furniture. "Good morning."

I stood back, then locked the door behind her. "Come in. I'm a little behind, I don't have coffee started."

"Did you have a bad night?" She pulled out a kitchen chair and settled in.

"No!" I launched into my story, waved my arms, started to feel stupid, didn't want it to sound like nothing. "He stared at his shotgun, rifle, whatever, then stared at me, Ida. I'm not making this up. He was trying to intimidate me!"

I slouched into the chair across from her, sagging, all my energy depleted by drama. "I heard his car stop behind me," I admitted, "and it was like I was going to be shot at again." I chewed my upper lip and rubbed the scar on my arm. It didn't look like much. It didn't look like I'd been grazed by a bullet. It looked like I walked into a fence. "I don't want to give up running outside."

She listened soberly, got up, and made the coffee. "He could be a killer, Abby. Even if he's not a very sophisticated one. Are you going to the police?"

"What would I tell them? He acted creepy, and had a gun in his car? I don't even know if that's illegal."

"It's not legal in Minnesota anymore," she said. "Under most circumstances. Used to be everyone drove around with gun racks in their vehicles. But I see your point."

"I want to do something, Ida. To him. I know where he works. Now I know what he drives. I need to come up with something to really stick it to him, without losing my licensure." The things they don't tell you in grad school. I'd like to go back and suggest a few courses.

"Well, alright," she said. "He's told on himself. It always surprises me, although it shouldn't at this point." She leaned back in her chair and thought for a moment. "Ernie's a weak link. We need to push on him, see what happens."

I got some mugs from the cupboard. "I'm in."

Ida dug out eggs and a pan, and made breakfast for us—no point trying to scheme on an empty stomach. "We need to find the right balance. Keep it mostly legal, but not so subtle it goes right over his head."

"I'm so grateful that you understand, Ida." I took a bite of eggs.

She refreshed our coffee. "You know horses establish dominance by making each other move. You get pushed, you either yield, or push back." She returned the carafe to the coffeemaker and sat back down. "We're damn sure not going to be dominated by the likes of that man. Please pass the pepper."

We both thought quietly while we ate. "Listen," she finally said. "There are vehicles and auto parts all over this thing. Doug Larsen, Patrick Lutz, Ernie Gates. Car guys. We come back with their language, it doesn't point to us."

"Say more."

"We go a couple counties over, no one knows who we are. Go to a U-Pull salvage yard, buy a rear view mirror, pull it out of a car. Wipe it clean of prints." She set down her fork and became animated. "We leave it on the hood of his car in the middle of the night, with a note: 'watch your back.' Then we find a way to keep an eye on him and see what he does." She beamed proudly.

"That could be just nutty enough to totally throw him," I said. "It has kind of a grease monkey Godfather vibe." I pushed my dishes aside, got out my laptop, and started researching salvage lots. "Couldn't we just buy a new one? Can't be a high-ticket item."

She shook her head. "That's not what they would do. They'd have one out in the back forty somewhere. If we want to confuse him, make it look like an inside job, we get one out of a seventies Pontiac. Or any old, scuffed up one, I guess. They look pretty much the same, don't they?"

She pointed at the screen. "Here. This place is forty-five minutes away. We'll go after our morning sessions. Now, I'll go bring in horses and get set up. You find out what tools we need, to pull out a mirror. We need to be smooth, not draw attention."

I searched for how to pull a rear view mirror from a window. Fingernail polish remover? I looked at my hands, frowned. Scrolled down. What else? Dish soap and a screwdriver, I can definitely do. I closed the laptop triumphantly, headed out the door and locked it behind me.

We chatted continuously on the drive—just like a road trip with a girlfriend, when you've both had too many energy drinks. We hadn't. We were edgy, but unwilling to admit it. I pulled into the dirt lot in front of the business, parked to the side a little, and sat.

"Well, alright," Ida said. "Here's our story. We need a mirror for a standard, four-door sedan, American made. For my nephew. He was driving through from Colorado, and his fell off."

"But he couldn't come get it himself," I added, "because...he broke his leg."

Ida stared at me. "Do you think that might be a bit much?"

I opened my door. "Let's go find out." I climbed down and headed for the door. Ida came in after me.

The man behind the counter was on the phone. "Hold on a second." He glanced at us. "Help you?"

"We need a rear view mirror," I started.

He jerked his head toward the yard. "Go get one." He went back to his conversation.

I squared my shoulders, turning confidently toward the door. Ida led the way, chin high. Row after row of junk cars sat with raised hoods—dozens of standard, four-door sedans missing doors, fenders, quarter panels.

"It probably doesn't matter." I opened the closest passenger door, sat down, took out my screwdriver, and tried to pry off the mirror.

"I guess we'll have to use the soap," Ida said. It was supposed to be a solution of soap and water, but we didn't have a spray bottle. Ida squeezed in behind the wheel, pulled a small bottle of dish soap from her purse, and smeared it around the edges. "How long do you suppose we have to wait?"

"I have no idea." I rubbed the soap in with my finger and wiped it off on the car seat. "We probably don't want to print the note on Walt's printer in the office."

"Can't you—" she laughed, and steadied herself on the steering wheel. "Oh my. Can't you just see the look on his face. No, I asked Betsy to print one off at the library. Could've been anyone in town. She got his address, too."

"Excellent." I pried at the edges with the screwdriver. "You know, it doesn't have to be good enough to glue back on anywhere." I put the screwdriver to the base of the mirror and popped it, hard, with the palm of my hand. I waved the mirror at Ida.

"Good, let's go." She wriggled out from behind the wheel and brushed herself off.

The guy in the store was still on the phone. He glanced at the mirror and held up five fingers. I dug out a five dollar bill and dropped it on the counter. He picked it up, opened the till, tossed it in. "Yeah, them things can be a devil to get out," he said, leaning against the wall, no longer aware of our existence. "You tell him, there's gonna be labor involved."

We really didn't want a receipt. I headed for the door.

I showed up at Ida's at midnight. She was dressed in all black. "Here I am," I said, "underdressed for yet another party. I don't have a cat burglar outfit."

Ida reached over and touched a picture of her late husband. "Johnny would've gotten such a kick out of this. I wish I could tell him all about it, just to hear him laugh." She put on vinyl gloves and moved to the sink, where the mirror sat in a plastic shopping bag. She picked up a dishcloth. "I've wiped every inch of it ten times, I'm sure."

I pulled out the can of cheap, nasty beer I found at a liquor store attached to a gas station, popped it open, and poured a little on the base of the mirror. "There, now it even smells authentic." I poured the rest of the beer down the drain and ran the water after it.

Ida smiled approvingly and produced a baggie with a note in it from under her sink.

"You know, Ida," I said, "The only way any of this would really be checked for prints, would be if Ernie turned up dead in his driveway."

"We're not taking any chances." She pulled the door shut behind us. We climbed into my truck and headed over to Ernie's neighborhood. Ida pointed down a side street. "Pull up here. It's a few blocks away, but we won't be in front of anyone's house. People get feisty about that, very territorial."

I pulled up by the alley and made sure my tailgate was locked. Good, there was a sidewalk. It would look more normal than walking on the street. "We should have driven by," I said. "Made sure he's home, and his car isn't locked in the garage or something."

"Well, you're right," Ida said. "There is a learning curve, isn't there? We forgot to case the joint."

"Great bag, though. Where did you get that?" I coveted her extra-large, roomy black handbag. It looked like something a woman might really carry, for something other than tools, or rear view mirrors, or vinyl gloves.

"Oh, I've had this for a hundred years. Here we are. Is that his car in the driveway?"

It looked like it to me. It was too dark to be sure if it was green, but it was the right size, shape, vintage. At the right address. We slid down a row of hedges between driveways, and stood with our backs against the shrubbery as Ida pulled on gloves and put the mirror on the hood of the car. She pulled the note from the baggie and tucked it under the windshield wiper, and we slid back along the hedges.

We continued down the sidewalk, two women leaving a friend's house after a nice visit. A large dog barked in a yard as we passed, but it was tied and couldn't reach us. Someone opened a window and yelled at it.

We walked around the block and cut a parallel path back to where we parked. Streetlights cast a yellow glow across empty, quiet streets. No traffic, no headlights. My pulse rate increased as we walked past shadows, potential hiding places. Cars and trucks in driveways, or by the curb in front of dark, silent houses. One window had the slight, flickering glow of a television. Ida chattered quietly while I scanned our surroundings. We came around the corner—I caught movement, looked again. Right by my truck. A man, in the dark.

Chapter Sixteen

I stopped short, grabbed Ida's arm, pulled her back from the sidewalk. She stopped immediately, snapped to attention, didn't make a sound. We were born for this.

I leaned over and murmured in her ear, almost silent. "Man by my truck." In the alley, even darker, was the outline of another pickup. We watched the man peer in my window, look at his watch. Try the door. Walk around, try the tailgate. He ran his hand along the tonneau cover, paused. Looked in all directions. In silhouette, he looked like a fairly big guy. Well built. Suddenly, this wasn't a lark. I fought down anxiety, bit my lip.

What would we do if he didn't leave? Two women, alone on the street in the middle of the night. My heart started pounding. Ida couldn't run. My Maglite was in the truck. It wouldn't help me there. A cold finger of fear trailed down my back. Think. The man slowly turned, scanning. He looked straight at us.

"Don't move," Ida whispered. "Don't move. He'll see movement."

Time stretched out as we stood, frozen. The man stared, as if trying to make out our forms in the shadows. I willed myself into absolute stillness. My mouth went dry. I started to feel light-headed. Don't faint. Don't move.

Finally, he looked away. A wave of nausea swept over me. We couldn't even retreat now, couldn't flinch. He wasn't leaving. The man raised a hand, ran it through his hair—

"Oh, my God!" I stormed towards him. He jumped, startled—snapped into a defensive pose, then registered me. I kept coming at him.

Ida gasped. I left her there. "What are you doing?" I yelled. "You scared the crap out of me!" I smacked him on the arm.

Ben took a step back and raised his hands. "I saw your truck! Do you have any idea what time it is?"

"Of course I know what time it is! I'm not five years old!" I smacked him again. "I thought you were a serial killer!"

He moved his hands into the universal Calm Down position. "I could have been! What are you doing out here in the middle of the night?"

"It's obvious what I'm doing! Walking back to my truck so I can drive Ida home! What are you doing, skulking around in the shadows? You know I just had a terrible experience! I'm going to have nightmares for a week, Ben! Thanks for that!"

"Walking back from where, Abby? Are you crazy? What are you doing out here, parking by another alley, walking around in dark clothing?"

"I am not wearing dark clothing!" I pushed past him and climbed into my cab. Ida caught up and got in beside me. I shot a final glare at Ben. A block away, I looked in the mirror. He stood, watching me drive away. I'd have to deal with this, eventually.

"Oh, man." My heart was still pounding. "Who does he think he is, demanding explanations from me?" I tried to slow my breathing.

"It's certainly none of his business what I wear," Ida said. "Some nerve! I'm wearing black for the next three weeks, in case I see him again."

"And what's he doing out in the middle of the night? Investigating, I suppose. Must be nice to be a man, go out alone at all hours," I muttered crossly. "What are the odds he'd drive right past my truck, in this whole town? Unless he's keeping an eye on Ernie! We might have gotten lucky, Ida. We might have just missed him."

We were quiet for several blocks, trying to ride out the adrenaline. I pulled up in Ida's driveway and looked at my watch. It was nearly one in the morning. Neither of us moved.

"We'll be tired tomorrow," Ida said. "But we've been tired before. It was worth it. It's been a long time since I've been on a caper." I couldn't hold back a snort of laughter. She turned. "What are you thinking about over there?"

"My tattoo," I said. "I decided what I'm going to get."

Approaching the ranch, I turned off my headlights before I left the road, like a teenager past curfew. I drove slowly past Max's house and willed my tires to crunch gravel quietly. Not that I couldn't be out late, that would be ridiculous. He'd have a friendly curiosity. I'd vaguely say I was out with a friend. He'd pick up on some nuance of body language or facial expression, or just read my mind. He'd be more curious. I'd get defensive. He'd be angry that

I'd done something reckless, whatever it was, Maguire! I eased my truck door closed and tiptoed up the stairs.

I pulled that little stand in front of my locked door, then dropped my jacket and purse. I sighed, pulled out my phone, and called Ben to apologize. He didn't deliberately frighten me, just stood by my truck. He probably didn't even know he looked like a serial killer.

His phone was either off, or on silent mode. Of course it was. He was out detecting in the dark. Free to go out on his own, doing what women can't even safely do in groups—and then lecture the women about it! I hung up without leaving a message.

I was groggy in the morning, but had the day off. Ida and I both emptied our schedules—it was tattoo day. I helped Max with the breakfast crew, but deflected his questions. Bum tattoos are private matters, I told him. He grinned, keeping any further thoughts to himself.

I wore my baggiest pants. Bring a small snack, they said. Bring water. We might need to nibble on something, for nausea. Sometimes people threw up. This might be a bad idea. There was still time to have sudden onset pneumonia.

I steeled myself, and picked up Fran and Janet—parking was limited. Ida brought Betsy. It was easier to be brave when the other women filled my truck with an air of excitement and adventure. By the time I pulled up in front of the building, I was energized. I trotted up to the door and held it for the rest of them.

We crowded into the lobby. "I'll tell them you're here," the receptionist said. "Since it's a large group, they're still getting things ready."

We looked at tattoo examples on the walls. Most of the décor—artwork, candles, knickknacks—featured skulls, skeletons, grim reapers. Motorcycles everywhere, Fran should like that. The Old Bats looked around, openly curious.

Voices drifted in from the next room—a loudly whispered argument with occasional shushing. We all leaned in.

"I'm not doing it," hissed a young woman. "I don't care. I will walk. I'm totally not kidding. I can literally walk, right now."

Murmurs I couldn't make out. Then a second voice, "Look, Rachel's doing Maguire. That still leaves two others, take one of those."

"I hope they know there are five of us," Janet said.

Another young woman: "Why does she get to pick from the other two? I'm totally not doing it either. I can't even."

I turned to the group. "Look, just so we're clear. If there's an issue here, I am not doing this by myself."

The voices came closer. "I'm not doing my teacher's ass. Either one of them. I'll take Clark or Gill."

Janet and Fran exchanged a glance. They sat straight and tall in their chairs, eagerly watching the doorway.

"At least you're a girl," a male voice whined.

"They're all women, Travis. There's no difference who you do."

Janet nodded. "Ahhh, Travis." She turned to Fran. "I'll bet you a beer that's Missy Tomlinson who can literally walk."

"I'm not taking that bet," Fran said. "I graded her essays, remember. Which she may or may not have literally written."

"What kind of grades did you give her?"

"I don't remember, so probably mid-range. Did you scold him for eating paste?" Fran turned as the door opened. A line of tattoo artists filed through.

"Hello, Missy," Janet said brightly.

One of the young women winced, forcing a smile and a little wave. "Good morning, Mrs. Elson. Travis here is going to take care of you today."

"Excellent," Janet said. "Don't worry, Travis, I came prepared. I wore a thong!" She beamed at the man, who visibly paled.

"Behave yourself, Janet." Betsy stood, introduced herself, and followed another tattooist through the doorway and down a short hall. Ida left with Missy. A slightly older woman projected a more businesslike demeanor. I hopefully met her eye. She nodded at me with a smile, and took Fran.

The remaining woman smiled nervously and led me into a small room. More of a cubicle, really. A large, open area was partitioned with thick, plywood walls. The tile floor was scuffed and chipped in spots, but clean. There was a fully reclining chair, a stool, and a wheeled, upright toolbox with several drawers. A basic shelf had spray bottles, ink supplies, black nitrile gloves. Framed certificates on the wall, that was encouraging. An array of electric needle pens. I swallowed hard. This was a bad idea.

My tattooist—Rachel, she said, with a forced attempt at confidence—had a hard look to her. Like it had been difficult for a long time, and she was already tired. She was young for it. Poverty, drugs? Jail? Maybe started with juvenile detention? Too many life stressors, that was clear. Why was she assigned to me, right off the bat? Unless she chose me, as the only outsider, the only one without history.

I didn't want to be face-down on the fully reclined chair, feet to the door. Rachel saw me hesitate, and explained that I would be covered, except for the specific area of skin to be inked.

"Oh, that's fine!" I laughed. "Gosh, have you been doing this a long time? How did you get started?" I could care less if she saw my butt. I don't like people behind me. Doorways behind me. You move on—you think you've moved on. Then you realize you've just arranged your life around not being vulnerable, which is quite a different thing.

Enough. Get on the chair.

I brought a picture of what I wanted, an ink drawing I found online. Rachel scanned it in somewhere and printed off a few different sizes. I picked medium. I wanted to be able to see it in the mirror, but let's not get carried away here. How big were the others going? We kind of assumed we'd all be done about the same time, but Betsy could be hours getting her griffin.

Rachel cut out the picture, positioned it on my exposed cheek, and held up a mirror. She made little dots with a marker, for placement. I started to relax. I could do this. I could let some woman make dots on my butt. It was fine. She left again and came back with some kind of a template that transferred the image onto my skin. It looked pretty good. Then she sat on the stool, wheeled right up close to me, and picked up the tattoo gun.

"You let me know if you need a break," Rachel said. "Especially for your first one. People have different pain tolerances, and it's a real different experience. Nothing wrong with needing a break."

It hurt more than I expected. I had a death grip on the edge of the chair, squeezing harder the more it hurt. Occasionally she paused the electric stabber, brushed my cheek with a gloved hand, and started again. We chatted casually the entire time. Rachel did business-like friendly, I choked out replies through gritted teeth. I suspected she just wanted real-time feedback that I was still conscious.

Rachel got an alert on her phone, but ignored it. "You're gonna need to hold completely still," she said.

"I am holding still." I was certain of it.

"Yeah, you're doing real great. You just need to keep holding still, okay? Just don't move."

"What?" I tried to look at her over my shoulder. "Is it going to change? What's going to happen?"

She put a second gloved hand on my lower back, as if holding me down. "Just hold still." The needle kept going. I faced forward again, willing myself to relax. The door opened behind me.

I craned my neck, twisting to see. A man, his back to me, closed the door. "What? Hey! What—".

"Don't move," Rachel insisted. "My uncle just wants to talk to you." She pressed a hand on my back again, and kept at it with the gun.

"Your—what? Are you—"

The man turned. Ernie! I grabbed the sides of the chair, pulled back against the vinyl, tried to shrink. Got loud. "What the hell?!"

"Quiet! You're gonna get me in trouble. And you gotta hold still," Rachel said sternly, "or you're not gonna be happy with this. You're gonna mess it up."

Ernie bent over and stuck his face right up to mine, his breath stale coffee and cigarettes. The sharp, burning pain of the tattoo gun intensified. Ernie stuck a finger in my face. "Look. I ain't looking for trouble."

"You what?! How—I'm—"

"Just listen! I know you saw me in a little bit of a bad position the other day," he said. "You don't talk about it, Abby. Not one word, not to nobody. Phyllis doesn't need any more trouble. You just mind your business and keep your mouth shut, you got it? Not one word to that investigator that lives with that cop. You ain't gonna be around here that long anyway, from what I hear. Just stay out of people's business."

I heard an inarticulate growl. It was me. Oh, God. Stabbing. Burning. I couldn't breathe.

"You tense up, it hurts a lot worse," Rachel said. "Just relax. It was better when you were relaxed. Grab the edge of the chair again."

I glared at Ernie. "Are you crazy? Are you both insane?!" I grabbed the edge of the chair again.

"You have no idea," Ernie hissed, jabbing a finger at me. "Things are outta hand. I gotta keep Phyllis outta this. You just stay away from her, you hear me? You keep your mouth shut! Understand?" He jumped at me suddenly, tried to make me flinch. I didn't.

"What the hell's the matter with you?" I shouted. "You don't do the damn flinch thing with someone's got needles in their ass! What are you, twelve years old? What the hell!"

"Hold still!" Rachel said. "Be quiet! Ernie, get out of here. Go! You're gonna get me fired! Lady, you gotta hold still."

"Oh, for—" I held still. They weren't going to kill me. If Ernie was going to pull a gun, he'd have done it by now. I glared at him.

He glowered back, but left. Rachel was quiet. Just the buzzing hum of the ink gun repeatedly stabbing me. I tried to relax my glutes. Neither of us pretended we had anything to chat about.

She was distantly professional when she was finished. She cleaned it up and held up a mirror. It was perfect—exactly what I'd envisioned. I grudgingly admitted to loving it.

She pressed a clear Saniderm bandage over it and gave me an aftercare handout. "Listen," she said quietly. "I'm sorry. Please don't get me fired. I need this job real bad." She waited just a moment for a response. I didn't give her one. If she thought I was going to gush some sympathetic crap at her, she'd be waiting a long time.

Janet and Ida stood in front of vinyl chairs in the waiting area. They glanced at me curiously. Their eyes cut from me, to my subdued tattooist, and back. Rachel worked the cash register, printing a credit card slip for me to sign. I took a pen and scowled at the charge slip. There was a line for a tip.

I squinted at Rachel, my pen hovering. A painfully hopeful glimmer flickered across her face, but she teared up and blinked it away. Her face hardened in a struggle for self-control. She turned away—and bit her lip. Just like I do.

Bit her lip, and she was just a young woman, born into this small town. This spider web community, this depressed economy. With a cultural expectation, as foundational as the granite and sandstone bedrock, that you do for family. Even if it costs you. Even if it's Ernie.

Oh, hell. I gave her a tip. The same generous one I'd planned, when I left home this morning. She met my eyes, and that lip trembled. She nodded, couldn't speak. Betsy and Fran bustled in, laughing, limping, sidling through the doorway. Rachel slunk away.

Everyone looked a little glassy-eyed as we gathered around Ida's pickup, grabbing a bit of tailgate or truck bed for stability. "Did you hear that yelling?" Ida asked. "It sounded like you, Abby. At first I thought it was you hollering at someone."

I glanced around the parking lot. "Ernie broke in! Halfway through! I'm face down, back to the door, with my butt hanging out! He started threatening me!"

"No!" Ida exclaimed. "What did you do?"

"What could I do? I had electric needles crocheting my back end," I complained vehemently. "I had his damn niece, she told me don't move no matter what, the little rat! She told him what room to come threaten me in!"

"Interesting," Janet said. "I left Warren and Ernie fixing my sink. He must have slipped out for a minute. Let's go jack him up."

"Let's sweat him," Fran countered. "Pretend nothing's off, watch him squirm. I always like to see how miscreants behave under pressure."

"I haven't done that in years," Janet said. "That's a good idea."

Ida tsked. "I wish we could all come. I'd like to be a fly on the wall and see the look on his face. This is too much, Abby. I want to hear all the details later."

Fran sat crookedly on one hip as I pulled into Janet's driveway. "I'm happy to get up for a few minutes anyway," she said. "Sitting may be dicey for a while."

We stood in the kitchen and surveyed the spread of wrenches on the linoleum. Warren's lower half stuck out from under the sink. Ernie sat on the floor, leaning back against the cupboards, the patched knees of his work pants close to his chest. His eyes flicked to my face and quickly away. He threw glances at Janet and Fran.

"Hello down there," Janet called. "We made it back!"

Warren pushed and pulled his way out of the tight space. "Did it hurt?"

There was a small silence. "It's supposed to be quite temporary," Fran said. She dug around in her purse as Janis Joplin started singing. "Betsy's calling. I hope they're alright. Yes, Betsy, is everything ok?" She chatted for a moment before returning her phone to her purse. "They're fine. Just reminding us to avoid ibuprofen."

Janet hefted her purse to the top of her refrigerator. "How did you know that was Betsy, before you answered?"

"That's her ringtone," Fran explained.

Perplexed, Janet stopped mid-stride. "How did she get that ringtone?"

"Well, I chose it for her, of course. You can pick one for everyone, so you know who's calling before you start trying to find your phone."

"For Pete's sake," Janet said. "You're going to have to show me how to do that. What's my ringtone?"

Fran missed a beat. "Well, I'd be glad to help you. Just make a list, and I'll show you how to set individual ringtones for each person."

Janet eyed her suspiciously. "I didn't get Janis Joplin at all, did I? Why does Betsy get Janis Joplin?"

Fran waved that away. "Betsy's the only one of us who was ever hip."

"You could just tell me." She frowned up at the top of the refrigerator. "I left my phone in my purse."

Warren, cross-legged on the floor, grinned at both of them. "Don't feel bad, Janet. I think you're plenty hip."

Janet sniffed. "Thank you. And now that you're out from under the sink, how about a cup of coffee? We can chat for a few minutes."

Warren and Ernie clambered to their feet and sat at the table. "I believe you've all met Ernie," Warren said. "We're having a fix-it day today, going house to house helping folks out."

"And I appreciate it. I hope you know that," Janet said. We remained standing as Janet filled cups from a thermos. "Well, the whole town knows what happened to us the other day, how we got caught up in the whole thing with Patrick Lutz. I'm sure you've heard gossip."

"Yes, yes, I have." Warren sampled his coffee. "I'm glad you're alright. That was a shock."

"It certainly was. How well did you know him?"

Warren took a drink and looked around, as if missing something.

"Oh, let me get out a few bars." Janet took a plate from the cupboard and loaded it with treats. Fran edged in to grab a bar.

Warren's face lit up as he happily reached out a grease-blackened hand. Probably just stained, not dirty. I thought of Papa and his friends, gathered in our garage to work on cars, motorcycles, lawn mowers. Gathered in our kitchen. I snagged a cookie while I could. Papa would've fixed a neighbor's sink without hesitation—a cup of coffee from a thermos more than enough thanks. Papa scrubbed and scrubbed his hands, but the stain from grease is hard to get out.

Warren ate an entire bar and took a second one before answering. "Worked in the same shop before I retired. I guess I can't think of much positive to say."

"Well, tell us something, Warren," Janet said. "More coffee?"

He held up his cup. "Well, now, Patrick was a mechanic, but not a good one. He was a lazy, dirty guy. Thank you, Janet." He set his cup on the table. "I can't tell you how many fellows have sat around a table at the café—you know we like to gather there—going on about how bad it was to work with him. Never pulled his weight, just pulled in a paycheck. Got out of working every way he could. Came in late, even when the lot was full of vehicles. Blamed his mistakes on other people. Got some good, hardworking folks in trouble for his errors. His family owns the business, you know."

While Warren talked, I watched Ernie. His face darkened. He ignored the baked goods, a horse refusing its bucket and putting the place on high alert. He drew in on himself, arms crossed in front of his chest, chin down. I tried to increase the power behind my stare, willed him to feel it. Didn't have the upper hand now, did he? Hadn't expected me to walk in the door—but at least he had his clothes on, a distinct advantage. "Ernie, you're being very quiet over there."

A slight head shake, almost imperceptible.

I glanced at Warren. Did he know what Ernie was up to? 'Oh, excuse me a couple minutes, I've got some terroristic threats to make. Want me to grab anything while I'm out?' Warren, seeming oblivious, took a cookie.

Everyone else stared at Ernie. He shifted in his chair. "Sorry. Can't bring myself to dishonor my mama's memory by speaking ill of the dead." Another tiny headshake. Ernie wasn't talking. We all waited a long moment.

"Okay," Janet said, "but would that be enough to kill someone? And what could it possibly have to do with Abby? Why would he be in her truck?"

Warren raised a finger as if making a point. "Now, Janet, we don't want to make assumptions. Very unscientific."

Here we go.

"We really don't know that Abby was targeted. Her truck may have just been handy, and her tailgate was unlocked. Even if they did know the truck was hers, perhaps they put the body there temporarily, planning to come back for it—" he looked at me. "But you moved your truck, and then you found him, so that put paid to that idea." He paused to take a bite. We all watched him chew. None of us had any response at all.

"I'm just saying the evidence isn't clear," he went on. "There is great precedence in nature of hiding things, planning to come back later. Chickadees are especially good at remembering where they leave seeds. Their brains function like bar code readers, differentiating specific locations—I'll admit the neurology is a trifle over my head. Of course, many animals store food. People will generally think of rodents or birds caching food for winter, but some animals stash food away to let it ripen. And it's not always food, of course."

Fran gave me a side-eye. I did a tiny shrug and pointed at Janet with my head. She started this—clearly she knew what she was getting us all into.

Warren waved his finger in the air. "Now, this is interesting. Primates. Orangutans and bonobos have been seen to transport tools and store them for future use. I don't imagine we know if they take other apes' tools or not." He nodded to himself and took a bite of a bar.

"Patrick wasn't the guy who never brought back your socket wrenches, was he?" Janet asked. "That's what you're talking about, with the monkeys, there. You're getting off topic, even more than usual."

He seemed to ponder while chewing. "He was, actually. Won't help him now. He'd steal tools from other mechanics at the garage, including Ernie here." He nodded at Ernie. "That's their livelihood, Janet. They're all making payments on those tools. I'm not completely off-point. This is really just an extension of our previous talk about camouflage. Hiding as protection. Sometimes self-preservation requires hiding objects, and keeping others from finding them." He shrugged. "Sometimes it works better than other times."

"Well," Fran said. "Thank you for the lovely visit. I really must be going. The dog needs to be let out."

Janet shot her a look. "If my purse wasn't on top of the fridge, I'd hear my ringtone right now."

Ernie quickly stood. "I can help you, Janet." He easily reached her purse and handed it to her. "Get you that Janis Joplin, right here."

Fran stuck her hand in her pocket, while leveling a piercing gaze at Ernie. "You see, there are still gentlemen in this world." A challenge, an unspoken accusation—a teacher holding out a plagiarized essay. "I'm sure your mother would be very happy to see how you treat women."

Ernie wedged himself behind Warren, and studied the baseboards.

Janet pushed a few buttons. "Now the truth comes out." We all waited. "Fran Winters! You turned off your ringer!"

"Look at the time!" Fran said. We made our way out the door.

I backed my truck into the street and turned towards Fran's house. "Do you even have a dog?"

"Of course not," she said. "Don't be ridiculous."

"Do I have a ringtone?"

"Not yet," she said. "You should really have a more recent song, but I'm afraid after the seventies I stopped paying attention. What did you make of Ernie's demeanor?"

"Clearly not a lead dog." I stopped at an intersection and waited for cross traffic to clear. "He's a scared coward, that's what I make of him. I don't know how that helps us." I pulled up in front of her house and shifted into park. "I could see him being sneaky. Both murders were sneaky."

Fran nodded thoughtfully. "That's a good word. Let's think about sneaky." She eased carefully from the cab, waved, and limped up her driveway. I watched until she closed the door behind her, then drove away.

I shifted my weight onto one cheek and turned toward the hardware store. I needed batteries for my Maglite. A man in the parking lot caught my eye.

Chapter Seventeen

The man was bent over, trying to maneuver a full-length mirror into his back seat. I looked again and grinned. It was Elson. I pulled in beside him and carefully removed myself from the cab. "You could've just asked me how you look."

Elson smiled, but shook his head. "Spending my day off dealing with emergencies."

I glanced at the mirror and raised my eyebrows.

"Yeah, yeah, okay," he said. "It's my mom. She won't stop climbing on chairs to look at her back end in the mirror over the sink. She's got all these pictures of handguns cut out, and Scotch tape, and I don't even want to know." Elson's eyes momentarily flickered to the side view he had of my bottom. He caught himself and switched his gaze from my rear bumper to my pickup's. "Are you okay? I didn't really talk to you about the DOA in your truck. Just got my mom out of there as quick as I could."

"So, I'm not a suspect, then? Should you even be talking to me?"

He smiled. "As of this moment, you're not a viable suspect, as far as I am aware. So, yeah. I can talk to you—about anything other than the details of the case."

"I'm mostly okay. Pretty freaked out, honestly."

"I'd be concerned if you weren't." He positioned the mirror on the back seat, sticking out into the parking lot, so he could let go of it. "Are you worried about your safety?"

"Not really. I was probably just parked in the wrong place at the wrong time."

Elson looked away, deciding whether to say something. He moved closer. "Listen, I gotta know. Did my mom really get a tat on her ass, or is she jerking my chain?"

"We all did—today, in fact. The Old Bats Club and their auxiliary member." I pulled the seat of my pants away from my butt a little, and tried to create an air pocket.

Elson straightened abruptly. "What did she get? Is it seriously a gun?"

"Sorry, there's an OBC code of silence. Anyway, I'm not going to help you picture your mom's butt."

He took several steps backwards. "Whoa! I'm not—that's not—no! She already offered to show me some prototype or something, just to get me to leave. She took hold of her waistband, I fled the premises."

I laughed at him. "Ok, come here a minute." There was no one near us in the parking lot, but I lowered my voice conspiratorially. "Now you tell me, do the cops all tell Detective Snake when they see me, or tell Ben?" I squinted at him suspiciously. "Everywhere I go, Ben either shows up, or nonchalantly brings it up in conversation. I swear someone's reporting on me."

Elson coughed. "Not hardly. Listen. Nobody's going to go out of their way to piss off Harmon, but no one's gonna scurry around trying to win his favor, either. You're totally overthinking this,

Maguire. You're making this way too complicated." He gave me a patient look. "If he's really doing that, if you're not just imagining things—he probably put a tracker on your vehicle."

"Maguire! Hey! Breathe! Abby! Look at me! You gotta breathe!" Elson grabbed my arm, shouting. I focused on his face, inches from mine, and took a breath. He pulled back, but didn't let go of my arm. "Geez! You can't do that!"

I looked at my truck, took another breath. Blinked. My mouth had gone dry. "How would I know?"

"You gonna be alright?" He studied me doubtfully.

I held on to my truck bed and nodded.

"You want me to look right now?" Elson circled the vehicle, felt inside the wheel wells, squatted in front of the truck, ran his fingers underneath. He found it—no more than a little, black button—tucked into a crevice inside the bumper. He continued to look and feel, in and around the truck. He verified that there was only one, and brought it to me.

My stomach clenched with burning anger. A piercing sadness—Ben and I were truly done. A hotter wave of absolute fury engulfed it all. He threw me away, chasing the win. The career-building opportunity. He'd expect to talk his way out of it. I held the tracker in my hand and pondered his destruction.

"Listen." Elson leaned back against my tailgate. "You want me to follow this up, obviously I will. These things have serial numbers on them. Just because Murphy's tight with Harmon—it's up to you, you wanna pursue this."

I studied the tracker. "How exactly does this attach to the vehicle? Is it just magnetic?"

Elson paused. "Why exactly do you want to know that?"

"I'm a lifelong learner."

His look contained an entire lecture. "You cannot put this on someone without their knowledge. Do not do that."

I gave him a slow smile. "I should put it on Detective Tom's car."

Elson pushed away from my truck. "I'm out. Not getting involved in that one. Don't tell me that."

"No, you're right. There's a better idea." I studied the pavement for a moment. "I know! What does the chief of police drive?"

Elson threw up his hands, warding me off. "No. No, Maguire. No. I like working in the same town where my mom lives. She's not getting any younger. I was never here. Wipe my fingerprints off that thing."

"Alright, alright." I blew out air in a great, theatrical sigh. "He can't just do this. Breaking up with him isn't nearly enough." Another wave of frustration swept over me. I kicked my tire, smacked my tailgate hard. "Rat! Dirty, lying—" I smacked it again and again, until my hand ached and I had to stop. "How did I feel guilty for not sleeping with him?"

Elson stared at me.

"Dammit! I said that out loud!"

"Listen." Elson moved closer, lowered his voice again. "Listen, Maguire. As a cop, seriously, never feel guilty about not having sex with anyone. Ever. I'm not kidding. I've seen way too much."

I paced a circle between our vehicles. I scowled, arms tightly folded over my chest. I walked awkwardly, because my pants rubbed on the Saniderm covering my tattoo, which just made me angrier. There had to be something I could do to him.

"Here," Elson said. "Give it to me. There's enough people that'll want in on this. I'll stick it in my pocket, carry it around, pass it on to another uniform. Whoever's got it when Murphy finally figures it out, it'll be on a cop, in a squad. He won't dare say a damn thing."

I liked it—but hesitated. "Promise me he doesn't get it back this time."

Elson missed a beat. "This time?"

I scowled. "It was bugs before. Listening. Twice."

Elson's face went blank. That deliberate emptiness you see on people who hide their thoughts for a living. He shifted his weight, nodded. "Yeah, prob'ly alright you didn't sleep with him." He held out his hand, took the tracker, and slipped it into his pocket. He angled the mirror into his back seat and got the door closed. "I'll see you later, Maguire. Let me know if you need anything, okay?" He slid into his car and started the engine. Then he seemed to freeze in place. He sat, unmoving. He turned off the ignition.

I stood with my keys in my hand, unsure what to do. Finally, he got back out. He leaned with one hand on his roof, face toward the ground, and grimaced.

I sidled and limped over to him. "Elson? Are you okay?"

He slowly raised his head. "Stupid. Stupid. Stupid. I'm such an idiot. Shit!"

I was afraid to say anything, so I waited.

He threw his hands up hopelessly. “I have to take this to Harmon. I’m sorry, I have to. I have no choice."

"You do not! Give it back to me! This never happened.” I was prepared to beg. “I don’t want to have to talk to him, Elson. Seriously. I’ll get myself in trouble. I lose my mind. He makes me insane.”

“I can’t help it. I’m sorry. Murphy was tracking your vehicle when the stiff was dumped on you. Or the killer put it there, so he could track the body. Now we’ve handled it, dammit. I can’t cover this up, I’m sorry. I have to talk to Harmon, I have to implicate his buddy, I have to bring you into it. I’m so sorry.”

“Harmon totally knows Ben does illegal surveillance,” I said. “Ben gives him confidential informant tips all the time. Tells his clients he’s getting the case closed faster, just using the police to do it. Harmon takes the information and doesn’t say where he got it. That’s how it worked last summer.”

“Well, hell. Either way, he’s not going to be happy with me for bringing it up. But I can’t assume he knows, I can’t withhold this. Listen, how long has this been going on, Murphy making comments about places you go?”

I thought. “Couple weeks, anyway.”

“Ok, so not just since this last homicide. Less likely it was anyone but him. I suppose it’s conceivable it’s related to whoever owned the truck before you. We’ll see what we can get off it, nail down the timelines.”

“Oh, perfect. So if I was off in any of my estimates, Harmon will be all up in my face about it. Like I tried to lie. Like he could say down to the minute where he's ever been. Just give it back to me. Come on."

Elson gave no indication he heard me. "I wish the crime scene people would've found it, but they didn't have any reason to be digging under the front bumper. This is going to suck so bad."

Ben the Rat was responsible for all of this. And I hoped it would come back on Tom somehow. They both needed to pay.

"Look," Elson said. "I'll do my best to just report everything thoroughly myself, so Harmon doesn't come looking for you. Best I can do."

I stood on a chair, trying to see through the Saniderm and check out my tat in the mirror. My phone rang. I bent down to pick it up—it was Ben. I rejected the call. A moment later, a text arrived. 'Please let me explain. I swear I had no intention of hurting you. Please talk to me.'

I let out a deep sigh and climbed down from the chair. I stood for a moment in the middle of my living room, but I was too angry to stay in that small space. I pulled on boots and clomped down the stairs.

At least the killer wasn't tracking me. I leaned on my hands on the wooden fence, took my weight off one leg, and wiggled my glute. I probably wasn't targeted. My truck was just convenient. I swung my foot sideways and tried to relax my muscles. It wasn't a murderer stalking me—just stupid Ben. Stupid, stupid Ben. Stupid!

"What's stupid?" Max appeared behind me.

I growled. Max took a few steps back. "I didn't mean to say that out loud," I told him. "Ben is stupid."

Max paused, raised an eyebrow, and very loudly said nothing.

"I heard that." Why was I scowling at Max? It wasn't his fault. My phone buzzed again. I turned off the ringer and shoved it in my pocket. Max's eyebrow twitched.

After Max walked away, I sent a quick text to Elson—the tracker was Ben's. That would be a relief to him, even if it left an impact crater in my life. He texted back. He already knew that. He traced the serial number.

Ida texted: 'OBC meeting tonight, Janet's house at six, let me know if you can't.' I checked the calendar. I could.

I was the last to arrive. Fran came in just ahead of me. She draped her coat on a chair, groped around in her purse, then set it on the floor. She reached for her coat and dug in the pockets.

"I've got you," Ida said. She poked some buttons on her cellphone. Nancy Sinatra started singing under the table, "These Boots Are Made For Walkin'."

Fran returned her coat to the chair and picked up her purse. "I was right in the first place." She rummaged around while Nancy sang.

"What a wonderful ringtone," Ida said. "Why, Fran, that suits me just fine. I'm very pleased with that."

"I thought it really captured you," Fran said. She shot a sideways glance at Janet, who had picked up her own phone. "I found it, Janet. No need to call." Janet frowned and set her phone on the table.

"Has anyone learned anything about the case?" Ida asked. "The affair between Ernie and Phyllis? What their alibis might be?"

Janet surreptitiously pushed some buttons on her phone, peering at Fran's. Nothing happened. Janet scowled and slid her phone into her purse.

Fran smiled. "Well, I think we've all been dutiful in our assignments, looking for a motive in Doug Larsen's extended family, or Phyllis's. But I wonder if that's a false trail, now that Patrick Lutz has been killed. Did anyone hear anything that might suggest a connection?"

No one had. Fran took the floor again, to describe our encounter with Ernie and Warren at Janet's house. Betsy and Ida listened with rapt attention.

"The look on Ernie's face," I said, "When Warren was talking about Patrick stealing tools and falsely accusing coworkers! With Doug gone, he gets the wife and probably the life insurance, if the insurance company decides Phyllis didn't do it. With Patrick gone, he might even get his tools back."

I paused. "And let's not forget him threatening me. Multiple times. He acted like he was just worried about the affair coming out, but I don't buy that. Making out behind the meat market on the busiest day of the year? He can't be harassing half the county, so why me? I know everyone keeps calling me an outsider, but still."

"Well, you're not from around here," Ida said, "and you developed a bit of local fame after those murders last summer. You may, perhaps, have a tiny bit of a reputation as a busybody." She waved away my appalled reaction. "We'll say you're relentlessly interested. But I agree, if he's only a philanderer, he's overreacting. He put himself at the top of the list." She pursed her lips thoughtfully. "We need to find out if he has an alibi. I'd like to have a go at him. Janet, does anything else in your house need fixing?"

"No, but I could break something," Janet said.

Ida nodded. "Do that. Make sure it's something they could fix, though. And ask for both of them."

"They'll come if you offer baked goods," Fran said. "Warren eats like a lumberjack. I'd like to know if Ernie gets his appetite back—he seemed too upset to eat, between Abby walking in the door, and Janet talking about Patrick."

Janet sighed. "I'll do it tomorrow. I don't want it to be Ernie, though. Warren would take that very hard."

"Listen," I said, "don't do this by yourself, Janet. We're potentially talking about a killer. Don't start grilling him, alone in your kitchen."

"Warren will be there," Janet said. "But you can come over too, if you're free. I'll let you know when they can make it."

"Alright," Ida said. "Abby and I are coming. What else?"

I thought about the tracker—it was Ben, though. We established that. But Elson said they would use it, pull off information. I should bring it up. I didn't want to talk about Ben.

"How is everyone healing?" Betsy smiled. "I notice a couple of us brought inflatable donuts to sit on."

"Mine is high enough up that my weight isn't on it," Ida said. "I'm glad I got a smaller one. Abby, are you alright?"

Everyone looked at me. I looked at the coffee table. This was incredibly awkward. I didn't know what Elson wanted me talking to his mom about. "There was a body in my truck. I keep thinking about it."

A few of them nodded, Ida suspiciously. I was glad we drove separately, so she couldn't interrogate me on the way home.

"Tobias fixed me up with an excellent mirror," Janet said, "if anyone wants to look at their tattoos. I've been keeping a good eye on mine." She led everyone into the hall and turned on the overhead lights. I waited in line while each woman half-bared her heinie, scrutinized her own and each other's in all their reflected glory, and effusively complimented every healing backside. I had to admit, they did look pretty good. Elson had gotten a nice, wide mirror. His thought process for that was better left unsaid.

"I might just buy one of these for the ranch apartment," I said, tucking the edge of my waistband under one cheek. "This is exponentially better than the mirror over the bathroom sink." I experimented with tightening a glute.

Betsy laughed. "I'm taking another turn! I didn't even think of flexing my griffin."

A half hour later, we returned to the living room. "Well, alright," Ida said. "This is one of the best meetings we've had in some time, but let's make sure it's productive. What do we need to cover?"

"I'll set the stage and get Warren and Ernie over here by late morning," Janet said. "Leave that part with me. We can tag team the interrogation."

"Abby, you swing by and pick me up around nine," Ida said. "Do you need us to bring anything, Janet? I always have bars in the freezer. If I take them out tonight, they'll thaw nicely."

Janet declined. She had it covered. She looked quite pleased with herself, whatever she had planned. Betsy offered to host the next meeting. She and Fran would dig around in the meantime.

"There's a fly tying presentation at Gundersons," Fran said. "They usually pull in a crowd. I'll see if I can glean anything."

I stopped for gas on the way home, then ran into the convenience store for eggs and milk. I noticed someone sitting in a parked car, looking down. Probably texting by the light that streamed out the store windows. Someone picking up groceries on the fly, just like me. Double-checking a list with someone at home, most likely. I thought I'd get less hypervigilant with a nice, quiet job. How many years before my heart stops kicking up a notch, every time I halfway see someone around a corner?

I grabbed my groceries, and threw in a box of marshmallow-filled cookie sandwiches as a surprise for Max. His favorite treat. The car was still there when I came out. The driver glanced at me, then did a double take. I slowed and looked more closely. Was it someone I knew? Hard to see, in the shadows. They looked away. Must have decided they didn't know me after all. Or was the person deliberately hiding their face?

Alone in my truck, I scolded myself out loud. "Oh, stop it. Dial it down, Abby." Every person in the world was not watching me. I shifted into reverse and backed out, then ignored my own lecture and checked out the car as my headlights washed over it. This person was watching me. Staring at me, but not with friendly recognition. She seemed to be talking on her phone, glaring in my direction. Phyllis.

I reached into the back seat, grabbed my Maglite, set it on the seat beside me and drove away. I checked the rear view mirror repeatedly, but no headlights appeared. I drove around a few extra blocks, looking for tails. Nothing.

I parked as close to my door as possible, and picked up my groceries before opening my door. I looked around before leaving my truck and trotting up the stairs. No one leapt from the shadows. I locked the door, but carried my Maglite with me, room to room, and set it on my nightstand when I went to bed.

Chapter Eighteen

We pulled in an extra chair to have five around the table. I got Janet talking. Dramatic stories and loud laughter would create a natural setting. She was in full swing when the men arrived.

"I'm sorry, Janet," Warren said. "You're having a coffee party. We can come another time." He took a step back. Ernie glanced around the room. He soured when he saw me, and turned to leave.

"No, no!" Janet exclaimed. "My, no. We won't be in your way at all. I so appreciate you coming over again, both of you." She wrung her hands, somehow looking ten years older and slightly feeble. I should learn how to do that. Could I stomach deliberately making myself look weak? My entire nature was to fake in the opposite direction. This was excellent spy craft.

"I don't mean to be so helpless," Janet went on. "I do hope I'm not a bother. Tobias can't get a darn minute off work right now. It's mandatory overtime, whether my kitchen falls apart or not."

Warren visibly inflated—stood tall, chest forward. "You know I'm always here, Janet. You couldn't possibly be a bother." Oblivious to Ernie's dejected slouch, Warren slipped off his shoes and padded toward the stove with a small toolbox. "Now which burner is giving you trouble, here?"

Janet pointed. "It worked the other day. I made chicken, potatoes and gravy —say, you could take home some leftovers! You both could." She beamed inclusively at Ernie. "Tobias can't get over for a decent meal, either, and it all turned out so well. I even pulled a pie out of the freezer, a lattice-top cherry. You won't believe the flaky crust. But now that burner just won't light."

Warren lifted the grate from the stovetop and set it aside. He tried to light the burner, then lit the others, one by one. "Well, your gas is coming in fine." He removed the disk covering the gas burner and peered at it. He straightened and turned to Janet with an expression of extreme patience. "Did your gravy boil over?"

Janet gasped. "Now, how did you know that? I cleaned it all up! There's not a speck of gravy on that range!"

Ernie leaned over the burner. "Well, there's your problem, Janet. The stovetop itself looks great, but you've got gravy in the little grooves of the burner here, see? Looks like the ignitor's clogged, too. We can take care of this with a toothpick."

Janet pulled a box of toothpicks from a cupboard. "Well, I never. Is that all it is?" She hovered for a moment while Ernie picked out dried gravy. "You men broke up your day to come over here. Let me get you some pie."

Far from irritated, they both seemed delighted to earn pie with so little effort. I leaned back, so Ida was between Ernie and me. He could get comfortable, loosen up. At the right moment, I'd suddenly move into his field of vision. I took a sip of coffee, to hide my smile.

Janet let everyone start on their pie. The crust was amazingly flaky. “What were you men doing today? I hope you didn’t cancel your plans for such a silly thing.”

Warren dabbed his mouth with a napkin. “Don’t feel foolish, Janet. You weren’t to know. That stove should work fine for you now. No, we were just over in my basement, talking about deer season coming up. Making sure everything’s ready to go.”

“Well, that’s interesting,” Ida said. “What does that involve?”

“We’ve already had our fall clothing out for grouse hunting,” Warren explained. “Of course, you’ll need a different shotgun for deer. Longer range, more stopping power. And different knives, of course, for cleaning.”

I stopped chewing. How many knives did they have? I imagined them in the basement, sharpening knives.

“I’m just completely unaware of this entire subject,” Ida said. “Tell me about the different kinds of knives.”

Ernie sat up straight and set down his fork. “You’re going to want a smaller, more flexible blade for smaller game, like grouse or waterfowl. That’s precision work.” He scowled. “Of course, you take your hide seriously, you’ll be precise there, too.”

Warren patted Ernie on the forearm. “Now, you’re thinking about that cape. No good dwelling on that. Water under the bridge.” He seemed to fight back a smile. “Larsen under the ground. So to speak.” He took a second piece of pie. “Ernie here has a particular skill with knives, takes pride in his work. Now, most will use a drop-point blade to open the deer. The small blade is for skinning and gutting. Detail work, as he said.”

Ida turned in her seat. "Do you mean Doug Larsen? What did he do?"

"Completely ruined my buck," Ernie blurted. He flushed and pushed his plate a few inches away. "No business touching it in the first place—then he used the wrong knife, hacked it up, wrecked it so it couldn't be a cape."

"What a strange thing to do," Ida said. "Do you think it was a mistake?"

Ernie scoffed. "You don't field dress someone else's buck, ever. And if you don't know how to do your own, you get someone to show you, or pay someone to do it right. Even just for the meat, there's a way to do it. Any ten-year-old who's ever watched someone harvest a deer knows that."

Warren shook his head. "Larsen was many things, none of them good, but he was never stupid."

"I don't mean to sound uneducated myself," Janet said, "but in this regard, I suppose I am. What in the world is a cape?"

"That's for mounting," Warren explained. "You want the head and shoulders intact if you plan to mount it. Otherwise, you don't have to be as careful with the hide, just for skinning, fleshing, gutting. Of course, you want to use the right knives for all of that. There's an art and a science to it all."

I felt light-headed. Warren absolutely could not get started on the science of whatever fleshing was. I'd confess to being a lesser spy. I couldn't take another minute. I leaned in. Ernie flinched and pulled back in his chair.

"Gosh," I said. "I remember when it first happened, you said no one would miss him. He sounds awful. I sure hope you both have good alibis!"

Warren chuckled. "How much attention do we really give our day-to-day movements? We don't expect to account for our whereabouts. It pays to be alert. There, now—that's another parallel with the natural world, Abby. Situational awareness, in both space and time. Not that there are wristwatches in nature, of course, but there's dawn, midday, dusk. Dark of night. Critical to be in the right place at the right time, for predator and prey, wouldn't you agree?"

"I was home that night," Janet announced. "Of course, I live alone. I believe they could verify that I was on the computer. I was researching tattoos that night."

"Abby and I were at the ranch," Ida said, "helping out with a moonlight trail ride. Although I did drive home by myself afterwards. How about you?" She looked expectantly at the two men.

"I'd have to consult my datebook," Warren said. "The days do run together." He finished his pie and Ernie's—Ernie lost his appetite again. Janet thanked them once more for the repair, as they left.

"Well, alright," Ida said. "We didn't get what we wanted out of that little maneuver. We might as well admit it, and move on." She crossed her arms and took on a look of determination. "We didn't learn their alibis, not at all. What did we learn?"

"One more reason that Ernie hated Larsen," I said, "and more about knives than I ever wanted to know."

"I wonder if they're being obstructive," Janet said, "or if they really don't know. I did have to stop and think about where I was." She threw a tentative glance at Ida. "Do we happen to know if Vig has an alibi for the second murder?"

Ida scowled. "He does not. He was out by himself somewhere, and I don't want to hear any nonsense about that. I almost never have an alibi myself, and I'll bet you don't either, living alone."

Janet didn't argue, a sure sign that she really was thinking something.

I was out of Diet Coke. I stepped out to go borrow some from Max—at least one, to sustain me—but his truck and Vig's were gone. I went back for my purse and keys. Jack Pine was five minutes away.

The sun was warm. I paused at the fence to look out over the woods. Horses moved through the shadows, slowly meandering, pausing to stand in their preferred mini-herds. I enjoyed the buddy groups, especially when Teddy, the kindly old gelding, befriended those in need. He'd taken in a horse that was bereft when its best herdmate came to end of life. He welcomed a rescue that someone donated here to have its best horse life with Walt and Max. I suddenly realized that Teddy had been the one to welcome me. He walked with me in the night when I first came, when I was still afraid of horses. He offered up his neck to be scratched, let me think I was doing him a favor. He'd taken me in, too—another herdless stray.

I shook that off and climbed into my truck. The convenience store sold cold Diet Coke in twelve-packs. I pulled three cases out of the cooler and laughed good-naturedly at the cashier's jokes about it. A couple of guys in line behind me bought cigarettes. One of them carried a bag from the attached liquor store. They both stared at me. I pretended not to notice, but kept them in my peripheral vision as I loaded my truck.

They came out behind me and climbed into an old beater pickup with a dented hood and a cracked grille. They eyeballed my truck and talked between themselves, making up their minds about something. I pulled out of the lot, watching my rear view mirror. They turned out of the parking lot and came right at me. They rode my back bumper, sped up and drove beside me, swerving too close. The driver made eye contact as I stared in disbelief—smirked at me. Swerved in again.

I wasn't going to pull over. They probably wanted me to, and who knows what they had in mind. I didn't want to lead them home. The cops, spread out over a large area, might be a half-hour away, or more. I had no idea what was going on. I felt a sudden surge of anger—enough being pushed around! Enough! I glanced at their truck. Mine could do over a hundred—thank you, Bobby. I floored it.

They reacted slowly and had to play catch up—tried, but failed. Their engine was older, and they probably spent their vehicle maintenance budget on beer and nicotine. I turned down a side road, fishtailed wildly on the gravel, steered into the swerving, straightened out. Hit a stretch of washboard, and the truck vibrated so hard my teeth clattered. Bits of gravel hit my undercarriage and side panels.

I thought about my beautiful, red paint job and winced, but kept going. A cloud of dust obscured the road behind me. I saw a field road ahead and slowed enough to turn into it, slid sideways with the curve, and drove right in between some farmer's rows of drying corn.

I followed the little one-lane, dirt road much more slowly, and crept all the way to the end of the field where it emptied out on another county road. I stopped at the edge of the cornstalks and sat, watching the plume of dust from the beater pickup travel down the road I'd been on. I let them get a good length of dust between us, pulled out, and went home.

Max's truck and Vig's were both in the lot now. I grabbed one case of Diet Coke, took it up to the house, and knocked. "I keep drinking yours," I told Max, holding up a case when he opened the door.

"No worries, Maguire. You don't have to buy me pop. Come on in, though." He looked over my shoulder. "What happened to your truck?"

I looked back. It was nearly gray with road dust. I hesitated. Strangely, I felt like I was confessing something. "Some guys chased me."

His curious eyes flashed into anger. Max ushered me into his kitchen, set the Diet Coke on the table, and steered me into a chair. Vig opened the case, took out a can and cracked it open. He handed me another one, cocking his head with interest. The story didn't take that long to tell—it all happened so quickly. Max, too furious to sit, paced between the table and refrigerator. "If this ever happens again, you call me, Maguire. Promise me."

"I will," I said. "But what would you do about it?"

"I don't know, but I'll damn well do something. I don't know what the hell is going on, but you take the brunt of things far too much. This is going to stop."

"Ditto what he said." Vig stretched. He didn't look relaxed, though. More like a panther stretching, feigning laziness, clocking a gazelle. "You got my number, right?"

"I do." I drank half my can and set it down. Fading adrenaline often left me glum.

"Nice job, though, Maguire." Vig toasted me with his soda. "Really. Well done on the losing a tail thing." Max scowled.

The whole episode, combined with the pointless morning at Janet's, left me with a sense of irritated futility. I grumped around my apartment, then finally decided I may as well use my crabbiness to accomplish something that needed doing. I pulled out my phone and called Ben. It rang four times, five. I waited, in case he was moving to a private location to answer.

"Abby!" His voice was happiness itself, and relief. I had reached out! I was over it. He could work his magic, talk his way out of another small transgression. "Listen—"

"You listen," I said. "Focus. Dig deep—pretend it's a case. Pretend this is a hostage negotiation, something with real consequences, not just a conversation with someone you're supposed to care about." I paused, registered the silence as he mentally backpedaled. I could almost hear his brain spinning, strategizing. "Don't insult my intelligence, Benson. This was purposeful. Planned, deliberate. I never want to see your face again. Never. Do not call me." I hung up, turned off my ringer. Shoved my phone in my pocket and blew out a long, slow breath.

I walked into the kitchen and looked at Papa. "I don't know," I told him, as though he had asked a question. I studied his eyes, the laugh wrinkles on his face. What would the question have been? He would have one, whether to seek information, or point something out. Papa used questions brilliantly. I'd give all the Bens in the universe to hear it. Just one more conversation. Oh, be honest. I'd always want one more, and another after that. I'd never be ready.

Papa saw right through people. It was a gift. He'd break it down for me sometimes, explaining what he saw in a glance. He taught me to read both printed and spoken words. Situations, people. "What should I have paid more attention to?" I sat on the counter and thought about it. "Ben really did like me, that part was mutual. That's the problem." I touched Papa's face. "But the chase is everything for him. I think he wanted me to be part of his life, but as a player in his game. In a subordinate role, of course."

I leaned my head back against the cupboard door, closed my eyes, sighed heavily. After a few minutes, I hopped down from the counter and went to the doorway. Fresh air. Change of scene. Shake it off.

Max had cleared more trees and hauled them to his staging area in the side yard. He'd been chopping—I'd heard the rhythmic whacks, the calming cadence that stopped as he carried and stacked, then started again. It took me a moment to spot him in the lean-to he was using as a wood shed. He had a few medium-sized trees left, and two different sized axes. Perfect. I picked up the big one and started swinging.

There was great satisfaction in heaving the weight of it, getting those large muscles going, sending the blood oxygen there instead of to the fretting center in my brain. It took focus to position and angle the axe head, balance my weight, engage the right body parts so I wouldn't pull or strain anything. Wreck my back, that would be all I needed. I muttered to myself with the lead-up and the swing, grunted with the loud thwack of impact.

Max came into my peripheral vision. I stopped, looked at him sideways. He studied me briefly. "You alright?"

I growled assent and moved along my log. Max picked up wood, and stacked. I kept chopping and tried to get a rhythm. I was nowhere near as smooth as Max. As soon as I started getting into a groove, the autopilot kicked in and my angry thoughts intruded. I should've known better. I should've paid attention—THWACK—to red flags. I should've stayed away when I found out he was capable—THWACK—of building a relationship—THWACK—and spying on me—THWACK—at the same time! Living a double life, knowing that I—THWACK—was not. He thought I was stupid, didn't he? THWACK. No. Oh, no. He enjoyed my intelligence. He thought dating me was like riding Lucy! He did! Smart, high-energy Lucy. He totally—THWACK—got off—THWACK— on the challenge. He loved that horse—THWACK—for the adventure of control. Damned if he would control me! I raised the axe but stopped in mid-swing and gaped. Ben's truck pulled into the drive. Of course it did! I tell him I never want to see his face again, what else would he do? He thinks he's oppositional? Bring it on! Watch and learn!

He swung down from the cab of his truck, stepped toward me, and smiled. Smiled! Completely dismissive! A hot flood of rage swept over me. Little spots appeared in my vision. I opened my mouth and a loud, guttural noise came out. I stormed towards him. He stopped abruptly. His eyes widened. He quickly scanned me and stepped back. I tried to yell at him, but it came out as an inarticulate growl. Ben ran for his truck, threw me an astonished look from behind the closed door, executed a perfect three-point-turn and sped away, throwing gravel.

I stopped, unsure what just happened. I heard Max laughing, and turned. He tried to stop, covered his mouth with his hand, coughed, choked. "I'm sorry—" He snorted through his nose. "That was the greatest thing I've ever seen in my life. You—" He propped himself against the side of the lean-to and shook, tears pouring down his cheeks. "His face—"

What? I started to wave my hands, and realized I was still carrying the giant axe. I charged at Ben with an axe, making wolverine attack noises. This is what it's come to.

Max bent over, arms wrapped tightly around his torso, nearly in a fetal position. He'd lost it. I stared at him. He blew out a few long, shuddering breaths, stole a sideways glance at me, and lapsed back into hysteria. After a few moments, he wiped his face with his hands and tried to collect himself. He couldn't look at me. "I'm—" he cleared his throat. "I'm sorry you're upset. I really am." He giggled.

I leaned the axe against a log and walked away.

The Old Bats Club met at Betsy's the next day. We sat around the table with notebooks and pens. Betsy and Fran had a diagram on a large whiteboard, outlining what we knew.

"Well, I know we need to discuss the case," Ida said. "And if it's too personal, Abby, just say, but I'm dying to know what Ben finally did. Max said you chased him off the property with an axe."

Fran and Betsy studied me with interest. Janet and Ida leaned forward eagerly. I took a drink of my coffee to gain a moment, then sighed. May as well get it over with. "He put a GPS tracker on my truck."

"No!" Ida gasped. "Again?"

The others goggled at her, then at me. "What do you mean, again?" Fran asked.

"Well, I mean, this is the first GPS tracker. Where is it? Can we see it?" Ida asked, wide-eyed.

"Elson took it." I glanced at Janet. "Tobias. He found it for me." I flicked a hand in disgust. "Ben kept bringing things up in conversation, places I'd been. It seemed like a bit much. Then I thought of people always calling Tobias on Janet—" I stole another glance at her. She nodded indignantly.

"I ran into Tobias in town, so I asked him if cops were telling Detective Harmon when they saw me anywhere. Or telling Ben. He said no. He knew right away the rat must be tracking me. Took him like ninety seconds to find it." I realized my fists were tightly clenched, and released them. I wiggled my fingers to get the circulation going again. "Tobias was going to carry it around, pass it from cop to cop on patrol, see how long it took Ben to figure it out. But then he realized it could have been the killer tracking me, so he had to take it to Harmon. He profoundly didn't want to."

Janet tapped her fork absently on the tabletop. "Tobias's plan was a good one. Did Ben confess?"

"Enough for me to know it was him," I said. "I didn't really let him get much further." I sighed. "I hope you don't feel like I was holding out. We've actually met since Elson found it. I just wanted to know for sure what was going on, before I said anything."

There was silence for a few moments. "Well, that's how you process," Fran said. "Thoughtful analysis. You are who you are, and you're one of us." She pursed her lips and paused for a beat. "I definitely want to hear the full story—it sounds like a doozy. But in the future, if there's any possibility a serial killer may have placed a tracker on your vehicle—well, I think I can speak for all of us in saying we'd like to know about it."

They nodded, around the table. "You're forgiven," Betsy said. "But I do want to hear about chasing a man with an axe, if only to experience it vicariously."

I had to smile. Impossibly, they were making me feel better. I took a breath, but exhaled without speaking. Just thinking about it was excruciating. I took another breath and started in. Their faces became grim as I went along—the bugs he planted on me last summer, how I let him talk his way out of it. Twice. In the full context, they didn't even find the axe quite as amusing. They sat in silence. "I think Max is still laughing," I said lamely.

"He is," Ida said. "He keeps talking about it. He adds a lot more detail, though. Does an imitation of Ben—the look on his face, running to his truck—and laughs until the tears flow. It's good for

Max to laugh, though. He's under too much stress. Walt thinks so, too."

I winced. I hadn't thought about Walt hearing. He hadn't said anything to me about chasing a man off his property, waving a deadly weapon. Even if I had been too furious to think about what I was doing, that didn't lend itself to a positive employment evaluation. I cleared my throat. "What did Walt say, exactly?"

"Nothing," Ida said. "But he got a twinkle in his eye."

"And on that note, helping Max," Fran said, "we should move on. I do want to say, though—" She paused, twisted her lips again. "Abby, I'm the last person on Earth to tell a woman what she should or should not do. I just want to encourage you—if you want a man, there are better ones, and you don't have to look too far to find them."

Betsy nodded. "Agreed."

"Hunh." Ida crossed her arms over her chest. "We probably never were on a police watch list. There was no surveillance on Phyllis at all." She frowned.

"We're not out of the woods yet," I assured her. "Deergrass doesn't have a whole lot of cops to put on stakeouts, but there's still time."

The Beatles started singing from the living room floor: "I Want to Hold your Hand." Fran dropped her fork with a clang. She hurried to the couch, grabbed up her purse and dug for her phone while the ringtone went on and on. She turned her entire body away. "Hello." Every gaze was fixed on her. "Oh, good, I'm so glad. Yes, I'll be there tomorrow. Thank you. Yes. Alright, then." She tucked her phone away, set her purse down, and turned toward us, flushed.

"Fran, who was that?" Ida asked innocently. We all stared.

Fran straightened her shoulders. "Just the store. An order came in, that's all." She took her seat again and retrieved her fork.

Janet gasped. "The bait guy! Fran! You did let him pick you up!"

Fran drew herself to her full height and leveled a steely gaze at Janet. "Let him, hell. I picked him up. Let's move on."

Ida clapped her hands and chortled with delight. "Good for you, Fran. Well done!"

Fran was so distracted, she didn't see Janet pull out her own phone. Fran's purse erupted into noise: The Yardbirds singing "The Bird." It was loud. Raucous. Wildly noisy.

Fran threw up her hands in defeat. "Alright, Janet, you got me." She picked up her purse again, and finally managed to stop the frenetic, blasting ringtone.

Janet's mouth hung open in shock. Ida sat wide-eyed, hand over her mouth. I bit my lip and tried not to giggle. Betsy flicked her eyes back and forth between Janet and Fran.

"Janet," Fran said. "Now, let me explain."

"Wha—" Janet was aghast. "How—"

"Now, listen," Fran told her. "I gave you that ringtone when Tobias was endlessly lecturing you, relentlessly, until you finally agreed to stop flipping people off in traffic."

Comprehension filled Janet's eyes. "Flipping the bird!" she exclaimed.

Fran nodded. "Exactly. Just a tiny act of defiance as a ringtone, Janet. Supporting you, really." The two exchanged a long, meaningful gaze.

"You know," Janet said, "people were more civil back in the day. Just flip each other off, back and forth, no one got hurt."

"Alright, you two." Betsy seemed to think she could rein in this meeting. She looked around the group. "Does anyone have anything intelligent to add about the work we're doing?"

Ida laughed out loud. She took a napkin and dabbed at her eyes. "I'm sorry, Betsy. I think I've got that out of my system, now. I guess we've only got Abby left."

"I don't have a ringtone," I told her, "but listen."

Chapter Nineteen

"They don't really believe Vig is guilty. That rat Ben has been tracking my every move, talking to Harmon. Using us." I looked around meaningfully. "Elson pointed out that Ben would know exactly where my truck was at every moment. The cops can use that tracker all they want, they aren't the ones who illegally placed it. They'll never tell me anything, but they're still digging around, is my point. They don't know."

"That whole conversation about hunting knives was unnerving," Ida said. "Ernie certainly perked up, talking about it."

"Incredibly creepy," I agreed. "But skilled enthusiasm with fleshing knives doesn't fit the MO of either homicide."

"I have something potentially critical," Fran said. "Or completely worthless. Gossip. Word is Phyllis may have another bit of side action, not just Ernie. Remember the photo Betsy and Abby found in their library research? City Councilman Swanson was reportedly missing in action just after the tornado, when his constituents were after him. Allegedly, his wife told the first people who called that he was at work. Except he wasn't. Then he was unavailable, unspecified, for several hours, until some downed trees were moved, and he could get his car out of the back lot behind the motel. A vehicle matching the description of Doug Larsen's truck was there, too. Or so rumor has it."

"Doug's cousin," Betsy said thoughtfully. "Interesting."

"If she had three men going," Janet said, "who choked her? If Doug did it, each of the others thinks he is her only solace. Justifies infidelity. If one of them did it, now it's an even bigger problem, because Doug will see it. She could file a false police report, invent a mugger, but that would get out of hand quickly."

"It would," Ida said. "Prominent citizen's wife attacked like that, we would've heard about it. Abby, you saw the bruises, you're the expert here. The red spots in her eyeball and around her eyes—how long would they still look like that?"

"Subconjunctival hemorrhage and petechiae, a few days, could be a little longer, depending on severity of the attack and personal factors," I said. "But the throat bruises were greenish yellowish, which should be five to ten days. Intersecting the two, we could say five days—assuming they both happened in one attack. You're asking if Doug could have been killed the day it happened. How many days after the murder did we go visit her, Ida?"

"Right around there," Ida said. "Well, alright. It's a possibility. Doug was killed to keep him from seeing the bruises and asking who did it. Or Doug did it, and one of the lovers reacted."

"Or one of the lovers complained to someone else, who wasn't judgy about the affair," I said, thinking of Bobby's theory. "People talk. That sympathetic listening ear decided enough was enough, and offed him. Maybe it was a mob action. If only Vig had an alibi, we could drop the matter, go get ice cream."

"We still have Patrick Lutz to deal with," Betsy reminded us.

"At this rate, I suppose he could've been sleeping with Phyllis too," Janet said. "Maybe he choked her. That would make a nice, tidy circle."

"We need to work on the signal-to-noise ratio here," Fran said. "I have no idea what's relevant. Let's make that our next assignment: cut to the chase."

Ben said that, from the beginning. He worked feverishly to eliminate possibilities, frustrated by the mass of them. "That was the point of the GPS tracker," I said. "Ben was looking for the signal in the noise. I was just one means to that end, but every time I talked to him, he asked questions, grasping for something to narrow the focus."

"Humph," Ida said. "He might be a good investigator. You just leave him there."

The meeting died down, but Ida was restless. She walked me to my truck. "Come to my place, Abby. Let's just sort through this one more time."

I followed her home and settled into her living room with a glass of water. I had enough caffeine onboard. "We need to think about this differently," I said. "Thinking about it like everyone else adds absolutely nothing to the situation."

"True," Ida agreed. "Go on."

"A few things keep getting stuck in my brain, over and over. My subconscious won't let go of them."

"Hold on." Ida leaned over and opened a drawer in her side table. She rummaged around and pulled out a pen and paper. "Alright. Spit them out."

"One of the men said you don't go back and kill a guy when you won the fight. You could teach a class on that statement right there, Ida. Plus, it fits with someone being treated badly for years, hiding themselves. Who has never won the fight? We have to think about that."

"Noted," Ida said. "Next?"

"I told Vig and Max this: we've all heard of threats that fly under the radar. Threats that are actively dismissed or scoffed at, and go on to create tremendous harm. Again, someone unseen, not taken seriously as a threat." I frowned at Ida. "They were dismissive, actually, when I said that. Didn't take it seriously, not at all. I had a professor who said you can't get mad at someone for displaying the symptoms of their diagnosis. Does that include being an alpha male?"

Ida made a rolling motion with her hand. "Stay on track. Focus."

"There really is a lot of detective work involved in diagnosis." I took a long drink of water, emptied the glass, stared at it. "Of course, if we were diagnosing, we could sit some people down and ask them specific questions. That would be nice. And, very much like doing diagnostics, it would be helpful if they had any inclination to answer honestly."

Ida tapped her pen on her notepad impatiently. "You're getting off track again. I'm not writing any of that down."

"Okay, okay. Roger talked about things that run deep. Something unseen causes erosion for years, eats away the foundation beneath us, as we go about our lives. Then something that's happened before, without incident, causes a disaster." Sinkholes appear suddenly, unexpectedly—but not quickly.

"What would motivate the city councilman?" Ida asked. "An elected official hasn't always lost, he doesn't fit that whole theory. But say Doug found out about him, threatened to ruin his career. Or just tell his wife."

"That's a good point," I said. "Is there any way Patrick Lutz ties into that scenario?" I struggled up out of the sofa cushions. "Excuse me. All that coffee." I moved from carpet to linoleum, lost in thought. Ida's bathroom was well-kept and quirky, just like her. The clear shower curtain she didn't have the heart to replace—her husband had loved it. The ceramic soap dispenser with splashes of color, in a white room. Ida was a splash of color, for sure. Something tickled the edge of my mind.

I refilled my water glass in the kitchen, and carried it past all those pictures of Ida and Johnny on the living room wall. Now, there was something that ran deep—but Ida was solid. Losing him didn't eat away at her, weaken her core. "How did you not lose your spark, when Johnny died?"

Ida looked up, startled. She paused. "I promised him I wouldn't."

I nodded. There was something critically important here, but it slipped away. I put deep, chronic stressors on hold, and moved back to the acute. What was finally too heavy, driving over the unseen sinkhole? What initiated the collapse?

"I want to know about that night at the bar," I said. "What happened before the fight with Vig? Who did Doug Larsen interact with? Specifically, did he laugh at someone? You'd be amazed how often that pushes people over the edge—someone laughed at them. People snap under humiliation. Sometimes I want to put out a public service announcement. Then I also want to know, what did Patrick do that day, or in the week prior, that might have humiliated someone, provoked a reaction."

Ida pulled out her phone. "I have Warren's number in here somewhere. He and Janet watch each other's houses if they're out of town, and she gave him my number as a backup, if he couldn't reach Tobias. He'll know how to get ahold of the man from the outhouse race, who was at the bar that night. Which one of them was it? It's a simple enough question, whether Doug laughed at someone."

"Joe was at the bar that night. Both bars, both nights. I don't know their last names, except Ernie. But listen, this could be a bad idea. Roger warned me off, Ernie threatened me. Just hold on. Let's think about this."

"Warren? Hello, Warren. This is Ida Gill, Janet's friend. Of course, yes—" Ida waved me away.

"Ida!"

She walked into another room. I heard her end the call a moment later, but she didn't return. She must be dialing. I paced nervously. I could hear Ida's voice, her cheery, conversational tone, but I couldn't make out words. What was my huge internal reaction to this? It felt like a very bad idea. Why? Compared to some of the things we'd done, this should be pretty benign.

I just wasn't quite myself, like Bobby said. That was probably it. All these threats left me feeling vulnerable. Really, the men only threatened me about keeping Ernie's secret. Don't forget you're an outsider here—mind your own outsider business. That kind of thing. What was taking Ida so long?

She returned with an air of triumph. "Well, you were right, Abby. Turns out Doug Larsen laughed at Ernie that night. Made a bit of a scene. Ernie walked out, leaving a fresh drink on the table. Larsen picked it up and drank it. Joe went on at some length, he's still angry. As far as Patrick, Joe wasn't aware of anything different. He always sneered at people, took their things. Acted like a child. Slammed doors, kicked the dog—one of the men brings his old lab, I guess—threw things. Mocked people, but with juvenile insults. Joe doesn't think anyone took that very seriously. Sounds like Doug was better at getting under people's skin, sticking the knife in and twisting it."

"Joe didn't say anything about Ernie being at the bar, when he was telling the story about that fight," I said. "All he talked about was Vig—not by name, he called him 'that guy.' Ernie was right there—neither of them said anything about Ernie having been there, but leaving too early to see the fight."

"Maybe he's afraid Ernie came back and killed Larsen," Ida said. "I wish we could find out what Ernie's alibi is for that night."

"Maybe Joe was so mad, he killed Larsen. Maybe the whole crew of the outhouse race did it together," I said darkly. "Maybe they have a murder club now."

Ida wasn't listening. "Janet's story about taking the BB gun after the squirrels—the night Doug was killed—and Warren having a visitor outside, you remember that? I'll just bet it was Ernie, that he went to Warren's house from the bar. You saw the way Warren patted Ernie's arm, calming him about that deer hide. Warren has probably kept Ernie from erupting, for years. Maybe he finally couldn't." She pulled out her phone.

"Do not call Warren again!" I shouted. "Don't, Ida! He'll talk to his friends about it. The whole murder club will come after us."

"Janet, hello." Ida waved me away, then pulled the phone away from her face. "Abby, go have a snack or something. I think your blood sugar's out of whack." She walked into the other room again. By the time she came back, I was pacing the kitchen, eating pickled beets out of the jar with a fork.

"Sugar," I explained.

"Well, alright," Ida said. "It was Ernie, over at Warren's that night. He left the bar, angry, didn't want to go home, ended up at Warren's. Of course, I'm embellishing, but he was there. Does that tell us anything?"

"We ask what their alibis are, and they were together at least part of the night, and won't say a word about it." I thought about that, and ate another beet slice. "Warren absolutely knows something. He at least has an idea. This whole time, he talks in circles, obscures things. Deflects through biology lectures and sheer quantity of words. His friends could very well be neck-deep in this. He's not going to give them up."

Ida pulled a chair out from the table and sat. She rubbed a scuff on the linoleum with her toe. Frowned at it. "Do you think he'd protect a murderer?"

"I don't know. What would you do, if you suspected Janet might have done it? Would you dismiss it, or make yourself pursue that line of thought? Or if you started thinking maybe Vig really was involved? More to the point, what if you thought Max did it?"

Ida refused to answer. She gestured impatiently: don't be ridiculous.

I went on. "There are a couple of people it could very well be. How could we get anyone to listen to us, much less prove or disprove anything?"

"We could leave Tobias an anonymous phone tip," Ida said. "From a pay phone. There's still one in the entryway of the library."

"I don't hate that," I told her. "He might recognize your voice and get mad, but what's he going to do? You could easily stonewall him."

"My voice?"

"We need to put the screws to Warren," I said. "Without Ernie or anyone else there. Warren's a performer—we need to eliminate his audience. No more nature talks. Steer the conversation. Go into therapist mode, instead of polite friend of a friend. Circle back on deflections, ask a different way, until he either answers or blurts out the reason he doesn't intend to. What do we specifically want to know?"

"I can certainly be direct," Ida said. "We could both go pin him down. He won't tell us who did it, but maybe he'll tell us who didn't, and how he knows they didn't."

"And no lectures about animals banding together against predators." I rinsed my fork and the empty jar. "We cut that right off."

"Just stick those in the dishwasher," Ida said. "You're behind my truck, you'll have to drive." She stood and picked up her purse, but set it down again. "Let me just use the restroom before we go. I don't want to be distracted. And if we're going to be direct with people, I'm not leaving you alone. Not for a minute."

I went out to my truck and climbed into the back seat, dug out a cloth shopping bag, and put my Maglite in it. Just in case Warren had company.

"We'll say we need Warren's advice," Ida said, as I drove. "His perspective. He'll like that. He did know both victims. Of course, most of Deergrass knew both victims, or at least their families. But we can still make him out to be some kind of expert, see what he does with that."

Warren's driveway was empty. I got out and peered in his garage windows. Empty as well. I climbed back into the cab. "Now what?"

We cruised by the café. "He drives an old LTD," Ida said. "Light blue. I don't see it. Let's go by the garage where those men work and see if he's there."

He wasn't. I drove another block, did a U-turn, and pulled over. I shifted into park, sat back, and looked at the garage. "I wonder which mechanics are on duty? Papa might have called this a fool's errand."

"He may have been right, but let's not give up yet," Ida said. "Warren is the most likely person to help us whittle down the list. If he can convince us that Ernie and Joe are innocent, we can move on."

"How are we going to justify questioning him? We didn't talk about that."

Ida paused. "I'll tell him straight out, I'm worried about Vig. We can't let an innocent man get dragged into this any longer. It will affect his job, his marriage. This has to stop."

We sat quietly and watched squirrels play chase in an upward ring around a tree trunk. An old woman waited at the crossing. I heard an ice cream truck. It seemed out of place—whimsical music as a soundtrack to a murder inquiry—but life just continued.

"I think we've done all we can today, Ida. We need to regroup."

She frowned, but had to agree. "We'll pend this forward, and figure out how to talk with Warren when Janet isn't around. Those two have been friends for so long, I think that shapes the conversation. He probably lapses into storytelling more readily."

"Easiest way is to conspire with Janet about it. You can work on that." I dropped her off at home, and drove back to the ranch.

Max walked out of the barn as I arrived. "I gotta get into Deergrass, go meet with a woman about a donation. This lady wants to cover some therapy sessions for people who can't afford it."

"That's wonderful!" I sniffed him. "Change your clothes first." I headed up the stairs and pulled a cold drink from my refrigerator. Maybe I should ask Max to swing by the grocery store and pick some things up for me. I rejected that, made a list, and grabbed my purse. It's not that far.

I sailed through the store, efficiently bagged my things, and stowed them in my back seat. Diet Coke on the floor, bread on the seat, never to meet—I hate squished bread. I pulled out of the parking lot and, on an impulse, turned the wrong way. I suddenly wanted to drive by again—not looking for Warren, but just to see where I was parked when someone left a dead man in my truck. It looked like nothing—a street, an alley. I slowed past the garage where all these guys worked. More nothing, really. A repair shop in a basically blue-collar town.

I drove past the bar where we had dinner that night, headed north, and drove past The Nail. I might never set foot in there, which felt vaguely disappointing. Not that I aspire to dive bars—I just don't like limitations. Maybe I should have a cold one there some evening, just to prove a point. Maybe not alone, though—I am still small and female in this stupid world. Who would go with me? I ran through the possibilities.

The list was short and futile. There was only one definite yes, and I was absolutely not doing it. Just no. I am not going to The Nail with the Old Bats Club. I turned for home. Just past the city limits, someone came racing up behind me. I looked, and stopped breathing.

The pickup with the dented hood, the cracked grille. I swore at my rear view mirror, debated my options, and slammed the palm of a hand against my dash. I cursed some more. They pulled up on my back bumper and hung there—must have been within inches. The mental pressure of having someone right behind me kicked up my adrenaline immediately. I should speed up, then slam on the brakes. I bet I have better insurance. But they're probably too stupid to wear seatbelts.

I could likely outrun them again, but why should I? If I'm going to drive a hundred miles an hour, it's going to be my choice, not some dirty, stinking bullies in a beater, pushing me. Any reaction I gave them would feed their twisted egos, jack them up, make them feel all big and tough. Why should I run in fear, give them the sick thrill of chasing me?

But what would they do if I ignored them? Run me off the road? Shoot at me? I told Max I'd call him, but he wasn't home. The adrenaline spike made me furious. Being thrown into a trauma reaction enraged me. Damn, stupid punks had no right to have control over me! My body betrayed me and started to shake.

I rummaged around in my purse with one hand, cursed, tossed things on the seat, the floor. Finally dug out my phone. Glanced in the mirror. The pickup was close—repeatedly backing off and speeding up, threatening to ram me. I called Vig.

Initially curious, he snapped into terse and direct. "How far out are you?"

I tried to think. "Seven minutes."

"Come home," he said. "Stay in your truck when you get here."

Chapter Twenty

They kept on me the whole way, turned on the gravel road, and followed me into the driveway. They skidded to a stop when Vig stepped out from behind his truck with a military-looking long gun aimed at their windshield.

I pulled up, killed the ignition, and turned to watch. The beater pickup spun backwards. The passenger waved his arms frantically and yelled at the driver, who over-accelerated, missed the turn, and backed right into the ditch. He glanced wildly out his side window, and there was Vig.

I slid out of the cab to hear better, hid behind Vig's truck, and peered over the hood.

Vig stood far enough back to cover both men, and ordered them out of the vehicle, hands first. His voice was loud, hard, with that violent edge that inspires immediate compliance. The driver popped out, empty hands raised. The passenger cowered, shrinking down in his seat. Vig repeated his order and threw in some vulgar cursing for effect. It worked. The man opened his door, but tried to hide behind it.

I recognized them from the convenience store. I was right about dirty—three-day-drunk dirty, sour looking. I was undoubtedly right about stinking. Vig gestured with the end of the gun, moved them both away from the truck, and had them turn around slowly. He visually scanned them. The driver had a large wet spot on the front of his jeans. Vig shook his head slightly. He barked at them, "What the hell are you doing, following her?"

The men glanced at each other. "We weren't—" one of them started. Vig took a half step forward, and the man shut up.

"I'm not asking again," Vig said. He pointed his weapon slightly to one side.

"We weren't gonna hurt her," the driver said. "I swear. This person in the bar just threw us some cash, told us to shake her up a little, that's all. I don't know why, that's all I know. Just let us go, she'll never see us again, I swear to God."

"What person?" Vig asked.

"I don't—" the man began. Vig's posture changed, and the man involuntarily took a step back. "Wait! Just someone at the bar! Dillon's, out on eleven? Out by that turn-off for the junkyard there? Gives us fifty bucks, says what her truck looks like, and to scare her off. We weren't gonna do nothing to her, I swear."

Vig calmly walked toward the car in the ditch, and aimed at the front tire.

"No!" the man screamed. "No! Don't! I ain't got money for that! I gotta have a way to get to work, I'm on probation. Please, man! Not the tire! Listen. It was a woman, okay? Just some woman, I don't know her."

One particularly expressive glance from Vig, and the driver fell the rest of the way apart. "Okay! Okay, wait. Her name's

Phyllis, okay? I swear to God I don't know her last name. Just don't—don't wreck my tires, okay? That's all I know."

Vig held the gun under one arm, and sternly pointed a finger at them. "Do not move." He pulled out his phone and took pictures of each man's face, the car in the ditch, their license plate. "You got any probation restrictions about harassment, stalking, reckless driving, terroristic threats?"

The passenger finally found his voice. "Please don't call the cops. We're gone. You'll never see us again. We'll never bother her again, ever."

Vig took several steps backwards. He held his weapon in both hands, pointed at the ground. He made a quick, sharp gesture with his head. "Get out of here. She never sees you again. You run into her in town, I will not believe it's an accident—you get the hell away, fast as you can."

They edged toward their vehicle, eyes on Vig the whole way. The driver managed to pull out of the ditch, leaving tire marks that would have to be explained to Walt. I profoundly didn't want Walt to hear about any of this, but nothing would make him angry like finding out something happened at his place and he wasn't told. I'd let Max call him.

Vig watched until the back of the truck disappeared over a hill, then turned to me. "Come on in the house."

We sat at the table. "Thank you," I said. My adrenaline started to level out. "I hate being helpless—it makes me so angry, having to be rescued. But that was very effective."

He nodded. "I fully understand now, why Turner wanted to bring you out, show you how to shoot. You should come on a regular basis, make some progress. Any idea who Phyllis is?"

"Yes," I said. "That's the wife of the guy you're supposed to have murdered."

"Huh." Vig unloaded the weapon and set the ammo on the table, the gun next to it. "What the hell do you think?"

I took a few slow breaths to counteract the dropping adrenaline. I tend to get light- headed otherwise. "That kind of threw me," I admitted. "I didn't expect him to say Phyllis."

"Give me a rundown on what you know."

"Okay, but—just, were you at all worried they might shoot you?"

"That's why I started with the AR," he said. "They got a handgun under the seat, they aren't gonna reach for that, looking at an AR. Not likely to have anything bigger than a handgun ready to just reach for. They do, it's a hunting rifle or shotgun. Not gonna be pros, screwing around with chasing a civilian woman down a country road. No offense."

"None taken." I started a messy recap, threw it all out there as things occurred to me. Oh, and this. And this. Vig didn't say a word, just sat, unmoving, focused on the middle of the table.

Through the open window, I heard Max's truck pull into the drive, pause by the ruts in the ditch, then come the rest of the way in. His truck door closed, but he didn't appear right away. I pictured him standing for a moment to assess, develop a theory. He came through the door and clocked the two of us sitting together, the weapon, the ammo. He immediately scanned me, saw that I was okay. He pulled out a chair and sat. "Tell me."

I told him everything, then repeated the entire recap I'd just given Vig, adding a few more things I thought of. Max's face hardened. His entire body tightened. He glared at the far wall.

"She's fine, Turner," Vig said. "This is not your fault, and she's fine. She keeps her head. She lost the guys once, decided on another course of action today, used her resources effectively. Never panicked, not for a minute."

Max didn't respond. At least he didn't lecture me.

"I really don't want to have to talk to Walt about this," I said. This was a therapy ranch. He couldn't have people bringing trouble here. I hoped he wouldn't fire me. Make Vig leave. Kick us both out.

"I'll talk to Walt," Max said. "He has to know, straight up. Everything. The worst possible thing would be to play around with what we tell him. I wouldn't worry too much, though, Maguire. He kind of thinks of you like a daughter, at this point."

I nervously stuck my head into Walt's office the next morning. He looked up at me. "Come in. Shut the door."

I sat across from him and waited for him to talk. Mainly because I had no idea what to say. We stared at each other silently, for what felt like an hour. Finally, he tilted his head a little. "Why exactly are you involved in this situation?"

I thought about that. I couldn't give Walt anything less than perfect honesty. About anything. How deep would he expect to go with this? Psychological development in childhood? He eventually noted that I was lost in the weeds, analyzing myself.

"Is it Ida?" he asked. "Putting pressure on you?"

"It started out that way," I said. No point pretending. He'd known Ida for decades. Walt understood Ida. "But honestly, after I saw for myself how upset Max was, it's been about him." I nodded, mostly to myself. "It's Max. Not pressuring me—quite the opposite. Just being so broken up about the whole thing, so determined to go to the wall for Vig, to do anything. I can't not help him."

Walt regarded me soberly. "We've talked before about your disregard for your own safety, Abby. I hope you've heard me and started to realize your own value. We don't want to lose you."

Caught off guard, I couldn't reply. I was just a temp worker. Had he forgotten? Finally, I nodded. Walt leaned over his papers again, and picked up his pen. Gently dismissed me.

I drove back into Deergrass to deal with some errands. I parked in a busy area and double-checked that my tailgate was locked. No line at the post office, a quick in and out. I mentally checked that item off my list, but stopped mid-stride when a squad car pulled in behind my truck. My pulse kicked up.

Elson climbed out, smiling at me. "Maguire, I was wondering if you'd be willing to provide me with a little cover some evening, fairly soon? I need to go somewhere and not look like a cop. A guy with a gal is way less suspicious. Especially with you being relatively new to the area, kind of an unknown factor."

"Huh. More camouflage." I tried to look normal, get my biology back under control. "Aren't you afraid to be seen with me? I'm not exactly the most popular person in the echelons of local law enforcement."

"I—" He paused. "First of all, no." He studied me, as if debating whether to continue. "Second, if I was going to care about people's opinions, everyone that would matter is actually inclined to like you, because you piss off Harmon so bad. It adds some much needed humor to the day." He laughed. "People love it when you show up and he goes nuts for hours afterwards. The way you went off on him out at the ranch, people quoted that for days."

He laughed harder, and put a hand to his abs. "That part about hoping he has a gloved finger up his ass when SWAT kicks the door in—" He leaned against my tailgate, laughed long and loud. He straightened, shook his head, wiped his cheeks. "Anyway. Are you by chance free tonight? It would be for a few hours."

This was a little disconcerting. Cops talking about me, imitating me? I had no idea how to respond. "At least I'm doing my part to support the rank and file."

He grinned. "And a few of the county folks as well."

Just when you think things can't get worse. "I am free tonight.," I said. "I'd love to help. What's the dress code?"

"Jeans and a t-shirt is perfect— maybe some kind of a plain t-shirt, without logos, so you won't stand out too much. Boots like you're wearing would be perfect, too. I can swing by and get you around seven?"

"Sounds good." I dug out my keys.

"Hold up a minute," Elson said. "What did you mean by more camouflage?"

I'd already forgotten I said it. I have more of an Etch-a-Sketch brain, my thought process easily shaken. Elson's was like laser etching. Anything he saw or heard was there to stay. "Warren Koenig gave your mother and me a long, involved lecture about camouflage in the animal kingdom. He made a good point—he's really very intelligent, even if he is a little bit off the bell curve. His theory is that Doug Larsen was so emotionally and socially threatening to people, they concealed themselves, made themselves either act like him or blend into the background, to avoid attack. He thinks that's at the heart of this whole thing."

Elson's serious demeanor was encouraging. "I've been thinking," I went on, "About how people use camouflage, socially. Warren predicted that this was going to be about a hunting mindset. Predator, prey, protective coloration. There's a whole textbook in this, Elson, just waiting to be written."

His radio crackled a garbled message. Elson somehow understood it, another skill that was beyond my comprehension. He stepped away, had a conversation with someone, and came back to lean on my fender. "Alright, go on."

"I feel like there's something there, but I haven't quite teased it out yet. You know, you're good at this. You should be a detective."

"I'd like to be," he said. "Wouldn't be a promotion—more of a job assignment than a rank, and obviously Harmon's got the slot here. Might have to go county, maybe a neighboring county, to stay close to Mom. But I think it would be interesting. I try to involve myself in things that will help, while I prepare for the exam."

He gestured at me with his car keys. "You, I just think you're an important source of information. You keep ending up in the middle of everything, and people talk to you surprisingly freely. I think Harmon's making a mistake blowing you off." He straightened and turned his body toward his squad, without breaking eye contact. "See you tonight, then? I really appreciate it."

I wore my clean boots, and brought a nice enough flannel in case the evening got chilly. Elson drove to a country bar in a neighboring town. "Ok now, we're just going to act like we're on a date, ok? Don't do your scrutinizing thing. Do you know how to line dance?" He threw an arm over my shoulders. He smelled good. His body heat and the muscled hardness under his t-shirt sent a tingle through me. I hoped he didn't notice.

Some of the dances I knew, others I mostly picked up. I sat out the quicker ones, not following the steps well enough to do it without tripping and falling. We did one slow dance—just to maintain our cover. He hummed, sang along quietly, one hand entwined with mine, the other firm on my lower back, holding me close. The vibration of the bass in his voice lit a fire in my core. He gently swayed, his chin rough when it brushed my face, his hip touching mine a few times, his breath soft on my hair, the length of his thigh pressing lightly against my leg just once, and I hoped to God he couldn't feel my entire being respond. I closed my eyes and tried not to think about my abs tightening, my toes curling, the feel of him. He stopped. I opened my eyes, looked around. The music had ended. Elson smiled.

He bought us some finger foods, covering the table with greasy, salty, delicious protective coloration. If I hadn't been looking for it, I wouldn't have seen him scanning, observing. We stayed until the crowd had mostly drifted away. He draped an arm over my shoulders as we walked to his car. I reached behind him and stuck my fingers in his back pocket, feeling the movement of his toned glutes with every step. Might as well enjoy the act. I refrained from giving his butt a squeeze.

"That was fun," I said, as he drove out of the lot. "Let me know when you want to go undercover and have barbecued wings again. Did you see what you were looking for?"

"I did." He held the wheel with his left hand, resting his right on the center console. He glanced between me and the road. "Who was there, who was together, who stood too close. Who disappeared together, who came back with a split lip and ordered whiskey. It's all good information."

We chatted and laughed about the crowd, the barbecue sauce on his shirt, the times one or both of us totally flubbed a line dance. I did not mention the slow dance. At all. Elson pulled into the ranch and turned off the engine. "Have you thought any more about that camouflage thing? I mean, if it's nothing, it's nothing. Just didn't feel like it was."

I paused. "Come up for a minute. It's complicated."

He looked around my apartment curiously. "This is nice. Didn't know what to expect, upstairs of a barn."

I sat at the table and gestured toward another chair. I didn't want to sit on the couch. Our knees might bump, and I wouldn't hear a single word he said after that.

"Listen," Elson said. "I appreciate your help tonight, but I don't want you involved. In anything. I don't want any bad elements having any reason to know you exist, alright? It gets ugly. I don't want to see you hurt, and I sure as hell don't want my mom getting hurt. I really can't stress that enough, Maguire. All I'm looking for is your take on the psychology aspect of all this."

"Yeah. I get it. All I'm doing right now is thinking. And talking with people, but that's what I do, and everyone's talking about the murders. I just have this niggling feeling that there's something right there." I stretched out my legs under the table and did a little circle with my toes to stretch my calves. "I keep thinking about Warren Koenig's nature talks. Camouflage, survival by hiding. Hiding in a social context is interesting—to some extent, we did that tonight. Hiding an object, but still to survive. He was talking about the body in my truck, but also about monkeys with sticks, and whether they steal each other's tools." I shook my head. I was tired. "I know I'm not making sense."

"Talk it out," Elson said. "Think out loud. Everything doesn't have to be spot-on relevant. Sometimes you have to just throw it all out there and dig through the pile."

I nodded. "Well, it has nothing to do with Vig, I'm convinced of that. It starts with Doug Larsen. It's someone who has a longer history with him—more than a scuffle out back of a bar. This was about taking back power. It feels like Larsen pushed someone over the edge—and while they were there, they took out Lutz. Death to tyrants." I drew circles on the table with my fingertip while I talked, then looked up. "I'm sorry, did you want anything? Soda or water?" Elson shook his head and gestured for me to go on.

I got up to get a glass of water for myself. "Say it is someone who became invisible around Larsen. I don't think a woman, although hundreds may have celebrated, considering his lifetime achievements of misogyny. I'm thinking a man who was shocked to be treated that way. Worst thing you can do to a man—treat him like the world treats women. Making a man feel weak, powerless, inconsequential is called emasculating, isn't it? As if it's only abnormal for males. If there even was a word like efeminating, it wouldn't mean taking away power, strength, significance. Oh, no. It would—"

I was getting off track. Elson's cop face was firmly in place. I wouldn't know if he was irritated or not. He probably did this the same way I did—listen for content. Separate out the opinions, the dramatics, and set them aside for later. Our jobs were probably more similar than one would think. That would be interesting to explore. He was staring at me.

I cleared my throat. "Anyway. I think it's about feeling powerless. Erased, invisible. It produces a deep, simmering rage, to exist as a supplement to other people, expected to sense what people want and give it to them. Whatever anyone does to you, your own experience of that is far less important than keeping up appearances, or keeping someone from ever being unhappy. Some people turn that rage outward, some turn it in on themselves until they can't anymore." And the whole time, a sinkhole forms.

"So, this person you imagine," Elson said. "Do they stop now? Score is settled, what do you think, they just go back to their normal life, like nothing happened?"

"Well, I'm not a forensic expert, a trained profiler," I said. "Let's be clear about that." I set my water on the table and sat next to Elson. "If, like you say, the score is settled—the grievance was against these two people—I expect it will stop now. It would take another impetus, a strong one, to make the jump to killing anyone else. That would feel like a separate act. It would make a separate statement about the killer's identity—I'm not a bad person, these two deserved it. It's not like I just go around murdering people."

I slid the glass in a circle on the table and watched the water gently slosh. "Once that line is crossed, though, once he decides there's someone else who needs killing—and doing it doesn't make him bad—I'd say he keeps going until a stronger, opposing impetus stops him. Whether it's, you know, the cops, or his dead wife appears to him in a dream and tells him he's going to be surprised how bad hell is, whatever. Something strong enough has to stop him."

"Him," Elson pointed out.

I shrugged, watched the water in my glass spin. "Just my guess. A man who was made to feel powerless. But what do I know?" I paused, let the room fill with silence for a moment. "I've been thinking about it with clients. Not like they could be involved, just the whole concept, camouflage. Do you want that?"

"Go ahead," Elson said. "I want to know everything you're thinking. It could trigger something for me, make something else pop."

"Okay. Camouflage is about being seen, or not seen. That's a huge deal psychologically. I used to have guys talk about the street smarts of getting people to underestimate them—not really see them—but they felt clever. They were outsmarting people. And they would counter it by bragging, making sure they were seen. It's completely different when the person hiding has no power."

“This family came in.” I paused, shook my head. “The mom spent the whole time doing what her husband wanted. She saw more clearly than he did, but she automatically did pointless things because he said to. Got mad about it, while doing it. Functionally invisible—couldn’t even see herself anymore. But—” I pointed at Elson dramatically. “Her daughter sees her, and sees that invisibility. She doesn’t want to become a woman, if it means she’ll disappear in a relationship.” I paused again, leaned back. “Seeing someone else live like that is powerful by itself. Strongly affects people. We should maybe think about that.” I started to think about that.

Elson shifted in his seat, nodded—go on.

“There’s this old couple,” I said. “Been fighting for years. They weren’t deliberately hiding, but didn’t see each other anymore. All they could see was their own anger. Then she almost keeled over, and he dropped everything to help her. When she actually saw him, it made him feel ten feet tall. She remembered being in love with him when he stopped seeing the argument, and saw her. Didn’t solve everything in one day, but they could see each other again. That anger was entrenched, for a long time. Blinding. Ida said they fought like some kind of animals, I forget what.”

“Alright,” Elson said. “This all makes kind of a picture. Potential motive, frame of mind. So what’s the upshot?”

I did a little head waggle and thought about it. “Larsen was cruel and dismissive to everyone. Maybe Warren was right—someone got angrier and angrier, and finally lashed out. Then covered it up lightly, like a cat covering its scat in the dirt. It’s not safe, cover it to survive. Maybe it’s about Larsen drunkenly fathering children all over the county, sometimes with married women." I raised a finger for emphasis. "Think of the rage there. Well, someone endured some kind of long-term relationship with Larsen, and finally blew." I nodded to myself. "And it felt like finally hitting back."

I got up to refill my water. The cowboy bar had made me thirsty—salty food, dancing. I raised my glass to Elson invitingly, but he shook his head. His expression was different, which distracted me for a moment.

"This generalizes to Patrick Lutz." I filled my glass from the tap. "Another person who behaved exactly how he wanted. Hurt other people, never held accountable. Entitled—no one can do anything about it. The same killer? Or a copycat, feeling empowered? 'Hey, look, Larsen's gone, it's wonderful! Here's another one.' What do you think? Same person, or not?"

Elson's eyes had changed. There was an intensity, a focus behind that cop gaze. Something had registered, struck a note. But what?

"Maguire, I know this is the last thing you want to hear, but you should talk to Harmon about this."

"No." In the following silence, I debated whether I cared how abrupt that sounded.

"Obviously, I will," he said. "I don't want to tell him I got it from you. Even that I talked to you. His brain will shut off if he hears that."

"You got what from me, exactly? What resonated, there?"

He said nothing, shaking his head.

I didn't push. "Tell him you thought it out yourself. Crack the case. Have him talk to Warren directly. Warren would love that, he'd be in his glory. Otherwise, you've heard people talking—bits of gossip, anywhere. Tell him you put it together."

The atmosphere had changed. Elson was tense. He stared at me for a long, slow, silent moment. "Tell me about the burying scat part."

"What? Why do you want to know about that?"

He shook his head firmly. "I'm sorry, I just need to know."

I waved my hands vaguely. "It was just the one comment, in the whole lecture about different species. Something about animals covering their scat with dirt as self-preservation, to keep predators from knowing where they are."

He disappeared inside his head for a moment, then focused on me again. "What happened with the girl who didn't want to grow up? Or her parents?"

"Mom came back for therapy by herself," I said. "She'll do well, I think. Learn how to take up a normal, human amount of space in this world. Give herself permission to live. Her husband, probably never see him again. How the marriage will do—" I shrugged.

"Tell me about the monkeys stealing tools."

I blinked. "That was really just an aside. Monkeys put tools somewhere, I assume sticks, and store them to use later. So, somebody could have stashed the body, but planned to come back for it, because look! It happens in nature! It sounds incredibly stupid now, actually. But he segued into saying that Patrick used to steal other mechanics' tools, and that's their livelihood, and they're all paying off tool loans."

Elson scratched the side of his face and frowned. "Mr. Koenig goes off on rants like that all the time. I used to know them by heart, but honestly, I stopped listening so long ago, I've lost the gist of it." A muffled banging sounded below us. Elson's eyes cut in that direction.

"That's just a horse in the med stall," I said.

He nodded, rearranged his legs, and turned in his chair. "Listen, don't repeat any of this conversation, alright? Your part or mine. Keep this between us, even if the old ladies' mystery group wants an update."

I had to smile. Janet wasn't fooling him one bit. "I'm an expert at confidentiality. Literally. Professional secret keeper. I'm incredibly good at boundaries that I see as legitimate."

Elson thought for a moment, then stood. "I need to go. Stick around the ranch for a few days, if you possibly can. Don't leave if you don't have to, okay? Don't go out alone."

"Hold on." I got up and stood between him and the door.

Chapter Twenty-One

"If you think I'm in that much danger," I said, "Tell me why. If my thinking is helpful, tell me what the kicker is, here."

He studied me, searched my eyes, trying to read something. He spoke very quietly. "Do you see this boundary as legitimate? Keeping this conversation between the two of us and God?"

His tone sent a chill down my back. I answered, almost in a whisper. "I do. I'm not trying to compel you to say something you'll regret later. I just want whatever truth you can give me."

"Come here." His voice was barely audible. "Leave your phone and your purse. And your jacket." He led me out the door and down to his car. "Get in for a minute."

We sat in his car with the doors closed. "All the times Murphy's bugged you, I don't trust him. I'm taking you at your word, Maguire. You can't repeat this. You understand?"

I got another shiver, but nodded. "Do I need to know?"

He did a little shrug. "Honestly, this is for my benefit. I'm not gonna lie, Maguire. I'm using you, like a consultant. Your take on the psychology here is helpful. But listen, the way you talk to people, really see people, puts you at risk. Small community. I guarantee people you've never met, somehow know who's talked to you. People sit around rehashing everything they've said to anyone about these homicides, to feel important, keep an exciting topic going. But you can see how the wrong person hearing your name over and over could be a problem. This stays in your head, no matter what. Don't even talk to yourself out loud."

"I get it."

"Larsen died by suffocation. Almost certainly passed out drunk at the time—suffocated, buried in a field."

I nodded. I had heard all that.

"He was suffocated by burying his head in manure. There was some in his lungs. His head was still covered in it. And he was buried lightly, not much dirt over him, less than you'd think for a shallow grave, even."

I paused to absorb that. "I'd heard the lightly buried part. So you're thinking it was meant to look like an animal kicking dirt over its own scat? Like killing Larsen is the same as getting rid of crap? Kicking dirt over it protects whoever dropped the crap there."

"I'm saying it's possible. I don't know how likely, but enough that we look into anyone who would've heard that camouflage lecture so many times, it was ingrained in their head." He paused, stared at the windshield, didn't seem to see it. "We need to look at that whole hunting group that used to go out together. I guarantee they've heard the whole spiel so much, they could recite parts of it with him. And they used to hunt right about where the first body was, that general area. I suppose the men's café group, too. See if anyone has any priors, any known mental health problems." He rolled his head around, cracked his neck. Stretched his shoulders.

"It's a place to start." He yawned, which immediately made me yawn.

I thought about the mental state of someone who would do that. "What about Patrick? Did he actually die from the blow to the head? Like, quickly?"

Elson nodded. "You and Mr. Koenig might have helped us there. Obviously, we knew it could be consistent with a wrench. No one would tell us about the stolen tools. 'I came to get my tools back, and my coworkers' tools, and bam. You won't be taking them again.'"

Like Ernie Gates. Stolen tools. Anger. Hatred. Phyllis. Threatening me. Close to Warren. In and out of Janet's kitchen—I couldn't say that. Or should I? "Do you think it's one killer?"

"I don't know, Maguire, and that makes it even more dangerous. If it's multiple people deciding who they've just had enough from, where does it end? There could be another body now, we just haven't found. I want you to stay safe, ok?"

I chewed on my lip. "I hear you." What if I didn't say anything and Ernie talked his way back into Janet's house? Checking on a repair, say. Decided she was an interfering old busybody, brought his knives. I couldn't tell Elson about Janet pouring gravy on her burner, to lure him in. I absolutely couldn't. Maybe we should go there right now, lights and sirens. No, we had a civilian car, so go pound on her door. No, Elson would have a key.

"Maguire, what?" Elson was annoyed. "What are you sitting there deciding not to tell me?"

I leaned back against the door and focused my gaze on the center console. I took a breath—long enough for an owl to hoot out in the trees, long enough for clouds to float over the moon, adding darkness. "Do you know Ernie Gates?" I checked Elson's face for recognition, saw none. "One of the guys at the garage. Friend of Warren's. They go out together fixing things for people, as a free service. It's very nice, really. Doing that."

I had Elson's full attention. If anything, he looked more irritated. I went on. "So, Ernie was there when Warren fixed your mom's sink, and we all started talking about the body being left in my truck bed. Warren talked about the guy, but Ernie got really angry, refused to talk. Looked like he could spit bullets. And Warren said Ernie had his own tools stolen."

"Oh, and—" I glanced at Elson. He'd be angry. Why hadn't I said this earlier? "He's actually having an affair with Doug Larsen's wife. Widow. He found out I saw them making out. Threatened me—don't tell anyone. He acted like he was trying to protect Phyllis. And—" I looked away from Elson's darkening face. "Ernie was apparently at The Nail the night Doug Larsen was killed. And Larsen publicly humiliated him. That same night." I would have loved to tell on Phyllis for hiring cheap thugs to chase me, but I had to keep Vig out of it.

Elson said nothing for a long moment—clearly thinking about a potential serial killer in his mother's kitchen while she played detective. His face hardened.

I went on. "Their coworker, Joe—I don't remember his last name, he was also on the outhouse team—he was at The Nail the night Larsen was killed. He saw the fight between Vig and Larsen. Joe was really angry about how Ernie was treated. He also warned me off, told me to keep my mouth shut."

"And," I tapped an index finger on the dash, making a point. "Joe was also at the other bar when Ben and I were having dinner—the night Patrick Lutz was killed, right around the corner. That doesn't mean Ernie is innocent, though. Maybe they both did it. Oh!" Another thought stopped me cold.

"When Joe described the fight, Roger said Larsen wasn't King Shit anymore. That's what he said, Elson. He called him King Shit." And I had liked Roger, more than any of them. I put my hand over my mouth, stared at Elson in shock.

Elson closed his eyes, as if getting a headache. "Anything else?" He looked at me, saw me shake my head. "I should go," he said. "Thanks again for your help tonight." He waited until I was back upstairs, then drove away.

I put my water glass in the sink and looked at Papa. I wanted to talk to him, but Elson had made me nervous. I leaned back against the counter and thought about all of it. Then I turned off the lights, double checked that my door was locked, and went to bed.

I found Rosie in the woods, standing with her buddies in the shade. She didn't stick her nose into the halter like she sometimes does, but she didn't walk away, either. We strolled along together, into the cool of the barn. I didn't haul her saddle out and balance it on the fence next to her spot. For now I just wanted to brush her, get the dirt off. Get out of my head.

Grooming is better for Rosie when I pay attention to her, notice, listen. She feels it when I'm mentally absent. When I go through the physical motions on autopilot, as though she were a wall or a fence to be painted, she pulls away. She's patient with me, most days. Probably giving me equine therapy. Probably gets back out to the herd and talks about what a hot mess I am. She and Rebel, Ida's horse. They could go on and on.

I explained this theory at some length, assuring Rosie that I didn't hold it against her. "Not that I gossip about clients, of course, but I don't have to work with me."

"You feeling alright?" Ida slid a hand along that smoothly brushed flank as she crossed behind Rosie. She studied me doubtfully over Rosie's back.

"I'm fine. I was just telling Rosie that I understand if she and Rebel talk smack about us. I don't blame her one bit."

Ida stared for a moment—then, I swear, she and Rosie exchanged a glance.

"Yeah, I saw that," I said. "I know. I'm owning it."

Ida cleared her throat. "Alright. Well. Did you know Janet's gone?" She nodded. "I can see you didn't. Tobias told her to get out of town for a few days, so she's visiting her sister. You know, he doesn't really order her around, normally. Oh, he sighs, shakes his head, argues with her. She plays it up for effect. He wouldn't give her a reason. Warren is watering her plants, bringing in the mail. She said he was worried about why she had to leave in a hurry, but she put him off. Well, we'll all be on edge until this is resolved. That's what it comes to."

I stopped brushing. Rosie eyeballed me, wiggled her hindquarters like she'd pull away if Ida wasn't standing on the other side of her.

"Your heart rate shot up there," Ida said. "What's going on?"

What could I tell her? "Elson wouldn't know about me being chased," I said, thinking aloud.

"What?" Ida's eyes were huge. Rosie squirmed between us.

"Let's get Rosie back outside," I said. "We shouldn't freak out if we're surrounding her." I put her grooming tools away. Ida snapped on a lead rope and walked Rosie to the corral, while I frantically thought through my talk with Elson. What could I say? What could I absolutely not say?

We started towards my apartment, but I stopped on the stairs and thought about talking in Elson's car, avoiding potential surveillance. "Let's take a walk," I said. We headed for the woods instead. Several horses looked us over, saw that we didn't have halters, and went back to grazing and grooming each other.

I told Ida about the barroom thugs hired to frighten me, and Vig's intervention. Max being angry, but not yelling at me. Walt's response. "Phyllis, though. What is that? Can you even picture that?"

"Funny that she's finally free to come and go as she pleases," Ida said, "and she picks that bar way out in the sticks. I tell you what, we poked at the right person with that rear view mirror. Just look at them, shooting at shadows. We should have thought, though, what to do when we got them unsettled."

"I supposed there's a learning curve to all this," I said gloomily. "I wonder if there's a training manual online somewhere." I went on to describe my evening with Elson, how I told him everything we know. I left out his side of the conversation—except his warning.

Ida thought silently for several minutes. My anxiety ran down, leaving me drained. I walked over and sat on a log, and listened to the birds calling, trilling. The leaves were drying out, falling early. A gust of wind pulled them from branches, sent them swirling on a long, gradual path to the ground.

Ida sat on a tree stump. "Tobias told you not to leave the ranch alone? Is that what he said?"

"Yes. I didn't tell him about being chased, or Phyllis hiring those guys. I would've had to talk about Vig."

She nodded. "Good. So, he knows about the affair, and Ernie threatening you. He can take all that back to the station, get things going in that direction. If Tobias thinks you're in danger, we need to stay sharp, Abby. Maybe we should go visit Janet—she's only an hour away. Talk through the whole thing, pull more out of her about what Tobias actually said."

"Good idea." Better than sitting around, verbally massaging the whole thing yet again. "Let's go."

Ida verified that Janet was free, and we wouldn't be intruding on family time. Her sister was working a funeral at the church. Janet could have gone, poured coffee or washed dishes, but chose not to. "We're on our way," Ida told her. She gave me an address. "Put this in your GPS. She said it's easy to find."

The route took us past Vig's house. I slowed, pointing it out. Ida craned her neck with interest and looked it over.

"We were sitting there in the driveway when the cops went by," I said. "We're going to go right past where Larsen's body was found." We headed in that direction.

"Stop! There's his car!" Ida shouted. "Pull over!"

"What?" I swerved to the shoulder and stopped. "Whose car?"

"There." Ida pointed. "Warren's." A light blue LTD, hitched to an empty trailer. Pulled to the side, on a flat stretch of land. "I'm sure that's him. He's got that union bumper sticker."

I pulled in behind it. "He doesn't have a trailer, does he? Someone told me that group of men hunted out by where Larsen's body was found. Around here. I've lost track of who said that. Probably Tobias."

"This is good grouse habitat," Ida said. "Good for a lot of wildlife, really. When you have a landowner willing to let you hunt, well, that's where you go. This is the Torgerson property—the extended family has some big parcels of land, all adjacent. There could be other people hunting at the same time. So he might not be right close here, Abby, is the point."

"But his car is here," I said.

"This is a nice, wide, flat stretch of road," Ida explained. "Good parking. Brings a few friends, someone has a four-wheeler. They can go together from here, or split up. Hard to say."

"Okay. He could borrow a trailer, and a four-wheeler. Or, someone could borrow his car to pull a trailer. He could be at home, drinking coffee."

We sat by the side of the road and studied the field, the treeline. "Probably not a very good idea," Ida said, "to go out in a field where people are hunting." We exchanged a look.

"I wonder if we could find him out there?" I said. "And what do we say, if he's with a group of people? Better if we were wearing blaze orange."

"It's grouse season, Abby, not deer. We don't look like birds."

I got out and peeked in his window. "There's a thermos. Why would he leave his thermos? Maybe he's coming back."

"There, is that him?" Ida pointed. "Look! No, to the left."

A man wearing camo slowly puttered out of the trees on a four-wheeler. A balaclava covered his face. Seemed unnecessary in the mild weather, but I wasn't out in it all day. He stopped, seemed to hesitate, then made a tight circle and drove back into the brush. He emerged on foot and stood by the treeline, a shotgun resting on his shoulder. I waved to him. "Warren!"

He didn't seem to hear me. I stuck my head in the truck door. "I'm not sure if that's him or not. I'm going to go find out."

"Hold on, Abby. What if it isn't him? What are you going to say?"

I grabbed my Shewee. "I'll say I gotta go, saw the trees. Can't make it to town. Sorry to disturb him. What if it is Warren? We saw his car. Don't mean to interrupt, just been thinking of a few questions, thought we'd seize the moment. Good enough." I turned and jogged into the field.

As I got closer, the hunter dipped back into the trees. It must not have been Warren after all. Warren could be a mile away, into the brush and scrubby wetland. Or in his basement, sharpening knives. This was a waste of time. I turned back toward my truck, but stopped when the man stepped out of the brush again. I watched him uncertainly. Was he looking at me? I couldn't tell for sure.

He looked around in all directions. I followed his gaze to my truck, parked on the shoulder. With the glare of the sun on the windshield, I couldn't see Ida. We seemed to be alone out there. I hesitated, unsure what he was doing. He definitely looked at me, I was the only thing standing in the middle of the field. He raised his weapon, aimed it right at me.

"Whoa!" I yelled, waved my arms. "I'm a person! Don't shoot! I'm a person!" Whoever it was, he had to hear me, but he didn't lower his gun. I awkwardly hit the ground, heard a shot, loud—over my head. I rolled, scrambled, pulled myself into the trees, looked back. He aimed at me again. I ducked into the brush and ran.

I tried to think, through screaming adrenaline, flooding fear. Was he crazy? What did I interrupt? What did he think I saw? I twisted, turned, tried to stay behind bigger trees. Put distance between us. Find other people, hunters, anybody. I didn't hear him behind me—what if he saw Ida? He'd know she saw him shoot at me. Oh, Ida. I left my car keys. She had to get away. I tried to project frantic thoughts in Ida's direction. Leave, drive away. Just go, Ida. Go!

I met barbed wire. Worked my way down the fenceline until I came to a post. Looked back, paused. Scanned the dried grass and weeds. Listened. Nothing. I put one foot on a middle wire, right next to the post—the strongest spot, the least bend. Tested my weight, quickly swung the other leg over the top, turned my foot to wedge my toe where the wire met the post on the other side. I snagged my jeans on a barb, wincing as the wire scratched my leg. I climbed down, headed for thicker trees, bent over in a fast walk, trying to be quiet.

I reached the brush and spent precious seconds scanning the fenceline. I saw no one, and tucked behind a grouping of poplars to breathe, look again. In my peripheral vision, I thought I saw motion. I froze and tried to be silent, as though someone that far away could hear me breathe. I willed myself to focus on the area where I thought I'd seen something, not let my gaze wander.

Something moved. It looked like the ground itself gently, slowly shifted. Something camouflaged, moving this way. He was coming.

I turned and ran through the scrub trees and brush. Branches whipped my face, stung. Leaves and sticks rustled and snapped under my feet. My breath came in ragged gasps as I lurched over a small rise. Something grabbed my foot—my shoe caught on a protruding branch, jerked me back. One hand flew forward to break my fall. A twinge of pain shot through my wrist. My chest and shoulder slammed into hard ground. My palm came up scraped and dirty, the side of my face smeared with soil still damp in the shade. I twisted around, reached awkwardly to pull my shoelaces free from the sharp end of the broken branch. Winded, fighting off panic, I rolled back onto my feet and started to run again. Keep moving. Put space between us. I crashed through dried leaves—my fall had been loud. He knew where I was.

Keep moving. I didn't see a low spot that was hidden by a covering of leaves. I stepped in it and pitched headlong down a small hill, slid and bumped over fallen branches, sharp rocks. Rolled, too fast, tried to stop, tasted blood, slammed into a log that rocked with my impact.

I rose to my hands and knees, reeled, put a hand on the log to push myself up. I looked around, tried to regain my bearings. Turned, and was surprised to see my truck. I had moved in a curving path, didn't realize I was getting closer to the field, the road. I'd stepped right over downed wire—I saw it now, a broken stretch of fenceline. I winced as I leaned on a scraped hand. Think. Something cracked behind me.

A rustle in the leaves. I looked around desperately for a hiding place, belly-crawled into the brush. There was an open space in the middle, a small patch of grass surrounded by thick bushes. I slithered in, knocked my elbow against something hard, bit my lip to stop from gasping in pain. Metal. Rusted pieces of old farm machinery, scavenged for parts, abandoned. I lay on piles of dark, rounded droppings from rabbits and deer, and flattened myself against the ground. I heard another rustle, and something faint that I couldn't make out. It almost sounded like singing.

Soft, quiet steps in the dry grass and leaves, coming closer. And yes, singing—a man's voice, soft, gentle. Janis Joplin. Fran's ringtone. The voice gave way to humming, then stopped. I pictured the hunter standing on the other side of the brush, looking for my trail. Waiting for me to move. I wouldn't be hard to track. He would find me.

He started humming again, close. I tried to stop shaking. Don't breathe. Don't.

The singing resumed. He was only a few feet from me. He chuckled, a deep rumbling. His voice was muffled by the balaclava. "Come on now, Abby. You wouldn't be out here if you didn't want to talk. People do say you're quite intelligent, you know. There's more than one person with their money on you to figure this whole thing out."

I heard his clothing rustle as he turned, looked around. He called to me quietly. Coaxing, cajoling. "Abby...you were listening, Abby. About camouflage. Very good. You weren't meant to be prey, you know. That wasn't my intention. Come on out, now."

He'd set his shotgun aside, held a handgun—he hadn't left home this morning only prepared to hunt grouse. He was quiet for a moment. Stood, waited. Then a bush off to one side rustled as he pushed the branches with his free hand, looked between, behind. He had a big knife strapped to his thigh, and three smaller ones on his belt. Ready for gutting and skinning. Cold clawed a trail down my spine, gripped me. I couldn't draw breath. I fought against the shaking, tried to be still.

He paused, pulled off the balaclava, stuffed it into a pocket. Warren stood, looked around. "It's the cage, Abby. Nothing in nature wants a cage. I do admire your determination, your attention to detail. But I won't have a cage. I'm afraid I can't be taken. I wish you had left it alone."

I felt around for the rusted pieces of machinery, gripped a metal bar, braced myself, waited. He moved closer, parted the bushes in front of my face, smiled, and raised the gun. I swung the bar as hard as I could, grunted with the effort, hit his arm. He yelped and the gun flew from his hand. I rolled after it, hurled myself through the brush, pushed off with elbows, knees, feet, scratched and scraped. He grabbed at me and I kicked him off. I landed on the gun, rolled to my back, and raised the gun as he leaned in, knife in hand. He froze.

"Don't do this." I aimed the gun. Center mass. Steadied it with my left hand, tried to breathe. "It doesn't have to be like this,

Warren. There's a way out. We'll find it. We'll find a way without a cage."

Warren studied me with bright, watchful eyes. He didn't look concerned at all—just interested. He'd encountered something unexpected. "Are you listening, Abby? What do you hear?"

Sirens. Faint, coming closer. "They'll be here in minutes, Warren. We can figure this out."

The hand with the knife moved, as if he were thinking about angles. "There's only one way this is going to end, Abby, but don't be afraid. I'm very good at this." He drew a preparatory breath, poised over me. "Innocent animals should never suffer. That's something a man needs to stand on."

"Don't do this, Warren. I don't want to do this. I don't shoot people."

He smiled kindly. "I know." He lunged.

I squeezed the trigger. The gun jumped in my hand, so loud it stunned me. Warren landed on me, heavy, hard. I tried to push him off and he stabbed at me ineffectively, too close, off balance. His arm didn't seem to work right. I pulled my leg out from under him, but he threw himself over it, pinned me with his weight. There was a red stain on the front of his coat.

"Warren, stop! We can get you help! Let me stop the bleeding! Just stop now!"

He leaned on my chest with his free arm, pushed me down so heavily I struggled to breathe. He crookedly raised the knife. Adrenaline screaming though me, I wedged the gun in between us and squeezed the trigger. The explosion stunned me. His body jumped. I pushed and shoved until I managed to get him off me.

I scrabbled backwards, kept my eyes on him, gasped for breath. Warren didn't move. I heard a shaky whimper, and realized it was me. I kicked the knife away, stuck the gun in my waistband, rolled Warren onto his back, tried to put pressure on the wound that was bleeding the worst. The sirens were closer, louder, right up to the edge of the trees. The squads had driven over the field, cross country, an SUV coming right into the brush.

"Get an ambulance!" I screamed, as if anyone under those sirens could hear me. My adrenaline was peaking. I started to shake. There was shouting. I couldn't process it. I felt dizzy. Blood seeped out around my hands, pressed to Warren's chest.

Elson appeared, stepping over fallen branches and logs, weapon drawn. He walked up and pulled the gun from my pants. He handed it to someone behind him, holstered his own, and pulled me away from Warren. I was covered in blood. "Maguire, where are you hurt?"

"Get an ambulance." My voice was unsteady. I looked at Warren, unmoving in the leaves and dirt. A county deputy pressed gloved hands to Warren's chest. I pushed away from Elson, barely turning my face from his uniform before vomiting.

Elson brushed my hair from my face. "I need to know if you're hurt."

"I don't know," I said. Heart pounding, I looked down at my bloody coat, slashed in a few places. "I don't know. It hurts where he was holding me down. I'm not sure." I tried a few tentative movements. Heard myself gasp with sudden, piercing pain.

Elson put an arm around my back and propelled me out of the trees and brush, boosting me slightly to step over logs. He deposited me in the back of a squad car. "Take her to the ER," he said to another cop. "Stay with her until I get there."

The cop executed a Y-turn and drove out of the field. I felt around under my coat, poked at the pain, winced when I found a deep, inch-long gash. Open wound. Bad idea. My hands were bloody, and it wasn't my blood. All those years of bloodborne pathogens exposure training. Leave it alone. An ambulance passed us, going the other way. I held myself together, arms wrapped tight, and leaned back in the seat.

The nurse who bandaged my stitches was a stabilizing force. She carried herself like a field general—'defy me, expect an artillery barrage.' I wanted to latch onto her, borrow some of that. I took a deep breath, tried to inhale some of her steely-eyed aura and gripped the side of the exam table when my head spun.

She printed off discharge papers and prescriptions. Wearing borrowed scrubs—the police took my clothes—I meekly followed her to a meeting room the cops had commandeered, just off the ER. She turned at the doorway and blocked it with her body, radiating disapproval. "Don't you take any guff from them," she said quietly. "You're a trauma patient. If we weren't getting slammed, I'd hold off on your discharge papers long enough to make them come to you, so I could run interference. I've got to go."

She leaned in, frowning. "I can see this won't come naturally to you, but you play the ER patient card. You hear me? They get pushy, you close your eyes, sway a little in your seat. They come into a hospital, they can damn well expect it." She walked me into the room, paused to level a death glare at each of the cops, patted me on the shoulder, and turned to go.

Harmon came in as she was leaving. She stood in front of him, interrupted his stride, and made him side-step around her. She met his impatience with a look that dared him to take her on, and left the room.

Elson stood, carefully maneuvering his duty belt around the arms of his chair. He waved me into the chair and joined a few cops standing by the wall. Harmon kicked another cop out of a chair and sat across from me. I willed myself to sit up straight. Damned if I would cower in front of Harmon.

Chapter Twenty-Two

Harmon looked me over in disgust. "Does everything have to be such a big, dramatic scene with you? Can you never leave anything alone?" He set a file on the table. "Such a damn mess, everywhere you go." He set down his phone and opened the app to make a recording. I scanned the room and thought about who was there, and why, and whether I really did ruin everything.

"Abby?" Harmon stared at me. He must have already started. "Do you need fewer people in here, to be able to focus?" He glanced at Elson, but apparently didn't want to ask someone of equal rank to leave. Elson stood, arms crossed, feet planted.

Harmon looked around at the others, called out a few by name, and excused them. After they filed out, he turned to me. "What were you doing out there in the field?"

Ida would have been questioned at the scene. I wondered exactly what she said. Ida was very good at oblique answers, pretending to miss the point. It was a particular gift of hers.

"I wanted to talk to Warren," I told him. "I saw his car."

"What exactly did you want to talk to him about, Abby?"

"You know I'm on morphine, right, *Tom*?" I frowned at his phone. "That should be clear for the record."

His look was menacing. "We need to get as much information as we can, while it's fresh, Ms. Maguire. Please answer to the best of your ability."

"We were on our way to see Janet. I heard Warren was concerned about her leaving town suddenly. I talk to people when they are upset." I gave him a dramatic pause, for emphasis—then forgot what I was going to say. What was left sounded lame, even to me. I was so exhausted, I could barely think.

"So you were doing spontaneous field therapy." Harmon blew out an impatient breath through his nose. "So, you didn't decide Warren Koenig was guilty and hunt him down to talk him into submission?"

"I didn't hunt anyone down. I was hunted down." My voice sounded flat, lacked the energy to be effectively antagonistic.

Harmon opened his mouth, but stopped as the door opened. Max came in and walked over to me, knelt on the hard tile floor so I wouldn't have to crick my neck looking up at him. I put a hand on his back, grabbed a handful of flannel by the collar, and grounded myself on him. He glanced at my scrubs, looked me in the eye. Murmured, "You okay?"

I met his eyes but couldn't answer.

Harmon cleared his throat, but Elson quickly spoke. "You're welcome to join us, Mr. Turner, as a support person for Ms. Maguire."

Harmon's face tightened. Max deliberately didn't look at him. For some reason, it seemed comforting that Max was not intimidated by the likes of Tom Harmon. Nor, probably, Godzilla. I felt my arms and shoulders relax a little. I really was getting light headed, but it might have been all the testosterone in the room.

The detective carried on. "If not to interfere in an active investigation, why would a supposedly intelligent person walk out into an area where people were hunting?"

"I don't look like a grouse. I saw him walking in the open field. By himself. With his shotgun safely against his shoulder. I was in full view of the road, until he started shooting at me and I ran for cover."

He continued as though I hadn't spoken. "And what were you planning to do after you got him to confess? Ask him how he felt about it?"

I smiled at him kindly, patiently—the look I gave Ben when I really wanted to annoy him. "People generally confess things to me in the confidence of therapeutic sessions. We've already established you have no respect whatsoever for that entire concept, but that's how it generally happens." I steadied myself, against nurse's orders. Not wanting to give an inch. My weight shifted slightly, just barely leaning on Max.

Max felt it and finally looked at Harmon. "You're not going to browbeat Maguire. You got any real information you'd like to get from her, I suggest you get to it. One more accusatory statement, and you can either arrest her, or I'm driving her home."

Harmon squinted. "This is not an accusation. It's an interview. She'll know if I decide it's an interrogation." Nonetheless, he moved to factual questions. I answered the best I could.

When we started plowing the same ground the fourth time through, Max stood. "I think that's enough. Maguire? You ready to go?"

I really did sway a little when I stood. "You know where to find me, if there's anything else I can tell you. I honestly do want to help."

I shuffled slowly down the hall, holding Max's arm. Ida saw us, and struggled up from her plastic waiting room chair. "Abby! Dear Lord. How bad is it? I called the police as fast as I could, I did, Abby! Are you okay?" She reached for me, but pulled back. "Where shouldn't I touch you? Where are you hurt?"

I pointed just below my shoulder. "A couple layers of stitches."

"Lord, help." She put a hand on my back. "Let's get you home."

They were quiet on the drive, clearly not wanting to bring up anything difficult. "Do you know...anything about Warren?" I asked.

"They took him into surgery," Max said. He left it at that.

"Ida, have you talked to Janet? I'm worried how all this is going to affect her."

"I did call her. Didn't want her to hear it on the news." Ida shook her head. "Well, she's very upset, of course. Thinks it's her fault. She should have seen something, you know how that goes."

"I'm just glad she didn't figure it out," I said. "She probably would've done something reckless, gone charging in." I stopped there. Profoundly hoped they wouldn't point out the obvious. They didn't. "Max, have you talked to Vig?"

"Not yet, but I'll call him. And Jules."

No one spoke until we reached the ranch. I was glad they held off on lecturing me. They both walked me up to my apartment, stood awkwardly in my living room, and watched me sit on my couch.

"Well, I'm going to go get your prescriptions filled," Ida finally said. She took the papers and left.

Max plopped himself into a chair. "You go ahead and take a nap, or whatever, Maguire. I'll be right here. You need anything, you don't want to be alone, I'm right here."

I nodded tiredly. We sat. Didn't talk. I jumped when Ida came back in—it felt like just a few minutes, so I must have slept. She gave Max a highly significant look.

"What?" I asked. "What was that?"

"You don't start these until tonight," she said, setting little bottles on the counter. "They gave you some IV drugs."

"Thank you. What was that look?"

"Word is they're searching the woods and the field. They say it's taking several officers just to keep traffic moving, chase away spectators. People are laying bets that another body's out there. I'd believe that, you know. It would explain why he'd shoot at you, just for seeing his car there." Ida looked at me thoughtfully. "Though I suppose, if he was all dressed up like that, scouting around for the perfect place to dump another body, he could've just been so into the moment that he saw you intruding into his fantasy, and something snapped."

"No," I said. "I finally get it." My hand looked odd. I held it up, studied it. It was fine. "My brain's a little foggy. We need to ban the word painkillers, I've decided. Starting now." I pointed at her.

"Change starts with you! Let's say pain alleviators. I'm going to start a petition."

"You're as high as a kite," Ida said.

"You're a kite." I squinted, tried to focus. "He thought I put it all together, that's why he reacted like that. Thought I understood, thought I was alone. Wrong on both counts. I get it now, though."

"Well, go on," Ida said. "I don't get it. Not at all."

"Honest to God!" Max looked like he might finally snap. "You two. Could you just not?"

"I wasn't looking for gossip." Ida frowned. "Just standing in line." She pulled a throw from the back of the couch and spread it over my legs.

"Could you not screw around with maniacs, then theorize about it?" Max scowled at her and rubbed his sock against his pant leg irritably. "You know perfectly well what I mean."

"Hmph. Well at least Vig is in the clear now, let's not forget that." Ida said huffily. "Some nerve. I'll bet he appreciates this whole thing is over with, even if some people don't."

"Warren saw us," I said. "We couldn't see him." I looked at my hand again. Ida and Max both stared at me, with that concerned, dubious look people get when they think you're alarmingly not okay. "Asking questions," I clarified. "He watched us the whole time. We never fooled him one bit. He sat there, eating pie, knowing full well we were picking his brain. Watched us tighten the focus, closer and closer to him." I put my hand down, so it would stop distracting me. "I told you he knew something."

Ida was more subdued than I'd ever seen her. Deflated, sad. "I provoked him. You're kind not to say so, but I did. You told me to stop, not to call him and his friends. You said they'd come after us. I'm so sorry, Abby."

I yawned. "Does Warren even have a backhoe? I never saw that flatbed trailer at his house. Maybe he borrows things. If he rented, there'd be a paper trail." I was glad to see a spark return to Ida's eyes.

She sat upright. "Just imagine loaning someone a trailer, and then—well, there's no point asking someone if they hauled a body on it, if you did have reason to wonder. They'd never say."

Max threw a pillow in disgust. "Neither of you should be allowed out, unsupervised!"

Ida waved him away. "But what was the point, Abby? What do you understand?"

"'Innocent animals should never suffer,'" I said. "'Something a man should stand on.' He meant that to be the last thing I ever heard. That was his confession, his explanation. It was all about the dog, all along. Warren never addressed the horrible grief of watching his dog die, the deep shame of not being able to do anything about it. It ate away at him for years, until he finally hit back."

They both stared. I could see it on their faces—is that true, or is she hallucinating?

"I'm serious," I said. "Walt even said. 'Grief is not willing to be ignored. Squeezes the life out of people, if they don't work it out.' This was about grief all along." Silence. I let it sit.

"And Patrick kicked the dog," I finally went on. "Remember? One of the mechanics brought it to work with him. An old lab—an old hunting dog, I'll bet anything. Probably on its last legs. It probably slept on a pile of rags or something, just for the comfort of being around people. That just hit too close to home for Warren. Another innocent dog getting hurt. That was why Patrick had to die."

I nodded to myself. "Patrick's obnoxious behavior, the tool theft, laziness, all of that was aggravating. But hurting the dog, that hit Warren right on that old wound that was still festering. The dog's owner couldn't do a thing about it, however angry he might be. That's what was too heavy for the sinkhole."

"Sinkhole?" Ida patted my leg. "You'd better let those meds work their way through your system, Abby."

"She's right, Maguire," Max said gently, "You need to rest. Do you want a nice pillow from your bed?"

"Well, yes," I said. "I do. But listen. Roger was right. Warren's shame over not being able to protect his own dog was so deep, it damaged his sense of self. Made him feel powerless. Ate away at him, unseen, for years. I'll bet anything it was Ernie who told him about Patrick kicking the dog just lately—and that was finally too much."

I made an exploding motion with my hands. "A sinkhole formed. Warren hit a critical mass, psychologically. He had to do something to stop feeling angry and helpless. Even as smart as he was, though, all he could think of was to lash out. It felt like self-defense."

I thought about Warren's pain and grief. I wondered if that iron grip, that refusal to release his own suffering and move forward, had been a conscious decision. If he purposely chose darkness, or if the emptiness pulled him in, and he got lost. The last of my energy dissolved into a dizzy nausea. Max and Ida resumed bickering as I fell asleep.

Elson and I went for another burger on his day off. He'd pay this time, he said. His turn to cook for me. His car was in the shop, so I picked him up at his house. My shoulder still hurt, but I could turn the wheel well enough to get by. Elson made no compensating wisecracks about a man being driven around by a woman. I considered proposing marriage.

I ordered the fruit, and pilfered some of his fries. Elson, off-duty and not on a case, was fun, and funny. We exchanged crazy work stories, and agreed our careers and our perspectives had a lot in common. He'd gone back to clean-shaven—I tried not to stare at his dimples. His leg bumped mine under the table, and my abs tightened. He eyed me thoughtfully.

Elson became quiet on the drive back to his house. He restlessly fiddled with a button on his shirt. Picked a tiny piece of hay off the dash.

"I haven't been to see your mom," I said, "since she's been back in town. Is she okay? It's got to be hard, living right next door to Warren's house. She's got to think about him all the time."

"She does," he said. "She doesn't even make smart remarks or get all dramatic about it. Doesn't really want to talk about it. They lived next to each other for longer than I've been alive. No way to make that okay. Hopefully it gets better with time." He paused, studied me. "Lotta damage, lotta fallout. Mr. Koenig looks so old, handcuffed to a hospital bed. Aged like twenty years, overnight. Just kind of caved in on himself. It's still hard to take it all in."

His eyes drilled into the side of my head. "Listen, Maguire. Harmon is smart, and he does listen. We're never going to be friends, but he does his job. I went to him with concerns about Mr. Koenig. Harmon paid attention. He was working that angle, breaking it down."

I didn't want to talk about Harmon. "You know what I keep thinking about? Your mom has a key to Warren's house—" I glanced at Elson. "He also has a key to hers. They watered each other's plants."

"Don't think that hasn't occurred to me. I'm going to have nightmares for years."

"You know what else I keep thinking about? How likely is it that Warren put a full grown man in the back of my truck by himself? I suppose he was strong for his age, before this. Being a mechanic, and hauling deer carcasses around."

Elson turned in his seat, to fully face me. "You know what I keep thinking about? I involved you in this by talking it through with you. I knew I could trust you—I still trust you, but I utilized your intelligence and your expertise, and completely underestimated how impulsive you are when you finally get out of your head. You have to leave this alone, Maguire. I mean it. That's why I'm telling you Harmon does his job. Whether Mr. Koenig did or didn't act alone, Harmon will figure it out. He's smart. He works hard, and he's determined. You helped us, alright? You did. Now, please, leave it alone."

I didn't say anything for a block or so. "I will," I finally told him. "Vig is out of it now. He can put his own life back together. Hopefully being dragged in by the cops hasn't hurt his future."

Elson didn't respond to that. "Feel free to use your counseling skills on my mom. She'll never go to a therapist about the whole thing, but she's pretty morose. I'd hate for her to lose her spirit. Maybe you and Mrs. Gill can help her get through it."

I pulled up in front of his house, but Elson didn't get out. He turned to face me again, with a smile I couldn't quite read. Warm, but purposeful. He slid the palms of his hands down the tops of his thighs. Gently slapped his hands against his legs a few times, rested them on his knees. Stalling. "Maguire—listen. In another lifetime, some parallel universe or something, I would definitely pursue a relationship with you."

"I—what?"

Quiet amusement joined the complicated smile.

I tried to lean forward. My seatbelt locked up, awkwardly jerked me back, hurt my sore shoulder. I groped around, released it, and pushed it off me. "What? Parallel universe? What's wrong with me in this universe?"

"I like you, Maguire. I like you a lot. But your heart is tied up elsewhere."

"What?" I willed myself not to scowl at him. "Are you talking about Ben the Rat? You'd better not be!"

"Uh, no. Murphy's an idiot. Maybe now he's out of the way, you'll see better. The point is, you might technically be single, but you're not really available."

I leaned back against my door so I could look straight at him. "I have no idea what you're talking about."

"I see that. Your head gets in the way. That's the whole thing, right there. Listen, I'd love to still do lunch from time to time, grab a coffee or something, if that's ok with you. I really enjoy your company, even if we're not dating. I really want to still see you."

What was wrong with me? I didn't even understand it this time. Not at all. "I would love to. And let me know if you want help studying for your detective exam."

His eyes lit up. "Really? That would be great."

I made the phone gesture with my hand, raised it to my ear, wiggled it. "Give me a call." Halfway to his house, he turned and gave me a jaunty wave. I drove a few miles down the road before I started yelling at the dashboard. "What is my problem with men? What does he think is wrong with me?" I smacked a hand on the dash, but stopped when the movement hurt my shoulder. "Does he think I'm on the rebound? He could just say that!" I glared at the windshield. "Another universe? What is that? How am I not available?"

I had a terrible thought. What if Ben was right? Was that even possible? Was I too guarded? Not that he had any room to talk, but had I really just bolted all the doors and put up barbed wire? I smacked the center of the steering wheel hard enough that my palm stung, and wondered how hard I'd have to hit it, to set off the airbag. What if there really was something wrong with me? I sounded like the mom who picked up manure. "There is nothing wrong with me!" I shouted angrily.

I got to the ranch, slammed my door and stood in the sparse, dry grass by the fence. The wood was rough and hot under my forearms. I felt the baking sun on my shoulders and the back of my jeans. The horses were entirely unconcerned about any of my problems, which seemed oddly comforting.

"Hey." Max leaned on the fence beside me. "What's up?"

I studied his open, friendly expression. The scars his neat, tidy beard almost covered. The rumpled flannel that smelled like the barn on a bad day. "Am I too hung up on my Papa?"

He pulled back a little in surprise. "Absolutely not. Why would you ask that?"

"Do you think I'm too obsessed with my job?"

Max frowned. "Why shouldn't you be career-focused? You're extremely good at what you do. Men's lives revolve around their careers all the time, no one thinks anything of it. What's this about?"

"Every single day," I said, "I understand less. About everything."

Max grinned, reached out an arm, and pulled me in for a hug. "Story of my life, Maguire."

"I'm not even kidding," I mumbled into his shoulder. "Maybe my IQ is plummeting. I don't even know what happened."

"I have just the solution," he said. "Come help me feed the dinner crew. Definitely cure what ails you."

I laughed, and pulled back a little to look up at him. Humor danced in his eyes. I rested my cheek on his chest for a moment. "Okay. Let's go."

Chapter Twenty-Three

The parking lot was full. Walt and Max had a circle of people in the outdoor arena. Vig was there, and a half-dozen men and women I didn't know. Most of the participants stood back and observed from the far edges. Vig talked, waving his hands expansively.

Ida came up behind me, draped a lead rope over the fence, and rested her hand on the wooden rail. "They've started a new group for first-responders and veterans." She tsked, shook her head. "You won't believe this, but it's really true, Abby. Max is calling it the 'Horse Calls Bullshit' group." She waved a hand, bewildered. "Lord, help. How that man's mind works is just a mystery to me. They're talking about making a separate one for women. You and I would lead that one, if we can get the gist of what that even means."

We leaned on the fence and watched as horses calmly kept their distance from people. One man turned to leave, but Vig spoke with him, seemed to encourage him. "Watch now," I said. "That guy will have a horse in his pocket in a couple minutes. I'm not telling anyone to do sniper breathing, though."

Ida threw me a suspicious glance. When I did not enlighten her, she shook her head, at me this time. She started to respond, but was interrupted by a chorus of children's voices chanting about how much fun it is to have a library card. "Oh, that's Betsy."

Ida pulled out her phone. "Hello! You know, it's really too bad you aren't here when you call. To hear your ringtone, I mean." She moved away. "Spill it. Everything." She listened for several minutes.

In the arena, Vig's reluctant participant was scratching a horse on the neck, and leaning his forehead against the horse's. The horse stood quietly. Vig beamed proudly. Vig might just make a good equine assisted therapist—I made a mental note to talk with him about certification.

"Well, alright," Ida said. She leaned beside me. The rough wood was hot under our arms. Ida squinted in the bright sun, as she turned to face me.

"What was that ringtone?" I asked.

Ida smiled proudly. "I found it online. It's from a cartoon called Arthur. Just listen, Abby. Betsy's librarian friends called her—listen to this! Apparently, they didn't find another body out there. But they followed Warren's ATV tracks to the edge of a marsh, dug around, and found a big wrench dumped in the reeds! It was even called a 'striking wrench,' which just sounds like Warren, doesn't it? I'll bet it was difficult for him, not being able to give a lecture about how to choose appropriate murder tools."

She held up a hand to keep me from answering. "But, listen, Abby, you'll never guess! Ernie got arrested as an accessory, and wait until you hear! Phyllis turned him in!"

I hadn't expected that. "Are they charging her with anything?"

"No," Ida said. "The cops pulled her in for more questioning, but they framed it like she was just guilty of being naïve. Encouraged her to think about how she'd been deceived, and she started talking. Said his behavior kept getting more erratic, and he wanted her to provide him with alibis. If that doesn't beat all!"

I idly picked at a loose splinter on the fence while I thought about Phyllis. And Ernie.

Ida looked around, as if anyone could hear us. "I guess Ernie was raving when they brought him in." She lowered her voice. "Yelling about someone being after him, leaving threats on his car in the night."

We stared at each other. I bit my lip. Ben would hear about that, and piece it together why Ida and I were out there in the dark. He'd feel better, having one less unanswered question, but he'd never tell on us. Ben was many things, but not petty, nor vindictive.

"I wonder," I said, "If they plan to follow up on that?"

Ida smiled. "He ranted about rearview mirrors until they scheduled him a psych eval."

I tried not to laugh. We both tried to suppress it, but I'm not sure why. Like laughing would make us look guilty. My shoulders shook, and a giggle escaped. Ida took hold of the fence rail with both hands, but couldn't hold back a snort. Then she had to take off her glasses to wipe her cheeks, and we both fell apart.

"Lord, help," Ida said, when we finally calmed down. "Can you imagine? What's going to happen next?"

www.ingramcontent.com/pod-product-compliance
Lightning Source LLC
Chambersburg PA
CBHW030353120726
47901CB00007B/2010
* 9 7 9 8 9 9 2 2 5 6 2 2 2 *